Master
Under Good
Regulation

By Kara Louise

Cover design by Kara Louise
Painting of "Reggie" by Larry Chandler, (1951-2007)
used with permission
www.larrychandlerart.com

ISBN 978-1-4357-3286-5

Published by Heartworks Publication

Printed in the United States of America

Library of Congress Cataloging-in-Publication Data

Kara Louise
Master Under Good Regulation

Note from the author ~

I hope you enjoy this story of Reggie
and how great an influence he was in the story, *Pride and Prejudice*.
While I had not intended for this story to go into such depth,
it could not but happen. In writing Reggie's narrative, I merely wished to tell a
cute little tale and ended up examining every detail, every supposition,
every possibility in the novel Miss Austen bestowed upon us ~
and how Darcy's faithful dog influenced or responded to those events.

I wish to thank Roya and her excellent work initially helping me
keep the tone Regency, keep me faithful to the book,
and for suggesting wonderful additions to my words.
Thanks also to Mary Ann, who gave this work
one final superb and thorough look through.

A special thanks to artist Larry Chandler and his wife, Donna,
for giving me permission to use his wonderful painting
of "Reggie" for both the book and on my website.
I regret that just weeks before readying the book for publication,
I learned of Larry Chandler's recent death.

Finally, and without question, I must thank Miss Austen
for her great inspiration.

Prologue

I have always enjoyed my life as the number one pet of my master, Fitzwilliam Darcy. I am not only his favourite sporting dog, but a faithful companion and fearless protector to him as well. Not that I have had much opportunity to display the latter, but of the two former, I am quite proficient.

This enviable position has allowed me to go places with him that others would only dream of going. Some of those places have not merely been geographical in nature. Some have been within the realms of his mind and heart. I am among the privileged few whom he has allowed into the deepest recesses of his thoughts and feelings.

I remember with great fondness my first meeting with my master as a puppy when he was but a young man of fifteen. His good father brought him to the modest home at which I was one of several litters of English Springer Spaniels born. I remember him looking over each one of us, picking us up, checking our eyes, teeth, and our frame. He had a look of gentleness and wisdom that I found appealing. I comprehended that he would indeed make a good master. He would take prodigious care of me, but he would be one that I could readily train.

The different litters of pups had been put into different pens when anyone came to see about selecting one. I soon discovered it was due to the difference in our breeding. I realized that somehow we were not of the finest breeding as the ones in the first pen, but were a little better than the ones in the third pen.

This young man's father, as well as the gentleman who had, up until now, been our prominent caregiver (excepting, of course, our faithful mother who gave us of her nourishment until we were whelped), apparently knew what to look for in selecting the very best dog of our breed.

"All these puppies would make an excellent choice," said the caregiver as he pointed to the puppies in the first pen. "Notice the markings, the sturdy build and well proportioned body, the alert expression in their eyes, the shininess of the coat, and the evenness of their gait."

"How do I know which one to choose, Father?"

"Son, look for the one that you feel in your heart will make a good companion and an excellent sporting dog. Look for strength and energy, but one who will relax when you hold him. In addition to not wanting a lazy dog, you do not want a dog that has a continual excess of energy."

The young man did not seem satisfied with any of the dogs in the first pen and walked toward ours.

"Now the dogs in that pen there do not have the breeding that these dogs here do," offered the man.

But the boy continued to walk toward us undeterred and I determined to put much effort into this time of scrutiny and to display only my best qualities. I was not sure how to accomplish it, but I found the wagging of my tail came most naturally. I looked up at him with my most beguiling expression in my eyes and was pleased when he kept returning his gaze to meet mine.

I had earlier noticed that Ambrose, a dog from the first litter, had been quite prolific in his attentions to the young man with very sloppy licks and I quickly perceived that the young Darcy was not responding with as much positive attention to this. I was of the impression that the young man could see that Ambrose was only trying to flatter him. Consequently, I kept my licks to a minimum; just enough to assure him that I liked him, but not enough to lather (or flatter) him with my drool.

"Son, narrow your selection down to a few dogs of the finest breeding and then choose the one that you feel in your heart," and here, the young man's father repeatedly tapped his finger against his son's chest, "is the right one for you."

The young man took in a deep breath and blew it out through puffed cheeks, seeming to struggle with making a choice.

His father laughed. "It is not as if you are choosing a wife, Fitzwilliam. Any of these dogs will suffice."

In time, he narrowed his selection down to two of us -- myself and Archimedes. Now Archimedes was larger and was quite strong and energetic. He was also from the first pen. I knew that if the very finest breeding was what the master was intent upon, I would quickly be out of contention. He had the two of us brought out and I could immediately discern that Archimedes was determined to exhibit his power and aggressiveness. I decided I would show a more loyal nature and stayed by the young man's side, content to display my faithfulness and dependability, which I believed were my inherent strengths.

The caregiver then gave some advice. "Archimedes is of the very finest breeding; both his mother and father are top of the line, and that goes back several generations. You cannot go wrong with him. Reginald, now, is a fine dog; however his parentage is not quite as prestigious."

The young man scrutinized the two of us carefully. He looked to his father. "Is the breeding that important, Father?"

"Fitzwilliam, just as in life, breeding is of utmost importance. As a Darcy, you must always keep that in mind."

I could see the young man was torn.

"Well, son, have you made up your mind yet?"

The young man finally answered, "Yes, Father. If it is acceptable to you, I have chosen this one."

His father seemed surprised. As was I. He pointed to me.

"Are you certain, Fitzwilliam?"

"I believe I am, Sir."

"And exactly what did you find in this dog that was superior to the other?"

The young man gave his father a most contemplative look. "I prefer his black colouring over the brown. He seems lively and playful, but not overly aggressive. He may not be of the most prominent breeding, Father, but I believe he will be most perfectly suited for me."

"And are you quite certain, son, that he is the one you want?"

"Yes," he answered and then added, "His eyes, Father... look at his eyes. I can see he is most intelligent. They are quite fine. Do you not agree?"

The elder Mr. Darcy nodded. "Yes, son, they are." He looked up at the caregiver and gave a slight shrug, "I believe we shall take Reginald."

I know not whether it was either of those singular qualities that I made an effort to display earlier or something else, but for whatever reason, he singled me out. I could not restrain my joy and may have been overly excessive in my response when he selected me. My tail went quite out of control and I could not help but give him a few good licks, which he promptly wiped away. I rationalized that I was still just a puppy and could afford to display more of an exuberant disposition when the occasion warranted it. In my opinion, his choosing me was definitely one of those occasions.

I often wondered whether his father was disappointed that he had not chosen Archimedes, but he accepted me into his home as much as I believe his disposition allowed. I did not allow myself to dwell too much on whether the elder Darcy would have preferred the other more well-bred dog. But I would be assured, before the man's death, that he held me in high regard.

As we approached the carriage, the elder Darcy put his hand upon the shoulder of my new master. "I want you to know, Fitzwilliam, that a man and his dog can grow quite close. A bond can grow so strong between you and that dog will grow to love you as much as you love him. Be kind, yet firm to him; you will find that this can be a most rewarding relationship"

"Yes, Father. I will."

On the way to my new home, my new master held me in his lap whilst his father set down the conditions for owning his own pet.

"Fitzwilliam, it will be your sole responsibility to take care of this dog, train him, and feed him." He paused, "Oh yes, and give him a good amount of exercise."

"I shall, Father." My new master readily agreed, as he squeezed me tighter and looked down at me, pleasure written across his face.

I was exceedingly grateful his father had bestowed my responsibility to his son and not to the servants, as I concluded I would be in much better care. I could tell that he had a strong regard for me already.

When the carriage stopped and he brought me out, I got my first glance at Pemberley, my new home. I could scarcely believe the grounds that stretched out before me. I squirmed to escape from his arms, wishing to begin my explorations immediately, but his grip on me held firm. I admit I was exceedingly anxious to at least put my mark on some bush, letting the world know I was here and this was where I belonged!

His father came up to us and slipped something around my neck. I was not sure what it was then, but I quickly learned that with it on, I did not have free reign as I would have preferred. It was a slightly painful learning experience when I tried to step out further than the parameters of the length that this thing, called a leash, allowed me.

My first night at Pemberley, I must confess, I was quite lonely and frightened. I was put in a crate that was kept off the kitchen. My master spoke to me as he put me in my new quarters. "Now, Sir Reginald Ascott Hamilton Darcy, I must put you here for the night. It is only until you are well trained and prove yourself to be obedient." He put both hands around my face and stared intently into my eyes. "If you learn quickly, Reggie, soon you shall be able to sleep with me in my room." He patted my head and closed the door.

Reggie, I thought to myself. *I liked that name. And because the young master called me that himself, I liked it that much more.* Yes, it was settled in my mind. *I think I will be quite content here.*

Needless to say, I whined for most of that first night because I was left alone, unaccustomed as I was to the solitude. But each night became a little easier and I soon accepted it; waking early each morning and looking forward to my master coming to see me as soon as he awoke. We soon became quite inseparable and I learned quite early on that he would allow me to become the one thing that he found difficult allowing any other person to become -- his close companion and confidant. And I came to learn what made this young man who he was and what those forces were that shaped him.

Chapter 1

My life as the preferred companion and sporting dog to young Master Darcy was unequalled. I shared my residence between two places; Pemberley, which was the grand estate out in the country, and a home in the city of London. I had nary a complaint about either, but my preference lay with Pemberley; its fresh air, its open and expansive grounds, and its endless supply of shrubs and trees.

But oblige me as I take you back with me to that first night at Pemberley. Sleeping alone off the kitchen was difficult. When my master left me, I suddenly felt quite fearful and abandoned, and I admit I did my share of whimpering occasionally throughout the night. His coming down several times in the darkness and quiet of the night did much to reassure me, but as soon as he left, all those feelings would return. I was most relieved when he appeared that next morning. I most enthusiastically greeted him when he carefully opened the pen and reached in for me. I could not resist giving him a fervent lick across his face, prompting him to attempt to scold me in his most authoritative voice and quickly wiping his face with the back of his hand.

"Come, Reggie. It is likely you need to go outside."

He slipped the leash over my head and set me down on the ground. When he opened the door, I was most anxious to get outside and tried to make a direct line to one of those fine shrubs, but the leash held me back.

"Mind yourself, boy," he said. "You will get there soon enough."

After we made a few stops at some strategically placed shrubs and trees, we began our leisurely stroll. I enjoyed sniffing out everything along the path, attempting to leave my mark whenever possible. Everything was new and I wished to explore it all!

We spent a good amount of time outdoors that morning and I was happy to discover that my master enjoyed walking. Now, I must confess that I would have preferred to walk without the restraint of the leash. How I wished to leap into a bush -- looking for some little creature to hunt down! How I wanted to run up ahead to determine what was there! When I heard the snap of a twig, I yearned to rush over and discover if there was some prey on whom I could pounce. But I could not do it with this leash that was attached to his hand and my neck.

As we walked along, I became fascinated with my young master's feet. They seemed unusually large for his frame. I have since come to comprehend that it is said that a puppy must grow into his paws; you may fairly accurately gauge what will be the adult size of the dog by the size of his paws as a puppy. I would garner that the same is most likely true for people. I deemed that my master, although reasonably tall (he was just about the height of his father when I first came to Pemberley), was likely to grow considerably more because of the size of his feet. I also ascertained that he would fill out quite nicely. Presently he was somewhat lanky and appeared to be adjusting to his tall and ever growing stature. His hands, however, were nicely proportioned and I thought them the perfect size, especially for easily picking me up.

But as we walked that morning, I sensed that he seemed to be heavily weighted down by something. I was not quite sure what it was. Although we walked as two companions, he seemed many miles away. I had noticed that when he had been in the presence of his father the previous night, his melancholy was even more pronounced. Although his demeanour was very polite, his manners were very reserved and formal, his posture rigid. On our walk, I was determined to display a more lively demeanour in the hopes that, at least on our walk, he might be cheered.

I ran circles about his feet, causing him to trip and prompting him on more than one occasion to have to disentangle himself from the leash, all the while making a futile attempt to keep his posture and deportment. As I had an abundance of liveliness and energy, being the puppy that I was, it was not difficult for me to give him a little bit of what I believed him to need.

I noticed him look back towards the house several times and as soon as it could no longer be seen, he looked at me and smiled, breaking out into a run and letting out an unrestrained, "Come on, Reggie! I will race you down this path!"

We ran down one path and then another, and even through some heavy woods. I made a mental note that I should be eager to return at a later time, as I would greatly enjoy exploring the vast array of flora and fauna through which we were presently running. My master soon slowed down and we stopped by a small lake. The water glistened, beckoning me to come and take a drink. Being a pup and having to work twice as hard to keep up with the long legs of my master (although I am quite convinced he did not run as fast as his legs would allow), I was more than pleased to see this enticing body of water before me, as I was quite thirsty. He walked me over to the lake and I eagerly stepped up to the edge, planting my front two paws in the water. I vigorously lapped up a considerable amount of water.

When I had satisfied my thirst, we walked over to the stump of a tree and he sat down. I sat down next to him, worn out and grateful for the respite. As I licked my front paws to rid them of the dirt that had been picked up in them, we had our first real conversation.

"I enjoyed that, Reggie." He took in a few deep breaths. "Do you think you will like it here?" He paused and then asked, "Do you think you will like me?"

I looked at him and sensed he wanted my approval. I cocked my head, looked at him with most accepting eyes, and wagged my tail in earnest. That was all he needed as an affectionate response from me.

He reached down and patted my head. "I believe you and I will become fast friends, Reggie."

He then slid down off the stump so that he was now sitting aside me on the ground. He brought up his long legs and reached over with his arms and picked me up, bringing me onto his lap.

"I am pleased Father allowed me to choose you. I feared he would not. Although Father told me to make my selection from the best litter, I could see something in you that none of those dogs of better breeding had." As he talked, his hand stroked my fur from my head down to my tail and I basked in delight.

He turned me around and cupped my face in his hands, looking directly into my eyes. "It is good to have someone with whom to walk these grounds, Reggie. Usually I walk alone, meditating a great deal upon who I am and what is expected of me. Father has instructed me my whole life on what it means to be a Darcy, to be proud of my name and connections, and how he has such high expectations of me."

He looked out across the lake, as if he were far away. "Mother was always there; ready to give me the reassurance I needed when it all seemed so overwhelming." He took in a deep breath now and was silent as a lonely tear appeared and trailed down his face. He quickly wiped it away. "She always had a way of tempering what Father said with the gentle reminder that no matter what, they would always love me."

I felt his arms tighten around me. "And now she is gone…" He was silent again and I wondered where it was she had gone. He quickly wiped away another tear that threatened to roll down his face. "Father says if I am truly a man, I should not cry. I am but fifteen and he says I should act like a man. But sometimes, Reggie, it is not particularly easy."

I noticed, with complete amazement, a sudden steeling of my master's faculties and the pain and grief quickly erased from his face, replaced by a stone-like countenance. As if no tear had been shed, no feelings had threatened to spill over, I watched him stand up and brush the dirt from his clothes, as if to brush away any trace of emotion that he may have just felt.

We walked slowly back to the house; both sensing the bond beginning to form between us. Instead of taking me to the pen off the kitchen, he took me over toward the stables. A larger pen was situated there and I discovered that this was where I was to spend a good portion of the day. There were several other dogs in nearby pens; some grouped two or three together. But I was placed in a pen by myself and hoped they would still accept me. As I was put inside, the other dogs greeted me with barking, and although it was quite intimidating for me being such a small puppy, I felt that they all accepted me fairly well. My master returned several times that day to bring me out for a brief walk or simply to reach over the pen and scratch my head. When evening drew near, he brought me back into the house and returned me to my indoor pen. And that is how my first few days at Pemberley passed.

~~*

My master awakened me one morning and when he brought me out, I was dismayed to find water pouring down from the skies. Huddling over me and partly covering me with his coat, he scurried me over to what had become my favourite tree and quickly returned me to the house. Now I must interject here that my outdoor pen does have a small shelter I may go into to avoid the elements if I so need, but I was very grateful to be allowed to remain in the house this particular day.

As he put me back in the pen indoors, he told me, "Reggie, your pen is going to be disastrously muddy today, so I am going to leave you indoors. Father says it is up to me to give you a bath when you need one and I believe this will prevent you from getting dirty."

With that, he closed the door. "Sorry about not being able to take our walk this morning. If it clears up, then I will come for you a little later."

He left and I heard him greet his father off in the distance. For a considerable length of time, I could just barely make out the conversation between my master and his father. Although I could not distinguish everything that was said, I believe my master's father was giving him instruction, as I would often hear my master say, "Yes, Sir. I shall, Father." The tone of their conversation was cordial, yet formal. But every so often, I would hear a very soft and high voice that I could not identify.

I sat in my pen, waiting expectantly for the first sound of my master's return. Occasionally, one of the kitchen help would come over to the door to look in on me and make some comment and smile. It was particularly gratifying when one of their visits was accompanied with some special treat from the kitchen.

Finally, after what seemed an eternity, my master appeared and walked very slowly to my pen. He was carrying something in his arms. It was a little girl. A precious little girl.

Our eyes met and she instantly buried her head against my master's chest.

"Georgiana, this is Reggie." He tried to turn her around so she would look at me. "Georgie, he will not hurt you. Look."

He stooped down and reached out his hand toward me, but the little girl kept her face hidden from mine. I heard him let out a frustrated sigh.

"Georgie, Reggie's feelings will be hurt if you do not at least look at him."

"I do not want to! I do not like dogs!" she cried.

My master's jaw tightened but then quickly relaxed. "Georgie, he is not like Storm. I promise you that he will not hurt you."

She shook her head vehemently against him.

"All right, Georgie. But poor Reggie will be sad all day because you think he is a mean dog. He is but the most gentle of puppies and you really should not judge him ill because some other dog frightened you."

"No!"

"Georgie, you know I would never let anyone or anything hurt you and Reggie will do the same. If you get to know him, you will see that he will always look out for you."

Georgiana continued to shake her head.

He turned to walk away and I was quite saddened that she did not seem willing to trust me. But as he walked out through the door, I saw her lift her head and take a quick peek at me. Just before they disappeared around the corner, I saw her eyes light up and felt that perhaps all she needed was a little time. I thought that indeed, someday, we would become good friends.

Being in the house that day gave me the opportunity to learn more about where my master's mother had gone. From what I heard from the servants, I found that she had just recently died. Being right off the kitchen, I heard the servants talk much about this and how heartbreaking it was for both my master and his sister. As they were scouring down the kitchen to make it spotless or were beginning to make the preparations for the next meal, I overheard much about this subject.

"The poor young master is still heartbroken, I ken tell ye that much!"

"His father puts on a strong face, he never lets anyone see his grief. But I think I have heard him cry when he is alone in his chambers at night. Methinks the young lad is holding in all his pain so he ken be strong like his pappa. He wants so much to be just like him."

"Terrible thing to go through at his young age. Not anymore a child, but not quite yet a man."

"And little Georgiana. One wonders if she will even remember her mamma, being such a young thing."

"I think letting the young man have his own dog was a right good thing. Have you noticed how his face just lights up when he comes down first thing in the morn and checks on him? I hadn't seen that expression on him in a right long time."

"Gives 'im something else to think about than missing his mamma, bless 'im."

One of the women came over toward the door where I could see her. "Yep, that dog might just be what Master Fitzwilliam needs to get him through this heartbreaking time."

I suddenly was hit with the overwhelming realization that the elder Mr. Darcy had great hopes that I might help his son through his grief. I realized that there were some heavy expectations laid upon my office, but I was determined to do whatever I could to help my master through it.

I could sympathize with my master in his loss, as I missed my mother heartily those first few days away from her and to own the truth, still did at times. I missed her cool, wet nose nudging me along when I needed some help. I missed her stern, but loving eyes warning me to behave properly around my brothers and sisters. And I missed the way she picked me up by the scruff of my neck when I was wandering too far away and licked my fur if it was not clean enough for her liking.

I let out a soft sigh. Yes, I did miss my mother. And I am sure my master missed his as well.

Fortunately, the rain did not linger long and soon we were able to venture outdoors on our walks again. I made a decidedly concerted effort to add a playful liveliness to our walks. It placated my heart to see my master smile and hear him laugh. Although I am sure he had not completely forgotten his mother, as I had not, I do believe I was able to help him experience a little bit more joy than he had when I first came to Pemberley.

~~*

Almost immediately, my training began. Whilst my master's instructions were simple and fair, it helped that I was also an eager learner. I was taught to sit, stand, stay, come, fetch, and a host of other commands. Once I learned the commands, he tried to improve the way I did them. He would say to me in a firm, but loving voice, "Reggie, sit up straight. You must never be in poor posture. You never know when there will be others watching you," or "Hold your head up high when you walk, Reggie. You are a Darcy. You must always remember that," or "Reggie, that was very ill-mannered to run off like that. You must behave in such a way that others will think highly of you."

Within a short time I had learned all the basic commands. Once I proved myself faithfully obedient, I was rewarded with the distinguishing privilege of being allowed inside the great home of Pemberley for brief periods of time.

I quickly learned that my behaviour indoors was to be of a calm nature and only let loose my energy whilst outside.

Initially, I was only allowed in select areas of the home, but as my temper was learnt to be most amiable among everyone, I was soon given almost full reign. There was in residence at Pemberley a Mrs. Reynolds, who seemed to be the person in command of the household. She was very adamant about where I could and could not go and what I could and could not do.

When my master wanted me to go with him somewhere in the house, she would often say, "Young man! That dog is not to go into that room!"

If I showed a little unrestrained enthusiasm, she would say, "Reggie, if you do not mind yourself, outside into your pen you will go!"

Although she sometimes seemed harsh, I knew she had a soft place in her heart for me as she would often bring me scraps from the kitchen that were most satisfying.

And Georgiana? Just as I hoped, she eventually did warm up to me. The next time my master brought her to me, she actually was able to look at me, although she still clung fiercely to her brother. Soon after, I sensed that a great amount of her fear had waned and she stood next to the pen whilst her brother reached in and she watched in awe as he stroked my fur. When my master brought her to see me the next time, he took me out of the pen and held me, coaxing Georgiana to gently touch my fur and see how soft it was.

I was so excited for her to have progressed this far that I forgot myself and almost squirmed out of my master's hands, which would have been disastrous for Georgiana. I remembered just in time that I needed to remain calm for her; all the while my heart was pounding that she would trust me not to hurt her. I could see the turmoil in her eyes. How greatly she wanted to do something that, for some reason, was going against her nature.

I sensed that she wanted to like me, but something was hindering her being able to trust me completely. Finally, after a few moments, she gingerly reached out and touched my fur, quickly pulling back her hand, but looking up at her brother with a triumphant grin on her face.

"You see, Georgiana? There was nothing to be afraid of, was there?"

I took a particular liking to this young lady in residence. I had to learn to behave with a restrained delicacy around her, not because she was frightened of me anymore, but because she was quite small and fragile. She was but three years old when I first came and it was with great joy that I watched her grow into a beautiful and compassionate young lady. After that first time she reached out and touched me, she often wandered in by herself when I was there and we would have a very pleasant visit.

But as I was generally the young Darcy's companion, he and I became inseparable and the strength of my attachment grew daily.

I looked forward with great anticipation to being trained to do what I was bred to do. I was to be a sporting dog for my master. Whilst it seemed to be inherent in me to nose out the birds, flush them out, and retrieve the ones that my master expertly shot down, I had to learn his signals and, the hardest thing for me to learn, restraint.

How I wished to scamper all about the countryside, following every scent and lead! But if I did not remain in close proximity to my master, it would all be lost to him. So I had to listen and learn to apply myself to his commands. After weeks and weeks of concerted effort and lessons, we soon become an admirable team.

I had been at Pemberley close to four months when my master came down late one night after everyone had gone to sleep. He reached into the pen, picking me up, and putting his finger to his lips to quiet me.

"Now you keep quiet, Reggie. We must not awaken anyone."

He took me up the stairs and into his sleeping chambers. He had made a bed for me on the floor next to his. He had collected a pile of old blankets and placed them in the corner. He then situated me on top of them all and told me that was where I was to sleep.

He told me to *stay* and then he climbed into his own bed. Once he was settled in his large bed for a considerable length of time, I decided I had *stayed* quite long enough, got out of my bed, and walked to the edge of his. From my perspective, being the puppy that I still was, the top of the bed appeared quite high. Nevertheless, I made an attempt to jump up, grabbing the top coverlet with my paws but unfortunately, slid back down, taking the coverlet with me, to the floor.

My master awakened, unsure what had just happened.

"What...?" He laughed as I looked remorsefully at him, feeling extremely mortified at my failure to stealthily join him. I think he took pity on me, or perhaps he did not want me to make another attempt and destroy his bed, because he lifted me up onto it.

"Now, Reggie, if you are to remain up here with me, you must stay on the other side; down at the foot of the bed. Do you understand?"

I made an attempt to lick his face and he promptly put me down at the far end of the bed. But gradually, throughout the night, I worked my way closer to him and was pleased to discover that he was more than willing to give my belly a scratching. I was in raptures and quite pleased how exceedingly well my scheme had worked out!

It was there, in the company of Master Darcy and in the private quarters of his bedroom that I really came to know him most acutely. How many talks we had there that burst forth from the depths of his being, I cannot say. Of course, I listened most attentively, giving him an occasional whimper or nudge with my cool nose to assure him I understood. Whilst he occasionally would talk on our walks as he had that first day, it was here, after a long, hard day, that he would quietly speak of those things that were on his mind; things that perplexed him or angered him; things that hurt him or greatly pleased him. I was privy to it all.

In the evening, when we would both retire, he would softly talk with me all the while he stroked my fur. I would listen to him faithfully, fighting the tendency to moan in ecstasy, as he knew exactly what pleased me. I sometimes felt as though his hand gently stroking my head all the way down to my back helped calm him as well; which I felt very privileged to help facilitate.

It was one night a few days after he first snuck me into his room (which was soon discovered but gratefully, I was permitted to continue), when I began to understand the demands placed upon him because of his prestigious birth. "Reggie," he confided in me, as his hand ran repeatedly down my back. "I hope you realize how happy you have made me. I do not have to be Fitzwilliam Darcy, Heir of Pemberley, in your presence. How I wish I could have your lively and playful disposition." He sighed and was still for a moment. I nudged his hand to encourage him to continue his ministrations. "It is not inherent in my disposition to be lively unless someone brings it out in me. Presently, the only other ones who do that are Georgiana and my cousin, Richard."

"At times I feel so burdened by who I am and the responsibilities that Father wants to ensure I possess. It is only when I am alone with you out rambling throughout the countryside that I actually feel free from all that my name requires."

With that he turned over and I am quite sure he immediately fell asleep. I lay there, content to listen to the sound of his steady breathing, and marvelled at how by sharing those thoughts with me seemed to lighten a bit of the load he felt in the face of all the responsibilities that would some day come upon him. As I pressed my head against his hand, breathing in his all too familiar scent, I closed my eyes, hoping I might be able to make just a little difference for the better in his life.

Chapter 2

Over the next few months, my master and I would take every opportunity to walk as the weather permitted. I sensed that he was exhibiting more and more of an unrestrained nature -- at least in my presence. He remained very formal and reserved in the presence of others, but he would toss sticks for me to return with wild abandon, challenge me to a fiercely competitive game of tug-a-war, or engage me in a race, as he had that first day. Sometimes, however, we would simply amble aimlessly about the grounds. We grew to have a mutual attachment and admiration for each other.

Apart from his family, the only other person that vied for my master's time was his tutor. He had been in the Darcy household teaching my master since he was a young boy. This gentleman lived in residence at Pemberley and even accompanied us to Town. Apparently, my master was required to spend a certain amount of time with him, although I do believe I would have been most capable to have been the one to guide him in all of life's most important lessons in life. I reluctantly, though nobly, relinquished that responsibility to his tutor.

Mr. Hannington, his teacher, was very formal in his manners and was of the firm conviction that the only truly significant achievement in life was the pursuit of knowledge. He willingly and gladly imparted his knowledge to my master.

It was fortunate for Mr. Hannington, as well as his lone student, that my master had an insatiable desire to learn; applying himself to his studies and going well beyond what was required of him. He and Mr. Hannington engaged in frequent discussions that ranged from history, current politics, economics, literature, and a myriad of other subjects.

My master was very grateful that he was allowed to be educated at home. For over ten years he was an only child, and his parents did not seem inclined to send him away to school. However, he acknowledged if they had not found Mr. Hannington, who had excellent credentials and in whom his parents had complete trust, there was always the prospect that he would be sent away.

Looking back, he confided in me, he believed it was a most providential decision to be allowed to be educated at home, as he would have most likely been away when his sister was born and would not have the opportunity to cultivate the close relationship with her as he had now. There was also the matter of his mother's recent death. My master reflected that had he been away when she had taken ill, he may not have been able to return home to Pemberley in time to see her before she departed for her eternal home and be there for his father and sister in their grief.

~~*

There was another struggle with which my master appeared to do battle. I recall evenings at Pemberley after he had retired for the night that he would be most grievously angry and resentful. He would toss and turn and betray a great sense of unrest, feelings erupting that he apparently strove to suppress throughout the day.

One evening, after he had spent the greater part of the day out with his father, he and I retired to his chambers. As he and I climbed the stairway, his posture and manner were stiff and the features of his face were firmly set in a mask-like countenance, much like that day he fought back his tears as he talked to me about his mother. I watched in fascination and fear as, with each step up the stairs we took, his true feelings became exceedingly exposed to me. I saw that he was especially provoked and I thought it prudent to keep a guarded distance from him until he had either calmed himself or invited me into the sphere of his confidence and presence, which I hoped he ultimately would do.

After incessantly pacing the room in agonizing silence, he suddenly blurted out, "I cannot believe Father is taken in by his falsehoods. He is nothing but a liar and a manipulative deceit and a..." Suddenly he appeared at a loss for words and he stopped, wiping his brow with the sleeve of his shirt.

His young face seemed to take on the features of an adult as he gazed off with a look of disgust. I took my place upon his bed and watched and listened, wishing there was something I could do to soothe my master.

He finally came and sat at the edge of the bed next to me. His hand absently came over and I looked forward with anticipation a soothing combing of my fur with his fingers. But as he began speaking, the intensity of his anger was conveyed through his hands and I received quite a vigorous kneading, instead.

"He has the impudence to tell Father how disciplined he is in his studies and how well he applies himself. My father has exceeded his duty towards him to secure him the finest schooling, yet I have seen how he neglects his studies in favour of carousing and unrestrained behaviour. His conduct and words exhibit that he is nothing but a scoundrel!"

I sat as motionless and wary as a trapped rabbit, as his hand grasped a handful of fur around my neck at this outburst. He turned, and looking at me, quickly let go. "I am sorry, Reggie. Did I hurt you?" His voice was filled with remorse and his chest heaved in and out as he attempted to calm himself. "He is no longer the friend I once had. I comprehend a darker side of him that Father does not see because he is blinded by his charms. I think perhaps Father does not *want* to see it because of his love for him."

I knew precisely of whom he was talking.

George Wickham. He was the son of the elder Mr. Darcy's steward and but a year my master's junior. The elder Mr. Darcy loved him almost as deeply as a second son. However, I was witness to this young man's duplicitous personality. He treated my master with contempt and scorn, all the while flattering and being most convincingly amiable to his father, from whom he hoped to receive condescension, education, and the promise of a patronage.

Not only did I determine that this rake had no redeeming qualities, but his dog lacked them as well. Storm was a black and brown dog of various and questionable breeding. He was much larger and stronger than I. The dog had a definite mean streak to him and I would not be surprised if Wickham ruthlessly encouraged and purposely trained him to be the vicious creature that he is.

It was apparent that most of the staff at Pemberley were fearful of this dog and Wickham had been told repeatedly to keep him either locked up or kept to the leash. But those admonitions to Wickham did not prevent him from taking Storm out on the grounds of Pemberley and, whilst off away from the house and the eyes of the elder Mr. Darcy, letting him off the leash. It was one of those occasions that I encountered them for the first time.

My master and I had been having a very pleasant stroll through the grounds at Pemberley. He had released me from the leash and I ran up ahead of him, stopped, and waited for him to draw near. At a small incline, I scampered up and suddenly found myself face to face with a large dog that was boldly baring his fangs and growling quite viciously.

I admit that I am not so exceedingly brave in the company of a dog almost twice my size, but I do have the very preferable trait of admiral loyalty towards my master, so I did what any loyal dog would do. I planted my paws firmly on the ground, gave a few convincing growls, bared my teeth back at this menacing creature, and kept at the ready for any indication on his part that he would attack. I bravely took a step forward, the fur on my back standing up on end, and turned my keenest attentions toward him lest he make any threatening movement.

Storm was not fooled by my feigned fearlessness. He took a step toward me and we were suddenly locked in a stare.

"Reggie," my master called out. "Come."

I was torn between obeying my master and continuing my protective stance. "Reggie," he repeated, this time more firmly.

We were both startled when suddenly, from out of the bushes off the road, a figure emerged. He looked to be about the same age and height as my master, but there was something definitely less refined about him and the iniquitous look upon his face did not settle well with me.

"Storm!" the young man called and the dog reluctantly turned and brought himself to the young man's side.

"Well, Darcy, it appears your little dog is either terribly foolish or has delusions of grandeur, attempting to engage Storm in a contest. I do not think your little dog would have fared well." I was quite convinced that the smirk on his face was at my expense.

"Wickham, you know your dog is not allowed to run free."

"Oh, come, Darcy. The dog cannot always be penned up. Your hound is allowed to run free. I don't see why Storm cannot."

"You know why not, Wickham. Even you can comprehend they are completely different dogs. Yours is wild and uncontrolled. Good Lord, he frightened Georgiana as well as her nanny when she had been playing on her swing. The dog is a menace and must be kept locked up!"

"You are making far too great a fuss about this incident with Georgiana. If you ask me, she is far too coddled and protected. If you continue to treat her in this manner, she will never know the real dangers in the world. You and your father will not always be with her."

Shivers coursed through my body at his ill-mannered comments about Georgiana. I could only be thankful that she was as young as she was and would have only limited society with the likes of Wickham.

I turned and looked upward at my master. Reigning in his anger, he spoke very commandingly, "How we choose to raise Georgiana is none of your concern, Wickham."

"And what I do with Storm is none of yours!"

"I would argue that point, Wickham. You have been told on several occasions to keep the dog locked up."

"By everyone but your father and I do not think he would insist on it. I believe that walking Storm out on the grounds unleashed would be perfectly acceptable to him as long as I am with him."

"I doubt that, Wickham. You may have charmed your way into Father's acceptance, but you do not fool me. I will not have you endangering others with that dog of yours!"

The two young men stared intently at each other.

Finally breaking the stare, Wickham gave a disdainful sneer at Darcy and then turned to me, letting out a scornful laugh. "That thing you call a hunting dog is rather pathetic," he decried. "Only good for chasing out pheasant from behind a bush, whereas mine," he angrily attached the leash to Storm and gave it a decidedly strong yank, inciting a yelp, "will take on anything. Strong as a bull and has not an ounce of fear in him. I only need say the word and he will attack at my command. If anyone crosses me, they will live to regret it."

The look on Wickham's face seemed almost a threat, but my master held his ground. "I give you warning, Wickham! Leave him on the leash, or you may one day come home to discover this menace gone."

Wickham narrowed his eyes at Darcy. "Come near this dog, Darcy, and you'll be sorry."

Wickham turned to walk away, giving Storm a severe yank with the leash. Storm followed him, but not before baring his teeth again. My master and I watched them until they were out of sight and then we turned to one another. I believe the same thought crossed our mind. Storm was mean-spirited because of the way Wickham mistreated and abused him, no doubt the same way he treats people.

That night my master was still uncollected from his encounter with Wickham. It appeared to me that my master wished to mollify me and needed to explain his relationship with this Wickham. His words seemed to indicate a wish to apologize for the ordeal we went through that afternoon.

"That was a rough encounter this afternoon, boy. Storm can be quite intimidating and Wickham can be quite threatening, but I will never let either of them harm you."

My master let out a deep, long sigh. "I just do not understand it, Reggie. From the time we were both walking, George and I were good friends. We would spend hours exploring the grounds of Pemberley and he treated me as well as any good friend would. But he has grown appallingly undisciplined and more deceitful." He spoke softly and with much deliberation. "I cannot trust him anymore. Whatever good opinion I once held of him has been lost forever."

From that day on, whenever my master exhibited traces of anger, I could usually attribute it to something that Wickham had said or done.

I came to learn that the only other person in my young master's life who gave him great cause for agitation was his aunt, Lady Catherine de Bourgh.

It was spring, and his cousin, Richard Fitzwilliam, who was a few years older, was making what had become a yearly journey to see her at Easter. Lady Catherine's husband had passed several years before, and her nephew had taken it upon himself to pay his respects each year. This year he invited my master to come along, as the two had become not only close cousins, but good friends.

I became aware of some ongoing discussion on whether or not I should accompany them. The argument in my favour was that my master and I were quite inseparable and I was, as my master proudly pointed out, exceedingly well behaved. We walked into the library one evening where his father was seated at his desk engaged in reading a book.

This was my first time to enter that sacred room where the elder Mr. Darcy spent a great deal of his time whilst at Pemberley. As we entered, I could certainly understand why. It had a very woodsy smell, (I quite had to keep reminding myself we were indoors and these large wooden bookcases were *not* trees!) The whole room had a strong, dark feel and scent to it and I believed I would have been quite content to spend much of my time idling here as I presume Mr. Darcy does.

My musings were interrupted by my master's voice.

"Father, I should like to talk with you about taking Reggie with me when Cousin Richard and I travel to Rosings."

"There is no need for Reggie to join you. He will fare adequately here without you. Besides, this is your first visit alone with your cousin. I do not feel it would be wise."

"But Father," my master pleaded, "At least if Reggie accompanies me, Cousin and I shall have some other pleasant company among us."

His father shut the book that he held within his lap and sharply looked up. "Fitzwilliam! You do not speak about your mother's only sister in that manner!"

My master steeled himself and took in a deep breath. "Father, if I may speak openly."

"Son?"

"Lady Catherine… she overwhelms me with her smothering attention, angers me with her critical assessment of everyone else, and completely frustrates me with her insistence that I am to marry her daughter!" I watched as my young master's voice gradually raised and he began to exhibit signs of desperation. He concluded with, "You *know* how she is."

I looked over to his father, wondering exactly *how* she was.

By the manner in which his father's jaw tightened, I was convinced that he inwardly agreed with my master. I could not help but notice that he did not address his son's comments about his aunt. "Compose yourself, Son. Personally, I have no quarrel with you taking Reggie. But I cannot guarantee that *she* will tolerate an animal roaming about her house. If he accompanies you, your aunt may insist that Reggie be kept penned up outdoors."

With that bit of news, my ears slumped and I dropped my head to the floor, resting it upon my front paws. From what I heard my master say about her, I was not quite sure I was going to feel any affection for Lady Catherine de Bourgh. Lifting only my eyes, I peered up at my master.

"I am aware of that, Father. I should like to take him all the same. I believe that once she sees how well behaved he is, she will make allowances."

Glancing over to his father, I watched him nod his head. "Yes, I believe you may be correct, but not because of Reggie's impeccable behaviour." I narrowed my eyebrows at this. "On the contrary, knowing her astute fondness for you, Son, I believe she may accommodate your wish for Reggie to at least remain in your chambers." He picked up his book and looked down at the page. "If I were you, I would not hope for any more than that."

"Then… you will allow me to have him accompany us?"

"I will allow it if your cousin agrees to it. He is the one who will have to suffer a full day's ride in the carriage with the animal."

"Thank you, Father. Thank you!"

He turned to me and ruffled the fur on my head. "I am sure he should have no objection! Reggie, you will be joining me on my first visit to Rosings with Cousin Richard!"

"There is no need for such an uncontrolled display, Son." His father said impassively. "Calm yourself."

My master took in a deep breath and straightened his stance. "Yes, Father."

We both walked out calmly and I took one last glance at the room and inhaled deeply, hoping to preserve that very appealing scent in my memory. As soon as he closed the door to the library behind us, my master dropped all formalities, leaned over and patted his upper legs, signifying it was permissible for me to jump up with my front paws. When I did, he vigorously rubbed both sides of my head with his hands and told me, "You do not know what your presence there will mean to me, Reggie! You have no idea how relieved I am!"

He turned to walk toward his chambers and I followed. "Come, we must prepare ourselves for the great Lady Cat!"

As he walked ahead, I was planted in my position, unable to move. I was not quite sure I liked that fact that she was referred to as a *cat*. After a brief moment, I felt myself a trifle more composed and followed my master, anxious to hear what more he had to say about her.

Chapter 3

After it was settled that I would be accompanying my master to Rosings, he told me more than I wished to know about his aunt. I must admit that when the time drew close for our departure, I believed her to be a most daunting, yet interesting woman. I looked forward to making her acquaintance with a hearty curiosity tempered with a healthy dose of fear.

A few nights before we were to leave, I was situated comfortably in my favourite place upon my master's bed, eager for whatever bit of conversation he was willing to furnish.

"Reggie," he looked at me intently, as he closed the book he had been reading and set it upon the table. "I must warn you that upon our initial arrival, my aunt will talk wildly about how pleased she is that we have arrived, quickly inquire after us but not wait for our responses, and then proceed to bring us into her drawing room where her daughter Anne will be waiting to acknowledge us. Anne will only be allowed to visit a short while, due to her frail health, and will be required to return to her chambers. My aunt will then begin a long tirade about her own ailments, bemoan profusely on how little she is appreciated, and enlighten us as to the tremendous amount of effort she puts forth to bring about resolutions to the disharmony among the cottagers." He let out a deep breath as he sarcastically unleashed this portrayal of his aunt.

He extinguished the last candle and fell upon the bed next to me. Bringing his hand over and gently stroking my fur, he continued, "As a young boy, I was unquestionably frightened by her. She is an imposing woman, tall with a very commanding voice. She does not tolerate her opinions and judgments contradicted or challenged."

I rolled over onto my back and he obligingly began scratching my belly. "And I find her completely unreasonable in her assertions, more often than not." He shifted onto his side and I could see in the dimness of the room that he was looking towards me. "Father says I must never disagree with her; that I must show her the deepest respect." He sighed deeply. "Sometimes I am so wearied by her words and complaints that I can barely wait to excuse myself from her presence."

Though he was now seriously engaged in conversation, he had reached that most particular place on my belly that causes an uncontrollable shaking of my leg. I could do nothing to prevent its incessant trembling and resigned myself to the pleasure of his hand upon me.

Suddenly he stopped and began to laugh. "Reggie, I would imagine that you are enjoying my scratching your belly more than you are my discourse on my aunt. I shall trouble you no longer with talk of her."

With that, we began a rumble and tumble of play upon his bed which prompted him to collapse in a fit of laughter. I contributed to our melee with the fiercest, albeit friendly, growl I could summon up as he playfully wrestled with me. The door to the room unexpectedly opened and we both abruptly stopped and looked up.

Standing at the door was my master's father, holding candle in hand and bearing a pained expression across his face. He took a deep breath and slowly issued these words to my master, "Son, there is no reason to behave in such an uncontrolled display. If you cannot behave in a more dignified manner with your dog, Reggie will not be permitted to accompany you to your aunt's."

We both watched silently as he backed out of the door and closed it behind him. In the darkness, my master quietly said, "Good night, Reggie," and rolled away from me in unquestioning obedience to his father.

I could not help but ponder his father's admonition. Just like my master, he was of a reserved nature himself. But there seemed to be a lack of tolerance for any sort of lively display in his presence. I wondered whether it could be due to the fact that he was still grieving for his wife. Perhaps he could not -- or would not -- allow himself to experience any pleasure and enjoyment anymore and, therefore, reproached my master when he exhibited the same. I was disconcerted that he considered it imprudent for my master to display any sort of a lively nature, for that was what I truly enjoyed doing.

Whereas I was more determined than ever to engage my master in playful jousting, I deemed it best to limit those times to when we were away from the house or when the elder Mr. Darcy was away from home.

~~*

The day before we were to depart for Rosings, as we awaited the arrival of his cousin, my master gave one further bit of information about his aunt.

Lowering himself to his knees, he grasped his hand under my chin and looked at me intently. "Most likely, my aunt will inquire after your lineage, believing it to be of utmost importance. Whilst your lineage is most acceptable to me, Reggie, she would be greatly displeased that you are not of the purest breeding. I confess that I will assert to her that you are of the finest breeding." He smiled down at me, "I do not consider it an untruth, for to me, you are finer than any dog whose breeding rivals yours."

I felt only the highest esteem for my master and my assessment of Lady Cat was quite complete. I had the daunting impression that she was formidable indeed!

‿‿*

With the arrival of my master's cousin, Richard Fitzwilliam, my fears and trepidations of making Lady Cat's acquaintance were momentarily forgotten. A lively gentleman, a few years my young master's senior, Fitzwilliam was the younger son of the Earl of Matlock, and never did I meet a man more eager to welcome me into his presence than he.

These two cousins appeared to thrive off of each other and I could readily see that Fitzwilliam had the same liberating effect on him that I do. He brought out a spirit of liveliness in him that so few could do. I eagerly welcomed him into this exclusive club that boasts only Georgiana and me as the only other members.

We set out for Kent early the following morning and the two young men enjoyed an endless discussion about every topic imaginable. Fitzwilliam had completed his education and boasting on the superiority of his school, which had educated future kings and statesmen in its time, found enjoyment in challenging his cousin on any and every subject. My master did not disappoint. Whereas his education had consisted solely of his tutor at home, he thrived on reading and gained much of his knowledge from the perusal of many books. Fitzwilliam was eventually forced to concede that my master's knowledge on every challenge could not be found wanting.

It is interesting for me to note that my master exhibited a completely different demeanour around his cousin. I did notice he was as lively in his company as he is in mine and Georgiana's, yet he was clearly stimulated by the conversation in which the two cousins embarked. Whereas his conversations with his father are no doubt intellectually stimulating, I can see that my master holds in all emotion, thoroughly thinking through what he is about to say before he says it, and never contradicts him.

Whereas, he and Fitzwilliam loved to argue and banter, laugh and cry. I comprehend, not for the first time, that he is a man full of passion and emotion and unfortunately, very few people have the opportunity to see it.

‿‿*

Upon arriving at Rosings, we disembarked the carriage; the two young men grateful for the opportunity to step out and stretch. My master motioned for me stay behind him and I gratefully obliged him as I saw what appeared *not* to be a cat, as she was so frequently referred, but instead, a giant pheasant-like bird coming out the door, marked by a disarray of large feathers protruding from her head.

Upon deeper scrutiny, however, I was able to comprehend that perhaps she could be likened to a cat - one that had surreptitiously devoured a large fowl of sorts, leaving the evidence of plumage to be seen by all.

She rushed up to my master, arms open wide, and after welcoming him, began lavishly praising him about how he has grown, asked why he had not visited sooner, and inquired after the family. After giving my master a superficial embrace, she instantly turned her attention to Fitzwilliam and it was all repeated.

She then abruptly turned and commanded the two gentlemen to follow her inside.

"Excuse me, Aunt," my master interjected.

She turned with narrowed eyes, as if this parting from her customary routine was an umbrage. "Nephew?"

"I hope you do not mind, but I brought along my dog, Reggie. He is very well trained and if it is agreeable to you, I should like to keep him in my chambers. He will be in no one's way."

I cautiously peeked around him and watched as she slowly looked down, raising one eyebrow with the sternest look of anyone I have ever seen. After studying me for a brief moment, she looked to my master, who was nervously rubbing his fingers together, but he did manage to eke out a disarming smile. Despite that, I was quite confident that she was *not* inclined to approve of my presence in the home.

"Springer Spaniel, I see. Breeding?" It was almost not a question. She spoke with great authority as if to say, *His breeding is top of the line, of course?*

"Only the finest, Aunt." I noticed a slight quiver of his voice. I wondered if it was simply because he was under interrogation by his aunt or because he slightly disguised the truth.

She turned her attention back to me, eyeing me with piercing scrutiny. "Good. Only the finest breeding will naturally grace this house. You are to keep him out of my way and do not let him venture too close to Anne. You know how frail and sickly she is and she is positively terrified of animals."

"Yes, Aunt!" My master gave his cousin a wide-eyed grin and then looked down at me, giving me a covert wink. We entered the great home and I recalled that in my master's chronicle of what to expect, he had told me we would next come inside, meet her daughter, and then would be made to hear all of her complaints. I wondered whether I would be allowed to remain with them and wished to make myself as invisible as possible, hoping Lady Cat would forget about my presence there.

We were led into the drawing room, darkened by the drapes being drawn across the window. A young girl, probably no more than ten years old, sat with a blanket about her. I found her to be a thin girl with pale skin. She shyly glanced up to her cousins as we all walked in and a very slight smile appeared on her face that very quickly disappeared. I wondered how much of her nature was due to her sickly disposition -- of which her cousins had spoken much in our journey hither -- or perhaps simply boredom with her circumstances.

Her two cousins politely greeted her and I watched as Lady Cat looked on with a gratified smile on her face. It painted a picture, in my mind's eye, of a cat that had just caught and eaten the pet canary. She was obviously very happy to have the two men here, particularly my master.

When Anne's eyes met mine, I sensed within her a conflict that likely stemmed from an inherent fear of dogs, (and therefore a fear of me), coupled, however, with a curiosity about me. I stationed myself in a secluded alcove, which was situated between the couch and small end table. Here I was able to watch little Anne and frequently met her hesitant and questioning glance with an affable one of my own.

She kept her head down for the greater part of her time with us, which allowed her to furtively observe me. I did not dare approach her, lest her mother send me out to sleep with the chickens in the distant barn of some neighbour. So the two of us quietly eyed one another as her mother continued her grievances about how little anyone in the neighbourhood appreciated all she did for them.

As I watched her, I also saw her look admiringly at her cousin, my master, the one whom she believed would someday be her husband. I could not help but notice my master strictly avoided her eye, as if any attention paid to her might encourage her hopes and her mother's very absurd assumption. But I liked this young girl and could not blame her for the sickly state in which she found herself nor the dreary conditions her mother forced upon her.

My strategically placed alcove was also completely out of Lady Cat's scrutiny. As I have aptly learned to make myself disappear from view and, therefore, from someone's recollection, by lying down on the far side of some piece of furniture, I was of the firm opinion that the great lady had quite forgotten about me. My strategy proved effective and whether or not she simply tolerated my presence or forgot I was there, I am at a loss to know. But I was allowed to stay.

However much she ignored me, I found I could not ignore *her,* let alone forget her. Her incessant complaints and grievances refused to escape my ears. On this particular day, Lady Catherine's complaints focused on how difficult it was to find capable servants.

"I have had to replace three of my kitchen staff and four of my maids in just one year's time. One would think they would be a little more willing to learn what my wishes are and anticipate them. How I dislike having to repeat a directive over and over! It is not to be borne!"

The two men sat quietly, hoping this tirade would end quickly and they would be able to politely excuse themselves.

"I only hope they get everything right for the small dinner party tonight."

From where I was situated, I was unable to see my master's face. As he was seated next to me on the couch, however, I could feel a definite tensing of his muscles and heard a slight intake of breath.

Fitzwilliam asked, "A dinner party tonight, Aunt? Here?"

"Of course! I would not wish to be derelict in my duties to you and not introduce you whilst you are here. It shall be a simple party. I have invited a small selection of families from only the finest circles in the surrounding neighbourhood. There are but a few. It shall be an intimate gathering."

I looked up and saw my master and his cousin exchange wary glances. Fitzwilliam gave a slight nod of encouragement to my master as if he were telling him that all would be well, there would be nothing about which to be troubled. I was not quite certain that it did anything to ebb my master's concerns. I could see it in his face that all he could envision was a room full of people that he did not know.

Lady Catherine stood up abruptly, bringing the two young men to their feet, and me, as well. She looked at her daughter and cackled out an order to her governess, Mrs. Jenkinson, to take Anne to her chambers as she had had enough activity for the day.

We watched as Mrs. Jenkinson helped the young girl up and quietly exited the room. Little Anne gave me one last glance before she walked out.

Then Lady Cat advised her nephews to prepare for the evening's activities as they would commence in less than two hours.

The two men politely excused themselves and I followed. Once we had climbed the stairs, my master, quite angrily, spoke to his cousin.

"You did not tell me she would be having social gatherings whilst we were here."

Fitzwilliam looked at him with a wide grin. "This must all be due to you, my young cousin. In all the years I have visited, she has never held a dinner party in her home on *my* behalf." He patted my master on his back as he continued his teasing. "Most likely, she will be showing off her future son-in-law to all her well-bred, refined acquaintances."

My master gave his cousin an annoyed thrust with his shoulder. "You know I will never marry Anne!"

"Quiet, Darcy! Someone may overhear you. She does have her spies throughout the house."

I could sense the desperation in my master's voice. "What am I supposed to do? I cannot have her continuing to spread that kind of falsehood around!"

Fitzwilliam put a calming hand upon his shoulder. "You are still young. Anne is even younger. By the time Anne is of age, you will be old enough to stand up to her. Presently," here, he gave an up and down glance at my master, "you may be tall and you may be disgustingly handsome, but you are still her inferior. If I were you, I would not speak to her of your contrary notions."

My master let out a frustrated breath. "So you are of the opinion that I should just let her inform all of Kent that I am promised to her daughter?"

"I believe you are."

"It was a promise *I* never made."

"I understand that. Just calm down, assure yourself you will get through this evening, smile graciously at our Aunt Catherine and all her guests, and tell yourself you will never see any of these people again… hopefully."

"You are a great help indeed, Cousin," my master spoke with resignation.

"Thank you! I have never been paid a kinder compliment! Since I am not entitled to everything that you are, being merely a second son, at least I can content myself with being considered a help to the great Master Fitzwilliam Darcy of Pemberley. If I accomplish nothing else, I shall die peacefully knowing that I once helped you." Fitzwilliam cheerfully smiled, my master groaned, and the two parted to their respective chambers.

~~*

I must admit that my master paints an exceedingly handsome picture when fitted with his finest clothes. It was no wonder to me, then, why his aunt favoured him so. And perhaps Anne, at a young ten years of age, had dreams of him coming and sweeping her away from this apparent dark and sheltered life that she led.

As the time drew nearer for my master to make his way downstairs, his pacing grew more intensified. He occasionally glanced in the mirror, straightening his neck cloth and tugging at his waistcoat. I could see that he was particularly nervous about all the acquaintances he would be forced to endure tonight.

I take great pleasure in meeting new people and thoroughly enjoy getting to know them (which, I flatter myself, I can do most proficiently with a few delicately, but strategically, placed sniffs); whilst my master, in stark contrast, stands back, sometimes in the shadow of his father, sometimes under the guise of indifference or pride, guarded and silent.

Whereas he is reserved by nature, as is his father, there is something else causing this reserved behaviour in him that I was at a loss to discern. I determined, from the first time I had noticed it, that I would watch and I hoped that someday I would discover the reason behind this. I believe it was this night that I first formulated an opinion on the matter.

~~*

For my own sake, as well as I believe my master's, before anyone else arrived he led me outside. This time I was able to survey the grounds without the ominous *bird-cat* woman intimidating me. Whilst opulent in size, it had a more forced and manicured appearance than Pemberley. It was very obvious to me that people had been involved in the shaping of the grounds surrounding her house. It appeared to have its landscaping imposed upon it, unlike the natural beauty of Pemberley's park.

But I could not complain as my master and I took a quick walk. He made several attempts to take in deep breaths, as if they would calm him. Finally, just as we were to slip back into the house, he paused. He looked at me and said in a clearly anxious tone, "Reggie, do not think me ill bred, but there is nothing I dislike more than a room full of people with whom I am not well acquainted."

That was all he said. We entered the house and he returned me to his chambers. I expected to see nothing more of him until he returned later that evening.

~~*

That night, I made myself as comfortable as I could, listening with a most acute ear to the sounds which had begun to stir below. As guests began to arrive, I began to assess that this was not the small gathering Lady Catherine had promised. In fact, it was quite the opposite.

I could hear only rumblings of voices and surprisingly, as hard as I tried, I could not distinguish my master's voice. Occasionally I heard Fitzwilliam let out a hearty laugh and even more frequently I heard Lady Cat raise her voice about some particular subject, but never once did I discern my master's voice.

I settled down on the floor, giving one hearty stretch before closing my eyes, anticipating a long evening of solitude. It was difficult to sleep soundly, however, as the noises from below kept sparking my interest. I was also acutely aware of the variety of scents that wafted their way upstairs from the kitchen. I could only imagine sitting at the feet of my master, hoping for some juicy morsel of duck, roast, or ham to be accidentally dropped at my feet.

I told myself that had I been allowed to join them downstairs, I would have behaved impeccably. No one would have even taken notice of me. Perhaps some of the kitchen staff would have taken pity on me and slipped me a little of the excess food, as they occasionally did at Pemberley. I know that I let out an audible sigh as I contemplated this.

I was laying there for some time when I heard the door knob rattle. I perked my head up instantly, anxious to see my master and hear how he had fared. The door opened slightly but to my surprise, no one entered.

I watched intently, waiting for someone to make themselves known. I soon came to know who it was because of the soft sound of feet scampering away and the discernable scent of the person. The door had been opened by little Anne!

I watched and listened curiously, before deciding upon what I should do. I did not see Anne nor did I hear anything apart from the commotion downstairs. I could not ascertain what she was about. Perhaps she was bored, having been confined to her room, and was now simply walking the hallway as a diversion. Perhaps she did not know I was in the room. Perhaps she wished to deepen her acquaintance with me.

I got up slowly and walked toward the door. It was open just wide enough for me to poke my nose through. I pushed open the door and it swung open wide enough for me to peer out. Looking to the right and then to the left, I finally saw her. She was lying in a prone position, peering through the railing at the people below.

She casually looked at me and then back to the goings-on below. I was unsure whether she was actually inviting me to join her or if she was terrified of me. I hoped it was not the latter and got down on my belly and edged slowly toward her. Whilst still a safe distance from her, I stopped and looked down through the railing at the vast array of elegantly dressed people beneath us. Occasionally, the young Miss de Bourgh let a soft sigh escape.

As I watched the spectacle below, I heard Anne say something. I perked up my head and looked over at her. She had reached out her hand towards me, but I was too far away for her to reach me. As I slowly came toward her, she timidly drew her hand away and I stopped again. She soon changed her mind and stretched her hand out again. This time I came close enough for her to reach me and she very softly touched my fur.

"Soft," was all she said.

My thoughts quickly reverted back to Lady Cat's words that Anne was terrified of dogs. I would have to strongly disagree. She was no more terrified of me than I was of her. I believed her to have simply not had contact with many dogs before and regarded me with curiosity.

She seemed content to lightly brush my fur with her hands. She would occasionally point to something below and giggle. I believe she was telling me the names of the guests attending the dinner party.

My attention was drawn back downstairs and I kept an eye out for my master. When I espied him, I involuntarily snapped to attention, just as Anne did. We both saw him at just about same time. I sneaked a peek at her and beheld her eyes momentarily brighten and her lips form the slightest smile. But again, the brightness in her eyes and her smile slowly diminished, a look of concern replacing them.

Turning my attention back to my master, I watched him walk out of the large ballroom and over to the fireplace in the great hall below, placing his arm upon the mantel. I could almost feel his discomfort as strongly as I saw it on his face. We sat silently, watching as his cousin approached him, making a futile attempt to nudge him back into the other room and back to the guests.

I could not help but study my master and ponder his conduct. When he had so much in his favour and so many advantages, what, I wondered, prompted such reticence in these types of situations?

As Anne and I watched the two young men converse, Anne scooted a little closer to me. Her hand continued to stroke down my back and I almost forgot about my master below until she spoke, again softly, "He does not like being there. All the attention he is getting makes him ill at ease. He does not enjoy being the centre of attention."

I lifted my head and looked at her, quite stunned. She had spoken hardly a word earlier when we were downstairs. I finally collected myself and turned back to the dinner party down below. I rested my head upon my paws, but was just barely able to see what was going on downstairs. I contemplated this young girl who was indeed small, frail, ordinary in looks, and restrained in conversation. But there was one thing I knew as a certainty. This little Anne probably knew more about what was going on in this house than anyone else!

Chapter 4

I must have fallen asleep because the next thing of which I became aware was the sound of people taking their leave from Rosings. I was surprised to feel something pressing down upon my belly. I groggily lifted my head and strained to turn it, only to see that Anne had fallen asleep as well, with one arm stretched out across me.

I moved as gently as possible so as not to waken her and turned my attention back downstairs. I saw that the last of the guests had departed and the house was empty now save my master, his cousin, his aunt, and the servants who were now busily cleaning up.

The two young men wished their aunt a good night and began making their way up the stairs, engaged in animated conversation whilst Lady Cat's callous demands to her servants on how to clean up more effectively echoed from below.

"Fitzwilliam, what do you plan to do with that stash of food! That is absolutely abominable of you!" My master spoke with more fervour than I had seen him display the whole of the evening. And although he tried to appear disgusted with his cousin, a small, teasing smile crept across his lips.

Fitzwilliam took a bite and mumbled, "I plan to eat throughout the night. I simply cannot bear to let all this epicurean delight go to waste!"

Fitzwilliam laughed and I observed my master give his cousin a censuring look, such as a father would, for speaking with his mouth full of food.

"But speaking of abominable... *your* behaviour tonight, Darcy..." Fitzwilliam swallowed and then continued. "What were you thinking? I have seen your dog exhibit better manners than you did in front of all those guests this evening!"

My master lost all sense of merriment and I was at a loss to know whether to take his cousin's words as a compliment or a censure.

"I did not feel at ease with anyone here," my master dolefully responded.

"Come, Darcy! You must learn to apply yourself in situations such as these! I know you to be a bit more lively and definitely more civil than you were this evening. You planted yourself against the mantel of the fireplace or stood at the window, disengaged from everyone far too often. There is no excuse for it! I found most of the people here tonight at least tolerable!"

"You were not the object of strained necks, stares with mouths agape, and whispers and murmurings to one another. I heard their comments about my 10,000 pounds, my estate… And the way our aunt paraded me before everyone! I felt as though I was being auctioned off… as if I were some prize horse to be bought or a piece of property to be surveyed," my master scowled.

"You are!" Fitzwilliam laughed softly. "I suggest you accustom yourself to it, Darcy. Just look at you! Handsome, wealthy, set to inherit one of the finest estates in the country! How else do you expect people to behave around you?"

"They could at least attempt to become truly acquainted with me. Everyone was so polite and agreed with everything I said. It became quite tedious! Their honey-drenched flattery dripped from their mouths at every opportunity, as if that was all that was required to secure my esteem."

"But certainly you see the benefit of being well-liked and admired by everyone. Just think of all the pretty young ladies who will do anything to secure your notice! Heavens, Darcy! If I did not like you as much as I do, if I did not hold you in the highest esteem, if you were not so completely faultless, I would positively loathe you!"

"But why?"

"Because, good cousin, if you did not notice all the eyes of the beautiful young ladies back there upon you, I did! You will be able to have anything you want in life. As for myself, I stand in the shadow of my elder brother and my cousin, with only tolerable looks, and no one takes an immediate interest in me as they do you. You have no idea how envious I am of you!"

"There is no reason for you to be." My master let out a breath of frustrated air. "How am I to determine whether it is *me* that they esteem and admire and not my estate or position in society?"

Fitzwilliam laughed again, but was prevented from answering when the two men reached the top of the stairs and stopped short. Both pair of eyes widened in surprise as they settled upon little Anne and me.

"Well, look at that, Darce! It appears as though your young wife has taken a liking to your dog!"

"She is not and will never be my wife!" my master said in a harsh whisper that I could only barely hear and I hoped little Anne did not.

I looked at my master with worry etched across my face. I narrowed my eyebrows, wondering if he would be angry with me for being out of the room and let out a trifling whine to assure him that I knew that I was not quite where he expected me to be. Hopefully he would understand that it was not all my fault.

"Anne must have opened your door, Darcy. It appears to me that our wise and infallible aunt was incorrect about Anne's fear of dogs. Just look at her, lying there fast asleep with her arm about him!"

"What are we to do?"

"We?" Fitzwilliam looked in helpless pretence at my master as he held out his hands. "My hands are full. I suggest *you* carry her back to her chamber."

With that suggestion, Fitzwilliam nonchalantly turned and continued on to his quarters.

"Cousin, wait!" Darcy's words hit deaf ears. Or perhaps ears that were not inclined to respond.

He let out a huff. "Very well, Reggie. Let me untangle her from you and return her to her room."

I watched as he easily scooped her up off the floor. As she was lifted, she turned her head into his chest and wrapped her arms around his neck. She never opened her eyes, but I had the feeling little Anne was not asleep and that this would be the closest she would ever come to having her promised one hold her. I watched and waited as he carried her the short distance down the hall into her bedchamber and almost as quickly as he entered, he stepped out, looking somewhat relieved. He took unusually brisk steps back towards me and we returned to our room.

~~*

For the remainder of our stay at Rosings, there were no more surprise dinner engagements at Rosings and therefore no more furtive spying trysts with little Anne, but the effects of that first night lingered with my master. Unfortunately for him, they did have invitations to several engagements in response to that first evening's dinner that they were required to attend. Although I could not observe as I had at that night at Rosings, I eagerly listened to my master when he returned and it was always the same.

As Anne had so discerningly put it, "He does not enjoy being the centre of attention."

He came in late one evening and had barely ridded himself of his formal attire when he threw himself upon the bed. He restlessly tossed and turned and I waited patiently, knowing he would want to eventually relate to me the events of the evening.

He finally rolled toward me and reached out to scratch my head. In the darkness of the room I could see his eyes drifting aimlessly about.

"Reggie," he began, "I am not quite sure I can handle one more of these affairs. Richard told me they are good for me. He says that in a few years I shall eagerly embrace every invitation extended to me and will accept and attend in good spirits. Or at least I had better."

Letting out a deep sigh, he continued. "I know these people are the very same people I will encounter in London and who will frequent the same circles of society as I. I just do not enjoy the fact that Aunt Catherine insists on making such a grand spectacle of me in front of all her acquaintances."

He was silent for a moment and I could see his brows furrow as if he was trying to determine something. He gave his head a slight shake and went on. "What I am at a loss to understand is, if she is so insistent on my marrying her daughter, why does she parade me in front of everyone, lavishing me with praise and accolades as if I am an eligible man in want of a wife?"

He continued scratching my head, moving his fingers to the area behind my ears that I find so pleasant and I let out an empathetic moan. At least I tried to make it sound empathetic. It could have been a purely indulgent one. He said no more and at length his fingers ceased their scratching and his breathing grew deeper. He was asleep. I consoled myself with the fact that it was because I was a good listener and he was able to share his deepest thoughts with me.

Whilst I came to expect my master's discomfiture when he returned from these engagements, even within the small confines of the family at Rosings he was not without consternation, either. Every time his aunt lavished praise on him, which she was moved to do quite often over the course of a conversation, he tensed. Her undivided and piercing attention towards him made him squirm uncomfortably more than once whilst visiting in the sitting room or eating at the dining room table. His aunt made more frequent assertions about the promised marriage, speaking of her expectations of their felicity. My master would turn to his cousin with a pleading look, only to receive a reassuring smile in return. My master knew he was not to counter her, at least not at his young age.

Each day Anne would come down at the prescribed time and join the family. She never spoke, but I began to understand through her eyes that she greatly feared her mother's disapprobation and therefore, dared not risk saying or doing anything that might irritate her. But as the rest of us sat in the drawing room and talked, I believed her to be listening and observing, storing it all up for her to meditate on over and over; especially every word my master said.

The one pleasant distraction my master and I shared was our walks around Rosings. I eagerly joined him in his early morning or late evening walks and we would venture off along different paths and lanes. I soon found that my master had favourite ones that he preferred over others. It was when he was outside alone with me that I felt he was truly himself and completely happy.

Finally, after enduring four dinner engagements, two dances, and one party at an elegant lodge, my master was more than eager to depart. Our time at Rosings was complete and we prepared to leave.

As we were gathered at the door on the morning of our departure, Lady Catherine belied her usual severe hand on Anne and allowed her to visit with us all in the sitting room and follow the party to the door as we were to leave. I believed Lady Cat had the hope that her nephew would give her daughter some sort of encouraging display that she might hold on to as a promise. But my master hastily bid her a simple farewell and turned to leave. I saw resignation sweep across the young girl's face. I comprehended that it was not out of hope disappointed, but from expectations met. She knew him too well to believe he would oblige her in any way.

Her attentions were turned to me and she kneeled down, wrapping her small arms around my neck. She hugged me a little too tightly and I felt a quiver shoot through her.

"Anne! Unhand that germ-infested dog!"

I jumped and Anne jumped. My master sharply turned around and came back. "Excuse me, Aunt, but he is *not* germ infested and in my estimation, Anne would likely benefit from an animal like him for her own." He looked at me and then to Anne, his eyes widening and turning toward the ground as he realized had contradicted his aunt whilst at the same time standing up for his frail cousin.

I cautiously looked to the great Lady Cat and noticed a fleeting trace of anger take hold of her, but she steeled herself. "Nephew, if that is what you believe is best for *your* Anne, I shall take it into consideration. I would do anything to secure her comfort and happiness for you."

My master closed his eyes tightly as a wide smile brightened Anne's face. But I do not believe her smile was due to the talk and hope of belonging to him. I believe she indulged the hope that she might soon obtain a companionable dog of her own. And truth be told, that gave me just as much pleasure.

Lady Cat walked out with us, leaving Anne to remain inside, in the dark, smothering world to which she was accustomed. It warmed my heart, however, to know that during our short stay, she was made just a little happier.

As we clambered into the carriage, Lady Cat issued her final words to us. "Now, nephews, I insist we make this a yearly event. I will not brook any disappointment on the matter. I do expect to see you often during the year as you visit with the rest of your family, but we shall plan on just the two of you coming around Easter from now on."

It was amusing to me that she completely disregarded the fact that Fitzwilliam had been making it an annual event for several years now. In her eyes, however, the addition of my master to the visit lent much distinction and she was quick to ensure he would return on a regular basis. And that we did.

~~*

My master and his cousin spent a few days in London. It was an enjoyable time that restored the liveliness back into my master that his cousin knew he was able to exhibit. The two cousins reluctantly parted ways and it was with much eagerness and joyful expectation that my master and I finally set off back to Pemberley.

It was a long day's journey and I was sleeping comfortably on the floor inside the carriage when the familiar scent of home penetrated my nostrils. I lifted my head to see my master gazing out the window with a serene look of contentment on his face. I jumped up onto the seat next to him and looked out, taking in a deep breath and revelling in that oh, so familiar aroma of the woods that surround our home.

My master looked over at me and could not help but notice the incontrollable wagging of my tail. "Yes, Reggie. We are finally home. It is good, is it not?"

I thought it appropriate to let out an affirming bark.

As the carriage pulled up to the front of the estate, the door was opened and I eagerly sprang out, anxious to expend a bit of the energy that had built up over the course of the day. I ran over to some bushes before I did anything else, but returned promptly and watched as my master conversed with Mrs. Reynolds, who had come out to greet us. As other servants came out to help unload the luggage, my head was tousled a few times by several who seemed to have missed me.

We walked indoors and I know my master, disappointed that his father had not come out to welcome him home, inquired of his whereabouts so he could greet him. Mrs. Reynolds informed him that he was in his study. As we walked to the study, I observed him watch for Georgiana, but we did not see her. As we approached the closed door to the study, we heard laughter and suddenly I was stopped in my forward progress by the detection of a particular scent of which I was not especially fond. I let a growl escape, but my master did not heed it.

As he approached the door, he heard laughter again and he looked at me oddly. He had not heard his father laugh like that in a long time. He tapped on the door and his father bid him to enter. As he opened it, his father stood up to greet him and the person sitting opposite him in a chair, beaming widely, stood up and turned around. My master was standing face to face with George Wickham!

Whether his father recognized the tension that suddenly spilled into the air, I do not know. He warmly came around from his desk and welcomed his son home.

"Fitzwilliam! You are home! I hope you enjoyed your visit with your aunt!" He stretched out his arms and placed his hands firmly on my master's shoulders. "It is good you are home. Come, sit down. George and I were just discussing schools. He seems inclined to attend Cambridge next year, as you are."

The two young men turned toward each other and a capricious smile again displayed itself on Wickham's face. "Your father is too good to me, Darcy. He has most generously offered to provide for my university education. It would appear that the two of us will be attending school together."

My master flinched slightly. "Is that so?"

"We have been discussing my desire that the church become George's profession and the living he may expect once he has completed school."

My master's eyes narrowed at this and he either seemed at a loss for words or simply refrained from speaking out of respect for his father.

"Well, Sir," Wickham quickly interjected, noticing the disturbing look. "I must go." He reached out and shook Mr. Darcy's hand. "You are most kind. I shall do all I can to live up to your expectations."

"I am sure you shall, George."

Wickham gave my master a nervous, but polite bow and quickly exited the room.

"Friendly, engaging young man, that George Wickham."

My master closed his eyes briefly and pursed his lips together. "Father, you have promised him an education and a living?"

"Yes, it is the least I can do. His father has been a most excellent steward for many years. He is my godson and I want to do this to assist him." His father looked over at his son, noticing the look of displeasure across his face. "You do not seem pleased with my actions."

My master took in a deep breath as if to say something, but then stopped. I could see the battle going on inside of him; whether to lash out against the young man his father seemed to favour.

The ensuing calm in him voice masked the anger I perceived roiling inside him. "His easy charm and amiability may not reflect who he truly is on the inside, Father."

"Oh, come, Fitzwilliam. You two used to be best of friends when you were younger. Certainly I can see that you both have grown apart, but that is no reason for you to think ill of him. You two may have very different dispositions, but do not allow that to sway your opinion of him. Just remember that he has not had all the advantages and opportunities that you have."

"Father," my master implored, "consider his behaviour of late. If I may be so bold, Sir, he is reckless and lazy. Certainly, he is not worthy of your patronage."

His father looked at my master sternly. "Fitzwilliam, he may have an uncultivated side to him, but that is only because he has not received the formal training you have received. Once I take him under my wing, I am quite sure he will apply himself. He has told me himself that he greatly appreciates all I have done for him and will gratefully accept and be faithful with whatever patronage I bestow on him."

"Father! He is…"

His father's eyes narrowed as he looked at his son, surprised by his outburst. "Son, George Wickham's father has been a most faithful and excellent steward for me for many years. George has always treated me with the utmost kindness and respect. I will do no less."

"You do not know him as I do!"

"That is enough, Fitzwilliam. You have had advantages and privileges in life that he will never come close to having. I will do what I must to secure him an education and a living that will situate him most comfortably. Now enough talk of that, tell me about your visit with your aunt."

My master stood silently for a moment, wishing he could detail all the times Wickham had been disrespectful, disorderly, and dissolute. How I wished my master could make him see how his behaviour was self-indulgent and reckless. But instead, he acquiesced to his father's request and related to him our stay at Rosings. I could discern all the anger and resentment seething within for the willing blindness of his father to George Wickham's true nature. I hoped that eventually, he would see Wickham for the rake he really was.

~~*

After that encounter, we easily and joyfully returned back to the routine we had before we left for Rosings. We spent the remainder of the spring and summer at Pemberley. My master seemed to flourish within the confines of the estate and soon the disquiet, which weighed heavily upon him at Rosings and immediately upon returning, was diminished to almost nothing.

My master and I eagerly set out again upon our favoured paths. He and his father participated in several shooting parties, and I displayed my excellence at being a well-trained hunting dog. I could not imagine a more pleasant occupation than roaming the grounds of Pemberley with my master and I could not quite fathom what it was about "society" that would be an improvement over this for my master; especially when everything about it seemed to cause him undue distress.

It was good to see Georgiana again and she was growing by the day. Her vocabulary was increasing considerably, although her shyness exhibited itself in her reluctance to connect more than two or three words together at a time. She was quite content to sit quietly and listen. Like Anne, I could see that she was a keen observer, and was absorbing everything around her.

Georgiana had a quick mind and learned rapidly, so her governess was inclined to begin teaching her to read and to play the pianoforte even at her young age. Georgiana was, by the summer's end, reading simple books and playing easy songs on the pianoforte; her governess assured her father that she was well on her way to someday becoming a very accomplished young lady. She became quite proficient at playing and even at the tender age of four, seemed to have a gift and an innate love for music. It seemed easier for her to express herself in music than express herself in words.

My master's father, still grievous over the death of his wife, sadly seemed more resigned than accepting of it. He spoke very little of her, but went about his day with a determination to keep himself busy; I think, to keep himself from dwelling on her absence. We had several enjoyable hunting outings where he joined my master and I. Father and son seemed to have a strong bond between them that may have grown a bit stronger in the time we were gone. I believe Mr. Darcy missed his son and although he did not show an overt display of emotion around him, I could perceive he was glad my master was home. I could not help but recall, however, the joviality and laughter that Mr. Darcy shared with George Wickham when we encountered them that first day back from Rosings. I wished there was something I could do to encourage this same liveliness between my master and his father.

As traces of winter teased away the pleasant fall days, plans were set into motion to travel to London, where, I understood, we would spend a great deal of time. Last year at this time, the move to Town for the Season was deferred for the period of mourning the elder Mr. Darcy was observing. He had no inclination to move about in the circles of Society without his beloved wife, and therefore he remained at Pemberley for most of that year.

So now I was faced with having to endure the whole of winter in Town with my master, who was more than reluctant to put the effort into making acquaintances with those who eagerly wished to seek out an introduction; his father, who now being an eligible, wealthy widower, was about to become a very much sought after gentleman, much to his disinclination and consternation; and little Georgiana, as shy as she could be, would keenly observe the discomfiture of her father and brother in the company of strangers, which would only serve to reinforce her timidity by their behaviour.

I sensed that it would be a very long winter.

Chapter 5

It was far too soon for my liking that we departed Pemberley for London for the winter.

Whilst I had absolutely no complaints about Town or the manor that the Darcys owned there, it was not as fine as Pemberley. Granted, the grounds were sufficiently laden with trees and shrubs, but my master and I could not take our long leisurely walks as we so frequently did at Pemberley unless we ventured beyond the grounds of the home and out onto the street. As I mentioned previously, I am of an amiable nature and I am most interested in the acquaintance of any dog we might encounter, but walking in town proved far too disagreeable.

The streets were heavily burdened with people in far too great a hurry; crowding the avenues with horses and carriages that appeared to care not of one's safety. I am ashamed to say that most of the dogs who aimlessly roamed about had, for the most part, very poor manners. Moreover, London was noisy where Pemberley was quiet. The smells in Town were quite repugnant compared to the fresh air of the country.

I willingly endured these distasteful conditions in order to remain by my master's side. I knew my particular reasons for preferring Pemberley and I sensed that my master shared the same.

For the first few days after our arrival, our time was occupied with settling in. The distinguished Earl of Matlock, Lady Matlock, and their son Richard were the first to pay a call. It was good to see my master and his cousin together again.

As we sat together in the drawing room that first evening, the conversation meandered to the parties, concerts, theatre performances, and other events that they all would enjoy attending together. Whilst all this was wholly perplexing to me, I enjoyed being in their company, especially as it was still early and Georgiana had been allowed to remain. She was happily situated by my side, brushing my coat with a small brush that, I assume, she also used to brush her favourite doll's hair.

The Earl, who was the late Mrs. Darcy's brother, attempted to broach a sensitive subject with my master's father. "Frederick… ahem," he cast a sly, nervous look to his wife who nodded her head in encouragement for him to continue. "There has been much talk amongst the ton recently…" He paused and appeared to swallow something with great difficulty.

"Yes?" Mr. Darcy looked curiously to him to continue.

"About your participation in society this season."

"And of what interest is it to them?"

"Well, it is not expected that you will remain in mourning forever."

"Excuse me, I am not sure I understand your meaning," the elder Darcy flatly declared.

An awkward glance again to his wife, another encouraging nod from her, and then, "I… we thought it best to advise you…" He stopped, struggling to continue.

"Just what are you trying to say?"

"Have you considered that you will now be looked upon as a most eligible match? There has been very animated conversation amongst the ladies who… who…"

At this point Mr. Darcy started, steeling himself to interject in as calm a tone as I felt he could muster under the circumstances, "I did not come to town for the season to humour ladies who are seeking a husband! There will never be another like Anne. I have no wish to seek out another wife."

Lady Matlock reached out and gently patted Mr. Darcy's hand. "Frederick, we know how deeply you loved Anne. And I believe we are of the same mind that you are not ready to consider remarrying. We just felt it best to advise you how you are going to be perceived."

The two young men were listening to the conversation and Fitzwilliam leaned over to my master and quietly asked him with a teasing air about him, "And you, Darcy, what are *your* intentions in regards to the ladies for the season? Will you oblige them with your attentions and irresistible allure?"

"You know I have no such intentions." Darcy declared resolutely.

"Come, Darcy! You missed coming to town all of last season and will be going off to Cambridge next year. Enjoy your last chance at gaiety with the ladies before your four years of studies consume you."

"There is plenty of time for that."

Fitzwilliam let out an exasperated sigh and shook his head at his young cousin in bewilderment. "If I did not know you better, Darcy, I would suppose you are actually acquiescing to the idea of Anne becoming your bride! How long are you willing to wait… five, six, seven years for her?"

My master's jaw tightened and he sent a threatening glance his cousin's way. Fitzwilliam softly chuckled as he reached over and tousled Georgiana's hair. "Perhaps Georgiana here may be your companion to the balls this season?"

A smile beamed across the young girl's face as she looked up at her brother. "May I go to a ball? Will you teach me to dance with you?"

"Someday, Georgiana, when you are a little older," my master reassured her.

Her eyes darkened and the smile was replaced with a pout. "I want to dance with you *before* I am older."

My master looked at his cousin sternly. "Now look what you have done!" He turned to Georgiana, "Georgie, I promise I will dance with you… *before* you are older. But you must learn first."

"Will you teach me?"

My master smiled at Georgiana's small, pleading face. "If you would like, Georgie, I shall be happy to teach you."

"Good!" exclaimed the little girl, who wrapped her arms around his neck.

Now I had heard of dancing several times, but was not quite sure what to make of it. I had certainly never espied any such activity in all my time at Pemberley. I was to discover just what this dancing was the very next day.

~~*

The next afternoon, after Georgiana had unceasingly implored my master to teach her to dance, he finally relented to her pleas in hopes of pacifying and entertaining her. He promptly placed her across from him and they stood facing one another.

"Now, we must imagine that Mother is playing the pianoforte. Do you remember how Mother used to play so proficiently?"

Georgiana nodded, but I doubted she had any recollection.

"She played very well. And I am sure you will, too, someday. You shall play as beautifully as she did."

He bent over and reached out his long arms to take her hands in his. "Now, we must take two steps together, like this," he said as he demonstrated, "and then two steps apart."

I was sitting on the floor just to the side of them, watching in amusement as they turned, walked, and occasionally, my master would pick her up and fling her around, much to her glee.

"Now we must pretend there are other dancers alongside us. You go to the partner over there and I go to the one over here."

My master pretended to take someone else's hand, but Georgiana had other ideas. The next thing I knew, she had reached down for my front paws and I was pulled up onto my hind legs. My master laughed, but Georgiana was decidedly serious.

I could not help but feel somewhat awkward at first, especially as Georgiana wished me to turn one way and then another. When she let go of one paw I almost went down, but in order to please her, I did my best to remain upright.

For me, that was my introduction to dancing and it was on many subsequent occasions that she would solicit my paws for a round or two. And I do believe I became quite proficient at it and was undoubtedly her favourite partner.

In addition to spending time teaching Georgiana to dance, my master also joined his father in paying visits to close acquaintances they had in town. Several people, in turn, stopped by the townhome to return the call.

My natural disposition was to eagerly greet these visitors as they entered. In truth, I was at the door to welcome them as soon as I heard the clapping of the door knocker. I could hardly contain myself and rushed to the door with tail wagging, eager to greet any guests who happened by.

It was unfortunate that I soon discovered my welcome was not always appreciated. I found it hard to believe that some of these acquaintances questioned whether a dog ought to be permitted in the company of guests, let alone be allowed in the house. As for me, *I* questioned whether these people with such narrow insight should be allowed in the house!

It became very apparent that Mrs. Linden, the housekeeper, preferred that I not be present when these guests, or any guests for that matter, were invited in. She looked down at me sternly, shaking her head and pointing her finger at me, calling to one of the servants to take me away before she even answered the door. To my dismay, I would be either confined to my master's quarters or sent back behind the kitchen.

I soon devised a plan that aided in my being left to observe. When I heard the bell ring, I fought that natural inclination to dart out and greet the unsuspecting guests and instead, surreptitiously hid under a conveniently placed table covered with a floor length lace cloth. To the casual observer it may have appeared that my hiding was the consequence of being timid of the guests, but quite the contrary, hiding there enabled me to be forgotten whilst the guests paid their civilities. No one seemed to take notice, with the exception of my master, who was well on to my scheme but fortunately never drew anyone's attention to it.

The guests who called upon us at the townhome were comprised of a diversity of people with a wide sphere of grand worldly influence, the finest connections, abundant wealth, and profuse advantage. Some displayed their position proudly and boldly, whereas others were more candid and humble. They all, however, were quick to offer sympathy and condolences to Mr. Darcy for the loss of his wife the previous year. I could perceive by the faraway look in some of their eyes that it was of no small consequence just who would garner his affections now that he was widowed. It also did not escape my notice that these same people were admiring his tall, handsome son and contemplating much of the same. They insisted that this fine, tall, handsome young man must unquestionably accompany his father to all the assemblies, balls, concerts, and plays that he might attend.

It became my habit to sneak my nose out from under the tablecloth to catch a glimpse of my master during these times of generous praise and overt perusals from these guests who were, I presumed, not particularly the closest of acquaintances. At least they did not know either gentleman well enough to value their reticent comportment. As I expected, my master sat respectfully still and managed to eke out a meagre, impatient smile. I easily recognized, however, the look of discomfiture spreading across his face. He looked as though he wished to be anywhere but here under their close scrutiny and open admiration.

Inevitably, they would ask if they could see Georgiana and she would be summoned. The poor little girl would hide behind the long dress of her governess, Mrs. Tallor, whilst her father gently encouraged her to come out and say hello. She was perfectly capable of saying a polite "hello," but her shyness exhibited itself in the company of those she perceived as strangers and prevented her from obliging. Her father seemed not inclined to press her further and she would be taken over to a corner of the room where she was allowed to sit with

Mrs. Tallor. She usually had a doll or toy with which she played as she sat and cast an occasional, curious glance up at the adults across the room from her. Her father's and brother's reserve did not go unnoticed by her.

Mr. Darcy made every effort to extend the same hospitality that had come so easily to his late wife, but it was obviously a great exertion for him. He struggled for equanimity as he spoke about her passing and how much he missed her. He graciously received everyone's words expressing their great sorrow for his loss. However, if anyone even hinted at his seeking out another woman to marry, he would adamantly refuse to consider it.

As Mr. Darcy made his feelings known, I could not help but notice the look of disappointment that swept across their faces. I am sure more than one of them had ideas for some fortunate lady, whom they hoped would sweep the widowed gentleman, or alternatively, his son, off his feet. No doubt more than one woman hoped they would be the one to win the heart of either of these excellent men.

~~*

We had been at the townhome several days when it happened. *It* being when Mr. Darcy could no longer deny that, despite his unwavering and quite vocal insistence that he had no intention of remarrying, the women of the ton had come to regard him as marriageable prospect Acquaintances of his, the Ludwigs, stopped by the townhome. Mr. Ludwig and his wife, whom Mr. Darcy seemed to know quite well, were accompanied by two young ladies that he knew not at all.

Mr. Ludwig made the introduction to Mr. Darcy of his younger sister, Elyse, and his daughter, Mirian. From my concealed position, which by now was known to most of the servants (and they kindly turned a blind eye to my presence as long as I behaved), I observed Mr. Darcy as he made the sudden realization that these two women had accompanied the Ludwigs in hopes of securing both of the Darcy men's regard.

As he recognized the subtle flirtations that both ladies exhibited, he cast a nervous glance at his son. To his credit, my master had comprehended it much sooner than his father and was already putting up that wall around him that shielded him from such unwanted advances.

From my concealed vantage point and overhearing the extent of their conversation, as well as being very observant of their manner and fashion, I determined that, from society's standpoint, both women apparently had good connections, adequate fortune, and excellent breeding. Both were comparatively attractive and fawned over the two men. However prized their attributes were, however, they were both dull, exhibiting very little ability to converse in an intelligent manner. I watched as both men responded in much the same way to these ladies. Both my master and his father exhibited an almost unnatural degree of self-control, as if any sort of animated outburst or engaging response might be mistaken by these ladies as an encouraging affection!

I thought back curiously to the day both men came to select a dog for my master. I was under the impression that breeding was of utmost importance in their consideration. However, I was pleasantly surprised when my master singularly pointed me out, when the dogs from the other litter were decidedly of better breeding. I believe that my personality -- and what I brought out in him -- had greater credence in his decision than did my breeding or lack of it.

I had a reasonable assumption that my master, although mindful of the importance breeding played, was most likely looking for something else of greater value. What that was, he was probably not even aware himself. But I heartily believed it to be something that would be stirred deep down inside when he met the right woman.

And seeing the similar way he and his father drew back in the face of such excellent prospects, I could not dismiss the fact that these two men were more alike than I ever imagined before.

Little Georgiana, sweet and impressionable as she was, closely observed her two favourite men as they squirmed in discomfort at the intrigues of several ladies who favoured the house with their presence. She watched as her father struggled with this new status as an eligible man in which he did not feel comfortable nor wished to embrace. She would watch her brother, whom she so admired, as he sat for the most part silent, harbouring a dislike for the many masquerades that the women wore, their shallow efforts at conversation, and whose presence, he found to his dismay, held little to pique his interest.

~~*

I sat comfortably on my master's bed one night as I watched Wheaton, my young master's valet, dress him in an elegant pair of trousers, vest, crisp white shirt, and then fashion a most constricting neckcloth around his neck. I crumpled my brow as I watched the discomfiture of my master as he was being so tediously dressed and fussed over. It was very apparent to me that he was going out that evening and that I would not be able to accompany him.

Wheaton departed after the neckcloth was in place and knotted to his satisfaction. Immediately after his taking leave, my master ran his fingers inside of it. I suspected that, much like my collar, it was too taut and constricting. He adjusted his coat and shirt in the mirror and ran his hand through his hair. Now, I rather admired his hair, as it was curly and unruly, much the same as my fur. But this evening he seemed quite perturbed with it and it was some time before he was able to get it to do what he wanted. Or he may just have resigned himself to the fact that there was nothing more he could do with it.

I watched as he and his father left the house, walking silently side by side, fastidiously dressed on the outside, but, I sensed, in much disarray on the inside.

My master was now taller in stature than his father and was not as lanky as he had been when I first made his acquaintance. He was growing into a fine young man and I could not have been prouder. I had the deepest conviction, however, that neither of these men were looking forward to their evening out together.

As I feared that I would spend the evening in lonely solitude, I determined that I would go and amuse Georgiana, at least until she was taken up to retire for the night. We had a marvellous time. She brushed my fur, we had a pretend tea party, and, of course, we practiced our dancing. Whilst I enjoyed my admirable status as providing for Georgiana's exclusive amusement, I wondered several times if my master was enjoying himself tonight. I certainly hoped so.

I waited patiently for their return, eager to discover what they might have done at this event called a ball. Now to me, a ball is something that is round and is thrown so that I may run after it, catch it, and return it. But considering the immaculate manner in which my master and his father were dressed, I was greatly convinced this was not the case.

When they returned, I eagerly greeted my master and his father at the door.

The both handed off their hats, coats, and gloves to the servants in complete silence. It seemed a hopeless business that either would utter a word of comment on their evening's activities. The elder Mr. Darcy walked straight to his study and closed the door. My master looked down at me; fatigue and weariness consuming his features.

"Come, Reggie. It has been a long night."

Those were his only words to me that night. A few days later, when our favourite cousin stopped by to take leave, as he was departing London for a few weeks, I was able to catch snippets of conversation about all that had transpired.

"So tell me, Darcy, what do you find to be your preference here in London during the season? Do you prefer the grand balls, the elegant dinner parties, or the small intimate gatherings?"

My master casually shrugged his shoulders. "I prefer very small gatherings with my closest friends!"

"What? What of all the available ladies at the balls? Are the ladies not pretty enough for you? I thought the ladies at the Gladstones' ball the other night were quite remarkable!"

"It is true, Fitzwilliam, there were several fine looking ladies at the ball."

"And so which ones struck your fancy? Was it Miss Enders? I believe I saw you dancing with her."

"Yes, I danced with Miss Enders, Miss Coulter, Miss Ralston, and Miss someone whose name I cannot recall."

Fitzwilliam clasped his hands together heartily. "All good choices, there, Darce. So who is she? Who is the one whose heart is now inexorably entwined with yours?"

"I have no inclination for any woman I met at the Gladstones' ball."

"I would find any of these women satisfying! Unfortunately none of them take notice of me. What is *your* excuse?"

"I found that when they opened their mouths, nothing protruded but idle chatter, meant only to flatter me and flatter themselves. If that was all I wanted, I would be a happy, content man."

Fitzwilliam slapped my master on his knee and laughed. "Perhaps my expectations for you are too hasty. You are still young, Darcy. I forget how much younger you are than myself. I will content myself to wait another year in the hope that you will then be so smitten with every woman who comes your way that you will be required to pass one or two in my direction."

A look of surprise, suspicion, and then relief passed across my master's face as he caught his cousin's teasing nature. "So, that is the reason you are pressing me to find enjoyment with these ladies. So that when I break their heart, you will be there to help mend it!"

"You have found me out, Cousin!"

Fitzwilliam soon left and I could not help but think that even though he had mercilessly teased and goaded my master, he had a great respect for him, albeit that he could not settle on the reason for my master's decided indifference for the women he had met. But I think if he knew him as I knew him, he would realize my master had a difficult time discerning the true character of any person he met for the first time. It was exasperating when they hid behind the deceit and charades that many exhibited, particularly when they had the ulterior motive to secure my master's attentions because of his wealth and connections.

But that was not all. I knew my master had a liveliness that was rooted deeply inside and wished to be freed. There were, at present, only a handful of us that could evoke that. I was convinced that he truly hoped, sincerely believed, that one day he would meet a woman who would bring that repressed liveliness out in him, who would also be honest, intelligent, and most of all, in love with him, not with the things he owned.

Throughout that first winter in town, I came to realize that even though my master preferred Pemberley, he did ardently embrace the finer accoutrements London had to offer. He greatly enjoyed accompanying his father to the theatre and concerts, the opera, and even literary readings. He confided in me that he was just now beginning to appreciate these culturally enriching activities.

His father was prodigiously proud of him. He had high expectations for his son and wished every advantage for him. Despite his own reticence, I knew he felt the need to introduce his son to Society properly and he took great pains to introduce him to those of polished society who, someday, might become the Mistress of Pemberley. Without actually saying it, he was making every effort to ensure that Pemberley would have a new mistress through his son. I believed him to be of the mindset that, for whatever reason, *he* would never remarry.

I saw the look of admiration in his father's eyes as he took note of his son, growing and maturing into a remarkably handsome and principled man before his very eyes. But I could not help but notice that look of apprehension as he anticipated bringing his son into a throng of ladies that would throw him, as well, into the foray.

This was, consequently, how we spent the whole of the winter season. Georgiana and I became quite proficient at dancing and tea parties. But I noticed that just as the reserve in her father and brother had increased and become more fixed whilst at London, so did hers. She had been very perceptive to the emotional climate that hung in the air that season, and whereas *I* made every attempt to overcome that outpouring of reserve, she absorbed it; her shyness becoming firmly entrenched.

Mr. Darcy and son endured their first season in town as conspicuously eligible men and both had come through with an adamant conviction. The elder Mr. Darcy was quite convinced he would never find and had no desire to find another wife as suitable as Anne had been, and the younger was quite convinced he would never find a woman who lived up to his meticulous expectations.

I rather hoped I would live long enough to find out whether he would one day find someone. I had the odd sensation it would take him a rather long time.

Chapter 6

I would be remiss if I did not comment briefly on our yearly visit again to Rosings. In the midst of our time in London, the cold winter days began to wane. The first warm days of spring cast upon our grateful countenances, announcing the coming of spring and consequently Easter, compelling us to journey again to Rosings. I must admit that I was a bit more prepared for this visit with Lady Cat, although I really cannot say whether that was good or bad, for she certainly remained a puzzle to me. As for my master, I knew that it would only be trying. I was conflicted in that I desired to further my friendship with Miss Anne whilst my master would most likely wish to distance himself from her as much as possible.

When we arrived, we found that not much had changed since our last visit. However, we were both pleased and surprised to discover that Lady Cat had kept her word to her daughter. Anne now had in her possession her very own dog. At least, I assumed it was a dog, but he was a tiny little creature who, for the most part was content to sit upon Anne's lap and did very little else. At first he was reluctant to accept my friendship, perhaps in part due to my larger size. Over the course of the next few weeks, however, we became quite comfortable with each other, particularly when he discovered that it was our shared intent to bring some joy and happiness into little Anne's life. Consequently, we got along perfectly well.

Anne seemed more like a young lady this year than last. But even though she had grown noticeably since our visit last year, she remained small and frail for her age. Her life was still a prison of restrictions, which in my opinion, did her more harm than good. She obviously longed for any attention that my master might extend her way, whilst he withheld any affection that would normally pass from one cousin to another because of his adamant refusal to give consideration to the promise upon which his aunt was resolved to insist.

Our short visit was comparable to last year's, and we came through it without a great deal too many hardships. I observed the slightest change in my master's dealings with his aunt. He still showed her great respect and did not counter her assertions, no matter how ridiculous they sounded, yet he appeared a bit more self assured. Unfortunately, he also continued to feel the greatest uneasiness as he came again under the scrutiny of those who wished to make his acquaintance or further their acquaintance from the previous year.

After our obligatory three weeks away at Rosings, we returned to London to finish out the Season. There was much to occupy my master's time with the theatre, opera, accompanying his father to his club, and of course the plethora of balls to which he was invited.

I honestly cannot say, however, who yearned more for the open grounds, fresh air, and sublime quiet of Pemberley. I knew I was anxious to return, and I believed my master was of the same mind.

At the end of the London Season, we joyfully returned to Pemberley and settled again into our familiar, comfortable, and altogether more preferable routines. I eagerly welcomed our return to pleasant times of walking, hunting, and simply soaking in the serene country ambiance. London had long ago worn out her welcome to me.

Our pleasant summer days were filled with numerous -- and I might add *very successful* -- hunting excursions. I had grown most proficient at questing, flushing, and retrieving game whilst my master was a most adept sharpshooter. We made an admirable team.

But my joyous days at Pemberley with my master that summer were soon to come to an abrupt end. I came to understand that he was to leave shortly to pursue further education beyond what his tutor was able to provide. He would soon leave for this place about which he had been recently speaking called Cambridge. All that I could decipher about the place was that I would not be allowed to accompany him and he would remain there several years, returning home only occasionally for short visits. This seriously grieved me as I did not understand what this place would be able to teach him that I could not. And I was of the impression that they would certainly not understand him as well as I did.

In consideration of my master leaving, we spent a good amount of time together the week prior to his departure. As much as I enjoyed his company, the knowledge that he was about to leave weighed heavily upon me. As each day passed, I knew it was one less before he would be gone from Pemberley.

~~*

Preparations were soon underway for my master to quit Pemberley. There was much to consider in planning for such a venture and my master was grateful for Wheaton's expertise on what he would and would not need.

The day before he was to leave, he and I took one final walk together. His eager anticipation for his future plans was tinged with sadness in having to leave his father and sister. I hoped he was saddened to be parted from me as well. I certainly was.

"Well, Reggie," he looked at me and reached down to stroke my fur. "Tomorrow I leave. I am not sure when my studies will allow me to return next. I hope it will be some time around the holidays."

Looking up at him, I saw him smile. "You really know how to get the best of me, Reggie, with those big, dark, beguiling eyes of yours. But Reggie, you need not worry. Father, Georgiana, and all the staff here will take prodigiously good care of you."

I whimpered to let him know I understood, but was feeling the ill effects of our imminent separation all the same.

"Most of all, Reggie," he continued as he stopped and crouched down, lifting my head and looking into my eyes, "You watch out for Father and Georgiana. Perhaps you can bring to their lives a bit more liveliness. I am afraid it is not in my constitution to do that, but I am persuaded that is something *you* might be able to do."

We walked on a little further, enjoying the warmth of the sun beating down upon us. I occasionally darted off after some squirrel or rabbit just to give them a good run, and promptly returned to my master to let him know I had succeeded in my feat. He smiled, knowing that I was merely practicing for when I would be out on a real hunt for real game. But it was a melancholy smile, as we were both cognizant of the fact that this would be our last time together for quite some time.

Our idyllic time together was suddenly interrupted when I sensed an unwelcome presence and let out a growl. My master looked at me curiously as we came to a turn in the path and found ourselves face-to-face with Wickham. Fortunately, he was without Storm. When my master saw that it was Wickham, he whispered softly, "That explains your caution, Reggie."

"Ahhh, Darcy," the young man forced a smile. "You are off tomorrow for Cambridge, I hear."

"That is correct."

"I expect you are anxious to get there. This place will not be the same without you."

"I was under the impression you were en route there yourself."

"I have decided it would be most beneficial if I were to defer it at least a year. There is much I wish to accomplish here first."

Darcy eyed him suspiciously as Wickham seemed smugly pleased with this decision. For my part, I shuddered to think of what Wickham would consider an accomplishment.

"Fear not, Darcy. I am most willing to see to your father's well being in your absence. As he has generously promised me an education at Cambridge, which I will take him up on next year, I am most obliged to him. It would only be fitting for me to do what I can for him in your absence. He has truly been an honourable godfather to me and I know he looks upon me as a second son."

Darcy took in a deep breath as he listened with building anger to Wickham's duplicitous and piercing words. "I doubt that my father will need any assistance from you, Wickham."

"You do not wish me to look in on my own godfather and see to his well being?"

"Perhaps I do not completely trust your motives."

"Come, Darcy. We have been friends since childhood. There is no need to think ill of me or my motives."

"We have long ago gone considerably different ways, Wickham."

The two men stood watching each other in a guarded silence. Finally, Wickham declared, "Well, I must be off. I am sure you must want some time with your dog before you leave. I suppose you heard that my dog disappeared," Wickham gave a wicked laugh and looked down at me, sneering. "'Tis nothing to me, however. I can get another dog as easy as that." He snapped his fingers quite forcefully. "But I suppose it must be exceedingly difficult for you to leave your only friend behind."

Now whilst I would pride myself on being my master's closest and most intimate friend, I did not particularly perceive his comment as a compliment. I was most relieved when Wickham took his leave with nary another word.

My master shook his head as Wickham turned and walked away. "I cannot believe my father has been so blinded by his deceitful charm. How can he not see his true character? I only hope he will inevitably show his true character to my father so he will recognize him for what he is." A kick to the path beneath his feet scattered some dirt and rocks as he expressed his contempt. "Come, Reggie. We have a long walk ahead of us. I do not want to return home until I am in command of my anger."

We finished our last walk together and that night, being our final night together, I snuggled up close to him in the bed. He reached over and rested his hand across my back, stroking it several times before falling asleep. I, however, slept fitfully as I felt that a part of me was going away.

~~*

The next day he departed for Cambridge early, and as I watched the carriage convey him down the long lane that led away from Pemberley, I could not help but feel as though something had been yanked from my heart. I watched as Georgiana clung to her father in tears, wondering why her brother had to leave, and I did not miss the tears that filled *his* eyes as he reached down to pick her up. I knew we all were going to miss him greatly.

I was obligingly allowed to spend nights in my master's quarters. Whilst it soothed my spirits to sleep upon his bed and be surrounded by his familiar scent, it was simply not quite the same.

What was this thing called 'education' that my master was obtaining? I wondered. Was it something that would enable him to understand me better? Would it improve our time together? I highly doubted that, as it was already as excellent as I could perceive it to be.

And whilst I knew I must endure a considerable amount of time without his presence, save for the occasional short visit home when it was allowed, I could not imagine how difficult it must have been for him to endure that strange place called Cambridge without family or friend.

Over the next few days it was not difficult to observe the depth to which his father and sister missed him. Georgiana often clung to her father, frequently asking for her brother and crying out for him, whilst I repeatedly witnessed his father walk over to a window and stare out, as if expecting or hoping to see him return at any moment. I deeply missed him and longed for our intimate talks and our meandering walks.

Up until this point in my tenure at Pemberley, my master's father had rarely taken any semblance of interest in my well being. However, several weeks after he left, we had a dramatic change in our relationship.

I was sitting in the drawing room one afternoon whilst Mr. Darcy was in his study. Georgiana was resting in her room and I felt a wave of intense loneliness take hold of me. The staff was attending their chores and I was left to myself. Feeling quite forlorn, I rambled about the house, sniffing out anything that still might have my master's scent upon it. I came upon the open door of the study and looked in, wondering what it was that Mr. Darcy was doing in there. He must have sensed that I was there as he looked up at me briefly, but then set his eyes back down to the book he was reading. I remained where I was until, after a few more moments, he looked back up and to my surprise, bid me to come in.

I came around slowly and sat tentatively beside his chair. "I know it has been very quiet around here, boy, but do not despair. He is not gone for good. My son will be home again, now and then, until his education is complete. I know you miss him." He reached down and hesitantly stroked the top of my head. "I miss him too."

Suddenly he stood up. "Perhaps you might join me for a walk about the grounds. Would you care to do that, Reggie?"

My tail wagged eagerly as he stood up. "Come, let us see how well those paths and lanes are being maintained by our grounds keeping staff. I have been neglectful lately in taking strolls through them as I ought."

Our eyes met and I recognized an amiable regard as he looked down on me.

We walked out and immediately I scampered down my favourite path that led down to the lake. It felt gratifying to give my legs a good run, my first since my master had left, but I most obediently returned to Mr. Darcy's side. We walked silently at first and then he reached down and picked up a suitable stick, which he threw ahead of us. I raced to retrieve it and returned it to him. As we walked, he continued to throw and I continued to fetch it.

The path to the lake took us through a copse, which afforded me several opportunities to scamper after creatures rustling in the thickets. Though most scurried away before I was even able to see what it was, I was thoroughly enjoying myself. We finally made our way to the lake and Mr. Darcy took in some deep breaths.

"I fear I am not as young as my son, Reggie. He is still youthful and can handle a walk such as this quite easily. For me, on the other hand…" He took in some more breaths. "Perhaps I should do this more often and then it would not be such an arduous task."

He sat down on a fallen log and looked out across at the water, its wind-whipped caps dancing across the water and the pale blue of the sky extending endlessly above. I believe we both felt a bond forming between us that sprang from our common feelings of yearning for one excellent young man.

I sat down next to him as he recovered from our strenuous walk. He seemed to be lost in his thoughts as his hand tentatively reached over and brushed through my fur, very much like his son often did. His eyes lit up as he began speaking of his son.

"Fitzwilliam is a fine young man. I am exceedingly proud of him, but I fear I may have been remiss in my behaviour of late." He let out a soft moan and I obliged him with one of my own. "Ever since his good mother passed, I fear I have allowed my grief to shape my conduct towards him and dictate my overall demeanour."

I looked up at him and he smiled back at me. "You have been good for him, Reggie. I think I may have been wrong in demanding restraint in my son's behaviour as I have over the years. Even before my dear Anne died, I insisted that he behave in an adult-like manner. Perhaps, as Anne told me so often, I never really allowed him to have a childhood. But that was the behaviour my father expected from me. When his good mother died, I fear I became even more stern. I wanted nothing to do with gaiety and laughter. I found any joviality to be distressing to me, my grief still so raw, yet deep in my heart I knew it was wrong to keep my son from moving past his own grief." He tousled the fur on my head and stood up. "I know, Reggie, that when he was with you, he was free from the constraints I demanded and he enjoyed himself. For that I am grateful."

He stood up and we began walking again back towards the house. "He is a lot like me, you know; perhaps too much. We are, I believe, both of a similar disposition; very reserved by nature. I wonder if I may have done him a disservice this past Season in Town. My response to being considered eligible again was to shy away from the attention. When I should have been encouraging him to accept the attentions of the fine young ladies he met, I was doing quite the opposite. I fear I set a very poor example for him to follow."

A soft laugh escaped his lips. "Rather than learning how to joyously receive the acquaintances of the finest young ladies in society, I believe, instead, he came to feel awkward in receiving them… just as I was."

He face and tone of voice took on a faraway deportment. "When I was Fitzwilliam's age, social functions were just as difficult for me as they are now for him, perhaps even more so." Sighing, and seemingly choked up, he continued, "Anne had an endearing liveliness and grace that made the demands of society much easier for me. I can only hope that my son finds someone to complement him as fittingly as I did with Anne."

We returned to the house and because of my elation in being taken into Mr. Darcy's confidence and regard, I noticed nothing unusual. Therefore, I was most alarmed when Mrs. Reynolds approached us as we walked into the house. "Young Mr. Wickham is here to see you, Sir. He wished to wait for your return and is in the sitting room."

"Oh, splendid! Thank you, Mrs. Reynolds."

As Mr. Darcy walked off, I chided myself at missing that particular scent that caused my fur to stand up on end across my back. I wondered whether I should follow him, remain where I was, or valiantly block his way, thus preventing him from going to that scoundrel. I decided it would be most prudent if I did not do the latter, but instead, compromised on the first two. I decided to follow him to the door. I would not enter, but I definitely wanted to hear what was said.

Mr. Darcy walked in. "Wickham, it is good to see you. Your family is well?"

"Yes, Sir. Very kind of you to inquire. They are all well, thank you."

"I am glad to hear that. I see your father regularly, of course, but not your mother."

"She would appreciate your concern, Sir."

"Come, let us go to my study so we may talk."

The two men walked towards the study and I followed closely behind. "So what can I do for you, Wickham?" Mr. Darcy asked as they walked.

"Sir, I have come to offer my assistance whilst your son is from home. I am most obliged that you perfectly understood my wish to defer my education for a year. And as you have so generously offered your benefaction at Cambridge, I hoped to be able to offer you my returned esteem in your son's absence. I know how much you will miss him. Please allow me to ask if there is anything I might do for you."

Stopping at the door of his study, Mr. Darcy put one hand on Wickham's shoulder. "Wickham, you are like a son to me. Indeed, you are my godson. As for the education, I could not have done any less. You owe me nothing, though I do appreciate your offering."

"I only wish to prove worthy of your patronage, Sir."

"You excel as I hope you will and I am sure you shall." Slapping him heartily upon his shoulder, Mr. Darcy indicated that the young man should enter the study.

The two men walked into the room and the door was closed. I was not able to discern any more particulars of the conversation, but I heard Wickham laugh frequently and Mr. Darcy followed suit. It seemed quite peculiar to me to hear Mr. Darcy laugh as he did. I could not recollect him ever doing so in the company of my master. I wondered if that was one of the reasons he enjoyed Wickham's company. He made him laugh. But I knew Wickham's charm deceptively cloaked his ulterior motives.

When Wickham and Mr. Darcy finally walked out of the room, I kept my head down, but looked up at them and could not help but notice a very smug smile on Wickham's face. Mr. Darcy had the look of pleasing regard upon his that only served to make me shudder.

That day set the tone for the following year whilst my master was away. When the weather was accommodating, Mr. Darcy would invite me to join him for a walk on the grounds. I believe it was good for him. He often told me of letters his son had written and informed me of his progress at Cambridge. He was applying himself faithfully to his studies, having very little time for any sort of social life, and doing exceptionally well. I was not surprised.

In the evenings, I would sit by Mr. Darcy's side. He would often have Georgiana join us and he would either read her a story from a book or tell her a tale of his early years and the three of us became very close. She and I became tireless playmates for one another. When she was not studying with her governess or practicing on the pianoforte, I was allowed to join her out on the grounds in her play area. She was just as reserved as her brother and father, and whilst I had not yet been able to bring out any excessive liveliness in her demeanour, she seemed to enjoy our time together.

We found great enjoyment in a good game of tug-of-war with any old slipper or good stick she could find. She loved to throw a ball as far as she could and eagerly waited for me to return it. Truth be told, her small arms did not allow her the length of throw to which I was accustomed with my master, however, I always made sure not to return it too fast, lest she felt her throw was wanting. Georgiana's idea of an enjoyable physical pursuit was very different from my master's. For example, often I would scamper about as she soared high on her swing. I must admit the motion made me quite nervous and she would giggle as I barked anxiously until she finally brought the swing to a stop and was safely back on the ground.

If it were for these things only, my days spent without my master would have been tolerably contented. But there was often an addition to our family gathering that year that I found quite disconcerting. Wickham was becoming a very frequent guest at the house. He and Mr. Darcy seemed to have an extremely easy friendship.

It was his attempts to befriend Georgiana, however, that concerned me. He was ingratiating and all ease to her, much to her delight and my chagrin. Unfortunately, I could easily see why. Her brother was gone and Wickham was there in his absence, being particularly attentive towards her. Georgiana relished this attention and began to exhibit a very strong regard for him.

Whilst I could hope that Mr. Darcy would one day see the real Wickham as my master and I did, I had my doubts that little Georgiana would ever think ill of him. She was still exceedingly shy around most people, but Wickham's recurrent presence in the home soon allayed all her inhibitions toward him and I believe she was growing to love him almost as much as she loved my master.

She had a captive audience in him as she practiced on the pianoforte to his unending praise and her shyness melted in his ingratiating presence. He seemed eagerly inclined to read Miss Darcy a story from one of her books or tell her one of his own. Mr. Darcy seemed pleased that Georgiana was less and less reticent in Wickham's presence.

These events weighed heavily on me and I looked with great anticipation to every visit my master made home. When word would start spreading that he would soon be returning, I could barely calm myself. When the day of his return arrived, if the weather was mild and the windows of Pemberley were open, I picked up his scent long before his carriage pulled up to the front.

I was in my usual place, lying on a carpet in the grand entryway, the first time it happened. I was resting after a particularly exhausting afternoon with Georgiana when suddenly my nose barely caught a whiff. *Could it really be him?* My tail wagged incessantly and I lifted up my head to get a better bearing on that scent. I sniffed around me, concentrating on that wafting aroma that I knew so well. He was returning!

I could not control my excitement! I began barking and whining, somehow accomplishing both at the same time. One of the servants, either annoyed by my behaviour or enlightened as to its cause, opened the front door and out I ran. I did not see the carriage immediately, but I knew precisely from which direction it was coming.

My legs could not take me to it any faster than what I was able to exert from them, and many an under gardener out on the grounds looked upon me in much amazement. Some thought I was about to run off for good and tried to corral me, but they were unsuccessful. I slipped through their grasping arms and ran around their blockades intent on one thing – meeting up with my master.

When I caught up with the carriage, I barked incessantly until it stopped. My master opened the door for me and I bolted up into the carriage and greeted him with a good, unrestrained licking across his face. He gently scolded me for such impolite behaviour, and then gave my head a good rubbing. It was so good to have him home!

When he and I pulled up in the carriage, all the staff marvelled how I had sensed his arrival. When it happened again the next time he returned, they realized it would be beneficial to pay attention, as they could have an early warning of his return.

Each time he came home, I could not help but notice how he grew, not so much in stature but in wisdom and maturity. I was usually able to rush out to greet the carriage and he always obliged me by opening the door and letting me jump in. I always enjoyed those greetings, as he and I had a few minutes to ourselves.

A few times, when he arrived at the door without my advance notice (whether it was due to inclement weather or because I had not detected his scent because of tightly closed windows), he always greeted me by allowing me to jump up with my front paws so he could give my head a good welcoming rub, something I was normally not allowed to do.

Once he was home, even if it was only for a mere week or two, I was able to sleep more easily at night. There we were, the two of us, exactly as we had been before he left! Wickham stayed away whilst my master was in residence and therefore, I did not need to be concerned for Georgiana and her father.

I marvelled at my master's stature, wisdom, and demeanour. He was becoming a man!

I was so relieved when that first year was finally over. I felt a complete failure in that I was not able to do anything to alert Mr. Darcy or little Georgiana about Wickham's true ways. At least I had the assurance that when my master departed again, Wickham would be leaving as well.

By the time Wickham did leave with my master for Cambridge, he had become a highly regarded and favoured companion of father and daughter. I was glad to see him go.

My master continued his education for several more years. Georgiana continued to grow into a sweet young lady. Mr. Darcy appeared to be slowing down, having to take more and more breaks on our walks. I accommodated him as well as I could, not wishing for him to be overexerted. I could say that those years seemed to fly by, but whilst I was in the midst of them, the days without my master seemed to pass by at a snail's pace.

I looked forward to his visits home when he would tell me of his lessons, his professors, and some of the friends that he had made.

He told me of the disgust he had in Wickham's choice of friends and the way he idled his time away. Their paths rarely crossed, but when they did, Wickham was more often than not behaving in a most imprudent manner. It seemed as though Wickham would never change, but somehow he managed to get through his classes and keep Mr. Darcy from ever finding out how little he regarded his education. My master believed he would never become a clergyman, *should* never become a clergyman, and I did not doubt him. .

Whilst my master vented his anger by telling me of Wickham's reprehensible deeds, he took much delight in talking to me of the friends he had made as well. Of those friends my master talked about, one seemed to stand out from the others. His name was Charles Bingley. However, it was not until after he completed his years at Cambridge that I finally had the privilege of meeting him.

Chapter 7

I rejoiced greatly when my master returned home permanently after receiving his education. I am not quite sure what he learned at that esteemed place referred to as Cambridge, but comparing the young man who left four years earlier with the fully grown adult man I now saw before my eyes, he certainly had been transformed in many ways.

I had designs upon his return to make up for all those years that were lost between us by claiming his precious free time. Sadly, he had but little. Almost immediately, my master and his father began working closely together in the management of Pemberley. My master had a vast deal to offer in terms of the decisions that had to be made and seemed to thrive on discovering more prudent and economical ways of doing things. His father and steward, the elder Mr. Wickham, seemed to greatly appreciate the profound wisdom and fresh ideas this young man brought to the table in their discussions.

Unfortunately for me, he began travelling more frequently; however, he would on occasion allow me to accompany him. I noticed that in his dealings with people, whether in business or in a social context, he never spoke without first taking the time to thoroughly think through everything he was about to say and was able to articulate precisely that which he wished to convey. He was always very polite and accommodating, yet he tenaciously remained distant from most people he encountered; not allowing them to get to know the man inside.

I noticed this particularly if he perceived that somehow they were not his equal. Thinking back to that first day he selected me over the other dog of more superior breeding, I remembered my first impression of him that he cared little for breeding. But now I perceived something else that looked very much to me as though it had become more and more important.

Perhaps it was what he learned at Cambridge or was something his parents had taught him from an early age. Whilst I had not particularly noticed it before, it was greatly evident to me now.

It was in my master's twenty-second year that we journeyed to Town for the winter season; the first since finishing his education. I wondered what changes there might be in our stay this time around.

I deliberated on whether he would graciously enter society with all the confidence that was due his lineage or whether he would persist in feeling unsettled and disquieted. Would he eagerly seize every opportunity to place himself with others of striking advantage or would he look upon these affairs and those attending them with perfect indifference? Would he finally allow himself to be known to others apart from that small circle of acquaintances or would he continue to master his emotions and remain firmly entrenched behind that wall he so long ago built around him? I knew not the answers.

After being in Town several weeks, my master informed his father that his good friend from Cambridge, Charles Bingley, was in town and asked if it would be acceptable if he invited him and his family to visit. His father willingly agreed and a visit was fixed for the following Saturday.

I had been sitting downstairs the day of their impending visit, eagerly and somewhat anxiously waiting for the arrival of these new guests. The kitchen help was busy preparing something that smelled heavenly and my master was making some last minute preparations for the visit. I was curious as to what his friend would be like. Would he be as reserved as my master or would he be lively and gregarious? Would he have an agreeable sense of humour or would he be dull and witless? I was anxious to find out.

When the doorbell rang, I eagerly ran to espy them, tail wagging and eyes firmly planted on the door just as it was opened.

Two gentlemen and two ladies were invited in. As I watched them enter, I restrained from making my presence known until I could observe them first. I noticed that one of the gentlemen had a beaming smile gracing his face and he cheerfully greeted Mrs. Linden, the housekeeper, announcing they were the Bingley party here to see Mr. Darcy. He had the stature of a grown man but was somewhat boy-like in his features with an innocence and artlessness that I found refreshing. I perceived him to be a little younger than my master. The other gentleman seemed somewhat bored, tired almost, as if he had been ruthlessly awakened from a nap and forced to come along on this visit. He said nothing, but in giving the entryway a thorough perusal, he suddenly seemed quite taken by his surroundings and I watched as he offered a slight nod of approval. I hoped that the former gentleman was Bingley and not the latter.

There were also the two ladies. One, the taller one, immediately made me think of Lady Cat because she was adorned with feathers. She was dressed rather fashionably and walked determinedly into the house with a noticeable sigh of admiration and a rather triumphant smile flashing across her face as if she had just realized something for the first time. She was the first to speak to the others when Mrs. Linden left to announce them to my master.

"Oh, Charles! You did not tell me your friend had such an elegant, exquisite home!"

"How was I to know, Caroline? I have never been here before!"

Well, at least now I knew which one was Bingley. Thank goodness it was the friendly looking one. When Mrs. Linden called for my master, I thought it would be a good time to extend my welcome to the party. I came toward them;

restraining my excitement as I had been taught over the years, but I must confess my tail did wag quite fiercely and uncontrollably. Caroline, the one whom I considered to have a rather suspicious smile, was the first one to notice me.

"Oh, heavens! What is a mongrel doing in this house? Keep him away from me, Charles! You know how I loathe those creatures!" Her hands frantically waved in my direction, shooing me away. Her eyes flashed fiery darts at me and she hastened back a few steps.

"I am sure he will not harm you, Caroline." Bingley bent down and reached out his hand towards me. "Come here, old boy. You are a friendly one. Do you have a name?"

"Oh, please, Charles. It is a dog! And why anyone would have such a horrid creature in a house as elegant as this is beyond me! What kind of man is your friend, anyway? This is too much to bear!"

I knew immediately I would not like this lady. I did not care who she was.

I heard my master's footsteps coming down the stairs. Bingley looked up and Caroline, who continued to belabour my presence with an inexhaustible diatribe of protests, suddenly stopped in mid sentence and gasped.

"Bingley, I am glad you are come."

"Hello, Darcy. It is good to see you. What a fine home you have here."

"Thank you."

"Darcy, may I introduce my sister, Miss Caroline Bingley, and my sister and her husband, Louisa and Geoffrey Hurst."

"A pleasure."

Caroline was apparently rendered speechless by the sight of my master, for which I was quite grateful. But her silence did not last long enough to suit me, as she immediately began to heap praises on him of the home, his friendship to her brother, and quite unexpectedly, of me.

"You have a beautiful home here, Mr. Darcy. We have heard so much about you! Our brother speaks so highly of you! And what a charming dog. Does he have a name?"

"Yes, this is Reggie." He leaned down to ruffle the fur on my head and I reached it up to him.

She turned to me, clasping her hands together. "Reggie! What a sweet name."

I nudged my master and looked up at him, wishing somehow to convey to him not to believe a word she said. *If only you knew her true feelings about me, Master!* Now it is not normally in my manner to *doggedly* discompose anyone, but with her deceitful and insolent manners, I just felt as though Caroline Bingley needed a little extra attention.

Seeing that my master was pleased with her words of praise for me, I walked right up to her and looked up. Lowering her eyes without lowering her head, she glared down at me. Whilst I could most readily read the warning in her eyes, I proceeded with my plan.

Before my master could say or do anything, my tail began wagging with all the enthusiasm I could muster. I came up on my back paws and rested, very momentarily, my paws upon her gown and whilst her arms were gesticulating wildly, I gave her a good licking with my tongue over her gloved hand as it swept toward me. I had to admit it would have been much more effective if her hand had been gloveless, but it did the trick.

A shrill came from her that could have been used as an effective duck call out on a hunting excursion. A pained expression overspread her features and she shook her hand violently, as if expecting something to fall off from it. Her other hand repeatedly brushed the area of her dress where my paws had lit as though I might have left behind a trace of dirt. Being the prodigiously clean dog that I was, I doubted there was even the slightest blemish.

"Reggie, no! Down boy!" my master scolded. He turned to Miss Bingley. "My profound apologies. He does not usually behave in such an ill mannered way."

Looking back at me, he gave me the sternest look and said, "If you misbehave again, out you will go!"

"Oh," Miss Bingley swiftly gathered her composure, "It is nothing. There is no harm done." She looked down at me with a disputable smile upon her face. "He is a very sweet dog."

I narrowed my eyes at her and wondered why she would say such a thing when she obviously did not believe it.

Turning back to Darcy and quickly forgetting me, she exclaimed, "I have been so looking forward to meet you! Charles often wrote about you and how indebted he was to you for your friendship at Cambridge and how you helped him out in so many ways!"

"Uh, that is very kind of you." I could see my master draw away somewhat from her as she drew closer. Good for him! In this case, I was fervently happy he did not respond favourably to her excessive praise. However, it was also apparent that Miss Bingley did not notice his discomfort as a smile remained somewhat permanently emblazoned upon her face.

"Will we make your father's acquaintance, Darcy?" Bingley asked.

"I regret that my father is not here to make your acquaintance. He had some unexpected business arise and asked me to give you his regards. He had been looking forward to doing so himself. Perhaps you will have the opportunity some other time."

"Oh, I should like that very much!" Caroline drew her hands together and tilted her head somewhat coquettishly.

Look out, Master! I thought. *She has plans for you!*

We walked into the drawing room and everyone settled themselves into chairs and easy conversation.

Of the four guests, Miss Bingley seemed particularly impressed by the home but even more so by the man. By the way she began mentioning names of her acquaintances who were, according to her, well established in society, the esteemed places she frequents, and casually mentioned some of her accomplishments, I was firmly of the opinion that she was trying to elevate herself in his good opinion.

Mr. Hurst took very little part in any conversation. I almost believed him to be somewhat displeased that they had to pay this visit. His languid demeanour hinted at this being an interruption of a well-established naptime. I noticed him begin to nod off several times, only to be nudged discreetly by his wife.

His wife, Mrs. Hurst, not quite as fashionable or outspoken as Miss Bingley, sat quietly by her husband's side, only venturing a comment when it was to agree with something her sister said.

Bingley was the odd man in the party, at least compared to the rest of his family. He was expressive and cheerful and completely unperturbed by anything anyone did. However, I took it as a sign of his good sense that he seemed to have a tremendous yearning to seek my master's guidance and approval.

He inquired of my master about where he ought to look for a townhouse to purchase in London and asked him if he knew of any that would be suitable.

"Perhaps you ought to let a place before you buy, Bingley. If your inclination for liking a house is at all similar to your fondness for young ladies, you will be tired of it in no time! Inevitably you will find that by the time you move in, you will be most unhappy with it and will be ready to move on! I wonder that you will find it difficult to find lasting contentment in any!"

"Hah! If *you* were in a position to have to look for a house, Darcy, you would never find one that meets your impeccable standards! It is a good thing you already have a home in town and in the country, for I dare say if not, you would be roaming the streets of London now a homeless man!"

"Oh, brother, do not say such things. How cruel you can be sometimes!" Caroline winced as her brother spoke in such a manner about his friend.

"But, oh so true!" he laughed. "Darcy is a rare breed, I must say. He has women constantly throwing themselves at his feet and he finds it all completely tiresome!"

A fleeting smile appeared and disappeared from my master's face. "Unlike you, Bingley, I want someone who is more than just a pretty face. She must have substantial depth and spirit, qualities I find lacking in most of the women of my acquaintance."

Bingley looked at his friend oddly. "My dear friend, I find most of the ladies of my acquaintance completely admirable!"

"And that is where we differ, Bingley."

Bingley laughed as he continued, "Back to finding a house, Darcy. Were you really serious about helping me find one? And are you are of the firm opinion that I ought to let instead of buy?"

"I believe it is the most prudent thing to do, Bingley. I know of two houses that would be most satisfactory for you in the area if you would like to take a look at them."

Caroline clasped her hands. "Oh, Mr. Darcy, how good it is for you to look after my brother this way. I am sure that any house you recommend would be more than acceptable."

I looked up at Caroline and thought to myself, *Get yourself up from off his feet, Miss Bingley! Do you not comprehend that he finds this all tiresome?*

Darcy gave the Bingley party a quick tour around the townhouse. With each room he took them into, Bingley would comment on some element of structure or design, Hurst would merely look around him and grunt, but the two ladies offered sugary words of such praise on the elegance, style, fashion, suitability, and anything else in the home of which they considered worthy of praise. By the end of the tour, I felt as though I was walking along a path of spilled honey.

After being shown the music room, the three men walked out and the ladies lingered behind a little. As I was following them, I had to wait for them to leave. It was then that I overheard Miss Bingley's comments.

"Oh, Louisa! I had no idea! Most of Charles' friends are so boring and dull! Mr. Darcy is quite engaging!"

"Caroline, calm yourself. With this man, you must play your cards right!"

"Oh, fear not, Louisa. I am going to do everything I can to make him notice me. How fortunate for us that our brother has befriended not only one of the most handsome man in London, but one of the wealthiest of our acquaintance. And just think of the positive influence he can have on Charles!"

Both ladies giggled softly. "He is handsome, Caroline. And his home is beyond words. I have also heard that his estate in Derbyshire is one of which any woman would desire to be mistress."

"Oh, and when he looks at me, Louisa, my heart absolutely flutters! Have you noticed those deep brown puppy dog eyes he has?"

Now if you asked me, she suffered under quite a misconception! *Puppy dog eyes?* Whilst I have every conviction that my master had begun to look remarkably like myself, we were both very much adults now and neither of us have *puppy* dog eyes!

The two ladies walked out and I sat there hoping beyond hope that my master would have more sense than to be taken in by this woman who unfortunately was the sister of his best friend.

~~*

Throughout those winter and ensuing spring months in London, the Bingleys called numerous times. My master took great pleasure in advising Bingley on matters in which his friend seemed deficient. He pointed out the suitability or non-suitability of homes in London to purchase or let, however finding none to Bingley's liking. To own the truth, Bingley admired practically every one that he saw and had nothing but praise for them. My master would then point out some aspect of the house that *he* considered less than acceptable, and Mr. Bingley's partiality would subsequently lessen and he would agree with my master, ready to move on to the next one. My master confided in me that he wondered whether Bingley would ever settle it in his mind which house he preferred over another.

My master also obliged his friend and invited him as his guest to his club and introduced him to several of his acquaintances that were in Town. They took in the theatre and opera and attended some of the finer private musical concerts to which my master had been invited. He took exceedingly good care of Bingley, advising him in areas he felt his friend required his guidance. Bingley was grateful for his kindness; Miss Bingley was profuse in her indebtedness to him for his care of her brother.

The two men had an easy friendship that seemed to be strengthened by what each offered the other. Bingley brought a liveliness into my master's life. He was of a spontaneous, cheerful, and sociable nature in contrast to my master's composed, controlled, and reserved nature. My master gave painstaking thought to all he did, whereas Bingley often acted impulsively and without a great deal of consideration to the propriety or acceptability of it. It was in those areas that my master often had to caution or admonish him, and Bingley graciously accepted any and all of my master's counsel whether or not he asked for it.

Bingley, from my perspective, was a great encouragement for my master, giving him the impetus he needed to put himself in those situations where he most felt uncomfortable. Having Bingley at his side as one who could feel at ease in any social situation compensated for my master's inability to do so. But I was anxious that my master's dependence on his friend came at the expense of giving Miss Bingley false hope, for I soon learned that she was of the opinion that he preferred their company -- her company -- to that of those he did not know or knew only slightly.

I overheard her more than once gloat to her sister about how he preferred to dance with her than with any other woman and that he would often not dance at all if she were already engaged. She would insist that he preferred her company in conversation over that of any other lady in attendance. Unfortunately, his obstinate preference to associate only with those with whom he was well acquainted, whether it be in conversation or dancing, was working well in Miss Bingley's favour. I inwardly groaned as I considered that she most likely did all the talking in those instances and as for the dancing, I knew he considered it a punishment to dance with a lady unless he was particularly acquainted with her. As I never heard him speak of one, I doubted he was getting particularly acquainted with any other young lady.

Whilst I was gratified that I did not perceive any particular regard on his part for Miss Bingley, I could not deny the fact that they were frequently in each other's company, which served to ease my master's discomfort in the larger social gatherings in which they found themselves. It appeared my master was entirely oblivious of Miss Bingley's misconceptions regarding his attentions toward her and did not suspect that his behaviour was only serving to give rise to her misapprehensions. This did not make me happy at all!

My master found himself accepting more and more invitations to social engagements that year, whilst his father turned just as many more down. But it was not due to his inclination to avoid the ladies who now looked upon him as marriageable material. His health was of increasing concern. He did not quite feel that he had the stamina to which he was accustomed, but could not pinpoint any reason for it. Consequently, that year he returned to the quiet and comfort of Pemberley, leaving his son to enjoy -- or endure -- the season without him.

~~*

At length we returned to Pemberley, obliged to forfeit our yearly Rosings visit in lieu of my master assisting his father with estate management due to his poor health. We were both quite alarmed when we arrived and perceived his thinning features, pallid face, and overall weakness. Convinced that the responsibility of running the estate was the cause for his worsened condition, my master was insistent that his father immediately relinquish his duties to him, whilst his father was just as adamant that he continue in them and tried to put up a brave front. My master and I could both sense that Mr. Darcy was not able to do as much as he used to. He no longer took walks. He slept more and ate less. We were both concerned for his well being and the doctors offered very little hope.

As the year progressed, his health declined even more rapidly. During the summer months, he was often taken outdoors to sit in the warmth of the sunshine, in the hopes that it would bring some comfort to his growing frailty. But despite being wrapped in a blanket, he spent most of the time shivering from the cold, though the rest of us found the heat stifling. Soon, he was too ill to do anything but remain indoors.

I knew his father's well being weighed heavily on my master. He was daily having to take on more responsibilities and knew it would not be long before he would be without his father's good wisdom and counsel. Only in the privacy of our chambers would he admit to his fears. He tossed and turned into the wee hours of the morning and often pulled himself out of his bed, walking to the window and looking out into the darkness of the night.

He was at a loss to know what to do for Georgiana. She would come to my master with every hope of an encouraging word about their father, but he abhorred any sort of pretence and therefore could not but tell her the truth. Their father was dying.

I often saw him looking at his young sister with a look of admiration mixed with fear. She was just now blossoming into a young lady. Taller than most girls her age, her formerly awkward, gangly stance was being transformed daily into a gracefully poised young lady before our very eyes. The brightly coloured pinafores that she once wore were now replaced by long gowns; her hair was drawn up instead of falling freely; and her slight girlish carriage was beginning to show tell tale signs of encroaching womanhood, all the while the youthful, innocent expressions of her face betraying the fact that she was still a child.

My master was well aware that with the death of his father, the management of Pemberley would not be the only thing placed upon him, but the care for his sister as well. I believed him to be well suited for the task of managing the estate, but I know he questioned his ability to be his sister's guardian. In the darkness of the night he would ask with much anguish, "How am I to bring her through all this? How can I help her bear her grief when I am at a loss to know how to bear it? Am I now to be father and mother as well as brother to her?"

Mr. Darcy weakened steadily throughout the course of summer and as the winter season approached, he grew even more gravely ill. My master remained at his side, forsaking the invitations calling him to London. He and Georgiana, who was old enough to know what was happening but too young to give up all hope, remained by his side. It was only when Georgiana broke down that I perceived my master had a difficult time reining in his emotions, let alone knowing how to be of any help to her.

She had been too young to understand when her mother died, but had felt the loss of growing up without one. Now she was facing the loss of her father. As hard as she tried to be as strong as her brother exemplified and her father admonished her to be, she cried frequently.

In due course, the family was called to come to his side as he grew weaker and weaker and there seemed to be little hope that he would recover.

I was the only one allowed in the room with my master when his father summoned the strength and asked for an audience with his son alone.

I had not been able to see Mr. Darcy for some time, as he lay upon a bed out of my sight. But as I heard his weak, shaky voice, I could only imagine how frail he must look.

"Son," he began and took in some deep breaths. "I know my time is short…"

"No, Father. I know you can pull through."

I was able to see his father wave a feeble hand through the air. "No, no. This is no time for empty words of hope. I know it is my time."

Darcy schooled his features, making every attempt to remain collected. "Yes, Father."

He took in a few more deep breaths. "I am entrusting Pemberley to you, as I am sure you well know. I am confident you will do well with its management. You have made me quite proud."

"Thank you, Father."

I saw Mr. Darcy reach out and take his son's hand. "Little Georgiana… take good care of her. I leave her care to you and your cousin, Richard. You two are of like mind and can be a support to one another in the decisions you will have to make in her regard. I am certain that she will be no trouble to you."

"I am confident of that, Father. We will do our best to do what would please you."

He coughed a couple times and it seemed almost that he could not catch his breath. Finally, "I have everything written out in my will."

"I would give everything up if only I could do something to help you."

"No, my son. I have lived a good life. I am ready now to go join Anne. It has been too long."

My master looked down and he rubbed his cheek, I think to remove a tear that escaped his eye.

"Do not forget the living I promised Wickham. When it comes vacant, it is his. Son, I ask that you personally see to his advancement."

My master tensed and said nothing.

"I have a fund set aside for him. His father knows all about it. If you have any questions, ask him."

"Yes, Sir."

"Fitzwilliam?" His father squeezed his hand. "I am prodigiously proud of you. I know it will be difficult at first, but you will do well. You are strong. Be strong for Georgiana, will you?"

My master's voice was shaky, but he answered that he would.

The rest of the family came in when they were finished speaking and whilst they gathered around him, I noticed my master slowly walk toward the door. He stepped outside of the room and I followed.

I could see that his grief was waging war with his anger. He was about to lose his father whilst at the same time he would be obligated to honour his father's dying request. He and I both knew that Wickham was not worth the admiration his father extended to him. He knew it was too late and it would be inappropriate to share with him Wickham's true nature now. He would allow his father to die thinking well of him.

He took in some deep breaths and leaned against the wall, his head falling back against it, shoulders slumping. My heart skipped a beat as his fists tightened, pounding the wall behind him. He suddenly seemed to lose all stability and began to sink slowly down the wall, letting out a brief sob, which he quickly stifled.

As if coming to his senses, he swallowed hard and took in another deep breath. He brought himself back up to a stiff, upright position, ran his hand brusquely through his hair, and steeled himself to return back into the room.

Chapter 8

It was not until the following day that the well-regarded and highly esteemed Mr. Darcy finally took his last breath. Family, close friends, acquaintances, and tenants hastened to Pemberley to pay their respects. In addition, many letters of condolences were received, remembering Mr. Darcy as a fine man of good standing, exceptional honesty, and exceeding generosity. Numerous preparations and matters of business now required my master's consideration and he could spare but little time to appease my desire for attention. But I understood. I faithfully and steadfastly stood by his side when I had the occasion, wishing greatly to help ease the pain, but unable to do anything but support him by my presence.

Among those who came to Pemberley was Lady Cat, who surprised us all by bringing her daughter, Anne. This was Anne's first return to Pemberley since being a young child and she appeared quite in awe of it. As she was ushered in, her eyes took in every detail from the wood floors to the high ceilings and every object of decoration in between. I believed her to be comparing her home and this place of which she had every assurance from her mother of becoming mistress. I wondered if she preferred the natural understated elegance of Pemberley to the garish opulent display that was Rosings.

Our annual visit to Rosings last year had been forestalled due to Mr. Darcy's illness and I noticed, even more markedly, the young woman who was trying to emerge from behind the constraints her mother imposed. I could look deep into her eyes and see her desire to become an admired and appreciated young lady instead of the pitied and often overlooked frail thing she had become. But it appeared that no matter how much she wished it, she could not wilfully bring it to fulfilment.

It did not surprise me that they had not brought along Anne's greatest and most faithful companion, her dog. I was of the persuasion that Lady Cat would never consent to travelling with one. It only made me more grateful for the delightful diversions in which my master included me. And I was more than willing to stand in his stead.

During their stay, Anne was frequently left with her companion and nurse, Mrs. Jenkinson, as her mother was often diligently -- and insufferably -- involved in either giving unsolicited advice or issuing outright orders. Therefore, I was able to spend a good amount of time in the company of Anne. There was little I could do for my master as he received the family members who came to pay their respects and give comfort and sympathy whilst at the same time having to step forward into his new role as Master of Pemberley.

Whilst the household was a flurry of people, it bid me well to remain out from everyone's path and I took to remaining faithfully by Anne's side. Georgiana often furtively slipped away from the others and joined us. I think the two young women felt a sense of camaraderie together out of everyone's way as one struggled with reserve and more than a little trepidation in dealing with the multitude of people in her home and the other struggled with the mere strength she needed to exert just to extend a polite greeting.

Georgiana was very appreciative of everyone's kind and comforting words, yet she was at a loss to know how to respond. I sensed that she was in some kind of a daze as each day passed, struggling to be as strong as her father would have wanted and her brother exemplified, all the while wishing to run to her room and give in to her tears. She found a respite with Anne and myself and took advantage of any opportunity to join us.

Consequently, the three of us could often be found sitting silently off in a room to ourselves. I would alternately situate myself beside one or the other and they would each methodically run their hands over my head and back. Whilst I confess I enjoyed the attention, I believed it also soothed their aching spirits and grieving hearts.

Neither felt compelled to say much, other than an occasional smile to the other. Anne would reach out and gently pat Georgiana's hand if she noticed that tears were beginning to pool in her eyes and Georgiana, in turn, would offer to call for some tray to be brought in if Anne wished for something to eat or drink. Other than that, they sat contentedly in hushed stillness.

Gradually, after several days of gathering and mourning, family members began to depart. As they took their leave of Pemberley, the house grew more and more quiet. When finally the last of the guests had departed, I hoped a sense of normalcy would return. But the emptiness and quiet almost made the grief in my master and his sister more pronounced.

My master, Georgiana, Fitzwilliam, and I stood together silently, watching the carriage conveying the last of the guests take leave. Georgiana let out a pent up sigh, Fitzwilliam remained still and silent, but I watched in compassion as the deportment of my master seemed to collapse slightly, no doubt propelled from a sense of overwhelming despair as well as all-consuming exhaustion.

In that moment I came to understand his character a little better as I comprehended that he had steadfastly pushed down his grief to the deepest recesses within him as he executed his newly assumed duties as Master of Pemberley in the midst of family and friends. He would not allow himself to grieve until everyone had departed.

The four of us turned back toward the house and walked in. My master affectionately and securely wrapped his arm around Georgiana's, anticipating that she might need his support as they walked. He was correct, as she soon slowed her steps, turned into him, and then collapsed against his solid chest. His arms instantly went around her as she let the tears and sobs, that had been somewhat held in check, come forth.

He looked at his cousin with a countenance of concern and questioning. I sensed that he was not only wondering what he could do to ease Georgiana's pain at this moment, but he was also likely looking ahead to the future and wondering how he would manage being the father figure to her.

Fitzwilliam walked around to the other side of her as she pulled away. "Georgiana, it is understandable to let your tears fall. It has been a difficult few weeks. Your father would be proud of how admirably you bore it."

He gave her a smile and she made a vain attempt to return one. He took her other arm and three walked in.

"If you will excuse me," Georgiana began with a trembling voice. "I should like to be alone in my chambers."

"Georgiana, are you quite certain you do not want to be in our company?" Fitzwilliam asked her.

"Quite certain. Thank you."

"Until supper time, Georgiana. If you need anything, Richard and I shall be in the library."

She turned and walked away and the two men watched the young girl slowly take the stairs to her room.

"I wonder, Richard. What is to be done about her? Do we even know how to begin to raise her?"

Fitzwilliam firmly grasped my master's arm. "We will love her and do our best. That is all we can do." He turned and pulled his cousin along. "Come, let us go to the library and we can discuss it there."

I followed behind as the two men entered the library and Darcy poured both something to drink. Richard seated himself in the chair in front of the large desk situated to the side of the room. My master eschewed the leather chair behind the desk and instead chose to seat himself in the chair adjacent to his cousin's.

"It is *yours*, now, Cousin," Fitzwilliam said, indicating the leather chair. "You *are* allowed to sit in it."

My master sighed. "Not just yet. I still see my father sitting there."

Fitzwilliam simply nodded his head.

The two men spoke of Pemberley, the elder Mr. Darcy, but mostly of Georgiana. They decided that Georgiana most likely would benefit from attending a school where she could meet other girls her age and hopefully it would allow her to move past her shyness. Like her brother, Georgiana had been tutored at home. Both men felt a school would give her more opportunities to grow as a young woman; however they both felt very emphatically that they would not make these changes for a while. She had just lost her father and they did not want to send her away just yet. They were both of the estimation that she would need one or the other to help her overcome her grief.

Fitzwilliam remained for several more days. I believed he wanted to ensure both cousins were in reasonable spirits before he took leave. Whereas my master tried to appear strong in his cousin's presence, I believe Fitzwilliam could see through his stoic veneer.

Sadly, unlike her brother's forbearance, there were times when Georgiana appeared to be completely inconsolable. Whilst she had clearly been grieving when all the family had been at Pemberley, it was now even worse. Unable to rein in her tears, she often isolated herself in her chambers, unwilling to see anyone other than her governess, brother, and occasionally her cousin. Even then, it would only be after persistent coaxing and for short amounts of time.

My master emotionally braced himself each time he would go to see his sister. He made concerted efforts during the day to seek her out and encourage her with comforting words and hugs whilst mastering his own emotions. He seemed to make it through the day on forced determination alone. Although his cousin's presence seemed to bolster his spirits tremendously, I knew he would not always be there.

For my part, I felt the loss of the elder Mr. Darcy as well. During those years when my master was away at university, I believe we came to a comfortable and secure understanding with one another. I wanted to give comfort to my master in the midst of my own portion of grief, but I was often at a loss to know what to do. In the past, I would engage my master in a diversity of ways, ranging from a tussle on the floor in the sitting room to a grand scheme of tug-o-war outside. But somehow I felt that any attempt at something of that nature was now not at all appropriate. All I could do was faithfully remain by his side and hope to be a comfort in that way.

In surprising short order, my master began pouring himself into the running of Pemberley. I could not believe the manner in which he suddenly changed. Heartened that perhaps his cousin had recovered from his grief, Fitzwilliam bade his cousins farewell. I believe it is fair to say we all felt a small tug at our hearts as we watched him leave. He had been the one who had given each of us encouragement when we felt down. Both my master and Georgiana felt his loss greatly.

It was not long after that I realized my master had indeed come through his grief. We entered the library just a few days later and he eyed the chair and desk. Slowly walking over to it, he very determinedly sat in the chair. From that moment on, he was totally focused on being the Master of Pemberley and was committed to nothing short of excellence.

Within a short time after his father's death, my master's responsibilities as Master of Pemberley soon took another adverse direction. The elder Mr. Wickham died suddenly. That left him without a steward and the necessity of hiring and training another. Unfortunately, with his own father's death, George Wickham returned from Cambridge.

The funeral for the senior Mr. Wickham was the first time the two men were in each other's presence since my master's days at Cambridge. Although he had heard that Wickham had returned from Cambridge briefly for Mr. Darcy's funeral, my master had fortunately not had any contact with him.

With the return of Wickham, my master finally spoke of what he witnessed when they were together at Cambridge. He relayed to me how Wickham's study habits were contemptuous and that he was often heard mocking those who took seriously their learning. He associated with those who were either of like mind as he or with those whom he could easily charm. It was usually through the latter that he was able to submit a paper that was due or somehow secure the answers to his exams.

My master was never able to verify it, but he suspected that it was only through Wickham's deceptive charm that he was able to remain at Cambridge. But he did know for a fact that he lived his life full of vicious propensity and want of principle. He regretted the fact that his former friend was not worthy of the honour and esteem his father had for him, let alone deserve the living that was promised, but there was naught he could do about that now.

Wickham departed Derbyshire without ever acknowledging my master, for which my master was grateful, and Wickham supposedly returned to Cambridge. We heard later, however, that rumour had it he never returned to finish out the year.

Nothing was heard from him for quite some time and I believed my master dreaded the day he would have to honour his father's wishes. One afternoon, just a few months after Mr. Wickham's death, we were sitting in the study and my master was going over some details of the management of Pemberley with his new steward. The post was brought in and in it was a letter from George Wickham.

My master had said nothing, but over the years I had come to recognize a certain look that crossed his face when something happened in regards to that man. I also had picked up a trace of his dastardly scent as the letter was brought in.

"Traynor, will you excuse me?"

His steward looked up. "Certainly, Mr. Darcy. I shall just look over these papers."

My master briskly removed himself from the room, taking the letter to the library. I knew that if I followed, there was a good chance that he would convey to me the contents of the missive.

He walked into the library and turned to shut the door behind him, but in seeing me, allowed me entrance. He walked over to a chair and sat down, ripping open the letter with little regard to the state it would be in from the force he used.

I watched his eyes scan the letter quickly. It must have been fairly brief, as he shortly dropped his hands to his side and let out a frustrated sigh. I tentatively reached my paw up and rested it on his leg. He looked down at me and I could see the all too familiar set jaw and pulsing temple that was normally brought about by a sense of irritation.

"George Wickham! He has the audacity to tell me he has no intention of taking the living my father provided and hopes I do not find it unreasonable that he expects some sort of immediate pecuniary compensation! He shook his head and pounded a tightened fist upon his desk. "Not that I ever believed he should wear a clergyman's robe, but now he states that he wishes to study the law and that the interest from the one thousand pounds that was left to him in my father's will would not be sufficient enough to live on."

Darcy closed his eyes and his head went back. "What say you, Reggie? Do you think he really intends to study law? Should I hold on to any hope that he has changed?"

I let out a soft whine.

"Me neither, Reggie. Me neither. I have a difficult time believing he will use any money I give him in a prudent way. But if it absolves me of my father's dying request and proves to be the last that I ever have to deal with him, I will do it. I am not inclined to bestow it with any sense of favour or pleasure, but I will do it."

My master sent off a cheque to the address Wickham had enclosed and hoped that would be the last contact he would ever have with him.

~~*

Once my master was assured that his new steward had a fairly comprehensive grasp of the workings of Pemberley and the manner in which he wished it to be run, the demands on his time were eased a little. I knew, however, that our times together would never be as carefree as they had been those first few years. He had more responsibility; both at Pemberley and in the raising of his sister.

He was most concerned for her education. She was still being privately tutored at home and whilst he considered her governess to be excellent, he felt strongly that she should be enrolled in a school.

It was a little over a year after their father's death, when Georgiana finally seemed to be in tolerable spirits again, and my master broached the subject with her to put her in one of the finer schools for young ladies in London. Though she was reluctant to accede at first, he emphasized that it would help her overcome her shyness and that she might find great pleasure in the society of other young ladies her age. As much as he reassured her that he did not wish her to be apart from him, privately he knew he had become too much like his own father. Whereas he had fulfilled the office of caring for her and protecting her admirably, he feared he was instilling in her the same coolness and reserve with which he struggled. He had talked with his cousin and they both concurred there was no better time to do this than now.

They assured Georgiana that it would be excellent for her and that they would see each other as often as possible. Consequently, she entered school, my master tended his duties, and I was left alone to entertain myself quite frequently as the demands of Pemberley intruded on most of his time.

~~*

Things remained as such for a good amount of time. Georgiana excelled in school, although my master and I were of like mind that she was not particularly happy there. As much as my master struggled with that decision he made to put her into a formal school, he had the greatest hope that it would benefit her in providing her with an excellent education and easing her shyness.

As for our walks, when we did have occasion to take one, I believe my master used them as his outlet for thinking through particulars of which he was dealing with the estate or decisions about Georgiana. Whilst we still enjoyed these shared excursions, they were fewer and farther between. Every chance I had, I attempted to bring liveliness back into our times together, but more often than not it seemed a futile effort. Though I knew my master cared deeply for me, I was dismayed that his responsibilities left little room for any enjoyment.

Georgiana seemed to fare no better than her brother. Being the sweet, compliant young lady she was by nature, she obligingly did her best and was well regarded. In desiring to please her brother, she made every attempt to break out from behind that wall of shyness, and whilst she did meet several young ladies of whom she was quite fond, it was clear to him from her letters and visits that she was unhappy. She had been twelve when she began and suddenly she was almost fifteen.

Seeing her discontentment, and believing the school had done all it could, my master again conferred with his cousin and they decided to have a more personal sort of schooling for her, so an establishment was formed for her in London. She would stay at the townhome and only the finest tutors and masters would be brought in to continue her studies. All that was needed was the right gentlewoman to preside over it.

My master knew that finding the right lady would take much time and effort on his part. He would interview each applicant and look through every recommendation and reference. But most of all, he knew he would need to find a woman with just the right personality whom Georgiana could trust and in whom she could confide.

It proved to be a rather daunting task for my master. Whilst there were many applicants, there were just as many reasons why he found them unsuitable. If I thought my master was impeccable in his responsibility as Master of Pemberley, it was nothing compared to the care he exercised in filling this position.

He always concluded each interview by taking the opportunity to introduce Georgiana to the potential candidate. He observed each of them vigilantly as they interacted together. I came to quickly gauge for myself whether a woman was too imposing and reinforced Georgiana's shyness, too strict and frightened her, or too lenient and did not challenge her.

Time and time again, when the interview was completed, my master would simply say, "Thank you for your time." He never gave them any encouragement or hope when there was none. But I could see he was getting quite desperate; knowing that it was crucial to find someone in whom he could entrust to oversee Georgiana's education.

Needing a respite from the arduous task of interviewing in London, we all returned to Pemberley. One fine afternoon, my master was called out to an emergency in regards to one of his tenants. He left in a hurry and I did not have the opportunity to join him. It was an early summer day and I was feeling all the ill effects of not having had a walk in quite a while. I believed there could not be a finer day for a romp, so I scampered up to Georgiana's room, eagerly wagging my tail and letting out an insistent bark until she acquiesced and agreed to accompany me outside.

It was a little breezy, which necessitated Georgiana having to hold onto her bonnet so it would not be carried away, even though it was securely tied under her chin. The ties trailed behind her, waving in the wind as she carried herself along. I found a stick, possibly one that had been a toy on some other walk, and eagerly brought it to her. She took it from me and gave a laugh as she gently threw it ahead of us. I retrieved it and returned it to her. I was grateful that even though she had become a lovely lady in appearance and form, she did not think it beneath her to cater to my whims to play. We continued in this way until we reached the path just above the lake. I took a little detour away from Georgiana to take a drink. As I was lapping up the water, I caught an alarming scent and then heard a voice.

"Good day, Georgiana."

"Oh, hello, Mr. Wickham."

I turned suddenly, chiding myself for not having caught the scent sooner. A surge of trepidation coursed through me as I rushed to place myself between the two, growling and baring my fangs at him. I was willing to risk life and limb to protect her from this scoundrel. What did I get in return for my act of sacrifice and protection?

"Now, Reggie, you be a good boy! You know better than that!" Georgiana gave me the sternest look and shook her finger at me. "It is only Mr. Wickham."

"Pray, dear Georgiana, call me George." I did not care for his voice, which was far too smooth and alluring. "After all, your good father was my godfather. I *am* almost a brother to you. "

Georgiana looked down, slightly embarrassed. She kept her eyes on her feet, which seemed inclined to push the dirt around.

"It has been too long," he continued. "Look at you; you have become a young woman! Beautiful, at that! I hope you are well. I know how hard it must have been for you when your good father passed away."

She looked up slowly, sadness filling her eyes. "It was. I appreciate your concern. But the years have eased the pain."

I watched him warily as he did not seem inclined to leave and eyed her with a far too familiar look. "I have heard it said that you are looking for someone to preside over an establishment your brother has formed for your education. Have you had the good fortune to find one?"

Georgiana shook her head. "No, my brother is very particular about whom he will employ."

"I can only imagine," he laughed. "Only the best for you, but nothing less than you deserve, sweet Georgiana," he said, cocking his head to one side. Leaning in a little too close for my comfort, he asked her, "Exactly what type of woman is he looking for?"

"Obviously he expects to find someone with a great deal of experience, who is very accomplished, and…" Georgiana paused, shyness overtaking her.

"Yes?" Wickham asked softly.

"Well, she is to be my companion. He wants someone in whom I … well you know how shy I am around people. He wants to make sure it is someone in whom I may trust and feel at ease around."

He reached out and gently touched her shoulder. I let out a growl and

Georgiana looked at me and again that finger reached down and shook so as to quiet me and put me in my place.

"Georgiana, I am sure your brother will find someone who will suit you exceedingly well. And whomever she is, she will be most fortunate to be your companion."

"Thank you, Mr. Wickham."

"George," he again reminded her whilst I made known my presence and displeasure with another growl.

"Thank you, George," Georgiana answered, looking down again in a blush and with what I would describe as a sense of confusion.

I watched as Wickham reached out for Georgiana's hand and brought it quickly to his lips. His eyes watched hers as he did this and when I let out an irritated bark, he narrowed his eyes and me, bowed to Georgiana, and went merrily on his way. Looking back up at Georgiana, I could see the look of trust and admiration in her eyes as she watched him leave and heard the slightest sigh escape her lips.

It appeared as though my fears had not been unfounded. When my master was at Cambridge that year whilst Wickham remained back, an abiding regard for that scoundrel had been deeply instilled in Georgiana that the years had not diminished.

The following week we returned to London to continue the interviews and a woman was found for Georgiana's establishment. Her name was Mrs. Younge and my master was impressed with the several recommendations to her credit, her gentlewoman-like nature, and her kind, encouraging nature. She and Georgiana seemed to get along nicely. Both my master and Georgiana were quite disarmed by her and she was hired.

~~*

With Mrs. Younge presiding over her establishment, Georgiana spent the greater portion of her time in London. As spring was upon us, my master began preparing for another trip to Rosings. We were preparing to leave Pemberley when a letter from Mrs. Younge was received asking permission to take her charge with her to Ramsgate. The letter said she had family there and she felt it would be beneficial and refreshing for Georgiana to branch out and take this trip to this seaside town.

My master was torn about what he should do. Though he was disinclined to acquiesce to this request, he knew he had the tendency to be overly protective of his sister, even when he knew she was in good hands. As his cousin was expected shortly, he decided to seek counsel from him before making a decision.

When Fitzwilliam arrived, the two men got into a lively discussion that verged on being an argument. My master held back giving his consent allowing her to go whilst his cousin was adamant that this would be a profitable experience for her. In the end, they both agreed that Georgiana could well afford to make this visit in the company of this fine woman. As they would be departing for Kent, as well, they would arrange to pay her a visit there after their three-week stay at Rosings. They requested that Mrs. Younge send directions of where they would be staying and a reply was promptly dispatched to their satisfaction. The two men then set off for another visit to Rosings, believing Georgiana to be in good hands. My master confided to me, however, that even though he and his cousin gave their blessing to Mrs. Younge's proposal, he was anxious for their visit to Ramsgate, as he had never entrusted his sister so far from him before.

~~*

When we arrived at Rosings this year, I noted how my master exuded the confidence that his few years as Master of Pemberley had shaped. Since that first visit twelve years ago, when he was a young boy of fifteen, he had become a distinguished man. I, on the other hand, was feeling my age. It was more of a struggle to take the long walks that I so cherished, although I refused to give them up. I would not allow the aches and pains that had begun to plague me to keep me from my enjoyable diversions.

My master and his cousin had grown considerably closer in the years they had been appointed Georgiana's guardians. Although quite different in behaviour and demeanour, they each complimented and held a great amount of respect for the other.

Likewise, it did not escape my attention that Anne had grown into a young woman; yet no one else seemed to notice it. It appeared to me that she lived in a sort of fantasy world, one in which she was no longer weak and confined. She sat quietly among our party, speaking hardly a word and doing even less. I wondered if her frailty was perpetuated by a truly weak body or her mother's tenacious shielding of her from any sort of activity, and restricting her access to the outside world. In her eyes I could often detect a look that went beyond her confined circumstances to some castle in the sky where she reigned, was beautiful and admired, and was free!

When we arrived this year, her dog was no longer with her and as neither of her cousins seemed curious as to his whereabouts and did not inquire of his absence, I never came to discover what happened to him. But I would not have been surprised if Lady Cat got rid of the dog, thinking he was a carrier of every germ and disease known to man. It was fortunate that Lady Cat had so much regard for my master, for in always wishing to accommodate him, she continued to allow me in the house.

Our visit this year, however, came to an abrupt conclusion earlier than expected, as both Lady Cat and her daughter found themselves suffering such ill effects of a cold that even my master's aunt, who possessively clung to every prospect of spending time with her nephews and prided herself on her hospitality, could not endure the presence of anyone. It was deemed best that we all leave.

So it was with great anticipation that my master, his cousin, and I set off for Ramsgate to have a joyful reunion with Georgiana. We hoped that our early, unexpected arrival would be a pleasant surprise for her.

Chapter 9

The day was warm and sunny and the air fresh from a recent rain shower. A few clouds were painted across the sky as we set out for Ramsgate. I situated myself on the seat next to my master and his cousin settled himself across from me. Both men stretched their legs out away from them, angled in such a way that they gave each other a good amount of space without crowding the other. It was a trifle too chilly for the window to be left open, so I had to be content watching the scenery go by without the benefit of the wind washing across my face, which I have always enjoyed.

My master pulled out a book he had brought along, although he did not read it. Rather, he let it rest in his lap as he watched Rosings Park pass by the windows of our carriage upon our departure. We passed the lane that separated Rosings from the parsonage and soon passed the road that led down to it.

He turned to his cousin. "Did you discern that the clergyman seemed to be feeling the affects of his age quite a bit more since our last visit? I would not be surprised if Aunt Catherine will soon need to interview for a new one."

"She will love that!" replied Fitzwilliam. "Remember how long it took her to instruct this one as to the proper way to deliver a sermon? I did not think she would ever be satisfied with his manner."

"Hmm," my master murmured as he nodded his head with a knowing smile. "I always wondered how he abided by all her demands."

"I believe she is *still* in the process of instructing him!"

At length we were on the main road and my master turned back to his cousin as he brushed his hand repeatedly from the top of my head down the length of my back. "Do you think Georgiana will be pleasantly surprised to see us?"

"I see no reason why she would not. Our plans are not to dampen any enjoyment she might be having there."

"I cannot help but think that our aunt falling ill was somewhat providential."

"In what way, Darcy?"

"We get to see Georgiana early and…" my master paused and cast a sly glance at his cousin.

"And?" Fitzwilliam looked at him curiously.

"And… we were able to remove ourselves from her company before she even once brought up the subject of my marrying Anne!"

Both men laughed and we all settled in for the journey.

We had left immediately after breakfast and I understood that we would arrive in Ramsgate in the afternoon. I could see the hopeful anticipation in my master's eyes that he would be seeing his sister shortly. I believe my eyes also reflected that same anticipation.

Before long, I had fallen asleep, lulled by the rocking and swaying of the carriage. Apparently Fitzwilliam had, as well. When my master called out that we were in sight of the North Sea, we both fumbled about, trying to get our bearings and comprehend what he was saying.

I looked out the window and saw the most beautiful body of water anyone had ever seen. It extended out as far as the eye could see and the sunlight danced upon the ripples that spilt toward the shore. I had never before beheld such a large expanse of water and wondered if my master would allow me to retrieve sticks from it as he did in the lake at Pemberley.

With tail wagging in agreement, I could not think of anything more appealing to me right now than taking a long stroll along the sand that lined the water's edge. I would even consider a moderate run along the shore, kicking up the water and splashing my master.

As the carriage conveyed us through this seaside town, I watched as people bustled about, enjoying the warmth of the sun. Many a couple, linked arm and arm, seemed to be out for a stroll, enjoying the breeze caressing their faces and the sun showering them with its warmth. Children gaily danced alongside and I spotted an occasional dog that seemed to be enjoying an outing with its master.

We passed a large type of platform that extended out into the water where several people were walking and to which boats were affixed.

"Ah!" cried Fitzwilliam. "We are at the harbour already!"

My master looked out and opened the window slightly. "The inn at which they are staying should be just down this…" He stopped, and by the way his eyes narrowed, it appeared to me as though he was trying to make something out.

"What is it, Darcy?"

He shook his head. "I thought I saw Georgiana." He let out a tentative laugh. "It looked very much like her from this distance, but it could not be, as the young lady was walking on the arm of a man. I must confess it gave me a start for a moment."

His cousin laughed slightly but I think we could both see a bit of uncertainty written across his face, as if he was not convinced that his eyes had deceived him.

The carriage soon arrived at the inn where Mrs. Younge and Georgiana were to be staying and it stopped. The door was promptly opened for us. My master turned to his cousin, "You wait here with Reggie and I will go see to things. I will see if they have accommodations for us and also inquire as to whether Georgiana and Mrs. Younge are in their rooms."

He slipped out easily, taking a moment to stretch, and then walked into the inn. I kept an eye out the window, watching for him to return and for anything else that seemed to be of interest in this new place. Needless to say, I was anxious to be free from the confines of the carriage!

He had not been gone very long when, with very determined long strides and a stricken face, he returned to the carriage. He barked up orders to the driver to take us to the harbour and hopped back in; the door closing quickly behind him.

"What is it, Darcy? Is something wrong?"

Shivers ran through me as I saw his face. I had seen that expression often enough, but I could not quite understand why he would have it on his face here at Ramsgate. He seemed to struggle for composure, for the right words.

"It *was* Georgiana!"

"Darcy, man! Of what are you talking?" his cousin asked. "*What* was Georgiana?"

"The young lady I saw at the harbour!"

"On a gentleman's arm? Are you quite positive? Tell me, what did they tell you back there?"

My master closed his eyes. His fists were clenched tightly and his breathing became very erratic.

"I inquired whether Mrs. Young and Georgiana were presently in their room. I told them that I was Miss Darcy's brother and was paying a visit."

"Yes?"

He swallowed hard, looking away and then back, directly at his cousin. "I was told that the three of them left some time ago to take a stroll about the town."

"The three of them?" asked Fitzwilliam. "What three?"

"That's exactly what I asked."

My heart began pounding. I cannot fix upon a reason, but I had a feeling I knew who the third person in their party was.

He looked gravely at his cousin. "I was informed that Mrs. Younge and my sister were accompanied by a Mr. Wickham!"

"Heavens! Darcy! What does all this mean?"

"I have no idea, but I assure you I intend to find out!"

We quickly made it back to the harbour where he thought he had seen them, and before the carriage even came to a halt, my master had opened the door and bolted out. Fitzwilliam followed, attempting to keep up with his cousin's long and brisk strides. No one even seemed to recall that I was at hand, but I was determined that I would not remain inside the carriage. If there was anything I could do to protect Georgiana from this villain... from this rake... from this scoundrel, I would willingly do it. And, I flatter myself, if there was anything I was ever good at, it was sniffing things out, particularly George Wickham! I knew his vile scent all too well!

The three of us took off in the direction my master last saw them, which led to the end of the pier. But I was not able to pick up any inkling of his scent. I know my age diminished my abilities somewhat, but I could not let it affect me now! I had to latch onto his scent!

I turned my head in every direction, and finally I detected a faint whiff. I barked excitedly to get my master's attention and head directly off away from the pier. The two men started after me. Thank goodness my master and I made such a good hunting team; he recognized my bark as the one meaning I had caught his scent!

As my legs took me in the direction of the scent, I also picked up Georgiana's scent. As I continued, the scent grew stronger. I hoped it would not be too late. There was a park located just down across the road from the harbour and I stopped when I came upon it. Using my keen eyesight and sense of smell, I discovered them walking down a path. I remained still, looking intently at our object. The last thing I wanted to do was to attract Wickham's attention and have him suddenly flee, much like I do when I come upon a flock of ducks or geese. I waited for my master's word to flush him out.

The two men caught up with me and my master noted the direction of my gaze.

"There!" my master called out and pointed in the direction of a walking path. "Good boy!" he called to me as he began to stride as swiftly as propriety would allow towards them. Georgiana was walking with her hand on Wickham's arm and Wickham's other hand resting over hers. Mrs. Younge walked ahead of them.

I could sense my master's anger as strongly as if it were directed at me. It was an all-consuming anger that was coupled, oddly enough, with a pervasive, intense fear.

I kept up with him and could have easily passed him. I suspected that my master was fearful of calling too much attention to us; therefore, I let him lead the way. Fitzwilliam lagged a few steps behind the two of us.

When he was within a reasonable distance, he called out, "Georgiana!"

The young girl turned, her eyes widened, a look of surprise crossing her face followed by a broad smile. At the same time, Wickham and Mrs. Younge turned, and I did not miss a mutual look of shock and concern that passed between them.

"William! Richard!" Georgiana cried. "And look! Reggie is here! What a pleasant surprise!" When her gaze drifted up to Wickham, she could not have looked happier.

Wickham made a vain attempt to return her smile and upon seeing this, I bared my fangs and growled.

"Wickham, unhand my sister immediately," my master demanded. "Georgiana, please come here."

The smile left Georgiana's face as she saw and heard the unbridled anger of her brother. Wickham immediately released Georgiana's hand and she walked warily over to her brother whilst Wickham, consumed with anger, and Mrs. Younge, overcome with fear, stood silent.

"Mrs. Younge, may I ask what this is all about? Why is my sister, who is under your care and protection, on the arm of Wickham?"

She looked nervously to Wickham, who was standing beside her. "We... we just happened upon George... excuse me, Mr. Wickham here at Ramsgate, Sir. I understood him to be an intimate friend of your family."

"Did you?" my master asked in a challenging tone.

He looked to Georgiana. "What are you doing with him, Georgiana?"

A guarded smile came to her lips. "We are to be married, Brother."

"Married!" He looked at Wickham and Mrs. Younge, who both seemed to shrink away at this revelation. His eyes narrowed as it seemed as though everything suddenly seemed very clear to him.

He turned to Georgiana. "Georgiana, we will discuss this later. Right now, you are to return with your cousin back to our carriage and wait for me there."

"But, Brother, we love one another!"

Wickham suddenly seemed to find his bravado and stepped forth. "You see, Darcy? You would not want to break her little heart by separating us now, would you?"

My master eyed him threateningly. "Wickham, you have no more regard for her than you ever had regard for the clergy!" I added my growl of agreement to my master's words. "The only thing you love about Georgiana is her thirty thousand pounds!"

"No, Fitzwilliam! That is not true!" Georgiana cried as tears began to stream down her face.

"And just how much was Mrs. Younge to receive for her complicity in this scheme?"

When he steeled his eyes at the cowering woman, she blurted out pointing to Wickham, "It was all *his* idea! He made me do it!"

At the sound of a cry behind him, my master turned to his sister who, upon hearing Mrs. Younge's admission, covered her face with her hands and began to sob uncontrollably. He reached over and wrapped her in his arms. After a few moments he told his cousin to take her back to the carriage.

I believe I was shaking as much from anger as Georgiana was from devastation. I waited by my master's side to see what would transpire. I was not going to leave him alone in Wickham's presence. I stood ready to attack if my master required that of me.

My master looked down, shaking his head once with an emphatic lurch. Bringing his hand up to his jaw, he clasped it over his mouth, almost as if he was keeping in check a torrent of expletives that threatened to explode. He looked back up and the objects of his accusatory stare remained still and silent.

Slowly, he walked toward them. I sensed that Mrs. Younge was disposed to run, but she may have thought that would not be a very ladylike thing to do and besides, she would not get very far, for I would easily be able to overtake her. Wickham squared his shoulders as if preparing himself mentally, if not physically, for a fierce battle. I was ready to do the same.

"What, may I ask, is the meaning of this?" The fury in my master's voice, though tightly reined, was unmistakable.

"Come, Darcy. There is no harm done," Wickham brusquely alleged.

"No harm done? You led Georgiana to believe you loved her and that you were to be married?" He was standing practically on top of Wickham's toes, now, looking him directly in the eye. Wickham tried to match his stare, but finally looked away.

"We have talked. She is old enough to know what she wants."

"Old enough to know what she wants? She is but fifteen! Fifteen years old!" My master's eyes narrowed and I believed him to be on the verge of some very violent, physical act.

Feeling all the intensity of the anger that my master was feeling against Wickham and this woman, I was unable to restrain myself any longer.

I must confess I do not have that ability, as my master so obviously has, to control my emotions; especially when they are a precarious combination of anger coupled with the unassailable instinct to protect. Baring my teeth and releasing a barrage of ferocious barks that exceeded anything I remotely believed possible for a dog my age, I tenaciously approached Wickham, feeling my skin rankle and fur along my back stand up on end.

With little advance warning, I saw his foot come toward me. I made a vain attempt to thwart the impact by taking hold of it with my teeth, but it hit me in the back leg, sending me off balance and off to the side. I tried to suppress a yelp, but one unwittingly escaped.

Struggling to get myself upright, I saw my master quickly advance toward Wickham and grab the collar of his coat. I sensed that this had infuriated him beyond all control and was about to engage in some violent action when his cousin, returning from leaving Georgiana in the carriage with the driver, came up from behind and took hold of my master's free arm, preventing him from making any contact with their adversary.

"Come, Darcy. No need to lower yourself to his kind. "

The initial pain had passed and I quickly pulled myself up, but had to admit that my leg was sore and I favoured it as I took my position again alongside my master, ready to assist him if he chose to do battle with Wickham.

It took my master a few moments to settle in his mind whether he would obey his cousin or every impulse screaming within him, but at length he steeled his emotions. He turned to Wickham and uttered a threat to him in the coldest voice I have ever heard. It sent shivers down my back for all its icy, calm menace.

"If I ever ascertain that you have been anywhere near my sister again, Wickham, you will find yourself on the receiving end of my full wrath and will be hard pressed to even crawl away once I have dealt with you!"

My master then turned to Mrs. Younge, who would not meet his eyes at all. "And you, Mrs. Younge. You are dismissed, effective immediately. You are never to see Georgiana again. It hardly needs saying that you may expect no references from me. In fact, your trespasses against the trust I placed in you are so egregious, if I hear that you are trying to obtain work with any reputable family -- with any family, for that matter -- in the whole of England, I will see to it myself that you are not hired! Make no mistake; I will take measures to ensure that you will never be in someone's employ again!"

My master took a couple steps back. "Now, my cousin and I will escort Georgiana to the inn to retrieve her things. If you know what is good for you, you will stay as far away from there as possible until we have departed. Do you understand?"

They both nodded mutely.

My master turned to leave without offering up any civil word or gesture of parting. As I turned to follow him, I brazenly gave the dirt path a good, quick kick with my good back leg, hoping that some of the kicked up dirt hit its mark.

As we walked back to the carriage, Fitzwilliam asked my master, "What happened back there? What did you say to them?"

"I made it quite clear that I never wanted to see either of them again. I told them that if either ever came near Georgiana again, I would settle the matter with them in a decidedly ungentlemanlike manner."

Both his cousin and I could see the disgust and dismay with which my master was tortured. "What are we to do now?" he cousin asked.

"We remove Georgiana from Ramsgate. I will not feel safe until we have placed many miles between her and that scoundrel. I told them we are returning to the inn to retrieve her things and that they had best not come anywhere near until we are gone."

"Are we to return to Rosings, then?"

"Lord, no! If our aunt were to discover what we just confronted, she would question our ability at raising Georgiana and would insist on raising her herself!"

"London is too great a distance to make before nightfall. Any ideas?" Fitzwilliam asked.

"Anywhere but here. Come, let us get started." As my master continued toward the carriage, his cousin put up his hands to stop him.

"Now, Darcy, for Georgiana's sake, you must rein in that anger of yours before you step one foot inside the carriage. She is confused, hurt, and, I think, distraught that she has so disappointed you that she has forever lost your favour and affection."

My master let out a frustrated sigh. "How could I have let this happen, Fitzwilliam? What did I miss seeing?"

His cousin firmly planted a hand on his shoulder. "Darcy, you had no way of knowing. Do not blame yourself. And we must not allow Georgiana to believe that you blame *her* either. This is all Wickham's doing and entirely his fault!"

I looked up and saw my master swallow hard and shake his head. "But she is my responsibility…"

"*Our* responsibility, Darcy. If you are at all to blame, then I am, as well." As sincere as the attempt was Fitzwilliam made to convince him, I believe my master wholly blamed himself.

"Look, Darcy. When we get in that carriage, you must do your best to console your sister and reassure her of your love. Now is not the time to ask her how she could have done such a thing, how you could have allowed it, or even… Lord help us… the details of what happened between them. There will be time enough later for you to interrogate her and censure yourself. Right now she needs reassurances from both of us that she is still loved. She is quite inconsolable."

"I do love her, but how do I let her know that when those feelings are presently being overwhelmed by my anger at Wickham?"

"Tell her you understand that she is possibly confused and hurt and that you will do everything in your power to help her overcome this. Make certain she knows she is not to blame, but the most important thing is to convince her not merely with your words, but your demeanour. Try to remain calm, for her sake."

My master looked at his cousin. "Is she really inconsolable?"

"Quite so, Darcy. Let us make every attempt to not make it worse. Do you think we can do that?"

"But Wickham had no right! I swear that man is the devil incarnate!"

"He is, Darcy. And even now, even though you have removed Georgiana from his presence, he has won if you let those feelings spill out to Georgiana. Now, Darcy, cast away all those thoughts, calm yourself, and let us retrieve Georgiana's things and depart from this place!"

I wondered whether my master was capable of dealing in such a way with his anger, but after taking a few deep breaths, he appeared ready to face his sister.

We arrived back at the carriage where Georgiana was seated inside and our driver was standing at the door. I gingerly hopped up first and placed myself at Georgiana's feet. Fitzwilliam entered and was followed by my master.

I settled myself in the carriage with my heart still beating thunderously. Instead of nursing my injured leg, I turned my attention to Georgiana to do what I could to soothe her gravely wounded spirit. I felt as though the severity of my injury was nothing compared to Georgiana's wounded and devastated heart, so I nuzzled up against her to assure her that my devotion was unchanged.

I could not, however, curb my thoughts from retreating back to Wickham's dog, Storm. Did Wickham treat him as he just now treated me? Was that his means of controlling his dog? Was Storm as mean as he was because of Wickham's brutal treatment of him? I would not be surprised.

Georgiana held a handkerchief up to her face, holding it to her eyes which were filled with tears. She looked up cautiously at her brother took his seat next to her.

My master slid close to her and put his arm about her. She turned into his chest, heaving uncontrollable sobs, and whispered a barely audible "I am sorry, Fitzwilliam."

"I know you are, Georgiana." He closed his eyes tightly as if trying to erase all that had just happened. When he opened them, his cousin nodded at him to go on.

"Listen, Georgiana, I know you probably do not fully understand now, and you must be hurt and confused..." The words did not come easily, and he seemed to struggle even more as she let out a heartbreaking cry.

"You must believe me, Georgiana, that we still love you and do not blame you for falling victim to Wickham's infamous schemes. You are young and he took advantage of your guileless nature with his deceptions."

She looked up at him with swollen, red eyes. "He said he loved me. I believed he wished to marry me because he loved me."

"I know, I know," I could feel my master fighting down his building anger towards Wickham.

"He talked to me about how much regard he and Father had for one another. He told me that Father would have been delighted at our marrying. He said it would be acceptable to you, as well; that you would be very pleased. He said that when we returned from Gretna Green as man and wife..."

"Gretna Green?" My master's voice boomed and Georgiana withdrew from him. Taking a deep breath, he pulled her towards him again and said in a softer tone, "Forgive me, Georgiana. He was going to take you to Gretna Green? To elope?"

She nodded mutely. I did not know all that my master was thinking, but I could pretty easily read in his face that it was probably a good thing that Wickham was not in the carriage with us at the moment. His hand tightened into a fist and his jaw clenched as he struggled again with maintaining his composure. He turned to look out the window -- at nothing I would guess -- and then turned back to Georgiana.

"Yes, he wanted to marry me as soon as possible and he said that was the only way to do it."

My master was silent. I believe it was to prevent him from saying something that would distress Georgiana even more.

We reached the inn and Fitzwilliam reached over and took her hand. "Georgiana, allow me to accompany you and retrieve your belongings." My master needed time to collect himself and fortunately, his cousin realized that.

The two of them stepped out of the carriage and as soon as they were out of sight, my master let out a mournful groan. Leaning over, he dropped his head into his hands. "I have failed the most important person in my life! How could I have done such a thing?"

I whimpered to console him and moved closer. Without looking up, he reached down and scratched my neck. "You were useful today helping us find them, Reggie. Sometimes I wonder what I would do without you."

Fitzwilliam and Georgiana returned in short order and we all settled back into the carriage. It was determined that we would set out toward London and find suitable accommodations before dusk. Once we were on the road again, it was a very long, quiet, and uncomfortable ride.

As the sun was slowly descending toward the horizon, we found a very pleasant inn that had two rooms available.

I could not help but limp a little as we walked toward the inn. Noticing it, Georgiana innocently asked why I was favouring my one back leg. I looked up at my master, knowing it would hurt Georgiana even more so to know the truth.

"My dear," he began, "Back there, Wickham kicked him. But I think our Reggie will be all right. I think he is but a little sore."

Georgiana gasped and crouched down, wrapping her arms about me and burying her head in the scruff of my neck. "I am so sorry, Reggie. I am so sorry."

"He is not badly hurt, Georgiana. It ought to heal in no time."

I felt her arms tighten about me. "He really was not a good man, was he, Brother?" Her voice trembled.

My master slowly and silently shook his head and with much self censure watched as her tears flowed unhindered.

Georgiana was given a room of her own and after barely eating anything at supper, she excused herself and retired for the night. Before she quit the room, my master called her over and drew her into his arms. He held onto her very firmly and for quite a while, I think for his sake as well as hers.

"Good night, Georgiana. Please try to get a good night's sleep."

She nodded mutely and walked slowly past her cousin. He reached out for her hand and brushed a kiss against it. "Good night, Georgiana."

When she left, the two men agreed that any discussion should be delayed until they were back at the townhome in London. Here, there was too great a possibility that she might overhear them or that someone else might unwittingly hear and her reputation would be jeopardized. They reasoned the tumultuous events of the day would leave her either too distressed to sleep or too exhausted to stay awake, but they did not want to take the chance of upsetting her any further.

Needless to say, my master scarcely slept that night. If ever he doubted his ability to be an adequate guardian for Georgiana, it was now. He looked over to his cousin who was, surprisingly, sleeping soundly in a separate bed in the room whilst my master paced, stared endlessly out the window, or went out into the sitting area to ponder over the situation.

I knew he was anxious to get more details from Georgiana, but he also knew he must use a gentle approach, lest he frighten her. Devoted to her as he was, I believe he wondered whether he would ever trust her to anyone else again.

The next day we departed early to cover the remaining distance to London. When we finally arrived at the townhome, it seemed as though everyone breathed a little easier. We were in familiar surroundings and we could almost believe that the previous day had only been an imagined thing. Almost.

As difficult as it was for my master, there were some things he needed to find out from Georgiana. Once they had been home and had the opportunity to rest for awhile, he called her into the library with Fitzwilliam.

"Georgiana, forgive me, I know this might be difficult. I would ask you to please relay to Fitzwilliam and me everything that occurred from the time you and Mrs. Younge arrived in Ramsgate until we arrived and found you with Wickham."

Georgiana's mouth began to twitch and tears pooled in her eyes, but she began to relate how they first encountered Mr. Wickham at dinner in the inn that first night in Ramsgate. He had moved Georgiana with a touching remembrance of her late father and she invited him to join them for the meal. Subsequently, he would always appear as if by Providence wherever Mrs. Younge had planned for their daily outing, paying solicitous attention to Georgiana, pleasing her with kind words of the excellence of her father. It was a matter of very little time before he was invited, with Mrs. Younge's approval, to join them each day afterwards.

My master looked intently at his sister. "Georgiana, were you ever left alone with Mr. Wickham?"

Georgiana blushed slightly. "No, no, not really. We sat together in the sitting room several times whilst Mrs. Younge was in the next room."

"What happened during those times?" His fervour to discover what all had transpired between his sister and Wickham caused her to tremble.

Fitzwilliam drew close and took her hand. "Georgiana, we only wish to ascertain whether Mr. Wickham displayed only gentlemanlike manners toward you."

"Yes…yes. He just… he just…"

My master's eyes narrowed. "He what?"

"Go ahead, Georgiana, it is all right," Fitzwilliam helped soothe the tension in the room.

"He was just very kind in all his words towards me. He told me how he had always admired Father and looked upon me with fond regard. He told me how he cared for me, thought I was beautiful, and could think of no one finer that he would ever want to marry."

When they had finished talking with Georgiana, they had pretty much determined that Wickham had used his deceitful charm to flatter her and taken advantage of her youth and innocence to convince her of his devotion and affection. Being so young and naïve, she believed him and believed herself to be in love with him, as well. They were greatly relieved that Wickham did not further compromise her.

That night the two cousins earnestly discussed what ought to be done. It was decided, for the sake of Georgiana's reputation, that discretion must be employed. The two cousins swore to each other that neither would utter a word of it to anyone, lest it harm her character and standing in society.

"You know, Darcy," Fitzwilliam began. "I think you were correct in your estimation that our aunt's falling ill was providential, but perhaps not for the reason you originally thought." He leaned back into his chair and closed his eyes for a moment. "I do believe someone is watching out for Georgiana!"

The two men then discussed plans to provide a companion for Georgiana. My master was naturally reluctant to place his trust in another stranger, claiming that he would see to Georgiana's needs. His cousin rightfully pointed out that he could not shoulder the responsibility for Georgiana's education in addition to managing Pemberley; that it was the office of a gentlewoman to do so.

Fitzwilliam gave a strong recommendation for a woman with whom he was well acquainted. Her name was Mrs. Annesley, a long-time friend of their family who was recently widowed, had an impeccable reputation, and my master agreed to give her strong consideration.

She was sent for and quickly came. My master was pleased with everything about her and she immediately took Georgiana under her wing. She was the only other person who was told about the incident with Wickham. At first, my master paid solicitous attention to Georgiana, insisting on taking all his meals with her, rarely letting her out of his sight. However, when Mrs. Annesley gently suggested that perhaps a return to their normal routine would be more beneficial to allowing the incident to be put behind us, he acquiesced. He could see that her maternal and gentle guidance comforted Georgiana, and for that he was grateful.

Once my master was convinced that Georgiana was well on her way to healing and moving past her guilt and shame, he gradually began to focus on other things. We spent a leisurely summer back at Pemberley, the once hot days of summer gratefully began to make way for the cool days of autumn, and a letter was received from his good friend, Charles Bingley.

Darcy,

I hope you do not think me too hasty or impulsive, my good friend, but I have found a most suitable country home -- Netherfield in Hertfordshire. I visited it Monday last and took an immediate liking to it. I did abide by your advice and inquired whether it would be available to let and Mr. Morris, the solicitor, agreed as long as another eligible offer to buy is not received. I will be moving in immediately, and will return to London in two weeks time to bring back my sisters and Hurst who are presently up north. I do hope you will join us when we return to Netherfield. I should very much like to have your approval on my new home.

CB

Chapter 10

My master deliberated long on the invitation from Bingley before finally settling upon joining his friend in a perusal of this new estate upon which he had so hastily decided. He laboured for days over whether it was too soon to take this first journey away from Georgiana since the incident at Ramsgate. Pacing back and forth in his study, he meditated on his options. I was a willing listener as he debated whether leaving her would be prudent and whether Georgiana would be in favour of it or not.

Despite his apprehension, he was fairly confident that leaving her with Mrs. Annesley would not give him cause to worry. Mrs. Annesley had proven herself over and over to be an excellent companion and had found her way quickly into Georgiana's broken and contrite heart. The two ladies appeared to be very pleased with the arrangement. Mrs. Annesley was also of a mind that this separation would be beneficial for both brother and sister and gently encouraged him to endeavour to make the trip with Bingley.

My master had not seen his friend for some time; Bingley's open and artless manner always served to raise his spirits. Therefore, with equal amounts of anticipation and ill-ease, he finally made his decision. He determined we would all set out for London where Georgiana and Mrs. Annesley would remain until all four of us could make the return journey to Pemberley together.

I was pleased with his decision, as I felt my master had become increasingly isolated in the years since taking on the responsibility as Master of Pemberley. In addition to that, since returning from Ramsgate, he had developed a rather cynical demeanour that was difficult for me break through. He had an armour about him that was not easily penetrated. Naturally then, I had every hope that time spent with his good friend would ease some of his burden and bring some light-heartedness into his life.

Once the decision was final, we set out almost immediately for London. Bingley's plans were to depart for Netherfield in a few days' time. My master occupied himself with the business that awaited him there and Georgiana and Mrs. Annesley spent their time cultivating Georgiana's accomplishments and providing her with culturally enriching engagements, so I frequently found myself with a great deal of idle time.

I must admit that at my stage of life, doing even the simplest things required more of an effort on my part. I found that I was enjoying my prolonged naps more than I ever did before. Do not misunderstand me; I still had it in me for a lively walk with my master or an occasional romp through the country. And I looked forward with great anticipation to be able to thoroughly explore the grounds of this new place called Netherfield we were about to visit.

On the day of our departure, my master spent the morning with Georgiana, reassuring her that he would return before long and that she should enjoy herself with Mrs. Annesley. However, he did not make any promises to her concerning when he would return, remarking only that he would allow sufficient time for Bingley to defend all the virtues of this country home to my master's critical assessment and that he also wished to get a good feel for the neighbourhood and grounds.

For the journey to Netherfield, my master and I rode together with Bingley, sharing his chaise and four. My master sent his own carriage on without us, as he greatly desired his friend's exclusive company. He knew once we arrived at Netherfield, their times together would be intruded upon by one or both of Bingley's sisters. They were, fortunately, riding to Netherfield in Hurst's carriage.

Along the way, it was clear that my master undertook his office of advisor to his less-experienced friend quite seriously. He used the privacy afforded to them in the chaise to interrogate Bingley on the particulars of his choice. I comprehended that my master was somewhat dubious of Bingley's discernment, for he had little praise of Hertfordshire society. "Bingley, this is a fairly rural area, you will find little society here."

"Oh, Darcy! I have met many of the neighbours already! They are a decidedly amiable lot!"

My master shook his head. "I cannot name one prominent family in the neighbourhood, Bingley. Are you quite sure this country estate is everything you want? For what the neighbourhood lacks in society, the estate will have to make up for in all its other amenities."

"Trust me, good friend; it is everything for which I have been seeking!"

"But will Netherfield live up to both of your *sisters'* expectations?"

"They will be pleased with it, I am quite certain."

"And what of the grounds? Will you find ample sport there?"

"The grounds are quite extensive, Darcy. Indeed, they are not as grand as Pemberley, but I believe they will provide us with abundant hunting."

My master took in a deep breath. He could readily see Bingley's enthusiasm as well as I could. For myself, I found it almost contagious, and I found my anticipation steadily rising. But my master seemed immune to it and finally said, "As it would be difficult as well as unfair to make an assessment of Netherfield without the benefit of seeing it, Bingley, I shall withhold all judgment until we have given it a thorough once over."

"I am quite certain you will be pleased with it, Darcy. I just *know* you will."

Bingley's words were intermingled with both the guarded assurance of his friend's approval and an optimistic effort at persuasion to sway his friend's opinion if it was not to his liking. I could see Bingley had every hope that my master would give his approval. I wondered how deeply it would affect Bingley if he deemed it an unwise choice.

~~*

As we approached a small village that Bingley referred to as Meryton, my master commented in abhorrence at the ogling of the common country villagers as the chaise and four in which we were riding ambled down the dusty street. Bingley's wide smile gave my master every indication that he felt these villagers were the friendliest neighbours for which one could wish and that he was looking forward to making their acquaintance. My master, on the other hand, did not share his friend's enthusiasm.

My master did not keep his feelings to himself. "We certainly appear to be attracting a great deal too much attention, Bingley. Have the people around here never seen a chaise and four before?" he grumbled. He turned to Bingley. "How far is Netherfield from here?"

"But a few miles."

I could see that my master seemed hardly impressed by what his eyes took in and that Bingley was becoming increasingly uneasy about his good friend's estimation.

Bingley's eagerness to portray Netherfield in all its glorious light prompted him to instruct his driver to take a divergent route to the estate.

In looking out the window as the carriage made a rather gruelling climb up a slight incline, my master agreed with his friend that the view from up here was quite pleasant. He lowered the window enough for me to stick my head out, which pleased me immeasurably. Our attention to the passing scenery was interrupted by the sight of a young lady skipping back down the hill on the other side of the road. The bonnet she was wearing covered most of her face, except her radiant smile.

As we passed her, she looked up and upon seeing my head protruding out the window, gave me a slight nod, her eyes sparkling, and I caught a most pleasant scent; flowery -- but not overwhelming, as Caroline's scents often are. I envied her for her youthfulness and the pleasure she seemed to receive from traipsing down the hill.

"Did you observe her, Darcy? She looked to me as though she was taking great delight in her journey down the hill!" Bingley exclaimed.

"Indeed I observed, her," my master declared, but in the next breath gave sharp censure to the young lady. "However, a proper young woman ought never to wander so great a distance alone! You never know what sort of unsavoury person might be lurking about!"

"Darcy!" Bingley countered. "May I inquire what you are about? What would give you the idea that someone such as that might be lurking about? We are the only ones up here, and unless you intend to be unsavoury, I cannot imagine such a thing!"

My master shook his head slightly. "One can never be too cautious."

Bingley said nothing more and a short distance ahead, he impatiently tapped on the top of the chaise and the driver brought it to a stop.

"Step out with me, Darcy," he said. "You must see this view of the manor and grounds."

The two climbed out of the chaise just as the Hursts' carriage drew up behind them and came to a halt. Bingley ushered his friend over to gaze at the view. I kept myself entertained by exploring the area whilst allowing my legs a little exercise and sniffing out the different scents that dotted the area; one in particular from a young lady.

Bingley's enthusiasm for his estate seemed to be mounting. He was just as eager as he was anxious to please his friend.

"Look! Down there! See between the trees? That, my good friend, is Netherfield! It is a fair prospect, is it not?"

I thought to myself, as I came back alongside the two men, that if Bingley were a dog like myself, his tail would be wagging viciously!

"It is hardly visible, Bingley," my master replied in a cool manner.

"Yes, I know," Bingley assured him, his enthusiasm refusing to be quelled, "but we shall see it shortly. Here, look at the grounds." With an outstretched arm and finger pointing, he said, "From that dip in the meadow towards the north to that cluster of trees to the south is Netherfield." He looked up at my master's face for some sort of response. "It is ample grounds for sport, do you not agree?"

My master nodded slowly. "Yes, Bingley, it appears that you shall enjoy good sport here."

Upon hearing my master's first compliment toward the place, Bingley seemed greatly appeased.

The Hursts and Miss Bingley were now approaching. The din of Miss Bingley's stridently plaintive voice shattered Bingley's hope of hearing his friend's approbation as well as the peaceful reverie the three of us shared as we looked down at the expanse of Netherfield below.

"Charles! I am beginning to wonder what you have done! Exactly where is this house and how do you expect me to live in such unpolished society! Did you see that village back there, Brother? I am sure you did! Not one fashionably dressed man or woman! I cannot imagine we shall be able to find one well bred person in the whole of this neighbourhood!"

"Nonsense!" Bingley cried out. "I have already met several neighbours who are simply delightful." He gently took her arm and gave a very temperate reminder. "I am quite confident, Caroline, that you will be perceived by the entire neighbourhood as the picture of fashion and elegance, and will be spoken of as a most accomplished woman. Think of your standing here! Yours will be the most sought after invitation."

"Mmm," she seemed to consider his words, "That would be true, Charles, but you must also comprehend that it will be highly unlikely that I will find anyone with knowledge of the latest fashions here. I will surely have to go to London quite frequently for all my gowns."

"I will do everything I can to accommodate you, Caroline!"

"I suppose it will not be too wearisome if you look at it that way, Charles."

"Good!" Bingley clapped his hands as he had it settled in his mind that his sister and friend would now be convinced of his good judgment.

We all returned to our waiting carriages and settled in for the short ride down the hill to Netherfield. When we were able to get our first good look at it, I noticed my master nod slightly.

"It appears in adequate condition, Bingley. Is the interior as sound as the exterior?"

I was quite proud that, as in all other areas, my master took his advisor role to his friend most seriously.

"It is in excellent condition, Darcy. Only a few minor repairs are needed to make it ideal!"

We pulled up and were soon waited upon by Bingley's servants, some of whom he had only recently hired and were still learning all that was required of them. As orders were being issued, young men obediently began removing the luggage from the carriages.

I easily noticed the gleam in Miss Bingley's eyes. She looked across the expanse of the manor and was well pleased with what she saw. I could only imagine that she was envisioning herself mistress here and being hostess to many a grand ball or dinner party.

Bingley, with enthusiasm literally emanating from him, gave us a complete tour of the home, heralding its favourable qualities and skimming quickly over its lesser features.

As it turned out, I need not have fretted about what Bingley would have done if my master disliked Netherfield. My master agreed that it would be a very good estate for Bingley. But he maintained his position that letting it instead of purchasing it was for the best and that Bingley had done the right thing. My master remained convinced that Bingley's inconstancy might lead him to tire of it shortly. He would also mention to me later that he strongly wondered of the society there and whether Bingley would soon find the neighbourhood quite dull, wishing to find another home shortly in a more superior district.

My master asked to see the stables and more of the grounds, so he and Bingley set out whilst the others clamoured over which rooms they would claim for their own. I was anxious to get outside, especially when Bingley looked down at me and exclaimed, "Reggie, I have a surprise for you, too, out by the stables."

I was eager to explore the grounds, but now he had my curiosity piqued. As we approached the stables, I could hear a yelping coming from off to the side. I caught the scent of another dog.

We came to a fenced in area and I found myself looking in the friendly face of another dog exactly as myself, only much younger.

"This is Lady Mercedes Belle Bingley," Bingley told us. "But I call her Sadie."

"So you have found yourself a hunting dog!" My master laughed. "Is she of a superior lineage?"

"Well," Bingley paused before he answered. "I must admit, I am not exactly certain. I acquired her from someone in Meryton. She is certainly beautiful, though."

My master pursed his lips in thought before continuing, "Is she well trained?"

"Her previous owner told me that she has been trained in sport, but we shall have to see if she is as excellent a sporting dog as Reggie is." He looked down at me and smiled. "Unfortunately, she will not be the indoor companion that you have in Reggie. Caroline would never stand for it and besides that, Sadie has never been properly trained to be indoors."

Bingley turned to me. "What do you think of her, boy?"

I approached the fence tentatively, unsure how she would welcome me. She came right up and our noses touched through the opening in the fence. Her tail wagged ferociously and she began to jump up against the fence. Like Bingley, I thought she was beautiful, but perhaps a bit too vigorous. I admit that in my younger days I would have been able to match her energetic amiability, but the years have quieted that tendency.

Bingley reached up to undo the latch on the gate and slowly opened it so he could reach in for her. She excitedly pawed at me as Bingley held her close and in her playfulness, she reached out and grabbed hold of my ear in her mouth, refusing to let go.

Unwittingly, I let a whine escape, and Bingley pulled her back to release her hold on me. "She still has a little puppy in her, as you can see. I had my stablehand fence this area in for her so she can come outside, or in inclement weather, she can slip inside the stable. Reggie, of course, is free to stay with you inside, Darcy, as he is accustomed."

"I thank you, Bingley. And I am sure, if Reggie could talk, he would thank you, as well."

Bingley placed Sadie back in the fenced in area and we set off to do some more touring of the grounds. Just as we were about to follow the path behind some trees, I turned back to steal one last glance at Sadie, who was watching our movement intently.

My heart felt a small leap when I looked back at her, but my mind was ill at ease. I could not dismiss the question my master asked his friend of her breeding. I thought again back to the day he came and selected me over all the others, even those of a more superior lineage. His father seemed more concerned that I was not from the finest bred litters. I was very grateful then that my master did not seem so inclined and had defended his choice as being the finest for him. Now, I wondered whether he regretted his choice. Did he now, as Master of Pemberley, see things differently? Did he now view that as highly important? I could not help but wonder.

~~*

Almost immediately upon our arrival, neighbours began making calls and leaving their cards. Bingley was in such good humour to receive everyone and felt inclined to approve of them all. My master did not seem to have a similar leaning. He did not join his friend in making the acquaintances when they called at Netherfield nor did he join his friend's visits when he repaid the call. Instead, he chose to sequester himself in the small, sparsely laden library, I suspect in part to stay out of the way of the sisters, whereas Bingley enjoyed the esteem and society of his new neighbours.

It was somewhat disheartening to me to see this young man enter into this new neighbourhood with such eager anticipation and joy, whilst his sisters, Mr. Hurst, and my master all bore it with such indifference. There were certainly no complaints about the house itself, but they found much to decry about the inferiority of the surrounding neighbourhood. To her credit, Miss Bingley did her best to exude hospitality and graciousness in her role as Mistress of Netherfield; however behind the backs of her new neighbours she was critical and displeased.

They were vigilant to keep their harshest remarks amongst themselves, although I do not believe it would have swayed Bingley's jubilance. He lived in a grand home and looked forward to everything that being its master would signify.

Bingley's enthusiasm became almost unbearable -- even to me -- when he and his whole party were invited to an assembly that was to be held in Meryton. Nothing could dampen Bingley's fervour, even as his sisters bemoaned having to endure such a tedious affair and my master grew exceptionally quiet. I immediately recognized the uneasiness in his demeanour steadily growing as Bingley grew increasingly animated in his anticipation.

~~*

As my master's valet was helping him dress for the assembly, I watched from my vantage point on the bed. As usual, he allowed his man to pick out his wardrobe that best suited the occasion, and was therefore dressed, on his part, with very little apparent interest or concern. He completely trusted his valet with the styles and colours and ultimate outcome of his dress, and worried not of it himself.

It appeared to me that the less thought he put into this evening, the easier it would be on him and the sooner the evening would be over. I could feel his anxiety building as his man added his final touches whilst he expertly tied his neck cloth.

"Anything else, Sir?" he asked.

"No, thank you. You may go."

"Have a good evening, Sir."

My master ran his fingers inside the neck of his shirt and neckcloth as he seemed to struggle swallowing. "Thank you."

The valet exited the room and there was silence. My master did not move for several moments. He looked over at me and I noticed a small smile briefly appear and then vanish.

"I know what you are thinking, Reggie. You are wondering why I endure all this for the sake of a friend!" He let out a laugh that was accompanied by a tight smile and took in another deep breath. "But this should be considered a small courtesy for such a friend. It has always given me much satisfaction how he has continually esteemed me and savoured the counsel I have given him."

I could certainly agree with him that his friend highly regarded his prodigious guidance.

My master turned toward the mirror and continued to nervously play with his neck cloth, loosening its strangling hold.

"Yet, to own the truth, Bingley and I are of such very different temperaments. I always wished that some of his ease of manner and light-hearted demeanour would find its way through to me." He slowly shook his head. "Tonight he will effortlessly make new acquaintances and strike up conversations with people he scarcely knows. He will dance with every young lady in attendance, admiring her and, I might add, giving her false hopes." He reached down and picked up a goblet that had been brought in for him earlier, downing its contents. Shaking his head once, he added, "I cannot do that, Reggie. It is not within me."

Giving his coat a sharp tug, he continued, "As a result, I will be most assuredly ill at ease the whole of the evening and will have the most dreadful time."

I let out a sympathetic moan and he walked toward the door. "Come, Reggie. I do not suppose I can delay this any longer."

We joined the others downstairs and I looked over everyone dressed up in their finest. Whilst I own that I know nothing of fashion, I believed they would all be admired and welcomed by the neighbourhood. I kept my distance from Miss Bingley, however, who had some horrendously strong scent splashed over her that was assaulting my nose.

My master bade me a good evening and I watched as a stone-like visage implanted itself on his face. Bingley's cheerful farewell was quite a contrast to the four other members of his party who, one would think, were on their way to their own funeral.

When the party stepped outdoors and walked toward the waiting carriages, I followed. As the servants were tending them, I caught Sadie's faint scent and decided to pay her a visit. She had frequently been in my thoughts of late and I had not had the opportunity to see her, so I quietly and imperceptibly slipped behind the carriages and then ambled down toward the stables. Because I had learned to be most proficient at keeping myself out from under the staff's feet, I was quite certain that I would not be missed by them.

As I came upon the stables, Sadie eagerly welcomed me. Her excited bark heralded my arrival to the stablehand. Coming out, he looked surprised to see me.

"Well, Reggie. What are you doing here? Did everyone leave you this evening?"

I let out a quick bark and looked over at Sadie.

"Ahh! You wish to spend the evening with your new friend, do you?" He brought his hand up and rubbed his chin contemplating this. I wondered if he would send me directly back to the house.

"Now I know, Reggie, that Mr. Darcy would not think kindly of you being out in the pen with Sadie with all that dirt, so..." He walked over and picked up a long leather lead. "I will allow you and Sadie to come into the stable, but she must remain on the lead. I must get some things done and cannot keep my eye on her. Will that do, boy?"

I barked again in agreement and he walked out, opening the gate and slipping the lead over Sadie's head. He brought her in and I could see that this was something he must have done often, as she seemed to know exactly what was expected of her.

He walked back out and retrieved a few of her toys. "Here are your toys, Sadie. Share them with Reggie." Then he looked directly at me. "Reggie, as soon as the carriages return, Sadie goes back in her pen and you go back to the house. I am not sure your master would be pleased knowing you spent your evening out here." Then he winked at me. "Just behave yourself."

Sadie tried to engage me in a sort of tug-o-war with what appeared to be an old stocking, with which I obliged her until I was too worn out. She looked at me curiously with her big brown eyes and I am quite certain she wondered why I did not scamper about with her. Most likely she did not comprehend that I did not have even half of the energy and playfulness that she had.

But I enjoyed myself. I found a comfortable corner and settled myself into it, watching as she ferociously and vigorously shook an old stuffed doll as if it had been some hunted creature, and rolled a ball around, occasionally tossing it into the air and making every attempt to catch it or rolling it towards me in the hopes that I would retrieve it. It was apparent to me that she had often been allowed to come in here tethered, as she very aptly manoeuvred around the lead, even quickly unravelling herself if she found her legs entangled. How I wished to join her. But I contented myself to simply watch.

The time passed all too quickly. When we heard the carriages approaching, I found myself not a little disappointed. The stablehand came out and ordered me on my way as he returned Sadie to her pen and began making preparations to receive the horses. I found myself quite eager to join my master, however saddened I was to leave my friend. But I had to admit that I had not even once, in the course of the evening, given any thought to my master and how he was faring.

The front doors were opened to the great house just as my master stepped down from the carriage. He looked down and saw me, a question in his eyes, but he warmly greeted me. I followed everyone in, curious as to the state in which I would find my master. Everyone walked in quietly, excepting Bingley, who was giving everyone a lively account of their evening at the assembly.

Then, with an eagerness to be to his room, my master bade everyone a good night. As we approached his chambers, he waved off his man when he offered to help him into his nightclothes.

I could see that he wished to be alone. That most likely meant that the evening had passed exactly as he had expected and he had behaved exactly as I had anticipated he would.

He quickly untied his neck cloth, letting it drop to the floor. He took off his coat and merely placed it over a chair. Unbuttoning his shirt, he stopped and took in a deep breath. Looking over at me, he said, "It was just as intolerable as I suspected it would be, Reggie! The neighbourhood here is an objectionable hodgepodge of inferior connections, ill breeding, and even a total want of propriety! There was not one admirable…" He paused here, as if probing his mind to the truth of what he was about to say.

However, that was all he said and I looked at him curiously, tilting my head, expecting to hear him elaborate on his last remark. But instead, he proceeded to divest himself of his clothes and impatiently put on the nightshirt that his man had set out for him. He climbed into bed and I eagerly joined him. I wished for him to tell me more of this evening, and yet, how I wished I could tell him of mine. But that was not to be.

When we were both settled in, I anticipated a good night's sleep, but instead, I laid there with my eyes wide open. I could not close them! My heart beat wildly as I thought back to my whole evening spent with Sadie. She was a pretty thing and very well tempered, I might add. She had a gentle spirit, albeit occasionally she would get a little too lively in her playfulness for my disposition. How grateful I was for this new friend. My only concern was that she might consider me too dull or too old for her liking.

I unwittingly let out a moan and turned my head. Fearful that I had awakened my master, I looked guiltily towards him. To my surprise, I saw something that quite arrested my attention. He was lying flat on his back with his hands folded up under his head and his eyes were wide open as well, staring off into the darkness! Now, I know why *I* had been thus engaged, but I wondered what it was that was causing this wakefulness in *him*.

Was he unsettled about something or was there some other basis for his behaviour? I knew he had not enjoyed himself at the assembly, but that was not enough to make him lose sleep. Typically, when he was troubled, he would talk about it. He would toss and turn, as if thrashing his body around would ease things. But tonight, he was lying perfectly still, yet wide awake for some unexplainable reason.

I nudged toward him to let him know I was awake and he could let me know what was on his mind, but he only took in a deep breath and let it out in a huff. Rolling over, he took his fist and pounded it into his pillow, fluffing it up only to make a soft landing place for his head, which he plunged into it.

All I heard him say, again, was an emphatic declaration, "No! There was not one!"

~~*

The following day, Miss Bingley did everything in her power to recruit my master to join in her disapprobation against the local populace. I could not discern if his distracted agreement was his attempt to be a polite guest or his true assessment of the neighbourhood, but there was something else to his demeanour that I could not place.

I listened with curiosity as Bingley prattled on in endless admiration about his most pleasant evening and Miss Bingley fumed in indignant disapproval. My master took little notice of either in his apparent preoccupation with something pressing more urgently upon him and he appeared miles away. He seemed somewhat reflective; less resolute in his words and actions.

Throughout the day, I was dismayed to find that whenever Miss Bingley had the opportunity, she cornered my master and raised her concerns. It was either about the insipidity of the neighbourhood, the most inappropriate way her brother was going on about one particular lady, or her impatience to return to London and refined society.

It was after the evening meal, when we were all gathered in the sitting room, when I began to get an inkling about something -- or perhaps I should say *someone,* that was partly responsible for my master's unusual behaviour.

Bingley had again brought up the subject of the most pleasant time that was had at the assembly the previous night.

"I have rarely enjoyed myself more," he declared. "And did you not think Miss Bennet the most beautiful creature you have ever seen? I could never conceive an angel more beautiful." Looking directly at my master, he asked, "What did you think, Darcy?"

"I will concur that Miss Bennet is pretty, however, to my taste, she smiles too much."

"Oh, but Darcy what a sweet smile she has!" Bingley said with a pronounced sigh.

Caroline interjected at this point, "It is unfortunate, Brother, that she has such a family! I was quite surprised to hear that the locals consider Miss Elizabeth Bennet to be a beauty as well."

My master stiffly walked over to the fireplace and rested his elbow on the mantel. "Which one was she?" he asked, averting his eyes from everyone in the room.

Bingley stood up from his chair. "She is the one you refused to dance with last night!" He walked over and stood next to his friend. "I cannot believe you meant what you said last night about her being only tolerable, Darcy! Granted, she is not as pretty as Miss Bennet, but you have to admit her pretty, as well!"

Waiting for my master to reply, I looked up at him and saw him pause. A faraway look had infused his eyes, but was quickly replaced with a straightening of his shoulders and a granite look coming to his features. "Miss Elizabeth Bennet pretty? I should as soon call her mother a wit!"

I turned to see Caroline beaming with pleasure whilst I was rather shocked at my master's callous rudeness.

"Come, Darcy!" argued Bingley. "You cannot believe that!"

His jaw tightened as he went on, "I hold to my assessment. She hardly has a good feature in her face!"

"Well, I say it was your behaviour last night that was barely tolerable. To refuse to dance with her and to speak of her so when she was within hearing! I am quite convinced she overheard you!"

My master cast him a sharp glance and I began to sense there was something about this merely tolerable young lady that was prompting the state in which he found himself. I looked despairingly at him, considering his behaviour. I had rarely witnessed such rudeness, except with the likes of someone such as Wickham. I was inclined to believe that his rudeness was due to the fact that we had been too long in Caroline's presence and her behaviour was beginning to have an affect on him. But then, I wondered if perhaps it was something else, instead.

As I pondered this, Bingley continued, "I have never met with more pleasant people nor prettier girls in my whole life! Everyone was most kind and attentive to me!" I looked up and seeing Bingley beaming, could easily picture him last night with his easy manners, enjoying himself immensely.

He smiled as he paused to sip from his glass, reflecting back on the evening. "There was no tedious formality that one finds so often in these affairs, no stiffness. I found it quite refreshing and quite easily and quickly found myself acquainted with the whole room!"

Either ignoring the look that was exchanged between his sisters or oblivious to it, his eyes took on a rather dreamy state as he let another pensive sigh escape.

My master, on the other hand, steeled himself against some unknown force and continued, "On the contrary, Bingley, I saw nothing but a collection of people in whom there was little beauty and no fashion."

"I heartily agree, Mr. Darcy!" Caroline's consensus was too swift for my satisfaction.

He continued, "I received neither attention nor pleasure from anyone." The image of a beaming Bingley gave way in my mind to the image of my master glowering in the corner, miserable and avoiding the society of anyone. I disconsolately put my head down upon my paws. It had been too long since he had truly enjoyed himself. I wondered if he ever would be able to enjoy himself again. I felt the smallest tinge of guilt for the delightful evening I had spent with Sadie. Now it was my turn to let out a long, drawn out sigh.

By the end of the evening, both Bingley's sisters agreed with my master on the plainness of the neighbourhood on the whole, but allowed that Miss Jane Bennet was indeed a pretty and sweet girl and therefore gave their brother the freedom to think of her as he chose; which he was more than inclined to do.

~~*

For the next few days, as inclement weather kept us indoors, I caught frequent snippets of conversation discussing either the sweet Miss Bennet, her tolerable sister, the younger sisters who were not worth talking to, or their intolerable mother. I was more than eager to distance myself from such disheartening discussion and looked forward to a change in the weather to allow my master and me the opportunity to walk about the grounds.

Now I must insert here that when we are in London, I am forced to be leashed on the streets and my master sets the pace and direction. In the country, however, I am free to choose the direction and my master considerately obliges me by following.

It is not difficult to speculate, then, that the few walks my master and I had enjoyed at Netherfield usually began in the direction of the stables. I admit I was hoping that my master would see fit to allow Sadie to join us. The first few days after we had arrived, my master was not quite convinced that would be a prudent idea and would not allow it. But, on a day that dawned bright and clear, he finally acquiesced.

The stablehand assured my master that she had learned her commands quite well and keenly obeyed. He had been prompting her on her hunting skills in anticipation of an upcoming day of sport for the gentlemen. He did not believe she would run off, except perhaps to chase after some game. However, he assured my master that should she run off, he was quite sure she would promptly return.

Sadie eagerly came out of the pen when it was opened; evidently, she needed to release some of her pent up energy and had to be called down for her behaviour. The stablehand commanded her to "sit" and she obediently sat down, wagging her tail ferociously, impatiently awaiting the command that would allow her the freedom to get back up on her feet. I found her liveliness most endearing.

When we finally commenced our walk, it was pleasing to find she generally remained by my side. She occasionally scampered into some bush because her ears picked up a sound or her nose caught a scent, but she would just as quickly return. How I remembered when I had such liveliness and curiosity! Now I was content to walk along the path and simply enjoy exploring what was before me.

When we returned after that first walk with Sadie, my master praised her for obeying his commands and informed the stablehand that she behaved admirably. I felt a great deal of pride swelling up inside, knowing that Sadie had proven herself well mannered and amiable to my fastidious master.

I was grateful that my master seemed to easily return to his self again after that evening spent at the assembly. But just when I thought it was all behind us, Bingley announced more pleasant news; that is… pleasant to him, rather disagreeable to the others.

"We have received another invitation!" Bingley exclaimed. "It is a gathering at Lucas Lodge. What great enjoyment that will be!"

As I watched my master's sombre response to Bingley's ecstatic announcement, I recollected how, over the past few years, I witnessed my master go through grief over the loss of his father, anger over the actions of Wickham, and regret and great concern for the welfare of his sister. In the midst of all those times I found that I was always able to give him some sort of comfort. But we had now come to this small country village in Hertfordshire and I was witnessing something in him that I had never witnessed before. I found myself at a loss to know how to handle it. And little did I know how it would change his life completely.

Chapter 11

Since settling at Netherfield, the gentlemen did eagerly await a fine morning to dawn that promised them an excellent day for hunting. I anticipated my first opportunity to exhibit my skills to Sadie and hoped that she would prove herself dutiful to all she had learnt. The perfect morning finally dawned -- it was the day after receiving the invitation to Lucas Lodge.

The air was still, but for an occasional breeze that captured and freed a smattering of leaves still lightly clinging to their branches, sending them gaily down to join the others on the ground. I enjoyed the sound and feel of the leaves being trampled beneath my paws as we walked toward the stables. As I looked ahead to a day spent hunting with Sadie, a sense of excitement augmented my vitality beyond what I thought was within me.

With unsurpassed eagerness, we set out, and Sadie was released from her pen. We all held out fervent hopes for an exceptional day. Whilst the ducks, geese, and game birds were not particularly plentiful, Sadie and I proved ourselves most proficient as we were able to sniff some out from around the several ponds that dotted Netherfield.

Sadie remained close by my side, and as a team, we obliged the gentlemen in flushing out a variety of game birds which were easily downed. My master, the ever excellent marksman, out shot Bingley and Hurst in bringing down four, whereas the other two gentlemen captured only three between them.

An excellent day of hunting soon came to an end. It was most rewarding to have teamed up with Sadie, who proved herself so proficient. Bingley blamed his poor aim on a certain "angel;" this lady he referred to as Miss Bennet, who occupied his thoughts, rather than anything Sadie may have done poorly. My master appeared to improve in his hunting skills with each year and I must confess I felt that this particular time out on the grounds I felt a youth and vigour I had not experienced in quite a long time.

As we all turned back to Netherfield, we passed the stables and I grudgingly watched as Sadie was returned to her pen. Whilst she exhibited no discontent in her accommodations, I greatly wished that we had more opportunity together. I thoroughly enjoyed my day and felt a great sense of admiration for my new young friend.

We walked around the manor to enter through the back, as the men's boots -- and my feet -- were more than a little muddy. As we passed through the courtyard, we noticed a carriage parked in front and an animated exclamation came forth from Bingley.

"It seems that we have visitors!" He turned to the two men who exhibited neither the enthusiasm nor the pleasure that their friend did from this intelligence. "Let us inquire who it is!"

When we entered through the rear entrance into the kitchen area, Bingley was met by his housekeeper who informed him that the Bennet ladies from Longbourn had called and were now in the sitting room with his sisters. A jovial cheer came forth from Bingley as he immediately prepared to join them whilst Hurst muffled a groan as he quickly made his own escape.

My master abruptly stopped his friend. "Bingley, should you not clean up before presenting yourself to your guests?"

"I am not wholly unpresentable, am I?" asked Bingley, hoping his friend would not believe him to be.

"Bingley, your boots are caked in mud! You cannot walk through the house, neither can you present yourself to the ladies with your boots in such a state."

"Then I shall remove them!" Bingley cried out with puppy-like enthusiasm.

"And walk into the room in stockinged feet?" My master's voice raised in frustration. "You must give more deliberation, Bingley, to your conduct as Master of Netherfield."

I could see the battle waging within Bingley; his desire to rush out and greet these ladies -- or perhaps just one in particular -- fighting against his desire to comply with his good friend's sense and instruction.

"Certainly, Darcy. You are quite right." He turned to one of the servants standing by the door. "Fetch me another pair of boots, quickly! Please!"

Bingley sat down and quickly began removing his mud encrusted boots and my master did the same at his leisure. One of the servants attended my paws and removed all traces of mud. I finished the task with a few good lickings.

Both men were provided with a clean pair of boots and Bingley had two servants assist him in getting them on promptly. My master, although not giving any indication of hurrying, was shod just as quickly.

Bingley stood up and looked to my master with a grin, "Come, Darcy, they shall be happy to see us now!"

My master shook his head. "I would rather not, Bingley."

Bingley placed his hand congenially on my master's shoulder and began leading him out. "For just a few moments, Darcy. Just to say hello."

I eagerly followed the two men, anxious to make the acquaintance of these Bennet ladies, particularly two of them, for the first time.

As we approached the door, a rather loud, high pitched voice came from someone inside, "We are so delighted you have taken Netherfield! We could not have asked for finer neighbours!"

As I peeked in, I watched as the two sisters exchanged a conspiratorial look toward one another as they responded with the barest hint of civility before we were noticed at the door.

"Oh, Charles, please come join us!" Caroline pleaded.

Bingley beamed in perfect agreement to such an invitation, seemingly forgetting my master and me. To my surprise, I perceived my master tense beside me, but his and Bingley's opposing actions were soon forgotten by me as I suddenly discerned a very familiar scent. As I gazed about the room, seeking to identify the source of that scent, I realized it was coming from one of the young ladies. I also realized at that same moment, that both the scent and the lady were one and the same with the young lady we had seen skipping down the hill.

As Bingley bounded in the room, the occupants stood and curtsied with alacrity, a smile on each face; the relief at the additional company obvious. But it did not escape my notice that not everyone was pleased by all the additions, as the lady whose scent I recognized earlier turned her head further and observed my master still standing steadfastly at the door. She raised an eyebrow archly and gave him a glare that was quite imposing.

Miss Bingley quickly made polite introductions, although I am quite sure, based on the easy amiability with which he addressed our visitors, her brother was already well acquainted with each of the ladies in the party. I, however, was grateful for the introduction and took particular note of the "angel" Miss Bennet and her sister, Miss Elizabeth, the one with the memorable scent.

Whilst indiscernible to the others, I saw a clenching of my master's jaw just before turning and walking away. I knew, from all my years as his faithful and loyal companion, that at the moment, he was not particularly inclined to be congenial.

It disheartened me to witness this poor display of manners on my master's part, especially when I was particularly inclined to know more of this Miss Elizabeth. Her refreshingly floral scent took me back to a more carefree time when my master and I would endlessly explore the grounds of Pemberley in the spring with all its flowers in bloom.

Instead of dutifully following him as I typically did, I made an exception and decided to enter the room. I watched as Bingley warmly greeted each lady and how his sisters bore up under his gracious and profuse words of welcome. I agreed with Bingley that Miss Bennet appeared very pretty and sweet. I admit that I could only but concur with my master that the other ladies seemed to exhibit a less refined manner, excepting, that is, Miss Elizabeth. And it was she in whom I was most interested.

Not wanting to attract attention to myself, being unsure how these guests would receive me, I slowly and quietly walked in, sitting down just out of everyone's way. Miss Elizabeth was the first to take notice of me.

"Why, Mr. Bingley! What a beautiful dog! Come here, boy. What is his name?"

"Oh," Bingley laughed. "He is not mine! He is Darcy's! The man hardly ever goes anywhere without his faithful companion." He looked back, expecting to see his friend behind him. Looking somewhat confused, he turned back to her and continued, "His name is Reggie."

Seeing her accepting countenance, I delightedly walked up to Miss Elizabeth and sat down before her. She leaned forward and patted the top of my head, whispering, "It seems I recall having seen you before, Reggie." I eagerly wagged my tail and bestowed upon her my most amiable manners. Seeing my well pleased response, she then scratched me about my ears. I looked up at her and saw that same sparkle in her eyes that I recollected from the first time I saw her.

Whilst everyone else's attention was on Bingley and his generous words of appreciation for their visit, Elizabeth leaned down and asked, "Will you give me your paw?"

I happily obliged and she took it in a firm, but gentle grasp.

Then she knelt down even more and whispered so no one would hear, "Well, Reggie, this is a pleasant surprise. How is it that you exhibit the most impeccable manners whilst, I am sad to say, your master, does not?"

My eyes widened at this. It was quite apparent that she did not esteem my master and I was quite of the opinion she *had* overheard herself deemed merely tolerable by my master at the assembly as Bingley had inferred.

No one else seemed to pay me any mind and considering Miss Elizabeth's warm friendliness, coupled with my instinct to discern character, I attributed her as being a most affable young lady. I felt for the first time in my life that my master and I held a very differing estimation of her. It was impossible for me to view Miss Elizabeth as anything but pleasant, agreeable, and, I might add, very pretty indeed!

I remained by her side, contented with her attentions to the top of my head, behind my ears, and an occasional stroke down my back, enjoying the feel of her gentle fingers occasionally twirling around my curly fur. I gazed up at her and she returned my gaze with a pleasant smile and those dark, sparkling eyes.

I suddenly became aware of a presence behind us; my master's scent was so strong that I knew he had returned. I turned my head towards him and began eagerly wagging my tail so that it was thudding heavily against the floor. I did this for the twofold purpose of allowing him to ascertain my cordial feelings for Miss Elizabeth as well as hoping to assuage his disappointment in me for venturing in here on my own accord. Miss Elizabeth noticed that my attention had been drawn away and looked up, her face still reflecting the joy from our encounter.

When my master saw Miss Elizabeth's bright face, he appeared unable to move as his attention was completely riveted upon her, and most likely would have remained permanently planted in that spot had it not been for Bingley distracting him by calling out and inviting him to enter.

His response was somewhat stilted, as he tore his eyes away from my new friend. "I… uh… no… I beg your pardon… I was merely looking for Reggie." He looked over at Miss Elizabeth and quite clumsily offered a most needless apology. "I… uh… please accept my apologies. Forgive me if he has been a nuisance."

"On the contrary, he is quite charming!" She looked down at me and smiled. I allowed my tail to thump a little faster to let her know I was smiling back at her on the inside.

"Come join us, Darcy!" Bingley exclaimed.

"No, pray, Mr. Darcy, do not trouble yourself on our account," protested Mrs. Bennet. "We have far exceeded our stay! We would not want to inconvenience you any longer." She looked around her and I could see from her expression that she held the same sort of contempt for my master that Miss Elizabeth did. *Curious indeed!*

My master politely, but stoically, followed Bingley and the ladies outdoors when the Bennets took their leave. I stayed right at Miss Elizabeth's feet and just before she stepped up into the carriage, she reached down and patted my head one last time with a twinkle in her eyes. I was quite charmed by her approbation, for Bingley's sisters had never even acknowledged me since my arrival at Netherfield.

I turned back to stand aside my master and saw an odd expression on his face. That he was fighting something deep within was evident; his jaw tightened and his eyebrows were drawn down. I hoped that he was not angry with me for taking the liberty to join the ladies without his consent. He said nothing to me but turned to walk back into the house directly.

Bingley lingered outside, keeping his eyes fixed on the carriage as it slowly pulled away until it was out of his sight. His sisters quickly returned to the house and as I followed, their critical assessment of the Bennet ladies did not escape my notice. Whereas they were pleased with Miss Bennet's manners, they were most displeased with the remainder of the Bennet family.

Later that evening, as we gathered after supper in the sitting room, Bingley continued his praise of Miss Bennet, which his sisters bore with surreptitious words and looks of disparagement passing between them. My master stalwartly adhered to a book he was reading, refusing to be drawn into the conversation. I wondered, however, if the book was not to his liking, as he did not turn the pages as frequently as he normally did.

Once we had retired for the night, he said to me, "So, you have made a friend of Miss Elizabeth, have you?" His voice seemed almost censuring. "It appears that she holds *you* in high regard."

These were the first words he had spoken of Miss Elizabeth all day. I had been encouraged that he had not joined Bingley's sisters in their assailing of her, as she was often the object of much derisive comments. But it seemed my encouragement was to be short-lived, for not one moment had passed in the privacy of our chambers before he seemed intent to shake something off himself (as I often must do when I am provoked by some unsolicited flying creature that assaults my ears) and he steadfastly declared, "Miss Elizabeth may have garnered *your* favour, Reggie, however in *my* estimation, she barely has an attractive feature on her face; she has more than one failure of perfect symmetry in her form, and her manners may be acceptable in the country, but are simply not those of the fashionable world."

How I wished (not for the first time) for the gift of speech to be able to assure him that her manners had been most pleasing towards me and I thought her to be without fault. If I could, I would enlighten him that she had been the one we had seen cheerfully skipping down the hill. But on the other hand, I meditated on the saddening thought that it might be best that he not be aware of this intelligence. Considering his censure of her that day, coupled with his disapprobation of her of late, it would most likely not put her in any better light.

I lay my head down on the bed that night and for the first time in my life, not so cordial feelings towards my master swelled up within me.

~~*

Miss Bennet was invited to dine at Netherfield later that week. I held on to the hope that the invitation would extend to Miss Elizabeth, but she was not to come. Bingley was most attentive to his guest and whilst his sisters politely discoursed with her, I could see that they were both in agreement that indeed Miss Bennet was very sweet, but that their brother should not raise her hopes by bestowing too much attention on her.

On those occasions when Miss Bennet joined Bingley and his sisters, my master accompanied them in eating the meal, but then left them to the company of themselves and opportunely occupied himself with reading or writing letters. It appeared as though he was willing to extend to her only a negligible amount of civilities that he was obliged to do.

I sensed more and more that my master's discontent here was increasing; that he saw little that prompted him to step out from his reserve and engage himself with others in this country neighbourhood. And that saddened me.

~~*

On the evening of the gathering at Lucas Lodge, I again watched as my master's valet gathered the clothes for him to wear. I was sure my master was not looking forward to having to endure the "inferior society," as Miss Bingley was wont to call it in front of him. My only conjecture on what constituted an inferior society was based upon my own experience. I recollected that years ago, when I was still in the care of my mother with my siblings, we often heard the gentleman who oversaw our care refer to our litter as being somewhat inferior to one of the others.

I gathered that it meant that we were considered less preferable in our parentage as the other litter of pups. But in observing those other pups' appearance and behaviour, I never noticed any particulars that would explain it satisfactorily to me. In the same light, even though it was hinted that Sadie was not of the finest breeding, she was, indeed, perfect in my eyes. I was of the same mind toward Miss Elizabeth, as well.

I now observed my master as he watched his friend, who was most gregarious and unassuming, cheerfully accept every invitation and wholeheartedly welcome these villagers into his home. Bingley found them all to be charming people and treated them all equally and graciously. My master, as well as Bingley's sisters, did not seem to hold them in the same high regard and there was much to decry about having to attend that evening, which left me in quite solemn spirits, if for no other reason than I hated to see my master be in accord with Bingley's supercilious sisters.

I looked forward, however, to spending the evening with Sadie again, and this time did not need to sneak out, as the stablehand had informed my master of my earlier rendezvous with her, and it was settled that I could spend the evening in the same way. As my master stepped up into the carriage, he waved me on toward the stables and I eagerly obliged.

Sadie was already tethered in the stables and the stablehand warmly greeted me. Sadie had been playing with one of her toys, but quickly dropped it when she noticed me and pulled at the tether, prancing about, and greeting me in her engaging way. I walked up and I acknowledged her by coming up and touching noses.

I settled down for an enjoyable evening watching Sadie continue to play with an exuberance of energy. Occasionally she would prance over to me, trying to engage me in her play. I would oblige her with a more subdued and brief version of her sport and then content myself with merely observing.

Reminiscent of the evening of the assembly, the evening passed quickly, due greatly in part to Sadie keeping me entertained, and again I gave no thought to my master and how he was faring.

When we heard the carriage entering the park, the stablehand sent me to await its arrival and I made my way back to the house. I was anxious to see my master and paid particular attention to his demeanour. I wondered whether he would be as plagued with distress as he had been after the evening spent at the assembly. His quick strides up the stairs gave me little inclination as to his mood, but there *was* something rather odd that caught my attention: my master was whistling! But it was not the familiar whistling to which I was accustomed when he called me, but rather it was melodic, rather like the music I would hear Georgiana faithfully practicing on the pianoforte at Pemberley. I was not aware of any particular tune, rather just little sounds that flowed in lively variance.

Just as we reached the top, Miss Bingley called up from downstairs, "Mr. Darcy, I do hope you can sleep well tonight and not be kept awake with thoughts of those *fine eyes*!"

His whistling stopped and he turned abruptly, looking down at her, eyes narrowing and a noticeable flush permeating his face. Making no response, he turned toward his room as Miss Bingley and her sister twittered with laughter.

When his valet offered his help to remove his evening clothes, again he dismissed him. This time, however, he neatly removed his neckcloth, folding it carefully and laying it on his dresser. Removing waistcoat and shirt, he hung them up carefully, alongside his discarded breeches. Putting on his nightshirt, he glanced in the mirror. A very contented smile found its way to my master's countenance.

"She *does* have fine eyes... very fine eyes! I see no harm in admiring a lady's fine eyes, do you, Reggie?" He took in a deep breath and then let it out slowly. "Perhaps the harm done was confessing the object of my admiration to Miss Bingley. She will most likely not show mercy with her teasing. At the time, I confess my mind was too agreeably engaged to consider how imprudent it was of me to make mention of it to her."

He turned and looked at me. "She does have beautiful eyes, Reggie. Dark... intelligent... beautiful eyes."

I greatly wished him to tell me more!

Did someone new attend this assembly that he finally found to be worthy of his admiration? I wondered. *Was it some superbly accomplished young lady?* My tail wagged in eager expectation of finding out more about this lady he admired!

He extinguished the candles, but instead of coming over to the bed, he walked over to the window. He crossed his arms in front of him and looked out. I knew that if I exercised some patience, he might be willing to confide in me. Therefore, I sat in anticipation upon the bed, my tail wagging as a sign of my trustworthiness.

His eyes remained steadfastly gazing out the window as he began to talk. "I regret to inform you, Reggie, that the fault is *yours* that this has happened."

My tail immediately ceased wagging and I put my head down in remorse as I began to wonder to what his censure of me was due.

He turned around to face me, but instead of a reprimanding glare, he smiled. "The day she paid a call, I walked in looking for you and observed her attentions to you. She had such an expression of warmth and beauty on her face that quite enchanted me!" He smiled in recollection, but it quickly left his countenance. "That is, of course, until she glanced up and noticed me standing there!"

My tail began uncontrollably wagging now, as I began to understand that it was Miss Elizabeth who had him so captivated! I was delighted that he had allowed himself to appreciate a certain quality of character over breeding, much as he had done when he selected me.

He walked back over to the bed and sat down, propping himself up on one elbow and reaching over to scratch me behind my ears. "You might recall me stating emphatically that I found nothing fashionable in her form and carriage."

He shook his head. "But, tonight, I could only find her figure as light and pleasing. Moreover, her manners have an easy playfulness to them that I found most appealing." He pulled his hand away and brought it up to capture his jaw, rubbing it in thought. "Nay, her eyes are only one of the many attractive features on her face."

He lay down on the bed, putting his hands behind his head and staring up into the darkness. "I must confess, Reggie, that again my behaviour towards her tonight was not exactly that of a gentleman."

I felt my heart sink as I pondered what it was that he might have done this evening that would put him further into Miss Elizabeth's disapprobation.

He brought one hand out from under his head and raked his fingers through his hair. His voice took on a soft, meditative tone and he appeared preoccupied and thoughtful, as if recollecting something from earlier that evening. "I could not take my eyes off of her the whole of the evening. I unabashedly stared at her as if I was some besotted youth! In addition, I was hard pressed not to eavesdrop on a conversation of hers, which did not escape her notice, I fear."

He turned towards me then and brushed his hand down along my back. "I had no wish to refrain from looking at her and cared little what anyone thought. You will be astonished to know I did not even take offence when she refused to accept my invitation to dance."

I chuffed in sympathy, and he patted the top of my head to show his appreciation for my concern. "She was only repaying me for the insult I paid to her at the assembly. But I only cared that I was able to gaze into her eyes."

He rolled onto his back, taking the same pensive position as before. "I am of the opinion that the moment she refused me was when I found her most beautiful!" He turned his head towards me, "Do you think that odd, Reggie?"

I let out a whimper to assure him that I did not. For in that moment, I realized part of Miss Elizabeth's charm was that unlike Miss Bingley, she did not hold him in reverence due to his wealth and status. She had no wish to use her arts to draw him in; in fact, she was doing quite the opposite... but with the same results!

My master continued, "Unfortunately, it was at that moment that Miss Bingley accosted me. I was meditating on Miss Elizabeth's fine eyes and pretty face. If I had more sense about me, I would never have confessed those thoughts to her." He groaned and scathingly spit out, "For the remainder of the evening, Miss Bingley was relentless in her wishes of marital felicity and comments on what a fine mother-in-law I would have! Now I must endure her teasing, when... when in truth," he suddenly turned wistful. "It is really nothing, nothing at all."

He lifted his head and took both his pillow in both hands, plumping it up before crashing his head down upon it again.

"Marriage to Miss Elizabeth! I barely know her!" His voice took a rather sullen turn, "I do comprehend that she is completely unsuitable for me. Her relative family situation is insupportable. Her connections..." He paused for a few moments, his deep breathing the only sound I could hear and I wondered whether instead of merely informing me of her inferior traits, he was trying instead to convince himself.

In an even lower voice, filled with something like regret, he continued, "But I cannot dismiss what a joy it was tonight to observe a lady who not only is pleasing in appearance, but is intelligent as well. She is well informed on almost every subject, able to articulate her opinions, of which she holds no small amount, quite admirably."

I noticed his eyes close and I closed mine with a great sense of satisfaction and anticipation of a good night's sleep.

But then he added very softly, almost as an afterthought, "And she is delightfully lively..."

~~*

My master, quite surprisingly to me, allowed himself the liberty to dwell on this young lady at great length. For the next few days, I knew at once when his thoughts meandered to her. Unbeknownst to himself and apparently, the others, there was a particular look that came across his face coupled with a marked increase in his breathing. I could barely resist acknowledging these observations with an enthusiastic wagging of my tail.

A few days later, Bingley received and accepted an invitation to dine with some officers in Meryton. To my surprise, this was somewhat acceptable to my master, who seemed quite disposed to accompany his friend, commenting that he hoped to find intelligent conversation amongst them.

When it was settled that all three gentlemen would go, Bingley subtly suggested that his sisters invite Miss Bennet to tea so they could spend some time with her alone and deepen their acquaintance. Whilst this was met with polite acquiescence, I sensed that they were truly not as delighted as they led him to believe.

On the day the men were to go out and Miss Bennet was to arrive, a cold darkness invaded the county. Throughout the morning, the sun fought the clouds for dominance in the sky, but it was finally quenched as a blanket of dark, thick clouds filled the sky. I could feel in my bones that a storm was imminent.

I watched my master don his heavy overcoat before setting out. Of course I was to remain at Netherfield and was grateful for the warm comforts afforded me indoors. I wished for Sadie to be given the same consideration, but I was somewhat reassured that at least she would be able to escape the harshest cold and wind by seeking refuge in the stable.

I curled up in front of the fireplace in the kitchen, eager for a relaxing afternoon and hoping for a sampling of the repast that was being prepared for Miss Bennet. Miss Bingley frequently made an appearance, ensuring that everything was proceeding as planned. Whilst she did not seem particularly eager for her guest to arrive, she did take delight in making sure all the preparations were being proficiently carried out.

At the sound of the bell, I stretched my whole body in anticipation of getting up and joining the ladies. As I slowly walked out toward the front door, I heard Miss Bingley gasp loudly.

"My dear Miss Bennet! Whatever has happened? You are positively drenched from head to toe!"

Miss Bingley and her sister quickly attended to Miss Bennet as she explained how she had ridden over on a horse in the hopes of escaping the upcoming storm but it had begun to rain much earlier than she had anticipated. The sisters ordered dry clothes to be brought forth and had their ladies escort her upstairs to assist her in changing into them. When she left the room, the two sisters could not hold their tongue about the foolishness she had exhibited by riding from Longbourn to Netherfield on horseback instead of taking a carriage.

"Upon my word, Louisa! I can hardly believe it! Such reckless actions!"

"I quite agree, Caroline. What could she have been thinking?"

"It shows an ill-bred thoughtlessness, if you ask me, Sister."

Mrs. Hurst and her sister both agreed that someone established in good society would never have exhibited such behaviour. It astounded me that they were upset more that her actions were not those of good society than they were concerned for her health and well being.

When Miss Bennet returned, she expressed her gratitude to the sisters and the three ladies proceeded to the breakfast parlour. I settled in a corner, out of their way, and rested my head on my paws. If they observed me, they may have thought I was sleeping, but in truth, I kept a keen ear tuned to their conversation.

Bingley's sisters evidently viewed this appointment as an opportunity to gather intelligence on their brother's favourite. They questioned Miss Bennet politely but with no little persistence on her family, her connections, and a variety of other carefully picked subjects. From their pointed glances at each other, I surmised that they were less than impressed by Miss Bennet's responses.

A deep grumbling escaped me as I realized the growing contempt the two sisters felt for Miss Bennet. I could not find fault with her, however the two sisters seemed inclined to view her connections as inferior. How unmerited their disfavour!

At first, Miss Bennet acquitted herself reasonably well to their interrogation. However, I began to notice that her appearance was ashen and she did not have the usual serene countenance that I had seen upon her. As the rain continued to pour down in torrents throughout the rest of the afternoon, the sisters repeatedly made reference to the hope that the gentlemen would return directly or that the rain would let up. Unfortunately, their hopes were in vain; Miss Bennet continued exhibit an increasing distress, the men were absent the whole of the afternoon, and the rain continued without intermission.

The gentlemen finally returned late in the afternoon. When Bingley discovered Miss Bennet was still there and saw her condition, he insisted that it would be best that she remain. Even my master concurred with his friend that the conditions of the roads due to the downpour would make a return to Longbourn hazardous. I was relieved by this decision. A letter was dispatched to Longbourn to acquaint the Bennets with her condition.

By suppertime, Miss Bennet had grown quite ill, and after eating only a small amount, she excused herself and retired for the evening.

The next morning we awakened to the sad news that Miss Bennet had become even more ill over the course of the night and even though the morning dawned clear and fresh, Mr. Bingley deemed it prudent for her that she continue at Netherfield. Mr. Jones, a local physician, was called for.

Bingley's sisters made Miss Bennet as comfortable as they could and gave reassurances to their brother that she was resting comfortably, however feverishly. They dismissed his heightened concern for her, insisting that it was merely a trifling cold.

Miss Bennet was ailing too much to join us, so we adjourned to the breakfast parlour to enjoy a late morning breakfast whilst she convalesced. I was settled comfortably at my master's feet, keeping an eye open for any morsel that might inadvertently fall down for my seizing. Do not misunderstand my meaning; my master would never resort to spoiling me in such a way, but I did find that I could usually depend on snatching a crumb or two near Hurst's place at the table.

The door was unexpectedly opened and at once I caught that familiar scent. With soaring anticipation, I watched from my vantage point on the floor as Bingley's housekeeper entered. Behind her, I caught the sight of very soiled stockinged feet and the hem of a dress encased in mud.

Even before the housekeeper was able to announce her, I knew the moment my master took notice of her. I heard his coffee cup clatter clumsily into its saucer and then heard a sharp intake of breath. Now I would have thought that breathing was a natural function that one does not have to give much thought. I know I rarely think about having to take a breath. But as I listened intently those first few moments, I could not detect any indication of an exhale. I was quite sure a good amount of time passed before he finally let it out, a bit shaky, at that.

The housekeeper announced that Miss Elizabeth had come to inquire after her sister.

Bingley promptly stood, followed by my master who seemed to struggle to his feet, and then Mr. Hurst, who rose, most reluctantly, from his plate. A small morsel dropped nearby, but at the moment I was not inclined to snatch it up.

Whereas Bingley enthusiastically welcomed Miss Elizabeth with a profuse greeting and assurances that Miss Elizabeth's ailing sister was being well looked after, I was only able to discern a very soft, "Miss Elizabeth," from my master in acknowledgement of her.

From the condition of her attire, I speculated that she must have walked some distance on her journey here. I know that the farther I walk, the better chance there is of my paws getting muddy. However, it appeared she cared little for the state of her appearance, but her concern was reserved exclusively for her sister. Despite her anxiety, her eyes were exceptionally bright and her countenance much more rose-coloured than the last time I saw her.

After being assured that my master's breathing was no longer impaired in any way (he was breathing normally again), I approached Miss Elizabeth and cheerfully greeted her with my wagging tail and looked up at her with great admiration in my eyes. She looked down at me warmly and with a ready smile, but was prevented from any further attention by Miss Bingley quickly approaching her.

Neither of us failed to notice the scrutinizing look Miss Bingley gave her as she came around the table, letting her eyes rest on Miss Elizabeth's feet. "Eliza, you have not walked all the way here, have you?"

"I did. It is but three miles."

Louisa then exclaimed, "Three miles in such dirty weather!" Her shocked outburst was then quickly tempered with a mild, "Such devotion you show to your sister, Miss Bennet."

Miss Bingley walked up to her and took her arm. "Certainly you did not make the trip alone?" Whilst her words were showered with concern, her tone of voice dripped with accusation.

"My two younger sisters accompanied me part of the way."

Miss Bingley gave a fleeting glance at the others at the table, widening her eyes in implicit scorn.

This censure was missed by Bingley, who was only of a humour to receive her and openly admire the affection she held for her sister. "I am quite certain, Miss Elizabeth, that your sister will greatly appreciate your coming all this way to see her. We shall do everything we can to accommodate the two of you."

"I thank you, Mr. Bingley. May I inquire how she is faring this morning?"

Miss Bingley was the one who answered. "Unfortunately, I believe dear Jane slept quite ill. Louisa and I took turns seeing to her. She awoke this morning with a fever and we have sent a dispatch for Mr. Jones."

"My family is deeply grateful for all you have done. May I go to her?"

"Certainly, Miss Eliza. Please allow me to show you to her room. I hope you will be most reassured that we are doing all we can to ensure her comfort." She eyed my master and I could see she was hoping he would notice her gracious hospitality rather than this country nobody's *fine eyes*.

As the two ladies departed the room, Bingley seemed gratified that Miss Elizabeth had come. "I cannot recall ever meeting two sisters who are more agreeable and close as the two eldest Bennet sisters! To think that Miss Elizabeth walked all this way for her!"

"Perhaps," my master began. "However, a simple cold does not justify coming so far... alone."

"But that only serves to show how great the devotion is!"

My master said no more and they continued to eat in silence until Miss Bingley returned. "Miss Eliza appears most pleased with our ministrations to Miss Bennet." She turned toward my master with a smile and I could see that she was gratified that he was attending to her conversation. But the smile quickly turned to an expression of hauteur as she continued, "But can you believe that she walked all of three miles in such conditions and without a proper companion? Only because her sister has caught a chill! Did she not consider that her sister would be in our good care?"

Bingley stood up and walked over to the window. "I am quite certain, Caroline, that she harboured no doubts about the care and concern we are showing her." Gazing out of the window, he surveyed the grounds. "Do you suppose it is too muddy for some hunting this morning?"

"Mmm," grunted Hurst between swallows of food. "I would be quite willing to entertain some sport today. I have had quite enough talk of ailing ladies and their requisite care."

"Darcy?"

I noticed him look toward the door through which Miss Elizabeth had just departed. "Yes, perhaps today would be a good day for sport."

The men decided to meet back in an hour and I followed my master upstairs, happy for this opportunity to be with Sadie again. As we passed Miss Bennet's room, although the door was closed, I noticed an almost imperceptible slowing down of his stride as we walked past and he cast a furtive glance at the door. After passing it, he quickened his steps and once in his chambers, set out to ready himself for a day of sport without delay.

I was not sure as to the wisdom of going out on the day after a rainstorm. In my younger days, scrambling in less than fine conditions would not have given me a moment's pause. But I have found that my tolerance for such activities has ebbed as my age advances. As I feared, Sadie and I ended up being quite covered in mud. The men also found themselves often trudging in the mud and on occasion, would find one or both feet well entrenched, a situation that would elicit curses from the victim and good-natured ribbing from his companions. Whether it was the precarious condition of the terrain, I could not say, but Mr. Hurst was the only one who seemed able to down anything. He returned later that morning with two, whilst my master and Bingley brought down not a one. I was of the opinion that both men had something on their mind and it was not the ducks and geese that were flying about the grounds.

When we returned back to the house, we all went our separate ways to get cleaned up. Bingley led both Sadie and I to the stables for our baths. I confess that I do wish the stablehand given the office to bathe me was a bit more gentle in his endeavour. Afterwards, I was given leave to return to the house and I immediately went to my master's chambers, where he was in the process of dressing after his own bath. My master and I were the first to return downstairs and we found it pleasantly quiet.

We were informed that Bingley's sisters were both visiting with Miss Bennet and her sister. My master settled in a chair in the sitting room with a book and I settled at his feet, anticipating another opportunity to see Miss Elizabeth again.

I wondered if those were my master's thoughts, as well. Every time the sound of approaching footsteps could be heard, he would anxiously look up and then upon seeing who it was, would turn his attention back to his book with uncommon concentration. For as tightly as his hands gripped the binding, one might assume that my master was reading a gripping account of some heroic battle, but I noticed once more that he was turning the pages quite infrequently, which gave me rise to think he was not as fully engaged in his book as he appeared to be.

Miss Bingley came downstairs next. Whilst I assumed that she had been attending to the Misses Bennet, I quickly readjusted my opinion as the scent she was wearing was overpowering and dizzying and the dress she wore I deemed to be one of her finest, which I found quite odd for an evening spent at home. Upon seeing my master, she came into the sitting room to join us. She informed us that the apothecary had come, declaring Miss Bennet's cold to be particularly violent and that he advised her to remain in bed and promised her some draughts. She told my master how she and Louisa had been most concerned for Miss Bennet and they were faithfully following the apothecary's advice, for the feverish symptoms had increased and her head ached acutely. Her words expressed care and concern, however her countenance did not.

More footsteps were heard and we both looked up to see Miss Elizabeth at the door. Her face was drawn and her hair somewhat dishevelled. Despite her appearance, however, one could not miss the compassion she felt for her sister.

"Pray excuse me. I must thank you for your hospitality, but it is almost three o'clock and as much as I regret having to leave my sister, I feel that I must go."

"I understand perfectly, my dear Miss Eliza. You must return home to assure your family of Jane's condition. Let me call for our carriage to return you to Longbourn. Nay, I will not allow you to refuse."

Mr. Bingley came in at that moment and agreed with his sister that Miss Elizabeth must make use of their carriage.

"Thank you," she said softly. "That is most kind of you. I believe I shall."

As Miss Elizabeth was preparing to leave, Mrs. Hurst came down. "I fear Miss Bennet is greatly concerned about your quitting Netherfield, Miss Elizabeth. I believe she does not wish for you to leave."

Concern and uncertainty became etched across Elizabeth's face whilst Miss Bingley's took on an even more agitated deportment.

Bingley looked to his sister, who was most reluctantly obliged to convert the offer of the chaise into an invitation to remain at Netherfield for the present. "Miss Elizabeth, please accept our offer to stay here with your sister, until she is well enough to return home." A smile graced her lips but I felt it was not touching her heart.

Miss Elizabeth most thankfully consented, and a servant was dispatched to Longbourn to acquaint the family with her stay and bring back a supply of clothes.

I was greatly pleased with this news. As I had not yet been able to spend any time with this young lady, it now appeared that I would have ample opportunity to do so. Uncontrollably wagging my tail in glee, I looked to Miss Elizabeth, who bestowed a warm smile back my direction.

I then turned to my master, who had observed this whole exchange in rigid silence. As Bingley and his sisters walked with Miss Elizabeth back to join her sister, I watched as he contemplated this news. His eyes narrowed, but they remained fixed on the door through which she had just walked.

At length, the sound of my still pounding tail caught his attention. He looked down at me and shook his head. "Control yourself, Reggie. It will never happen." He looked back toward the door and drew in a deep breath. "I cannot let it happen."

Chapter 12

My master and I sat in the drawing room alone. I knew that he was pondering the announcement that Miss Elizabeth would spend the night at Netherfield as it was clearly reflected in his demeanour. Attempting to remain collected, his nervous mannerisms -- repeatedly tapping his fingers against the arm of his chair and his foot against the floor -- betrayed his true lack of composure to me.

I turned my attention to the rich smells from the kitchen as they grew stronger and began assiduously tempting me to wander in and beg for a sampling. I was prevented from pursuing such endeavours when Miss Bingley and her sister returned from escorting Miss Elizabeth to her room near Miss Bennet so that she might easily tend her sister during the night. Bingley entered, more distracted than I have ever seen him, and we waited impatiently for the announcement that the meal was ready to serve. Miss Bingley offered repeated assurances to her brother as to her devotion to Miss Bennet during her ailment, but they seemed to be more directed for my master's approbation than for any selflessness on her part. At length, a servant announced the meal to us and Miss Elizabeth was summoned.

As we entered the dining room, we found Mr. Hurst already seated at his place. Miss Bingley artfully manoeuvred herself beside my master, and when Miss Elizabeth entered, she found the only remaining chair adjacent to Mr. Hurst.

Bingley seemed most concerned for Miss Bennet and inquired of Miss Elizabeth if she had at all improved.

"I fear I cannot answer favourably. She is by no means better."

Bingley's stricken countenance showed full force his distress. His sisters repeatedly expressed how much they were grieved, how shocking it was to have a bad cold, and how excessively they disliked being ill themselves. Though their declarations were ardent in their expression, they just as quickly ceased, with little real feeling behind their words. They then began a far more animated discussion of the latest fashions described in *La Belle Assemblée*. It was apparent to me -- and I am certain to Miss Elizabeth -- that they thought no more of the matter.

Whereas Miss Elizabeth appeared not to be particularly pleased with the seating arrangements, nor her dining partner, I was quite delighted. It not only allowed me to situate myself, as was my preference, in close proximity to Mr. Hurst in the hopes that I might glean some crumb dropped by him, but I was near enough to Miss Elizabeth to again become the object of her attentions. Once Mr. Hurst ascertained that she preferred a plain dish to a ragout, all conversation between them ceased. With a gentle nudging of my paw upon her shoe, she discovered me hidden under the table and I was treated to some surprisingly pleasant stroking through very clever -- and quite discreet -- manoeuvring of her foot against my head and belly.

Bingley was the only person who attempted to engage Miss Elizabeth in conversation. He was, however, often thwarted in his civility by his sister, who seemed intent to be in command of the conversation around the table. Whilst everything she said was chiefly addressed to my master, she held no little expertise in deflecting her brother's attention away from their guest.

Consequently, as Miss Bingley held court on all manner of fashionable news, Miss Elizabeth ate her meal in bemused silence whilst her foot continued to stroke my fur and in due course, when it found a most pleasurable spot on my belly, a moan of ecstasy unwittingly escaped from the depths of me.

At the moment of my unfortunate outburst, my master had been responding as disinterestedly as politeness would allow to a question Miss Bingley had posed to him. He abruptly stopped in the middle of his sentence, and at that moment, Miss Elizabeth sharply pulled her foot away.

It was a few moments before my master was able to again attend to his conversation with Miss Bingley. Being out of his view, I can only surmise that he had heard my moan and was perplexed by it. He would often remark that he knew exactly where to scratch my belly to elicit that particular response from me. Whether or not he was aware that it was due to Miss Elizabeth's pleasant ministrations I knew not, nor could I be sure of his reaction, but for the remainder of dinner, her foot remained sadly but firmly planted on the floor.

When dinner was completed, Miss Elizabeth excused herself to return directly to her sister and unfortunately, as soon as she had stepped out of the room, Miss Bingley began abusing her.

Her manners were pronounced to be very bad indeed, a mixture of pride and impertinence; she had no conversation, no style, no taste, no beauty. Mrs. Hurst concurred, adding, "She has nothing, in short, to recommend her, but being an excellent walker. I shall never forget her appearance this morning. She really looked almost wild."

They continued to berate Miss Elizabeth as I wondered what it was about her that was so appalling to them. I could not understand why they disdained her for walking all that way from Longbourn to Netherfield. Walking is a wonderfully exhilarating pastime. My master and I took great pleasure in walking! And whilst she may not possess the same style and taste of Miss Bingley -- thank goodness! -- she had an unassuming and congenial air that I found most appealing.

I became increasingly unsettled at their contemptuous words accusing her of looking almost wild and her petticoat being six inches deep in mud. How I love to run free with nary a care about whether my fur is getting matted or my paws are coated in mud. Miss Bingley, so it would seem, viewed this as impertinent and unmannerly. I doubted that she knew how to take pleasure in such things. I considered it her loss, for I doubt very much that my master ever looked upon her with as much feeling in his eyes as he looked upon me during our jaunts. Or as he did upon Miss Elizabeth after hers, for that matter.

I came out from under the table and settled myself in a corner of the room, out of everyone's way. My master shot a curious glance in my direction when he took notice of me, eyeing me most suspiciously.

"You observed it, Mr. Darcy, I am sure," said Miss Bingley; "and I am inclined to think that *you* would not wish to see *your sister* make such an exhibition."

He turned back to Miss Bingley. "Certainly not." His voice quivered slightly, to which I attributed his likely contemplation of the harm that might befall Georgiana from one rakish lout if she were to encounter him whilst out on a walk unaccompanied.

"To walk three miles, or four miles, or five miles, or whatever it is, above her ankles in dirt, and alone, quite alone! What could she mean by it? It seems to me to show an abominable sort of conceited independence, a most country-town indifference to decorum."

"It shows an affection for her sister that is very pleasing," said Bingley, coming to her defence, for which I was most grateful.

My head turned from one to another as she was at first criticized by Miss Bingley and then defended by her brother. I could barely conjecture what my master was contemplating through all this as he remained for the most part silent.

"I am afraid, Mr. Darcy," observed Miss Bingley, in an eager half-whisper, "that this adventure has rather affected your admiration of her fine eyes."

I waited, my heart beating expectantly, to hear what he would say.

"Not at all," he replied. "They were brightened by the exercise." Though his response was mild in tone, there was no mistaking the defiance flickering in his eyes to Miss Bingley's challenge.

Hurrah! I thought to myself. *We are making progress!* My tail thumped in exuberance at his open and honest admiration.

Whether she actually heard and understood the significance of his words, I know not, but it did not lessen the enjoyment between the sisters of issuing more derisive remarks and for the most part, I ceased listening. I have found the workings of human relationships to be needlessly complicated. It was evident that Mr. Bingley esteemed Miss Bennet. To me, that should be the end of the matter, but his sisters were determined to dissuade his affection.

I heard the ladies begin to disparage the Bennets' connections. Bingley made an attempt to dismiss them, but then I heard my master's response.

"But it must very materially lessen their chance of marrying men of any consideration in the world," he replied.

I turned and regarded my master in complete puzzlement. His words were blunt and harsh. I wondered why his praise and admiration for Miss Elizabeth had so suddenly and unexpectedly ceased.

I watched him as he stood up and walked over to the sideboard to refill his coffee cup. His steps were brisk; his demeanour resolute. In that moment I comprehended that he was making a greater effort to convince *himself* that she was completely unsuitable, as he was not merely a man of *any* consideration, but of *great* consideration.

To my master's declaration, Bingley made no answer, much to my disappointment; but his sisters gave their hearty assent, and indulged their mirth for some time at the expense of Miss Elizabeth's vulgar relations. I dropped my head upon my paws in anguish, realizing that the great chasm that separated dogs and people was so vast, I may never fully understand them. And in the present circumstances, I found my master the most perplexing of them all.

~~*

It was some time before Bingley's sisters left to grace Miss Bennet and her sister with their indifferent presence. The satisfaction that had permeated their features during their abuse of her was opportunely masked by calculated expressions of care and concern. They remained with her until summoned for coffee. Miss Elizabeth stayed behind with her sister, unwilling to quit her at all, until later in the evening, when her ailing sister fell asleep.

I was seated at my master's feet waiting expectantly for Miss Elizabeth to join us. My master had been persuaded, much against his inclination, to join the others at the loo table, so he was seated with them. I listened as the five engaged themselves in this peculiar diversion. It was interesting to take note that this was the only time I had witnessed such animation in Mr. Hurst, other than when out hunting. He seemed to take delight in bidding high and crushing everyone's enjoyment and success in the game.

Bingley invited Miss Elizabeth to join them in the game when she entered, but she politely declined, and making her sister the excuse, said she would amuse herself for the short time she could stay below, with a book.

"Do you prefer reading to cards?" Mr. Hurst looked at her with astonishment. "That is rather singular."

"Miss Eliza Bennet," said Miss Bingley, "despises cards. She is a great reader, and has no pleasure in anything else."

A slight growl escaped as I contemplated the ankles of Miss Bingley, which were within an easy reach. I was quite tempted to throw away years of discipline and give one a slight nip!

"I deserve neither such praise nor such censure," cried Miss Elizabeth; "I am not a great reader, and I have pleasure in many things."

Mr. Bingley came to her defence, reminding everyone that she obviously took pleasure in nursing her sister. To my chagrin, my master remained silent. With growing agitation towards him, I arose and walked over to Miss Elizabeth, sitting down aside her to demonstrate my approbation.

Evidently hoping to distract everyone's attention from Miss Elizabeth, Miss

Bingley proceeded to flatter my master as she compared her brother's simple library to my master's grand one. I know my master must have thought this quite amusing -- I certainly did -- as we both observed that whilst she quite frequently had a book in her possession, her eyes rarely perused it. And even though she requested from my master a recommendation for good reading, she rarely took the trouble to actually read what he had suggested.

I looked up at Miss Elizabeth, who reached down and gently stroked my head, a smile touching her lips. I believe she was quite amused by Miss Bingley's concerted effort to speak highly about anything and everything that pertained to my master. Her attention appeared to be riveted to the conversation ensuing at the table whilst I could comprehend my master's attention was riveted to her. I cannot be sure that she was aware of being the object of his regard, but at length, she set her book aside, discontinued her attentions to me, and walked over to the group.

In addition to Miss Bingley's praise for the library at Pemberley, she also had endless words of praise for Georgiana. Whilst I could not disagree with her estimation of my favourite young lady, I did not believe it to have come from her heart.

From there, the conversation digressed to what constituted an accomplished woman. Whilst I doubt very much Miss Bingley would consider Miss Elizabeth even minutely accomplished, my master, who had taken notice of the extent to which Miss Elizabeth read, subtly included this quality in his measurement of accomplished women. My heart soared at this display, clearly designed not to draw Miss Bingley's ire, but still convey his admiration. To my disappointment, however, Miss Elizabeth did not comprehend any such estimation on his part and left the room, apparently feeling quite set down by the party.

After another callous remark by Miss Bingley about Miss Elizabeth, the remainder of the evening was spent in relative silence. My master was not inclined to join in any conversation, which dampened any eagerness Miss Bingley had to engage him. Elizabeth returned later in the evening only to say that her sister was worse, and that she could not leave her.

It was quite apparent that Bingley was concerned for his ailing guest; his sisters declared that they were miserable. I imagine that had more to do with boredom than anything else. They solaced their wretchedness, however, by duets after supper, which only added to my misery.

My master and I endured the duets silently. I was grateful when he expressed a wish to retire and excused himself. Obediently following him upstairs to his room, we passed Miss Bennet's room as we normally did. This time my master walked briskly past. However, I paused ever so slightly, cognizant of Miss Elizabeth's pleasant scent emanating from within.

My master turned and uttered a stern, "Come, Reggie! I will tolerate none of that now!"

We entered into his chambers and he dismissed his man, declaring a wish for some time alone before preparing for bed. He seated himself askance upon a chair, facing me instead of the desk at which it was situated. He planted one elbow upon the desk and rested his jaw upon his hand, looking down at me pointedly.

"During the meal tonight, Reggie, you allowed a somewhat peculiar sound to escape. Precisely what transpired that prompted you to moan so impudently?"

His eyes narrowed into mine with such accusation that I lowered my head onto my paws, averting my own.

"I might harbour a suspicion that Mr. Hurst was inadvertently dropping you morsels of his dinner."

I peered up at him, knowing he was not finished.

"However, I know you too well to believe that to be the cause. You tend to snatch food very quietly." He paused and stood up, walking over to the window. Folding his arms across his chest, he turned slowly to face me.

"That only leaves the possibility that Miss Bennet had something to do with it. Was she, perhaps…" He paused as if struggling for the correct words. "Was she, through some peculiar manoeuvrings, the instigator of your moan?"

I let out an affirming whimper.

"As I thought." He unfolded his arms and braced his hands against his hips. "And very clearly I recollect both of her hands were upon the table. As such, I must conclude that one or both of her *feet* to be the culprit. Might I be correct?"

My tail wagged in eager concurrence, hoping to enlighten him as to my partiality towards her.

A partial bemused smile began to form but was quickly replaced with a frown. He turned and began untying his cravat as he paced about the room, fighting for some sort of control that appeared to elude him. Finally, after several moments, he pulled sharply on his neckcloth and threw it disgustedly on the floor. "This is ludicrous! How is it that I am envious of my own dog?"

He walked over and sat down on the edge of the bed. I jumped up and sat down beside him. His hand gently stroked my head and trailed down my back.

"Tell me, Reggie, what is your secret? To what do you owe this ability to garner Miss Elizabeth's favour?"

I placed a paw upon his lap, but he stood up abruptly, causing it to crash back down to the bed.

"It is just as well. Miss Bingley is correct. Her relations are completely unsuitable." He looked down at me with a grave look in his eyes. "It is not that simple. I cannot allow…" His demeanour became more rigid and his breathing deepened. "I cannot allow these feelings… which have intruded upon me with no provocation or invitation… to take hold."

He began nodding his head slowly. "She shall be gone soon and with her, this unreasonable allure that has me in its grip."

I lay my head down, wishing for some way to influence my master's wavering opinion in her behalf. He had remarked to me that it was not that simple, but I knew not why. Having spent thirteen years with my master I was well acquainted with him and somehow, stirring from the depths of me, I believed the two of them to be entirely suited for each other.

I knew that my only opportunity to do something lay whilst she remained at Netherfield. I hoped that she would remain long enough for me to exert some influence over my master's unreasonable conviction.

My master paced quite a long time before finally retiring to bed, and then once in, tossed and turned until the wee hours of the morning. At length, I recognized the familiar deep breathing that indicated sleep had finally overtaken him. But I lay awake a short time longer, formulating a plan that would facilitate him seeing Miss Elizabeth as he ought, and not give in to what he perceived as others' expectations or pressure. After giving it much thought, I realized that somehow I must arrange it so that my master and Miss Elizabeth would find themselves together on the one diversion they both took great delight in -- a walk!

~~*

The next morning Elizabeth sent word that her sister had improved and requested a note be sent to Longbourn asking for her mother to come. The note was dispatched and forthwith, Mrs. Bennet and her two youngest daughters arrived at Netherfield, soon after the family breakfast.

After Mrs. Bennet's visit with her ailing daughter, she came into the breakfast parlour, where we were all awaiting her. Whilst she expressed pleasure with the care her daughter was receiving, she was insistent that it would not be prudent to move her yet, prompting a look of displeasure to pass between Bingley's sisters. A feeling of gratefulness, however, spurred my tail to wag excitedly, as I knew this meant Miss Elizabeth would remain at Netherfield and my plan could continue unabated.

As I watched the exchange that went on that morning in the breakfast parlour, I must admit I was quite concerned about Mrs. Bennet's indignant consideration of my master. It was quite apparent to me that she also held a strong dislike for him, seeking every opportunity to covertly rebuke him in the sharpest of tones.

To my knowledge, my master was not particularly accustomed to being subjected to such brazen disapprobation, and I fear that the shock of it caused him to be less than politic in his conversation. Therefore, I was somewhat gratified that Miss Elizabeth did attempt to rectify a misunderstanding between them, putting the best possible light on his clumsy mutterings. The fact that he entrenched himself behind a wall of reserve as he turned away from the party to gaze out a window -- no doubt lest he offend again -- did nothing to raise their esteem of him.

It was with great relief that the three Bennet ladies finally took their leave, but not before the youngest daughter secured a promise from Bingley to host a ball. Even Miss Elizabeth seemed most gratified when they finally departed; she appeared as stricken as my master at her mother's rude and outspoken manners.

With the departure of her family, Miss Elizabeth excused herself to return to her sister. At once, Bingley's sisters took advantage to scorn the Bennets and all their relations and cuttingly reminded my master of his fondness for *fine eyes*. Whilst happily he was not inclined to join them in their censure of Miss Elizabeth, neither did he choose to defend her nor declare his admiration for her.

I knew something had to be done directly!

~~*

That evening I was hopeful for another opportunity to staunchly display my approval for Miss Elizabeth by faithfully remaining by her side. She finally entered the drawing room with some needlework in hand. My master was writing a letter to his sister, though I suspect its progress was somewhat impeded by Miss Bingley annoying him with repeated attempts to praise his style or request that he include her words of praise to Georgiana in his missive.

Again Miss Elizabeth appeared quite amused by Miss Bingley's relentless commendations to my master, either of his sister or of his writing and on the evenness of his lines. And again, as last night Miss Elizabeth set her employment down to fix her attention on the diverting conversation.

But rather than moving closer to the party, this time she remained seated, and I took advantage of that by nuzzling up to her. May I be so bold as to say that my charm worked its magic, and she soon began scratching my head as she listened to the conversation.

When at length my master finally attended to my whereabouts, he froze as his eyes travelled down her arm to where her hand was running through the fur on my head, taking up the curls gently around her fingers. I looked up at Miss Elizabeth with admiration in my eyes, only to see contempt in hers as she beheld my master's stern gaze. She let out a quiet huff and I noticed that my master seemed no longer able to attend to his letter.

When Miss Bingley asked another inane question, my master's answer was fraught with tension, but that did not deter her from continuing. The conversation turned from praise for my master to a discussion of Bingley's shortcomings and I watched in dismay as my master and Miss Elizabeth began a lively disagreement at Bingley's expense. Or perhaps it was at my master's expense, as again, it did nothing to elevate him in Miss Elizabeth's regard. Still, I do not believe that I was the only one to see the spark of genuine pleasure on my master's face at their banter.

Bingley ended the tête-à-tête with, "By all means, let us hear all the particulars, not forgetting their comparative height and size; for that will have more weight in the argument, Miss Bennet, than you may be aware of. I assure you that, if Darcy were not such a great tall fellow, in comparison with myself, I should not pay him half so much deference. I declare I do not know a more awful object than Darcy, on particular occasions, and in particular places; at his own house especially, and of a Sunday evening, when he has nothing to do."

My master smiled tightly and I am quite certain he felt somewhat offended. I thought I could depend upon Bingley to portray my master in a good light, but this time, even though it may have been in jest, both of us felt the damage of his words. I settled down at Miss Elizabeth's feet, confident that although my master was still stinging from his friend's words, he had thoroughly enjoyed his repartee with Miss Elizabeth.

Whilst two of my favourite people spent a good portion of this evening in sparring dialogue, I curiously observed Miss Bingley during it all. She seemed perplexed, even somewhat jealous, that Miss Elizabeth had so engaged my master in a conversation, albeit an argumentative one, when he rarely answered her in more than one or two words.

Music was soon requested and whereas Miss Bingley politely suggested that Elizabeth play first, she did not appear overtly dismayed that her offer was turned down. Unfortunately, that meant we were subjected to Mrs. Hurst and Miss Bingley playing and singing. Just like the previous evening, there was little for me to enjoy in their performance. What I did enjoy, however, was watching my master.

Miss Elizabeth again turned her attentions back to the top of my head and stroked down my neck and back as she listened to the sisters. I enjoyed Miss Elizabeth's ministrations to my head almost as much as I enjoyed watching the comportment of my master. That he was greatly suffering whilst watching me receive such pleasuring attentions was most apparent, at least to me.

I believed the evening to be another exercise of futility as there appeared to be very little improvement in her regard and very little expression of his. When Miss Elizabeth glanced at him and discovered him staring, she pursed her lips tightly and let out that little breath of air that I unfortunately took to mean she was quite displeased.

How I wished my master would allow all his feelings of regard to be expressed upon his face! Instead, he bore a rather severe demeanour as he struggled to maintain his control when it came to Miss Elizabeth Bennet. My master was, at the moment, *not* under good regulation, something I knew to be an uncharacteristic prospect.

It was with great surprise, then, when my master suddenly blurted out, "Do not you feel a great inclination, Miss Bennet, to seize such an opportunity of dancing a reel?"

Dancing! I thought. *How I would love to see the two of them dance!* My master never dances with ladies whom he does not esteem. Surely Miss Elizabeth will not mistake his regard now. I did not even consider that I had never beheld dancing in a drawing room, save for Georgiana and myself when she took me as a partner to learn.

Miss Elizabeth apparently did not hear him or perhaps she believed his request to be insincere, for she did not answer him at once; however, a slight smile touched her lips. I watched as confusion filtered across my master's features, but smoothing his countenance, he asked again.

"Oh! I heard you before," she answered, "but I could not immediately determine what to say in reply." She said this with a challenging sparkle in her eyes, but as she continued, my master's confidence appeared to wane. "You wanted me, I know, to say 'Yes,' that you might have the pleasure of despising my taste; but I always delight in overthrowing those kind of schemes, and cheating a person of their premeditated contempt. I have, therefore, made up my mind to tell you, that I do not want to dance a reel at all -- and now despise me if you dare."

I easily recognized the hurt that suddenly flooded my master's eyes. It was the same hurt that I had seen when his father died and when he would ponder the hurt his sister experienced. It was disheartening to realize that Miss Elizabeth did not recognize my master's attempts to bridge the distance between them. Perhaps this was going to be more difficult than I anticipated.

He softly answered, "I do not dare."

A subdued silence took hold of everyone for the remainder of the evening. I believe that although Miss Elizabeth seemed oblivious to the fact, Miss Bingley was becoming strongly suspicious that she was gaining my master's favour. My master, on the other hand, whilst succumbing to some wayward yearnings to engage Miss Elizabeth, knew not how to do it in a way that his admiration would be evident to her without opening it to the scrutiny of Bingley and his relations. Struggling openly with me on the subject of her unsuitability, I suspected he inwardly rejoiced at her set downs, hoping they would make his task at putting her out of his thoughts easier. I flatter myself that in this matter, I understood his heart better than he, for I believe he found that they caused her to have an even greater appeal to him.

That night he was tormented with sleeplessness again, although he remained silent on the subject of Miss Elizabeth save for one utterance. With a great sense of desperation he looked at me and said, "There appears to be nothing she can do to affront me, Reggie. I truly believe that, were it not for the inferiority of her connections, I should be in very great danger!"

For much of the evening, as he tossed and turned, I contemplated what that danger might be. I knew Miss Elizabeth would never harm anyone. I had to surmise, however, that the danger of which he spoke referred to allowing himself the liberty to fall in love with her. Would it certainly cause him such great distress to give consideration to this woman simply owing to her "inferiority of connections?" I could not construe one reasonable answer.

It was my turn, then, to feel the full force of the affront that eluded him. I was disconsolate in the realization that he was allowing those inferior connections to interfere with what I believed would be a more than suitable attachment. It was perplexing to me that this was the same young man who eschewed superior lineage to choose me as his companion. I was determined to show that judgment of merit over bloodlines should hold for Miss Elizabeth as well.

I knew I had little time left. I knew he was aware of how she treated me and how much I held her in my regard. I had to do something desperate! And soon!

~~*

Morning dawned with bright rays of the sun shining through the window. A beautiful day beckoned and my master promised me a walk later that morning.

After eating a light breakfast, he and I furtively stepped out, hoping to escape the company of Miss Bingley. To my disappointment, Miss Elizabeth had not as yet come down from her sister's room.

As we stepped out, I made every effort to devise some means by which Miss Elizabeth would join us on our walk, but nothing came to mind. I was interrupted from my musings when Miss Bingley unexpectedly and quite lamentably appeared in the lane, assaulting us with her presence. We were both taken aback as she insisted upon joining us.

My master and I both held out hope that the extent to which we wished to walk would soon become tiresome for her, but unfortunately she remained steadfastly by his side. Thus, our anticipation for a leisurely and pleasurable stroll as well as any plans I might devise to include Miss Elizabeth were thwarted quite cruelly.

When Miss Elizabeth and Mrs. Hurst unexpectedly came upon us, I was rapturous, as I believed Miss Elizabeth's lively and amiable presence on our walk would endear her to my master wholeheartedly. This would certainly make for a more enjoyable diversion!

But to my dismay, neither sister seemed inclined to show any civility toward Miss Elizabeth. I watched incredulously as Mrs. Hurst sidled up alongside of my master, taking his one free arm, thereby effectively excluding Miss Elizabeth from joining us on our walk as the path only admitted three. I felt the rudeness strongly and could only hope that Miss Elizabeth would not blame my master for the sisters' lack of courtesy. Apparently my master felt it as well, for he offered that they take the avenue instead, which would accommodate all four of them.

The two sisters looked at him with much displeasure for his suggestion, but Miss Elizabeth laughingly answered, "No, no; stay where you are. You are charmingly grouped, and appear to uncommon advantage. The picturesque would be spoilt by admitting a fourth. Good bye."

Miss Bingley and Mrs. Hurst seemed content with Miss Elizabeth's response and in unison turned so that my master was forced to walk away with each lady on an arm. I watched as he guardedly turned his head to see Miss Elizabeth gaily run off. When he turned his attention back to the ladies, I decided to leave him and follow my new friend, hoping it would compel him to come after me and join Miss Elizabeth.

She ran a short distance and stopped when she espied me dutifully following her. Looking down, she laughed. "Why, Reggie! What are you doing here?"

I offered up a paw to her in apology for the rudeness to which she had just been subjected, wagging my tail to show my earnest. She stooped down and beckoned me to come. When I approached her, she cupped my face with her hands.

"Reggie, how pleasant it is to witness such gracious and affable manners! I asked you this once and I shall ask you again. How is it that *you* are so polite when *he* is so ill mannered?"

She reached down and picked up a stick and I waited with great expectancy for her to throw it. But instead of letting it go, she held onto it; resolutely pounding it into her open palm.

"He certainly is an enigma, Reggie. If he is not brooding and silent, he is critical of everyone and everything he sees. I sense his disdain for me as sure as I do Miss Bingley's."

I found it difficult keeping my eyes adhered to the stick whilst attending to her words about my master. Unfortunately, the words were neither heartening to me nor complimentary to him.

"One would think that a man of education and striking advantage would somewhere along the way have acquired even the most basic civilities." She paused contemplatively. "Perhaps he does not oblige himself to attend to those for whom he sees no advantage to himself." She let out a breathy laugh. "If that is the case, Reggie, I can hardly expect that he would concern himself with satisfying my demands for well-mannered behaviour."

She continued to tease me with the stick as she dispirited me with her words. "And his idea of an accomplished woman! Has he ever met a lady who has attained all that? I would imagine that even all the ladies he has met in the ton would scarcely meet his unrivalled expectations."

I sadly realized that she was completely unaware that my master considered her to be most accomplished. Miss Elizabeth may not be all the things Miss Bingley had in her list of accomplishments, but she certainly possessed the ones my master deemed essential. My tail gave a few fervent thumps against the ground, surging from a deep sense of frustration at the manner in which my master and Miss Elizabeth continually misapprehended one another.

She unexpectedly gave the stick a spirited toss and with a great laugh, called out, "Fetch!"

My legs responded with little thought as I quickly set out to retrieve it. But at my old age, my eagerness to please her propelled me more than my vigour, and I returned to her panting, but in proud possession of the stick.

"Good boy, Reggie. You are an infinitely preferable companion," she affirmed, as she took the stick and patted the top of my head.

We began walking again and I glanced about me to ascertain whether my master had come in search of me. I was disappointed that he did not seem inclined to oblige my scheme by coming after me.

I turned my attentions back to the path along which we were walking and found myself even more dismayed at Miss Elizabeth's next words. "You must see how he looks at me, Reggie, when I am petting the top of your head. I am quite sure he is of the opinion that a fine, well-bred woman should refrain from bestowing her attentions on a mere dog!"

I could not but whine in commiseration as I realized I had seen that look as well. However, rather than condemnation of her actions, I believed his severe countenance was due more to his imagining that instead of her fingers combing through my fur, they were running through his hair.

"Forgive me, Reggie. I did not intend to refer to you as a "mere" dog. You are quite special and it is only for that reason that I enjoy bestowing my attentions to you." Her voice softened. "Sometimes I feel that save for Jane's excellent Mr. Bingley, you are the only friend I have at Netherfield."

She threw the stick again and then walked over to a fallen log, upon which she sat. I laid the retrieved stick carefully before her and rested my head in her lap.

"Tell me, Reggie," she whispered. "What secrets can you divulge of your master?" She looked at me with her shining, dark eyes. "I pride myself on being an excellent studier of character and he has proven to be the most difficult I have ever encountered."

It was difficult for me to give any thought to what she was saying as her fingers found the place behind my ears that caused me to moan unwittingly again. At any rate, she did not seem inclined to wait for an answer on my part.

"Do you recollect how last night he seemed to take great delight in arguing with me about whether Mr. Bingley would readily yield to another friend's request, and then -- quite unexpectedly -- in the next moment, he asks me to dance a reel?"

She stood up laughing, taking my forward paws in her hands. As dear little Georgiana did when she first learned, Miss Elizabeth pretended to dance with me. I gladly assumed the role of her partner. "Dance a reel! In the drawing room! But I would not let him get the better of me! I cleverly foiled his attempt to discredit me. I remained silent and refused to accept his absurd request."

Taking several more steps forwards and backwards, she abruptly stopped, a puzzled countenance overtaking her fine features. "And yet there was something else." She tilted her head to the side as she tried to put her finger on what it was. "A hint of gallantry, perhaps?"

She looked down at me, the sudden sound of her laughter as refreshing to me as a spring rain. "Mr. Darcy gallant?" She laughed again. "Ludicrous, Reggie! Simply ludicrous!"

Miss Elizabeth continued to hold my paws and dance. As much as I enjoyed our play, I suddenly became aware of my master's scent, and in looking around, I discovered him, somehow disengaged from the sisters, watching us furtively and quite intently from up the road.

Chapter 13

It seemed too short a time before Miss Elizabeth thanked me for honouring her with the spontaneous dance and for being such a delightful dance partner. She released my paws, and with a ready smile, beckoned me to join her on the walk back to the house. I gave a final glimpse back to where I had observed my master earlier. He was no longer there.

I took as great a delight in my walk with Miss Elizabeth as I ever did with my master. Her love for the outdoors was clearly exhibited in the manner in which she leaned over to smell the flowers that we passed or ran her fingers across the leafy branch of a tree. At one point, she leaned over and picked up a fuzzy little creature which she called a *caterpillar* and brought it down so I could see it. She let out a gleeful laugh when she noticed my head tilt as I watched the funny way it inched along in her hand.

When we arrived back at the house, Miss Elizabeth prepared to go inside whilst I decided to remain outside to await the return of my master. She turned and looked down at me. "Waiting for Mr. Darcy, are you? Very well, I should see to Jane. It was a lovely walk, Reggie, and between you and me, I have not enjoyed a dance more than the one I just shared with you." She reached down and tousled the fur atop my head. "If truth be told, I have not had a more delightful diversion since coming to Netherfield!" She smiled, and with a firm nod of her head said, "Thank you, my good friend!"

When she stepped inside the door, I turned back to watch for my master. As I lay down and waited, I pondered the predicament before me.

Since his father's death and assuming the role of Master of Pemberley, my master had become far more serious than any man of his age ought. But he had exhibited more spark and liveliness in these last few days in the presence of Miss Elizabeth than I had seen from him in the last five years put together. Her wit and vivacity evoked something in my master that I knew had been sorely lacking in his life.

For that reason I had always treasured those times when my master and I took to the grounds at Pemberley together. It was on those walks that I beheld more of an unrestrained nature on his part. He laughed openly at my antics, exclaimed in marvel at some beautiful sight, or even took off in a run when incited by me to do so.

I lowered my head onto my paws, letting out a mournful groan, wishing for some way to enlighten him as to the pleasure he would truly know if he were but to walk with her. I could easily envision the two of them walking the grounds of Pemberley; Miss Elizabeth taking great pleasure in the sights and smells and sounds as my master escorted her down every path and lane he had ever traversed throughout his years there.

I was not ignorant of the fact that I was aging. I acutely felt my aching muscles that slowed my movements considerably and my propensity to fatigue with little effort. And I knew that the time would soon come where I would no longer be a proper companion for him. At that moment I made it my office to do everything in my power to persuade my master to pursue his happiness with Miss Elizabeth.

Before I was blessed with any sort of reasonable scheme as to how to achieve my plan, I espied my master walking toward me with a brisk and resolute stride. When he came to stand before me, he locked his arms behind him and took a firm stance as he regarded me sternly.

I wagged my tail in an earnest, yet somewhat apprehensive greeting, uncertain of his disposition toward me.

"Without a doubt, Reggie, you have been exhibiting the most uncontrolled behaviour of late." He shook his head at me. "Do you truly believe, in your wizened old age, that your designs will have sway over me?"

I let out a quick yap to protest my innocence and he leaned over to ruffle the fur on my head, much like Miss Elizabeth had just done.

"In spite of my misgivings toward your conduct," he began reflectively, "I must confess that I have not had any greater pleasure in the past few days than observing Miss Elizabeth's particular attention to you." He brought up one foot and placed it on the first step, resting one arm across his knee to more easily facilitate his leaning down to scratch my head. He took in a deep breath and let it out slowly before continuing. "It appears that she has a great fondness for you." His eyes looked out toward the place where she and I had been dancing.

"And she honours *you* with a dance when she has refused *me*… twice!"

He reached under my chin to scratch it as well as lift my head up and our eyes met. "I know you are fond of her, Reggie…" He paused and his voice softened, "and I concede she can be most beguiling when she chooses." He sat down upon the step and looked out again across the grounds. In a contemplative yet resolute voice he declared, "But it cannot be."

We sat for a few moments in silence as I pondered why it was so easy for me and yet so difficult for my master to garner Miss Elizabeth's favour.

I looked up at him and noticed the struggle in his eyes. I was confident he was not battling Miss Elizabeth's desirability nor her pleasing behaviour, for I had seen the look of admiration and longing in his eyes. Indeed, even in their spirited disagreements, he had each time come away from it with a stronger sense of Miss Elizabeth's merit. No, he was continuing to address the issue of the inferiority of her relations and all I could hope was that he would be reminded of how, as a young boy, he chose me over the puppies of superior lineage because he wanted a suitable companion for himself. Should that not be of greater merit to him? All I could do now would be to assist my master in seeing all that was excellent in Miss Elizabeth and hopefully every other argument against her would fade.

After we had been sitting for some time in silence, my master finally spoke. "Come, Reggie, we must join our hosts directly! I told Miss Bingley and Mrs. Hurst that in your old age you had a very disagreeable tendency to wander away and get lost and that it was vital I found you immediately." He let out a soft chuckle whilst I let out a low growl to voice my displeasure at such a characterization of faculties. "I am sorry to say that was the only thing of which I could think to separate myself from Bingley's sisters. It is very likely they will return at any moment!"

At least my plan had separated him from the two sisters; however it fell short when it came to bringing my master and Miss Elizabeth together. All the walks my master and I had ever taken were where he and I forged our acquaintance and where we deepened our attachment. I remained confident that a walk together was all that my master and Miss Elizabeth needed.

∼∼*

True to her word, Miss Elizabeth continued at her sister's side for the remainder of the day. When Miss Bingley inquired after them later in the day, she returned with a more tolerable report. Miss Bennet was improving, and although she would nevertheless take dinner in her room, she might feel inclined to join us afterwards in the drawing room. Whilst I was grateful for her recovery, I was aware this meant Miss Elizabeth would soon be returning home.

After the evening meal, Elizabeth excused herself to return to her sister to see if she was well enough to join the others in the drawing room. The men quit the dining room to take some port in Bingley's study. His sisters proceeded to the drawing room, with whom I reluctantly followed, hoping Miss Elizabeth would return directly.

At length, Miss Elizabeth entered the drawing room with her sister.

"Why, Miss Bennet," exclaimed Miss Bingley, clasping her hands together, "How good it is that you are feeling well enough to join us tonight! You are certainly looking much improved!"

Miss Bennet, in a soft voice, answered, "Thank you, Miss Bingley. I am feeling much better and I wish to thank you and your sister for your gracious hospitality."

"My dear, it is the least we could do, is it not, Louisa?" She looked over at her sister, who nodded. "You may be assured that we would have done *anything* to help speed up your recovery!"

I was quite certain they would have, solely to remove the Bennet ladies from Netherfield!

I sat and listened to the ladies as they talked and Bingley's sisters continued to be most gracious in expressing their pleasure at seeing her improved and attended to her every need. I knew that their anticipation of the Bennet sisters leaving soon made their pleasant conversation and attentiveness much more effortless.

When finally the men returned, they each expressed congratulations to Miss Bennet for her recuperation and their satisfaction to see her downstairs. My master then claimed a rather large chair and picked up the book he had brought to read. Mr. Bingley took the open space on the small sofa next to Miss Bennet and his attentions were forthwith attentive only to her. Mr. Hurst sat at the empty table, petitioning someone to join him in a game of cards, but when no one answered favourably, he removed to a sofa in the corner and, stretching out upon it, promptly fell fast asleep.

My master soon found himself the regrettable focus of Miss Bingley's attentions. It appeared to me that Miss Bingley was no longer interested in Miss Bennet and her improvement. She placed herself in front of him and to my surprise, loudly proclaimed the book in her hand as the finest she had ever read. As this declaration was directed primarily at my master, I can only assume it was one upon which she had solicited his recommendation. Oddly, she did not seem to be as devoted to the book as her words would indicate, for her eyes appeared far more often employed at stealing coquettish glances at my master than in taking in the text.

For his part, my master directed all his attention to his book and seemed intent to devour the pages. I believe he did this as much to dissuade Miss Bingley from pursuing any further conversation as he did to avoid being distracted by Miss Elizabeth, who had seated herself in a nearby chair and had picked up her needlework again.

I watched as Miss Elizabeth occasionally glanced over to her sister and Mr. Bingley. It was quite apparent that Miss Bennet was grateful to finally be well enough to be out of her room; although she still appeared somewhat weak. She and Mr. Bingley sat close to the fire so she would not catch a chill and his face lit up as he conversed with her. Miss Elizabeth bore a well-pleased smile of her own each time she beheld the symptoms of peculiar regard Mr. Bingley was demonstrating.

In a room overflowing with so much bliss, I felt that my master and Miss Elizabeth could have no choice but to behave most amiably toward one another.

I looked over at my master who was bearing up admirably under Miss Bingley's focused attention. But his rigid and focused demeanour eventually accomplished its purpose, for Miss Bingley most reluctantly turned her attention to the book she had brought into the drawing room. I surmised that her book must not have given her much pleasure, or perhaps she was not given to much understanding of it, for she was once more drawing to his side, asking him questions about *his* book, which was apparently the third volume of the set, hers being the second.

When all attempts at securing my master's attention failed, she gave up entirely on her book and paced the room restlessly. I was becoming quite agitated myself as Miss Bingley made every attempt to garner my master's favour whilst Miss Elizabeth did not seem inclined to engage in conversation at all. How I wished to be able to persuade them to converse rather than idle at their separate pursuits!

At first, things began to look more positive when Miss Bingley began addressing her brother about the inadvisability of his giving a ball. Warming to her subject, she insinuated how there were some present that would not enjoy such society, obviously trying to show her consideration for my master. Given how much Miss Elizabeth enjoyed dancing with me this afternoon, I was convinced that this was a subject of which much lively debate could occur, which would only increase her allure in his eyes. However, Bingley simply refused to consider her complaints and considered it a settled thing. A careless remark about my master preferring to go to bed instead of the ball if he chose to do so brought a glance up from my master's book as well as Miss Elizabeth's employment.

My master gave a slight scowl as a smirk danced upon Miss Elizabeth's lips. The hoped-for tête-à-tête between them was thwarted by my master's friend. I feared disappointment would be mine this evening.

Miss Bingley glanced at my master, who had resumed reading his book with his jaw clenched, and then returned to walking about the room. She held herself tall as she walked with graceful strides, slowing down ever so slightly as she passed close by my master. He resolutely adhered to his book and I watched as a sense of desperation passed over her. It was pathetic to me how much she coveted his attention. Clearly, she knew not the futility of her actions. Indeed, if she had been attentive at all to my master's deportment, she would have noticed a slight sense of exasperation on his part!

In one final astonishing move, she walked over to Miss Elizabeth and asked her to join her in a turn about the room.

I believed Miss Elizabeth to be just as surprised as I. If she had only a small portion of the insight that Miss Bingley did into my master's propensity, however, she would have understood that her invitation was a sure way to secure his attention. Not fully comprehending Miss Bingley's motive, Miss Elizabeth immediately agreed.

As Miss Elizabeth drew alongside Miss Bingley out of politeness more so than pleasure, Miss Bingley finally succeeded in the real object of her civility. My master looked up to attend their movement. I believe I was as pleased as Miss Bingley, although not for the same reason.

The two of them walked together only briefly before Miss Bingley turned to my master and invited him to join them. He had no doubt been surprised when Miss Bingley invited Miss Elizabeth in a turn about the room. When she extended the invitation to include himself, he was more than startled. I hoped that he would at least oblige her. Even though it meant taking Miss Bingley's arm, he could just as easily take Miss Elizabeth's as well.

I watched him as a gleam unexpectedly appeared in his eye. I sat and observed this unfolding before me in awe as he began a most... how can I put this... *uncharacteristic* teasing -- dare I say *flirtatious* -- dialogue I had ever witnessed.

When he admitted to the ladies that he could observe their figures from where he was sitting much more readily than if he joined them, I do believe Miss Bingley was thrilled even though she chided him; Miss Elizabeth, for her part, looked slightly shocked and blushed! From my vantage point on the floor, I waited for Miss Elizabeth to notice the admiration in his eyes directed towards her.

Her manner, however, was devoid of any hint of admiration toward him. A look of censure and challenge overspread her face as she retorted with a determination to tease and laugh at him.

The two of them stared unflinchingly at each other whilst Miss Bingley proclaimed that he was impossible to tease, as he had such calmness of temper and presence of mind. Not to contradict our hostess, but I believe I was the only one with a presence of mind, as my master's complete attention was on admiring Miss Elizabeth whilst she appeared solely to be calculating what my master's faults might be.

I had the unnerving sense that this conversation would not proceed as I wished, either. It was true that a sense of spirit had suddenly taken hold of my master, but he was so far in Miss Elizabeth's disapprobation, I held grave doubts that whatever transpired next would not raise him in her esteem.

I was startled out of my musings by Miss Elizabeth declaring, "Mr. Darcy is not to be laughed at! That is an uncommon advantage, and uncommon I hope it will continue, for it would be a great loss to me to have many such acquaintance. I dearly love a laugh."

She spoke with such a sparkle in her eyes and conviction in her words that a distressed whimper escaped me. Here I had hoped that they might find a way to converse amiably and bridge the distance between them, and instead, the chasm seemed to grow larger with every word.

I noticed the flicker of distress in my master's eyes as he considered thoughtfully his response before answering.

He owned that Miss Bingley had given him more credit than she ought and Miss Elizabeth supposed that follies and nonsense and the like were precisely what he was without. Did I dare hope that they would carry on a conversation that shed a good light on my master?

"Perhaps that is not possible for anyone." *No,* I thought. It seemed at the moment to be impossible. He continued, "But it has been the study of my life to avoid those weaknesses which often expose a strong understanding to ridicule."

"Such as vanity and pride." Miss Elizabeth answered back.

"Yes, vanity is a weakness indeed. But pride -- where there is a real superiority of mind, pride will always be under good regulation."

Why must my master insist on being under such good regulation? Elizabeth must have likewise wondered as she turned and tilted her head down toward me, suppressing a smile from him. Miss Bingley took advantage of the silence to step in. She had been watching each of them intently at their verbal sparring, wondering, I am quite certain, why it was that a simple country lady appeared to have such a hold on my master.

"Your examination of Mr. Darcy is over, I presume," said Miss Bingley; "and pray what is the result?"

Elizabeth turned her attention back to my master as she studied him. I waited expectantly for her answer.

"I am perfectly convinced by it that Mr. Darcy has no defect. He owns it himself without disguise."

I believed that she was not being serious or, if she was, she was not paying my master a compliment.

"No," my master remarked. "I have made no such pretension. I have faults enough, but they are not, I hope, of understanding. My temper I dare not vouch for. It is, I believe, too little yielding..."

As he continued, I comprehended something profound. My master was exposing certain deficiencies of his character to Miss Elizabeth in a most atypical and vulnerable manner. He had always tenaciously clung to his guarded mien as a way of protecting himself and his sister. He was not one who readily shared his thoughts and feelings to anyone, let alone his faults.

Yet here he was, openly declaring his defects to Miss Elizabeth! If only she realized what a compliment he was paying to her. If only she could see beyond his actual words and realize the import of his openness and honesty.

I caught the end of his declaration. "My temper would perhaps be called resentful. My good opinion once lost is lost forever."

"*That* is a failing indeed!" Miss Elizabeth cried. "Implacable resentment is a shade in a character. But *you* have chosen your fault well. I really cannot laugh at it. You are safe from me."

"There is..." my master began, and I sensed that whilst he was struggling to defend himself to her, he was enjoying the banter. "...I believe, in every disposition a tendency to some particular evil -- a natural defect, which not even the best education can overcome."

"And *your* defect is a propensity to hate everybody."

"And *yours*," he replied, with a smile, "is wilfully to misunderstand them."

The silence seemed to hang heavy in the air, as did my head. Miss Elizabeth stood defiantly before my master, taking umbrage at his accusation. Miss Bingley wished for any sort of diversion to disrupt the solicitous attention my master was bestowing upon Miss Elizabeth. Whilst the essence of their words may have outwardly appeared insolent, she knew, as well as I, that my master savoured every moment of it.

She asked for the pianoforte to be opened directly and for her sister to play music.

For the remainder of the evening, my master had difficulty keeping a smile from creeping up the corners of his mouth. His eyes travelled repeatedly in admiration to Miss Elizabeth, who had returned to her stitchery. Since both her hands were employed with her work, I knew sitting at her side would be to no avail in receiving her attentions. I was only concerned, however, that whilst my master's affections towards her appeared to be steadily growing, hers toward my master were waning.

As we retired to his chambers for the night, it was with a great sense of hope that I looked forward to the next day. With Miss Bennet much improved and able to join the others, Miss Elizabeth would no doubt grace us with her presence throughout the day. In due course, I was certain she would begin to see the good in my master as much as he had begun to take delight in her; provided that my scheme to show him in the best possible light was successful.

I pounced upon the bed, awaiting my master to join me, but instead, he settled in a hard backed chair. Leaning over, he rested his elbows on his knees and spreading out his fingers, he lowered his head so that they cradled his face. He began massaging his temples quite brusquely, as if he was attempting to expel demons that were residing within.

"How is it that a man of my upbringing and education, with connections to the elite of society, cannot resist the charms of a country lady?" His eyes glanced up and met mine. "Why is it, Reggie, that I find her so arresting?"

I gave him a sympathetic whine and he closed his eyes as he continued to rub his forehead.

"One would think," he continued, "that being the rational man that I am, I could put aside these… these…" He shook his head as if it would assist him in finding the exact word he wanted.

He stood up with a fierce determination. "I have allowed this unseemly infatuation toward her to go unchecked far too long!" He looked down at me, shaking his head slowly. "I know you are displeased, Reggie, but I cannot allow my attentions toward her to mislead her. I cannot raise her hopes that I am singling her out." He paced a few steps in one direction and then the other.

"From this moment on, until she departs this house, I shall avoid her like the plague. I shall refuse to engage her in a discussion or debate, even to discuss the weather with her!"

He threw the coverlet back and came into the bed with such force I thought I would bounce off. "By the time she is back at Longbourn..." he swallowed deeply, "I will have completely forgotten that she was here, what effect she had on me, and I… I shall own peace in my soul once again!"

~~*

The following morning Miss Bennet came down with Miss Elizabeth and joined us for breakfast. The discussion around the table that caused me alarm was that the Bennet ladies desired to return home. Miss Bennet felt herself well enough and Miss Elizabeth concurred. When Miss Elizabeth affirmed that she wished to write home to request the carriage be sent for them that very day, Miss Bingley and Mrs. Hurst readily obliged. A missive was sent off to Longbourn directly.

I sat in the corner of the room downcast, wishing for Miss Elizabeth to engage my master in any sort of discourse. He had not forgotten his resolve from the previous night and remained steadfastly silent throughout the meal and I had little hope left within me. With Miss Bennet joining our party for breakfast for the first time it was of little surprise that Miss Elizabeth was engaged in conversation with her and Mr. Bingley. My master listened, but seemed to have no inclination to join them.

I became increasingly unsettled as we awaited the response to Miss Elizabeth's letter. I could only hope that the carriage would not suddenly appear and whisk the young ladies away without further opportunity for my master to reconsider his regard for her.

When a letter came back in reply, I was greatly relieved to hear that they could not possibly send the carriage before Tuesday. Miss Elizabeth was distressed and Bingley's sisters directed insolent smiles towards one another. My master sat silently, his eyes not straying from the page of the book in front of him.

I had an inkling of hope that they would remain a few more days, but it only lasted for a moment, as Miss Elizabeth was resolved to leave as soon as possible. She urged her sister to ask if Bingley's carriage could be borrowed. It was settled then that they would leave on the morrow and I did not believe that to be enough time to accomplish what had become my sole ambition.

~~*

Miss Bennet and Miss Elizabeth adjourned to the drawing room with Mr. Bingley immediately following. He made every attempt to encourage them to stay longer to allow Miss Bennet to improve considerably more, but they would not. He declared he would spend every moment he had remaining by Miss Bennet's side.

Directly after they left the room, Miss Bingley turned to my master. "So, Mr. Darcy, you shall have the benefit of her *fine eyes* but for one day more. Do you think you shall miss them when she leaves? Perhaps you have etched them in your memory? Are they truly so fine that they have erased every trace of her objectionable family?"

I let out a growl, which, unfortunately, only my master heard, giving me a censorious glance. For the past few days, her remarks had continued unabated and I knew it was discomfiting my master exceedingly. Today, however, it appeared as though her snide remarks simply slid off him.

I had grave doubts that the delight he took in his repartee with Miss Elizabeth the previous night lingered. The spark of liveliness that I had witnessed in his countenance had completely faded and the façade of being in strict command of his faculties had unfortunately returned.

We removed ourselves to the library and he settled in a small chair in the corner. I lay down at his feet, quite disconsolate. I believe we had come here because he was making every attempt to avoid her presence.

He sought his asylum in the library for quite a long time. I fell asleep several times. At length I awakened when I heard soft footsteps enter. Both of us looked up as Miss Elizabeth stepped in and walked to the far corner of the room. She did not see us and went to a shelf, perusing it for something suitable to read.

I stood up and began to walk over to her. I felt, rather than heard, my master's attempt to stop me. But he did not succeed and I continued toward her.

I came by her side and she looked down at me.

"Hello, Reggie. What are you doing in here?"

I lifted a paw up to her and she leaned over and grasped it. I breathed in her light floral scent that wafted over me and looked up into her eyes sparkling with mirth. At the sound of my master adjusting himself in his chair, she turned towards him and an awkward glance passed between them. He had been observing us with the sternest of expressions etched upon his face. She gave a slight curtsey and nodded her head. "Mr. Darcy."

He reciprocated with barely a nod and whispered, "Miss Elizabeth."

She turned back to the shelf and he turned his attention back down to his book. I looked from one to the other, waiting for some further conversation to ensue. Certainly she could inquire of my master a recommendation or he might make a suggestion himself! Miss Elizabeth was content to pull several books down, opening each one and glancing through the pages before she found one that suited her.

She took a seat in a chair on the opposite side of the room. I watched incredulously as neither seemed inclined to further acknowledge the other. I planted myself alongside Miss Elizabeth and she obliged me with a hand upon my head as she read her book, but my master did not allow himself the liberty to look up.

As I regarded him, I noticed that he was tense and his breathing somewhat laboured. He held his book in one hand and the fingers of his other hand soundly tapped against the arm of the chair as his foot did the same on the floor.

This resolve by which he had commanded himself to abide was apparently not the easiest task he had ever performed! Indeed, the task of *not* singling out Miss Elizabeth appeared far more strenuous than he most likely ever imagined.

As I lay there, I hoped for some sort of dialogue to commence. The folly of human relationships lay before me. One would think they could find *something* to discuss in the solitude of this room! Some spirited discussion! Even a lively debate! If my master was so intent to refuse to engage her in discourse, why did not Miss Elizabeth challenge him on some topic?

It appeared to me as if an agreement was formed by both parties to remain steadfastly silent, much to my disappointment. After a full half an hour elapsed with nary an acknowledgement on either side, Miss Bennet arose and left the room with her book in hand. My head sullenly dropped to my paws and the demeanour of my master noticeably relaxed. He closed his own book and leaned over to temple his fingers to his forehead. He glanced over at me and in his eyes I beheld that familiar struggle that I had noticed throughout Miss Elizabeth's stay. It appeared to overwhelm him. But unfortunately, the unsuitability of her connections was gaining in consequence over her suitability in every other manner.

I continued in my disappointment throughout the rest of the day. Miss Elizabeth was to leave the following day and neither she nor my master seemed at all inclined to converse. My master took his resolution seriously; he adamantly forbade himself to pay her any particular attention. Was I wrong in clinging so voraciously to the conviction that she was admirably suited for him?

He and I took a rather leisurely stroll later in the afternoon. We found ourselves down by the stable and it helped cheer me up greatly to see Sadie. Since Miss Elizabeth had come to Netherfield, I had practically forgotten her. She was allowed to join us on our walk and her playful enthusiasm and company helped greatly to ease the heavy burden I was carrying. Unfortunately, it did little to ease my master's burden, as I suspected he wished despite himself, for the society of one very particular person.

Later that evening, my master and I returned to the library. We sat silently in the cold darkness, the only light a small flickering flame from a single candle nearly burnt out. The house was peaceful and silent, as everyone had retired for the night. I was certain that but a few hours remained before the sun would make its morning appearance. My master nursed some strong drink from a goblet he held tightly in his hand. I looked up at him with grave concern as he stared across the room. His eyes were fixed to the place were Miss Elizabeth had stood earlier that day as she looked through the small selection of books for something suitable to read. I still could barely comprehend that in spite of the good amount of time they had passed in close proximity in the room together, they had spoken barely a word to the other.

I rested my head upon my paws, fighting the urge to close my eyes as I was feeling the effects of having slept very ill these past few nights. The pacing back and forth in the early hours of the morn, the tossing and turning when in his bed, and the debates my master held with himself on the merits or defects of Miss Elizabeth had not only wearied my physical body, but elicited feelings of melancholy, as well.

He filled his goblet again and took another sip. His unexpected words, though softly spoken, startled me, causing me to look up.

"So she leaves on the morrow? So be it! Let her depart this house and allow me peace of mind again!"

His voice was slurred, to which I attributed his drink, but I surmised that rather than numbing his feelings, as was likely his desire, it heightened them.

"So you displayed your country manners, Miss Elizabeth Bennet, by walking three miles through muddy fields and along soggy roads only to boast a glowing countenance when you arrive! Did you suspect the effect that would have on me? Was that a purposed employment of your arts to entrap me?"

His rigid and erect comportment, to which I was so accustomed, was slumping gradually into his chair with each gulp of his drink.

He lifted up his goblet into the air. "Challenge me on every thought and opinion, even when I am extending a compliment your way!" He lowered his glass and swirled its contents, looking down into the liquid. His person swayed as well, as if every fibre of his being was in a swirl of conflicting thought and emotion. "Dare to weaken my defences and my resolve with your sparkling eyes and delightful smile, even as you confront me!"

"Then astonish me by defending me to your mother when she misconstrues my meaning! Yet you clearly comprehended my intent when I stated that in a country neighbourhood one moves in a very confined and unvarying society. How am I to remain collected in your presence when one moment you defend me and the next you pronounce judgment?"

He shook his head slowly and he took another sip. "Refuse my offer to dance a reel or walk into the avenue. Laugh at my attempt to placate the incivility directed at you by Bingley's sisters."

His head dropped back and his eyes stared vacantly at the ceiling above.

"Disappoint me by remaining silent when I wish so much to hear your lively voice and your clever and thought-provoking opinions."

He let out a huff. "Mock me, that I am without those follies and nonsense that allow for teasing! Examine me, Miss Bennet, and proclaim all my defects!"

He brusquely ran his hand through his hair. "Torture me with your relations! How can one be so suitable for me in so many ways whilst at the same time be so completely unsuitable because of her family connections?"

The flame of the candle extinguished and in the darkness, he set his goblet down. In a whisper, he declared to himself, "Come tomorrow, all will return to the way it ought."

He looked down at me. "Come, Reggie, I think it is time we retire."

He began to stand up, but just as suddenly, he grabbed for the armrests of the chair. Bringing one hand up to his head, he crumpled back down into it. "Perhaps not."

He sat quietly for a moment, leaning his head back and closing his eyes.

At that moment, the sound of soft footsteps could be heard approaching. My tail unwittingly thudded against the floor several times as I caught the scent of Miss Elizabeth. I was about to get up to greet her when a large foot came down upon me, successfully preventing any movement on my part, and my master whispered in a coarse voice, "Stay, Reggie! Quiet!"

I was sorely tempted to disobey, but thought the better of it. For Miss Elizabeth to see my master in the state he was in would not improve him in her regard. We sat quietly, in the back corner of the library, as she walked in.

She was carrying a single candle and walked directly to a bookshelf, apparently returning the book she had taken this morning to its place. She had on a long white nightgown, modestly covered with a shawl. As she lifted her arm to place the book on the shelf, the shawl slipped from one shoulder. She was unable to retrieve it until she set the book on the shelf. My master took in a sharp breath and held it until she had returned the shawl to its proper place.

I have never seen an angel before, but I would have to surmise that she must have looked exceptionally like one. Georgiana had often told me stories of angels, confiding in me that she was quite certain her mother was one. Miss Elizabeth's long, dark hair was let down and highlighted by the flame of the candle. Her white gown practically glowed against the darkness of the room. Her graceful movement across the floor, as she turned back to the door, made her appear to float rather than walk.

We remained steadfastly silent, listening to each footstep that took her farther away from the library and then up the stairs. At length, we heard a door close.

My master's voice shook with derision. "Dare to despise me, Miss Bennet, for admiring your figure clandestinely in the darkness of this room! I own that as a true fault of character! But as I sit here, fighting every urge to act on my impulses, one fault you will never be able to ascribe to me is *ungentlemanlike* behaviour towards you!"

After a moment's pause, he said, "So depart, Elizabeth, and give me peace!"

His breathing was heavy and he leaned his head back. Within a short time, he had fallen into a deep, but restless, sleep.

Chapter 14

The next morning, my master and I awakened in the library to the sounds of servants readying the house for a new day. My master shook his head and brought a hand up to rub his temple vigorously as he made an attempt to get his bearings.

"It would appear as though we slept all night in the library, Reggie. I fear I drank a trifle too much last night. Remind me never to do that again!"

He stood up slowly, grasping his head. "Come. Let us see if we can escape to my chambers and freshen up before anyone takes notice of our situation. All that I require is a good splash of cold water upon my face and a cup of coffee to return to myself again."

I wondered whether he truly *would* return to his self -- ever again! I knew that my acquaintance with Miss Elizabeth had changed me. From the very beginning of our acquaintance, I felt a kinship existed between us. What I beheld in her had given me hope that a lady suitable in every way had been found for him. Could he not see that? Had making her acquaintance not somehow altered him in the way it had me? Despite his determination to argue that it had not, I was of the opinion that his uncharacteristic behaviour last night rather proved that it had.

~~*

Later that morning, as the party gathered in preparation to depart for church, I gave one last perusal of my master and Miss Elizabeth. Though I knew he was still feeling the effects of his intemperance, my master did not display any outward indication of it, other than an unusually large share of coffee at the morning meal. Perhaps if Miss Elizabeth had been aware of his impressive recovery, she might have been more obliging. Instead, she ignored my master entirely.

Miss Elizabeth's attention was wholly occupied with her sister, a joy she shared with Mr. Bingley. He took every measure to ensure that she was well enough to join them and to affirm that he was most delighted that she was. Even Bingley's sisters expressed great delight in her recuperation and commented on how the Misses Bennets must anticipate their return home. My master stood resolutely apart from the others, abstaining from entering their conversation. I confess I remained in my own corner and sulked. I was downcast, disheartened, and not a little disappointed. I knew any opportunity for me to see Miss Elizabeth again was negligible and my master did not appear inclined to appease me nor to allow himself the liberty of enjoying her company any further. He was steadfastly determined to exhibit naught but the most basic civilities towards her.

I awaited their return from church with very little optimism that my master might break his resolve to avoid Miss Elizabeth. Unfortunately, he lived up to my expectations and it was very soon after that the Bennet ladies made preparations to depart Netherfield. My master politely joined Bingley outside as they approached his carriage to embark, but he kept himself back. With an eagerness to express my admiration and pleasure at being in her company, as well as to exhibit my disapprobation towards my master's resolve, I approached her with a fervent wag of my tail.

As Bingley bid farewell to her sister, Miss Elizabeth came down and cradled my face. "I thank you, Reggie, for making my stay here so delightful." She nuzzled the top of my head and when I lifted up my paw to her, she took it gently and a ready smile danced upon her face. "It has been a pleasure," she spoke softly as she released it.

With a twinkle in her eye, she reached into her satchel, saying she had a little token for me. She pulled out what looked like a short piece of rope.

"This is for you, Reggie. I found it on one of my walks and thought you might like it as a toy. I tied some knots into it on both ends so it may be easily grasped."

She held one of the knots in her hand and dangled the rope in front of me. When I grabbed the other end with my teeth, she pulled and I held on tighter.

"Oh! It appears as though you have played tug-o-war before!" She leaned forward and whispered, "Pray, do not tell me that Mr. Darcy has engaged in such diversion with you!" She laughed and stood up, letting go of the rope. I kept a sure hold of it within my jaws, hoping she might continue our game. But to my utter disappointment, she turned to allow Mr. Bingley to hand her into the carriage.

I turned to my master, who did nothing more than bow and politely say goodbye. He had such a severe look on his face! I do not doubt that it said to everyone around him, 'Let us get this tedious farewell over with directly.' But I, as his most constant companion, knew that in fact he was thinking, 'I find her so beguiling I know not what I shall do.'

As the carriage drove away, I was left with an emptiness that pervaded my whole being. I could not imagine our remaining stay at Netherfield to be half as enjoyable as these last days in the society of Miss Elizabeth Bennet.

~~*

For those first few days after the Bennet ladies departed, my master displayed but the barest civility. Miss Bingley made every attempt to engage him in conversation -- even in an animated debate, as she had observed the attention he had bestowed upon Miss Elizabeth when she challenged and argued with him -- but Miss Bingley's attempts were wholly futile. As she grew more and more desperate in her attempt to find a topic -- *any topic* -- to which he would respond, my master grew proportionately less forthcoming.

He was making a concerted effort to rein himself in even more tightly under that rigid control that he had found himself lacking the past week. Little could Miss Elizabeth guess how easily and unexpectedly she wore down his meticulously formed defences during her stay at Netherfield.

Despite his dogged determination, however, it became quite apparent to me by how easily he became distracted; how little he was satisfied with his book, a meal, or even a day spent out hunting that his efforts were to no avail. He could not concentrate and found himself the object of much chiding for his lack of attention when Bingley or one of his sisters addressed him. His day was fraught with aimless meanderings, futile endeavours to distract himself, and impatient rejoinders to his friend and his hosts.

Did I dare hope that he found himself missing Miss Elizabeth just as much as I missed her? Did the expression of bewilderment that frequently permeated his countenance indicate that he was not quite sure how to stifle such a relentless partiality towards her?

One can hope, can they not?

I began to comprehend that whilst he had been convinced that her departure would bring him peace of mind, it seemingly was having the opposite effect. The more effort he exerted attempting to forget her, the more difficult he discovered it to be.

We were all gathered in the sitting room one afternoon a few days later. My master was holding a book in hand but staring aimlessly at the fire flickering in the hearth. Quite unexpectedly, Bingley announced, "I cannot help but wonder how Miss Bennet is faring. I believe I will set out directly for Longbourn and inquire after her!"

He stood up with a noticeable eagerness and was walking toward the door when a voice halted him.

"Bingley, allow me to accompany you."

I believe there were three of us in that room who were quite surprised by this request. Miss Bingley turned with visible astonishment; I glanced up with a great deal of pleasure, and my master, who had uttered those words, collected himself forthwith.

"Allow me... if you will, Bingley, a moment... whilst I tend to something upstairs before we depart."

He excused himself and hurriedly quit the room with me following close behind. As he darted up the stairs, I heard him mutter, "Whatever prompted me to make that offer?"

Entering his chambers, he walked before the mirror and took in a deep breath as he glanced at his reflection. He straightened his coat and suddenly began arguing with the man staring sternly back at him.

"It is no use! I find myself with no other option but to go to Longbourn with Bingley with the hopes of seeing her again! Inferior connections or no... "

He ran both hands through his hair, combing it with his fingers and then stared down at me with a nervous smile.

"You find me at a complete loss to know what has taken hold of me. I find myself most uncharacteristically wavering in my regard for her. Despite every argument against her unsuitability, I find I cannot disregard what great pleasure and delight I find in her company!"

My tail resoundingly thumped against the floor at this quite satisfying, but not surprising, news. He attributed to himself as wavering in his regard, whilst I begged to differ. I wholeheartedly believed that he had remained *constant* in his regard for Miss Elizabeth from the beginning. He merely wavered in his attempts at dissuading himself that his feelings for her were natural and just.

As he returned his attention back to the man in the mirror, he straightened his neck cloth and declared most vigorously, "It appears that there is nothing I can do to relieve my suffering but to go to her. The days have been positively torture for me since her departure! With each passing day, I find myself hoping to walk into a room and find her there. On our walks, I wish to catch sight of her down the lane! I catch a scent that reminds me of her and I turn my head, expecting to see her!"

He looked down at me with a tentative smile slowly breaking out upon his face. "I am resolved to make no attempt to hide my attentions toward her at Longbourn this day so she will be unmistakably confident of my regard, even at the expense of raising her mother's hopes!"

I responded with a most ill-mannered jump, planting my front paws upon his upper legs and putting forth a highly charged wag of my tail. I then jumped down and retrieved the knotted rope that Miss Elizabeth had presented to me, holding it proudly in front of me. He regarded me with a shake of his head. "If only I had the optimism that you had, Reggie."

The men's decision to ride into Meryton and then to Longbourn on their horses prevented me from accompanying them. In my younger days, I would have cared not a whit, but a distance of three miles would have proven far too wearying in my advanced age. My disappointment in not being able to see Miss Elizabeth was lessened with the comprehension that my master was going to her with the intent of making clear his regard for her.

I watched as they rode off together, two men with very different objectives. Mr. Bingley, with his open artlessness, simply hoped to enjoy Miss Bennet's society, with little consideration as to her suitability. I believed that my master's decision to join Bingley was a very good indication that he was listening to the leanings of his heart like his friend rather than the strictures of his familial obligation.

I settled myself in front of the fire in the sitting room, the drawing room, and occasionally the library, depending upon which room Miss Bingley was *not* occupying at the time, for she was in a most disagreeable state, a look of grave suspicion infusing her countenance. It was clear to me that she was not at all pleased by my master's decision to accompany her brother to Longbourn.

With a rapidly beating heart, I made every attempt to sleep, but my thoughts refused to be still as I deliberated what might be happening. Would my master truly be able to display exceptional manners and particular attention to Miss Elizabeth? Would he come away held in a more favourable regard in her eyes or would they somehow find themselves at odds with each other again?

The sound of heavy boots coming in through the back kitchen door alerted me to the return of my master and his friend. Their return was much sooner than I had anticipated and I wondered what may have prompted their call on Longbourn and the Bennets to be reduced to such a short one. Perhaps the Bennets had been away and they had not been able to see them.

I trotted eagerly to join the men as they came in. Bingley's countenance glowed and he cheerfully answered the staff's inquiries about Miss Bennet. His answers gave every indication that he had indeed seen her. He declared that she was completely recovered. As I approached, however, there were two things that became quite apparent to me.

The first was that my master was deeply troubled. This was a silent anger overtaking him that I had not seen in a very long time. His movements were abrupt and harsh. His demeanour was rigid and unresponsive. He was not even wont to acknowledge me! His features were overspread with a reddish hue and his breathing was almost forced. I had a grave suspicion that the morning had not gone well at all! Based on his state of agitation, it would appear likely that it was nothing short of a disaster, and my heart sank. Could he have sunk further in Miss Elizabeth's approbation?

As I tentatively approached him, I passed close to Bingley and it was then that I detected something else. I caught the scent -- albeit a very slight scent -- of Wickham! My fur bristled across my back as I turned with alarm toward my master and recognized the expression of anguish that only Wickham could produce upon his features.

He brusquely excused himself from Bingley and marched directly up the stairs, taking every other step in a hurried and determined manner. I followed behind, concerned for his well-being and wishing to know exactly what had transpired!

Upon coming to his chambers, he stopped abruptly and glanced down at me, finally realizing I was at his side.

His eyes grew dark as he slowly shook his head and spat out, "He is here, Reggie. Wickham is *here!*"

He opened the door and I followed him in, bestowing inadequate tokens of compassion to soothe his fury and rage. I sat at his feet peering up to him, offering up a paw of companionship. My tail wagged only slightly to assure him I understood and was not at all pleased with this news.

He brusquely raked both hands through his hair and paced back and forth in silence, shock and suspicion overtaking his features.

"Why is that detestable leech here?" he spewed out. "Of all places, why must he suddenly appear in Hertfordshire? What is there *here* to lure him away from his debaucheries in London? Did he somehow discover I was here and he has come to harass me?"

He walked over to the window and gazed out, silenced by his own question. His breathing became increasingly laboured as he fisted and unfisted his hands.

"No, I believe he was as surprised as I. He had no previous intelligence that I was in the neighbourhood. But why here? Why now? I readily believed all my dealings with him were history!" He pounded a fisted hand against the frame of the window.

"Of all people to encounter…" His jaw tightened as he kept his gaze fixed to something off in the distance. "And what kind of cruel twist of fate would have me come upon him when he is addressing *her?* Such an unsuspecting and pleasant expression upon her countenance, such delight in her eyes as they exchanged civilities. I am quite certain she esteemed him as a most charming gentleman! Certainly, she has enough sense about her that she will not allow his deceptive charm to have sway over her!"

I listened with wide eyes as I realized he must have encountered Wickham whilst he was engaging Miss Elizabeth in conversation.

His voice grew softer and was laced with regret. "Will he once again come between me and someone…" He was unable to finish and was silent for a moment. I could see the pain in his eyes.

He had difficulty formulating the words; his unsettled behaviour causing him much suffering. "This morning… I vowed to display nothing… but the most polite and attentive manners toward her. I cared for nothing… but to garner Miss Elizabeth's esteem!"

He walked over and sat down upon a rather large chair and rested his head in his hands, shaking his head. "But when I saw Wickham with *her,* I was so filled with rage that I did not -- I *could* not -- extend even the basic civilities toward her."

I approached him and sat at his feet, leaning into him, feeling the crushing weight of what had transpired as if I had experienced it myself.

"So instead of singling Miss Elizabeth out, instead of exhibiting to her that I can be attentive and pleasant, instead of doing all I can to improve in her regard, I behaved in a most impolite and rude manner… quite the opposite of what I had intended."

He looked down at his hands, which were clenched tightly together. "I ignored her, driven by a fierce anger and overpowering compulsion to distance myself from that man. I rode away, leaving Bingley to shower his attentions toward Miss Bennet whilst I neglected to even acknowledge Miss Elizabeth, her sisters, or her new friend."

My fur bristled at these words. How could Miss Elizabeth consider such a worthless man -- such a devious rake -- a friend? Knowing Miss Elizabeth as I did, I heartily believed she would see him for who he truly was! But just as suddenly, my heart sunk, as I realized she had never come to know my master for who he really was. I could only hope that she would see through any sort of deception that Wickham might cloak about himself.

My master's eyes darkened and narrowed. "Wickham tipped his hat at me but I refused to return any salutation. I saw Elizabeth's spark of disdain directed towards me as I rode away, but I could do nothing. Her fine eyes lashed out in contempt at my manners. I wish, even now, that I could divulge the truth to her about him and explain my behaviour, but I cannot. My only hope is that his stay in Hertfordshire will be short and the damage he inflicts here minimal."

I gently pawed at him and he responded with a tousle of my fur. "It appears, Reggie, that my dealings with Wickham will never cease."

~~*

For the next few days the knowledge that Wickham was in the vicinity weighed heavily on my master, and whilst Bingley was filled with joviality as he began making plans for the ball he was about to host at Netherfield, my master became increasingly disturbed. It became apparent even to his good friend.

Bingley commented one evening as the two men gathered in the study, "Darcy! If you are this unsettled because of the ball, you are by no means obligated to attend. You may remain in your chambers if you chuse, however it would mean a great deal to me if you agreed to attend and... if at all possible... make an effort to enjoy yourself!"

My master turned to his friend, commanding a reticent smile to emerge. "It is not the ball, Bingley, that has me so disconcerted and pray, accept my apologies for my behaviour of late."

"Then what is it? I have never seen you in such a state! I have always observed you to remain collected and cordial even in the most bothersome of situations! What, may I ask, has caused you such distress?"

I wondered what my master might say to Bingley. His behaviour of late had been inexcusable if one was not aware of the situation, but I was quite certain he was not willing to divulge Georgiana's involvement with Wickham.

My master appeared to be contemplating what to say. He was torn between being open and honest with his friend and yet would not divulge anything that might hurt his sister's reputation.

At length, he pronounced, "The gentleman in Meryton that was with the officer and the Misses Bennets the other day... Wickham... is a long-time acquaintance of mine."

"He is!" exclaimed Bingley. "I was not aware that you had a previous acquaintance with him."

"We grew up together at Pemberley; his father was my father's steward."

"Go on," Bingley urged, noticing the grimace taking hold of my master's features and realizing there was more.

"We came to be at odds with one another. My father offered him every opportunity to do well in life... promised to provide a living for him... but Wickham proved to be dishonest, most undeserving, and an idle miscreant. I cannot divulge the nature of his transgressions. But, as I was responsible for all dealings after my father's death, Wickham holds me responsible for certain decisions I chose to make as a result of his disrepute. Suffice to say, Wickham may attempt to pass himself off as a gentleman, but he is not a man to be trusted."

"Heavens, Darcy! What are we to do? I understand he is now an officer in Colonel Forster's regiment and I have informed Forster that all the officers are invited to the ball!"

"I doubt that he will come. He has no greater wish to be in my company than

I do to be in his. At least that is what I surmise." He eyed his friend as if wondering what more to tell him. "It was unsettling to me, Bingley, to have encountered him when I least expected or wished it."

That appeared to satisfy Bingley as to my master's demeanour as he continued to press on along with his sister to make all the arrangements for what would be the finest ball ever held in the neighbourhood. She took a great deal of care to ensure that the plans were coming along to her satisfaction, all the while lamenting the lack of society there would be at this ball. Bingley later compounded her complaints when he advised her briefly on some of the details regarding Wickham and she vowed to do all in her power to ensure my master would not have to suffer in his presence.

When the invitation cards were ready to deliver, Bingley and his sisters set out to extend some personal invitations. Even though the Bennets were one of those so privileged, my master was not inclined to accompany his friend and sisters. I believe he was still stinging from his encounter with Wickham and consequently, he decided against it.

Whilst they were out extending the invitations, my master suggested we take a walk about the grounds. I was grateful for the diversion, as I felt in my bones that rain was on its way and would settle in for several days. Before we quitted the house, I ran up to my master's chambers and found my cherished toy.

My master allowed me to lead the way; he was not inclined to go any particular direction. I conveniently led him to the place where Miss Elizabeth and I danced the other day. When we reached the small area along the path, I sat down and dropped the rope, glancing up at him. My master returned to me a knowing smirk as he realized where we were.

"Dare you to boast, little fellow, by bringing me to the very place where you and Elizabeth danced so amiably whilst she was staying at Netherfield? Do you wish, you little braggart, to call attention to the fact that she obliged *you* with a dance yet she has yet to honour *me* with one?"

I yapped in affirmation. "And what would you have me to do about it? She is the one who has refused me!"

I yapped again.

"Oh, I see. You are of the opinion that I ought to ask her for a dance at the ball!"

This time I yapped and wagged my tail fervently.

"Well, I have already made up my mind in the quarter."

I peered up at him eagerly, waiting for him to tell me what he had decided.

"Since seeing her with Wickham, I cannot erase the image from my mind of her ease and friendliness towards him. A great deal of my disquiet these past few days stemmed from the expression she had as she spoke with him, especially as I cannot but compare it with the ensuing look of disdain she flashed at me."

He took a few steps, giving a rock that lay on the path a good kick off into the shrubbery. "I fear that if she persists in this estimation of his character, Wickham will have won yet again -- whether he knows it or not!"

He returned to me and kneeled down, picking up the rope that still lay on the ground. He turned it over and over in his hands, meticulously eyeing it. "I have given this every consideration and I have concluded that all I can do is single her out at the ball, Reggie. If she does not come away certain of my regard, then there is little else I can do. But I am at least determined to ask her for the honour of a dance!"

~~*

From that day until the day of the ball, it rained incessantly as I knew it would, giving us no further opportunity to walk the grounds. I kept a close watch on my master, however, and whilst he still was mistrustful of Wickham's presence, I believed him still to be of the mind to apply for Miss Elizabeth's hand for a dance. He was aware, as was I, that singling her out would be tantamount to publicly declaring his admiration for her to the whole of this Hertfordshire neighbourhood, especially if he were to apply for her hand for a second dance. Now in my opinion, that would certainly be a splendid idea!

Bingley's enthusiasm for his own prospects at the ball was only slightly dampened when he learned he must make a trip to London the very day following the gala event. When inquiring of my master as to whether he wished to accompany him, my master declined, replying he would prefer to remain at Netherfield and await his friend's return. I was grateful and could only surmise that meant he was hoping to further his association with Miss Elizabeth after the ball.

Early on the evening of the ball, my master kept to his chambers. He was noticeably tense and on more than one occasion, he stood before the reflection in the mirror asking his reflection if he was being prudent. He had dressed with an uncharacteristic amount of care and prepared with not a little unease with the hope of being accepted for one simple dance, trusting that Miss Elizabeth's heart might be won in the course of the evening. Straightening his jacket and neckcloth for the hundredth time, he appeared neither completely satisfied with his appearance nor confident of his forthcoming actions.

I, however, was of the opinion that no one could be more handsome than my master, nor could one be on a more exceptional quest.

He must have sensed my growing enthusiasm and eagerness, for he regarded me with a sombre eye.

"Reggie," he began, "securing Miss Elizabeth's regard may have been effortless for you, but it has proven to be much more complicated for me! Never in my life have I had to work so hard to attain something!" He reached down and scratched under my chin. "If I could take you with me and present you to her as a testimonial to my good character, I would!" He took my head in his hands. "But tonight, my friend, you are confined to my chambers. I will not trust you to be let free to roam about this house even with the strictest of instructions, for I know you would have no qualms but to march down there with every intention of seeking out Miss Elizabeth. If you were to do that, Miss Elizabeth would most likely be quite delighted but you would send Miss Bingley and everyone else at her precious ball into pandemonium!"

He stood up and returned to eye his figure in the mirror one last time. "I will send my man in here in a couple of hours to take you out back. But you will remain tethered on your lead and you will behave! Do you understand?"

I let out a whimper, fully disappointed that I would have no opportunity to observe this most gala affair, but acknowledging that I understood. He was not inclined to trust me one bit. I do not believe he even trusted himself. Whilst he was probably correct in his assessment of my predicted behaviour, I was not accustomed to being locked up and was certainly not looking forward to it.

The music began playing and my master and I glanced at each other.

"I must take my leave now, Reggie." He took in a deep breath. "Were it not for Miss Elizabeth, I would have nothing to look forward to this evening. As it is, I will be required to endure much in the course of the evening with the likes of the folk in this country neighbourhood."

As my master stepped out the door, he turned and glanced at me, flashing me that nervous smile and a firm nod of his head, as if he were convincing me, as well as himself, that this evening his plan would be executed to his satisfaction. It was difficult for me to settle down as the sounds from below only prompted me to conjecture when Miss Elizabeth arrived, when he asked for her hand, and when they began dancing. Needless to say, I paced the floor for quite some time in restless anticipation.

~~*

From my perspective, the night lingered on and on. I anxiously awaited the return of my master and yet I knew that if things were going well between him and Miss Elizabeth, I would not wish him to rush back to his chambers and to me. I forced myself to wait patiently and passed the time contemplating the day Miss Elizabeth would be Mistress of Pemberley.

When finally my master returned to his chambers, his entrance startled me. I confess sleep had taken hold of me and now I struggled to awaken. He strode in forcefully, followed by his valet, who proceeded to help him out of his clothes. But he did not speak a word.

Casting a very inquiring and eager eye his way, I made every attempt to determine his state of being. He was exceptionally silent, answering his valet in only one or two word responses. He was tense; I sensed that immediately. My forehead furrowed in concern as I watched him turn to me with an expression of disgust consuming his features.

No! I thought. I deliberated what possibly may have occurred. *Had Wickham appeared? Had Wickham somehow ruined my master's evening and his chances with Miss Elizabeth?*

I had to wait patiently for his valet to finish and to leave us to ourselves.

When his man finally departed, I turned to my master with all the encouragement I could muster under the circumstances. I wagged my tail in as much concern as eagerness as I awaited any enlightenment he might divulge to me as to the details of the evening. His gaze was averted from me, as if he was not inclined to meet my glance. The only words out of his mouth startled my senses and shocked my very being.

"I have certainly been suffering under a foolish misapprehension in my regard for Elizabeth Bennet! Her family displayed themselves with an ill-bred vulgarity such as I have never before been subjected! And Wickham has… has poisoned her against me by some means, with some outright twisting of the truth! I should never have allowed myself to indulge this fanciful yearning for her as she… her family… is far too ill-suited! The only sure way to overcome these powerful feelings that have taken hold of my heart is to take drastic measures. I have no other alternative but to leave Netherfield. I am compelled to return to London, as far away from her as possible, and as promptly as it can be arranged!"

Chapter 15

Upon awakening the next morning, I hoped rather than believed that I would find my master wholly recovered; his ardent regard for Miss Elizabeth returning in such strength as to replace the ill-feelings that had so engulfed him last night. But it was not to be, and throughout the morning I was able to piece together something of what had occurred at the ball from conversation that took place between my master and Miss Bingley.

As my master and I came into the breakfast room that morning, Miss Bingley was the only other person at hand. My master greeted her and asked the servant for a cup of coffee, seating himself at the table.

Without glancing up at her, he asked, "Do you know what time Bingley is departing today for London?"

"I believe as early as possible. But considering how late everyone stayed last night -- *particularly the Bennets* -- I doubt he will be leaving any time soon. Why do you ask?"

"I am not inclined to remain here any longer. I believe I shall accompany him."

Miss Bingley looked at him sharply and quite unexpectedly uttered a commanding, "Mr. Darcy, you cannot leave!"

My master's head jolted toward her in astonishment at her exacting demand. "I beg your pardon, Miss Bingley?"

"Mr. Darcy," she recovered her composure, a smooth smile replacing the panicked countenance, "please accept my apologies for my outburst. I see we are both of like minds; neither am I inclined to remain even one day more! The society here is intolerable! However, what I meant to say was I have something of the utmost import to discuss with you and it can only be done whilst Charles is away. I see no other alternative but to request that you stay here at least one additional day!"

We both turned to her; my master out of curiosity and I with misgivings.

"What is so urgent that I must remain behind, Miss Bingley?"

"We must discuss this Miss Bennet disaster directly! It is imperative that we devise a plan to separate him from her! You must agree with me after what we witnessed last night that he must be made to see the imprudence of this prolonged affection. Naturally, we cannot discuss it whilst he is in our midst, and I am relying on your counsel, for I know he will listen to you. I fear it may prove to be too late if we delay discussion of this until you both return!"

I watched my master slowly lift his coffee cup, gazing deep into the swirling liquid as if it held the answer to the dilemma he faced, and he finally took a sip. Never in my life had I so fervently hoped that he would not acquiesce out of a sense of politeness to something so blatantly unsound!

"Mr. Darcy, you beheld her family last night. Have you ever witnessed such undignified behaviour? And all from members of one family? Certainly you were appalled at the lack of breeding displayed. It would be insupportable for Charles to marry into that family!" She continued in a softer, yet more determined manner, "Please, I beg you to consider remaining back so that we may have time to discuss what we shall do without fear of Charles overhearing!"

My master lifted his eyes to her and was about to reply when Miss Bingley added, "You heard her mother, last night, did you not, Mr. Darcy? Miss Bennet is a dear, sweet girl, but her mother! Is it not quite clear that her sole purpose in promoting a marriage between her eldest and my brother is to elevate their family in society?"

I listened in astonishment as Miss Bingley accused Miss Bennet of something of which she, herself, was guilty in her attempts to garner my master's favour.

Miss Bingley's pleading was halted by the entrance of Bingley himself and she turned in shock towards him, fearful he may have heard her just now. Even with just the few hours of sleep he had, he entered the room in a buoyant manner and with a most jovial greeting. By the expression on his face, it was apparent that he had not overheard his sister's scheming words.

"Good morning, Caroline! Good morning, Darcy! Beautiful day, is it not?"

Miss Bingley's eyes darted to my master as she simply answered, "I suppose it is."

He looked to his friend, who merely took a sip from his cup of coffee.

"I simply hate to quit Netherfield today," he continued, "after such a pleasant evening last night. I do believe everyone enjoyed themselves. I know *I* did."

A smile beamed from his face as Miss Bingley rolled her eyes and looked away. "Yes, Brother, but I believe *some* enjoyed themselves more than *others*!"

"Tell me, Darcy, are you quite sure you do not wish to accompany me to town? I should thoroughly enjoy your company on that tedious journey thither!"

I lifted my head towards him as I anxiously awaited his answer. I believe Miss Bingley was apprehensive, as well. I did not know whether I preferred him more to accompany his friend to town or to remain here! *I* certainly did not wish to leave, hoping for the opportunity to see Miss Elizabeth again, but I knew that if my master chose to stay at Netherfield, it would be for the sole purpose of plotting with Miss Bingley a strategy to separate her brother and Miss Bennet. And in doing so, my master would be sealing his fate concerning Miss Elizabeth, much to my disappointment.

"I thank you for the invitation, but I think not, Bingley. I have pressing business which needs my attention and I know you are anxious to be away. More than likely, when I do quit Netherfield, I will not return for some time. I shall remain on with Mr. and Mrs. Hurst and Miss Bingley until you return."

Bingley accepted the words of his friend good-naturedly and unquestioningly. Miss Bingley, upon hearing his words, resembled nothing so much as a contented cat about to toy with its snared prey before devouring it. A disgruntled groan expressed my opinion on the matter. My master quickly glanced at me, to which I returned his gaze forthrightly before each of us turned away.

Immediately after finishing his breakfast, Bingley set off for London. I, unfortunately, was left to a scheming household and bemoaned my master's willing complicity with Miss Bingley.

As he and Miss Bingley sat with Mr. and Mrs. Hurst in the sitting room, I listened to their plotting and scheming with disbelief as they attributed a most disheartening account of the Bennet family's behaviour at the ball last night.

Miss Bingley's eyes pleaded with my master as did her argument. "Certainly you heard her mother, Mr. Darcy! Such a presumptuous woman! How dare she speak so openly and freely about her expectations for Charles and Jane to become engaged directly? I am quite certain she has the whole of Meryton prepared to offer felicitations."

"Quite imprudent," agreed her sister.

"Now exactly how did Mrs. Bennet phrase it as she was enumerating the many advantages of the match?" Miss Bingley pointedly asked my master. "I believe it was something to the effect, 'It is certain that their marriage will be such a promising thing for my younger daughters, as Jane's marrying so greatly must throw them in the way of other rich men!'

I was quite dismayed at Miss Bingley's accusation, but in looking over to my master and noticing his grimace, I had to concede that he was recollecting Mrs. Bennet's very words.

"And the youngest sister; you observed her, I am sure, displaying such unrestrained manners! Is there a redcoat in Hertfordshire unworthy of her flirtations? I could barely keep my countenance!"

Her eyes locked onto those of my master. "Mr. Darcy, surely you must agree with me that we cannot allow any sort of attachment between Charles and Jane Bennet. He is far too guileless to withstand the arts of a family looking to elevate their status. And if they succeed in their scheme -- what will become of Charles then? Left to care for an ambitious mother-in-law, obliged to entertain soldiers for the sake of flirtatious, ill-bred sisters? It is not sound!"

My master took in a deep breath as he seemed to deliberate on her words carefully. Before he could reply, Miss Bingley offered up one more observation from the previous night that clarified some things for me and appeared to be all that was needed to secure my master's alliance with her.

"It must have come as quite a shock to you, Mr. Darcy, to learn of Miss Elizabeth Bennet's admiration for someone of the likes of Mr. Wickham. I could not understand myself how she had come to be so enamoured of him." Casting a glance at my master and appearing to be pleased at the effect of her words, she continued. "Miss Bennet did not cease to question me all evening of what I knew of his acquaintance with you. Miss Elizabeth related to me how simply charming she found him to be."

Clasping her hands together and looking down at them, she confessed with an air of feigned humility, "Do you know, I tried to warn Miss Elizabeth about him? I thought it was an exceedingly friendly gesture on my part, but she was quite quick to defend her favourite and dismiss my counsel."

His jaw set tightly and his mouth grim, my master stood up and walked to the sideboard, setting down his empty cup. "You are correct, Miss Bingley. What you have said about separating Bingley and Miss Bennet is something upon which I wholeheartedly agree," he said firmly.

At his assertion, my head sunk to the floor between my paws. I felt a sense of hopelessness that there could be nothing now that would improve my master's regard for Miss Elizabeth, as he regrettably appeared to view her family as completely unsuitable. My spirits sunk to a new low as I came to the realization that all hope was lost.

I truly had believed that my master, unlike Miss Bingley, would be willing to overlook status and birth. His selecting me was a prime example of that as well as his deep regard for Miss Elizabeth. Unfortunately, he could not overlook behaviour. His prodigious attention to my training attested to that!

I wondered if he might be more concerned about how an alignment with a family of that nature would reflect back upon himself; however I was also confident that he did not trust people who looked to others solely for elevating status or purses. And of this, he believed Miss Bennet guilty.

My master turned to his co-conspirator. "We must never allow Bingley to ask for Miss Bennet's hand in marriage. Though Miss Bennet is unquestionably pleasing of countenance and manner, in all the times I have had the opportunity to observe her, she displayed no outward regard for Bingley. I believe you may be correct in that she is receiving his attentions to secure a husband of a certain fortune so as to benefit her family and that is solely due to her mother's encouragement. I would be doing a disservice to Bingley to allow him to ask for Miss Bennet's hand in marriage."

He spoke in a deliberate manner, as if he had thought this out thoroughly beforehand. It did not escape my notice that he did not address the subject of Miss Elizabeth nor Wickham, as Miss Bingley had just pressed him.

"Yes, you are so correct, Mr. Darcy," Miss Bingley agreed. "She shows no affection toward him. None at all! I have never beheld any open regard on her part whilst in my brother's company. It is as though she cares nothing for him!" Miss Bingley appeared ready and eager to seize and agree with any argument in support of her objective.

"Mr. Darcy, what can be done about this? Once Charles returns, he will wish to seek out Miss Bennet! You know that is not wise!" Her manner suddenly changed from one who was controlling the discussion to one appealing to my master's astuteness. But it was not to last long.

"That is true," my master answered, "but we cannot prevent him from seeing her."

Miss Bingley looked to her sister and then back to my master. "Perhaps there *is* something we can do."

My master looked over to her. "And what would that be?"

"Might I suggest we all depart tomorrow for London? We shall instruct the servants to close up the house for the rest of the winter; inform them that it is very unlikely that we shall return any time soon."

"This will hardly please Bingley," my master countered.

"He will be displeased for but a short while. You know how easily he falls in and out of love. Once he has been away from Miss Bennet, she will soon be forgotten, as will any attachment for Netherfield."

"Of this you are quite confident?"

She leaned in toward my master and whispered in a most conspiratorial voice, "We shall ensure that he begins to harbour doubts about her. We shall only talk of her indifference toward him, how little she esteems him, and how unsuitable it would be to make an alliance with her because of her family. He listens to *you*, Mr. Darcy. He regards *your* opinion most highly."

I turned away in disgust. I could not believe that just yesterday, he was so inclined to openly acknowledge his regard for Miss Elizabeth. And now *this*!

"I believe it *would* be prudent… *for him*… to be separated from Miss Bennet to discourage any sort of admiration to continue." My master let out a raspy breath. "I heartily concur. We must leave on the morrow! This unsound attachment must be obliterated in its entirety!"

My master spoke with such force and command that I believe he surprised even Miss Bingley. But I knew the weight of his argument was directed chiefly towards himself. He needed to distance himself from Miss Elizabeth and he was going to destroy his good friend's prospect for love and marital felicity, as well as his own, by doing so. I wondered if this indeed was the true measure of a friend.

Yet despite the outcome, I saw a tiny glimmer of hope in all of this. My master had never once dismissed the persons of Miss Bennet or Miss Elizabeth. He may have agreed that the family behaved abominably and that Miss Bennet had never displayed any outward sign of admiration. But he was careful to avoid condemnation of either lady. Perhaps I was exhibiting foolish hope, but I clung tenaciously to the fact that, in truth, he did esteem them, even in the midst of his determination to separate himself and his friend from the Misses Bennets.

The remainder of their talk that morning was spent in a most disheartening discussion on how best to approach Bingley and dissuade him from his attachment. Despite my miniscule bit of hope, it was almost more than I could bear to remain in the same room with them.

When their strategy was finalized, preparations began for the following day's journey and ultimately, the closing up of Netherfield for the winter. I made a grand effort to stay out of everyone's way, in no small part due to my abhorrence of their scheme. My master, although outwardly satisfied with the decision that had been agreed upon, was not completely settled within himself. Whether he was willing to *admit* it to himself or not, I understood his regard for Miss Elizabeth had taken a fervent hold upon him that permeated his whole being.

Whether he *knew* it or not, I believed he would not be able to dismiss the leanings of his heart as easily as he wished. He may make every attempt to command himself to put aside these foolish yearnings, but when it came to matters of the heart, my master was enmeshed in something quite unlike anything he had ever before experienced. And the decision which he had just allowed himself to agree upon, I believed, would inevitably cause him a great amount of distress.

~~*

The next morning, I came downstairs to find Miss Bingley at a desk writing a letter with a very pleased expression upon her face. As she issued orders to the servants, it occurred to me that she may have been planning this for a long time. She knew exactly what needed to be done and she presented the servants with a long list of tasks. When the stablehand came in for his instructions, I came instantly to attention, suddenly recollecting Sadie and wishing to hear how she would fare.

Miss Bingley's concern lay chiefly with putting all the animals for sale at the market. She informed him that it was of no use to keep these creatures as there was little chance that they would be returning.

"And Miss Bingley, what of Sadie? Will you be taking her with you to London? She has proven to be an excellent hunting dog for Mr. Bingley. I shall put her in a crate for you, if you wish."

"Absolutely not! What need would we have of a hunting dog in Town?" She shook her head vehemently. "Take her into the village. Someone will certainly buy her." She emphasized her final directive with a sweep of her hand. "And be sure to get the highest dollar for every one of the animals!"

"Yes, Miss Bingley." The stablehand bowed and turned to leave. My heart pounded as I realized Sadie was going to be left behind. I did not think I could bear yet another heartache.

Once he left the house, she presented the letter she had been writing to another servant. "Once we have quit Netherfield, deliver this letter to Longbourn; but only after we are gone."

I wondered what was contained in the letter, but from the look of delight on Miss Bingley's face as she composed it, I doubted I would be happy with its contents.

I stood up, finding it difficult to even breathe. I could no longer remain in the house. As servants were busily coming in and going out, it was with great ease and determination that I slipped out.

My destination, if you have not already construed, was the stable where Sadie was kept.

To my delight, Sadie greeted me most gregariously. Her tail wagged fervently and she began pawing at the dirt as if she wished to dig out. When her initial excitement at seeing me had waned, she calmed down and eyed me curiously, extending her nose through the slat in the fence.

I touched her nose with mine and as our eyes met, she let out a whine. I am quite confident she sensed there was something troubling me. I closed my eyes briefly, enjoying her unique scent, when she began fervently licking my nose as if to console me. But I could see that she was agitated as a result of my own distressed demeanour.

I lay down alongside the fence, and that accomplished its purpose in calming her. She lay down as well, and stretched her paw through the fence, placing it alongside mine. We were so close, nose to nose, and yet that fence and the prospect of what might happen to her, in my mind, had already separated us. I covered her paw with one of mine and determined that I would do everything to ensure we would remain together.

At length, quite as I expected, I heard my master's voice impatiently calling out my name. It took everything within me to keep my head turned away, refusing to acknowledge him. Sadie let out a whimper and a fearful tremor as he pounded closer, his feet stomping so hard it shook the ground.

"Reggie! Come! We are about to leave!"

Although I could not see him, I felt his presence and knew he was standing over me.

"Reggie, I will not tolerate this any longer. Either you return to the house with me and get yourself up in the carriage or I will…"

I did not allow him to finish. I stood up and took an offensive stance opposite him. I had never barked back at my master in the entirety of my life, but I did that morning. I barked and barked; anger and frustration compelling me to defy every discipline that had ever been instilled in me. I was so zealous that with each bark, my front paws came up off the ground.

Each bark countered every argument he ever waged against Miss Elizabeth's unsuitability and why he was mistaken. Each bark chastised him for his blind obstinacy. And each bark was a proclamation that I would not leave without Sadie.

My master stood in silence, somewhat taken aback by my behaviour. He waited for me to finish. He knew I would, as I became quite weary from all the exertion. When I stopped to gather my breath, we merely eyed each other.

Finally, he spoke. "There are some things, Reggie, that you will never understand. It is best for everyone concerned that we all depart… today! Now, come!"

I looked over at Sadie, who had been observing this all with a cautious posture. Turning back to my master, I gave one more bark and sat down obstinately in front of her.

"Mmm," my master mumbled. "You wish to have Sadie accompany us, am I correct?"

I barked again to concur.

He wiped his hand across his face and then up through his hair. "We cannot take her with us, Reggie. I am sorry. Now, come along."

I growled in response and held my ground.

"Reggie!" He came toward me and the fur bristled across my back.

"May I be of service, Sir?" The stablehand suddenly appeared and walked over to my master. "I heard a dog barking. Was Sadie behaving defiantly?"

My master folded his arms across his chest. "No, it was Reggie. It appears as though he is not inclined to leave Sadie behind."

"They are fond o' each other," the stablehand replied. "She is an amiable dog. Do you wish to take her, Sir?"

"No, no. Reggie has me spoilt with his *usually* impeccable behaviour."

"Ah, but Sadie has improved considerably in *her* discipline, sir. Oftentimes I take her home in the evenings. My young'uns, they enjoy her very much. I've worked quite a bit with her and she now behaves most amiably. She's a good dog, Sir, just like Reggie."

Darcy looked at him. "Why do *you* not keep her?"

"Oh, no, Sir. My wife would not be wanting me to bring her home for good. Truth be told, I could not afford the price Miss Bingley has fixed for her. 'Tis a shame, for she deserves a fine and loving home. You need not worry, Sir, I am sure I can find her one. Such a sweet spirit she has, I am sure some gentleman will be able to see the value of a companion like Sadie."

My master could see that I was going to be unyielding in this. "As it appears that Reggie is determined to remain at Sadie's side, I suppose I shall have to take her myself. I hope you are correct in your assessment of her demeanour. Secure her in a crate and put it on my carriage. I shall arrange for her purchase with a generous amount that should satisfy Miss Bingley."

"Yes, Sir, and I am certain you will be quite satisfied with her. You can see her intelligence and devotion in her eyes. Just look at that sparkle in 'em. You know she would be saying something sharp and witty if only she could talk."

My master looked at him oddly and then looked at me. I let out an assenting bark and looked back at my master with pleading eyes.

My tail began wagging and I gratefully approached my master. He knelt down and wrapped one of his arms about my neck. Ever so softly he said, "It is settled then, Reggie. One of us ought to be contented of heart." He took in a deep breath and looked off into the distance. I knew at that moment he had put aside his strict regulation and allowed his heart to speak. And in the next few months, I would see just how much of a struggle it would be for him to remain under good regulation, for an occasional morsel of remembrance, tenderness of regard, or expression of yearning would inadvertently exhibit itself in my presence.

~~*

My master informed the others that he would ride a good part of the way on his horse, whilst I would ride in the carriage. I felt guilty that Sadie had to be confined to a crate and secured on top, but I knew she would bear up admirably as she was not as accustomed to the same comforts to which I was.

I watched my master mount and give his horse a firm kick. He was off directly in a determined gallop. I knew he wished solitude as he left this place and that the thunderous rhythm of the horse's movements would jar every complacent or amiable thought that might still be lingering for Miss Elizabeth. But I also knew that his heart, deep down inside, was likely to remain unfaltering in its regard for her, and that he would not any time soon be able to cast it aside.

Before I took my place in the carriage, there was one more thing I needed to retrieve. Slipping past the servants and Miss Bingley, who stood watching my master until she could no longer see him, I returned to my master's chambers. In the corner of the room lay my rope, which I had left behind earlier that morning. Quickly snatching it, I was grateful to have this keepsake from Miss Elizabeth in my possession.

The carriage was ready to depart when I came back out. I was grateful that the Hursts' carriage was far from ready and we most likely would not be meeting up with them on our journey to Town. Our driver was anxious to leave and I hopped up inside. I situated myself upon the bench, as I wished to look out the window as we left this place that had so indisputably changed our lives this past month.

As the carriage pulled away, my nose and eyes were fixed out the window, searching the road, the paths, the woods, and the valleys for any scent, any glimpse of Miss Elizabeth. As we were soon far beyond the boundary of the neighbourhood, I conceded defeat and settled down in the seat, quite worn out from my earlier display of animosity. Sleep soon came upon me, induced by the gentle rocking of the carriage.

~~*

At some time in the afternoon, the carriage stopped in a small village where my master was already waiting for us. I was let out and set free to run about. It felt invigorating to walk about after being in the confines of the carriage. Sadie was let out as well; however she was kept on the leash and tethered to a tree.

Sadie ran circles about me, tangling both of us in the leash. On more than one occasion my master or his man had to disengage us from the leather lead wrapped around our legs. Despite my earlier sullenness, I was cheered up greatly just by being in her presence. Although she occasionally behaved with a lack of restraint, she lifted my spirits and made me feel young again. Impeccable manners have their place, make no mistake, but I found her liveliness in attitude of equal merit.

I watched as my master stretched his legs, walking briskly up and down the lane by which the carriage was stopped. He pressed his hands behind him kneading his back as he held himself erect. I knew he must be stiff from the long ride. I wondered whether the ride had accomplished what he had hoped or whether it had merely given him a backache.

After stopping for a cold lunch at the small village, we returned to the carriage. I hopped inside and Sadie was returned to her crate. My master's horse was tethered to the carriage and he climbed in after me.

Upon entering the carriage, I immediately picked up the knotted rope in my mouth, lay down on the seat, and dropped the rope onto my paws, where I let it rest in plain sight. I looked up at my master as he took note of it, but he made no response, save for a tightening of his jaw that revealed to me some direction of his thoughts.

He sat rigidly upon the seat, turning to view the prospect out his window, and I turned away towards mine. It appeared that neither of us wished to look at the other. Whilst I was pleased that he agreed to take responsibility for Sadie, I still felt very strongly that he was making a grave mistake in disallowing his regard for Miss Elizabeth and going along with Miss Bingley's scheme to discourage his friend's attachment to Miss Bennet. I finally lay my head down, although my eyes refused to close. To punctuate my displeasure, an audible and most disturbed moan repeatedly escaped from the depths of me.

It appeared my mournful state finally assailed my master's nerves for he suddenly slammed his book closed, causing me to cautiously lift my head and look up at him.

"See here, Reggie. I am no more inclined to be pleased with the outcome of events the past day than you, but believe me when I say; it is for the best that it has transpired as such."

I noticed that immediately after he had spoken those words, his rigid demeanour loosened somewhat; his posture seemed to slump against the comfortably cushioned seat. He closed his eyes briefly before he continued.

"I know you found Miss Elizabeth to be most pleasant company."

I let out a whine to help refresh his memory.

"So be it. *I* found her to be most pleasant company, as well; pleasant, attractive, inspiring, intelligent…"

He reached over with his other hand and ran it down my back. I responded in kind by stretching out my paw and in a manner displaying our affable bond, I placed it on his leg.

"I have always desired to marry a woman I could love and respect, but wondered if such a woman existed who could look at *me* and see me for who I am and not for my name and fortune." He paused a moment. "It seemed as if I might have finally found such a woman. She did not go out of her way to flatter or please me, was not hesitant to challenge my every word and action, and impudently taunted me at every opportunity."

He leaned his head back against the seat of the carriage and closed his eyes. "It was quite a refreshing change!"

I whined again in sympathy and he continued.

"Despite every argument against her, I quite unwittingly found myself to be very much in love with her."

He turned toward the window, gazing out and continuing to stroke my fur, but just as quickly straightened up and shook himself out of his reverie.

"However, I have exacting obligations to my name and my family, Reggie, and in weighing her suitability as my wife, there are far too many factors that would make her an unbefitting choice."

He turned back to look at me. "It is not as though I am abandoning a woman whose heart became inexorably entwined with mine." He laughed sarcastically. "Well, it may be entwined with mine, but wrapped in shards of censure and scorn rather than cords of love and admiration."

His jaw tightened again. "On the evening of the ball, the impropriety of her family's behaviour as well as her impudence towards me convinced me that I must cease any and all display of regard towards her. Miss Elizabeth may have been in her person everything that was engaging to me, but her family's situation is too intolerable. I confess she garnered my favour, but I had to make the requisite decision that I could not, in deference to my obligations, marry a woman with such inferior connections."

He paused and then turned away from me and towards the window again. "My feelings of esteem toward her became far too powerful. They interfered with all my rational reasoning and I consequently had no choice and resolved to disregard her." He took in a deep breath and huffed it out. "The only way I could reasonably accomplish that was to leave Hertfordshire."

He looked down at me with the sternest expression. "I am sorry, Reggie, but she is to be forgotten."

I laid my head down upon my paws, a great sense of defeat washing over me. I had to face the truth that my master knew that Miss Elizabeth did not hold him in high esteem and he was of the firm conviction she would never meet the requirements needed to become his wife.

~~*

We arrived in London at dusk. As the sun set, a brisk air settled over us. My master pulled out a blanket and tossed it over his legs as we made our way through the streets toward his townhome. The London air, which was rife with a variety of assaulting odours, provoked me to cough several times as I attempted to catch my breath. My master looked down at me and asked if I was faring well. Fortunately, the little episode passed. I only hoped that our stay in town would be brief and that we would set out for Pemberley and its pristine environment without much delay.

When at last we pulled into the wide lane that led to my master's townhome, I was anxious to get out and see how Sadie had fared. The carriage halted and the door abruptly opened. I waited impatiently for my master to gather his things and step out. I could hear the sounds of the carriage being unloaded and wanted to be there to greet Sadie and reassure her.

When I finally was able to jump out, I saw that her crate was still secured on top. Two men came over and carefully lifted it up, bringing it down.

"What shall we do with her, Sir?"

My master looked over at Sadie and then at me, as if he had completely forgotten about her.

"Do not let her out without a tether. Take her to the back and put her in the pen. She probably needs to run off some of her energy and I would not want her to scuttle off with Reggie darting off after her.

He then looked down at me. "If you wish, you may go with them."

I eagerly set off, hoping to make Sadie's transition to our household here go smoothly, so that no party had cause to repine the addition.

The townhome had several pens that had housed dogs throughout the years and whilst I hoped that she would not always have to remain penned up, I knew it would have to suffice for now.

When she was let out, she ran into the pen and around in circles for some time. I stepped in before they closed the gate and dropped my knotted piece of rope. I watched in delight as she picked it up and tossed it into the air and then pounced down upon it. Just watching her made me feel young again and I joined her in a little bit of play until I was quite fatigued and began coughing again.

One of the servants, who had been working nearby, heard my coughing and came over to unlatch the gate for me.

"Sounds like you need to take it easy, Reggie. Now don't you worry about your friend, here. I can see that she is one who will adapt very easily. I am quite sure of it!"

Sadie looked at me curiously. I do not know whether it was due to concern over my coughing or over the strangeness of this place, but she seemed somewhat troubled. I settled myself just outside the pen and watched her for a few moments before going inside the house. Her attention was quickly drawn to an array of toys that had accumulated over the years and were strewn about the pen.

Yes, I believe he was correct. Sadie would adjust easily. I was grateful that my master granted my wish and conceded to bring her back with us, but I was still quite forlorn that he did not make a similar resolve regarding that lively young lady who so enchanted both of us back in Hertfordshire.

Would my master adjust easily? He had resolved to put Miss Elizabeth out of his mind. I knew it would not be any time soon that *I* would be able to forgot her. I wondered how long it would be before my master did.

Chapter 16

After I saw to Sadie's comfort in her new surroundings, I entered the house, finding my master in his study. His steward had wasted little time in securing him to attend to the work that had accumulated over the month that we were away. I curled up in the corner, as he was thoroughly engaged by all the information before him.

When his steward finished and was about to excuse himself, my master gave him two sealed letters. My ears perked up when I heard him mention his sister.

"Please see that this is delivered to Georgiana at Mrs. Annesley's home promptly. It is alerting her to the fact that I am returned to town and wish to see her tomorrow morning, if at all possible."

I was more than pleased and very anxious to see my master's sister once again and wagged my tail in eager anticipation. Then he handed off another letter.

"And see that this one is delivered to the Hursts' townhome. It is for Bingley, explaining my sudden and unexpected presence in town and extending an invitation for him, Miss Bingley, and Mr. and Mrs. Hurst to dinner tomorrow afternoon. Please inform the staff that we will be having these guests."

"Yes, Mr. Darcy. I shall see to it immediately. Is there anything else?"

"No, thank you. You may go."

Whilst I looked forward with great eagerness to seeing Georgiana again, I knew that the invitation to the other party was inevitably going to result in the demise of any hopes Bingley and Miss Bennet had for one another, unless he stood firm. I was doubtful that he would be able to withstand this united front that had been planned to bear witness of the disheartening and discouraging accounts of Miss Bennet's deficient displays of admiration and unsuitable family connections.

For the remainder of the evening, my master immersed himself in work. He spoke not one word to me since I entered his study. But the silence between us only heightened the thought that Miss Elizabeth was first and foremost on both of our minds.

He had resolved to forget about her and he was carrying through on it;

outwardly, at least. I wondered if it gave him pleasure to be under such strict regulation. I doubted that it truly would. With little hope of ever encountering Miss Elizabeth again, all I could do was hope that my master might some time soon come to his senses. At least I had a sense of gratitude in that Sadie had been allowed to join us.

~~*

The next morning I was awakened by the sound of a howling wind. I could sense, just by its sound that a cold, north wind had invaded London. I was grateful for my warm coat of fur and that I was sheltered in the warmth of the house. A wave of regret swept through me as I considered Sadie outside with only the shelter of a small wooden dog house to protect her from the elements. But again, I reminded myself I had been pampered my whole life whilst she most likely had a coat of fur that sufficiently kept her warm.

Once I began moving about in the bed, my master followed suit. He lifted up his head slowly and looked around and then towards me, giving me a faint smile. He swung his legs out from under the warmth of the blankets and reached for the servant's bell, giving it a sharp ring.

Even before the lingering peal of the ring ceased, a servant came in and lit the fire, which sent its warmth throughout the room. My master's valet then entered and proceeded to set out his clothes, informing him that his bath was almost ready. I jumped off the bed and made my way down to the kitchen, where a hearty meal was awaiting me. How wonderful it was to be back where I was indulged and spoiled!

After my master's breakfast, he and his steward sequestered themselves again in the study. I retreated to one of my favourite corners of the house and settled down, quickly falling asleep.

The sound of voices eventually awakened me and looking up, I beheld Georgiana entering the house. I struggled to arouse myself quickly to greet her, but aches and an overall stiffness prevented me from doing so in a timely manner. I felt as though the cold had not only taken hold of London, it had taken hold of me, as well.

I walked as briskly as I could to greet her, maintaining an enthusiastic wag of my tail, and saw her eyes light up when she saw me.

"Reggie! It is so good to see you!"

She reached down and wrapped her arms tightly about my neck. I gave her face a very polite licking, which made her giggle. "I have missed you, my good friend. It is a joy to have you back."

Georgiana stood up and when she inquired after her brother, was told he was in the study with his steward and they would inform him she had arrived. We proceeded to the sitting room to await his beckon.

"Tell me, Reggie," she said as she sat in one of the chairs and leaned over to stroke my head. "Did you enjoy your stay at Netherfield?"

I let out a short bark and wagged my tail in response.

Georgiana smiled and we both turned when we heard the familiar gait of my master approaching the room. She stood up and when he came to the door, he returned her smile and they quickly drew toward each other. They held each other in an embrace that my master did not seem inclined to bring to an end.

Keeping his arms partly about her, he pulled away slightly and regarded her admiringly. "You are grown since I last saw you."

Georgiana laughed. "You always say that, Fitzwilliam, and if you insist on continuing to do so every time we reunite after a separation, I shall have grown so exceedingly tall that I shall be a giant by the time I am old and grey."

Smiling, he took her hand, and walking in, espied a bowl of fruit that had been provided. "Come, let us sit down and visit. Would you care for some fruit, Georgiana?" He escorted her over to the table and they each selected a deep red apple.

My master picked up a linen napkin and began rubbing the apple within its folds, whether to clean it or make it shiny, I know not, but he seemed very intent on his task, turning it over and over in his hand. Georgiana, politeness demanding that she not take a direct bite out of it, as was her brother's intent, handed the piece of fruit over to the servant who was standing nearby, and asked that it be quartered for her.

As my master was about to take a bite, the servant let out a cry. "Mr. Darcy! Stop! I am so sorry, Sir!"

My master abruptly stopped, his mouth wide open as he was about to sink his teeth into the fruit he was holding.

"It has gone bad inside, I fear."

The servant nervously picked up the whole bowl of fruit and went to retrieve the potentially rotten culprit from my master's hands.

"I shall dispose of these directly, Sir. They were purchased just this morning from a shipment that arrived from Spain. They must not have been inspected thoroughly. I am so sorry."

"No harm done, Hannington" my master reassured him. "You might as well throw out the whole lot."

Georgiana looked at her brother and smiled softly. "It looked like such a perfect piece of fruit… at least on the outside. I would have never guessed that it was unsuitable to eat."

My master looked at her oddly for a few seconds and then suddenly jumped up. "Hannington! Bring those apples back, please!"

The servant, who had just stepped out the door, turned around. "Pardon me, Sir?"

"Bring those apples back." He waved his hand as he said, "You may dispose of the one that was cut open, but leave the others."

"But Sir, if the one is spoilt, the others are most likely, as well."

"Yes, I am well aware of that."

The servant gave a slight bow, albeit with a quizzical expression on his face. "As you wish."

Once he left, my master took Georgiana's hand and led her to the small settee, where they sat down. "Tell me, how are you, Georgiana? How is your establishment with Mrs. Annesley?"

Georgiana giggled and I was certain she was as mystified by her brother's odd request as was the servant. "I am quite well, Fitzwilliam, but would you oblige me and tell me exactly what is the meaning of this peculiar request?" She gave her head a slight nod toward the bowl of fruit.

My master shook his head and poked Georgiana's nose with his finger. "It is merely for a material lesson to be used later this afternoon. Nothing that concerns you, my dearest." He appeared to be oddly satisfied with something. "Now, you were about to tell me about Mrs. Annesley."

"It is an excellent arrangement. Mrs. Annesley is firm, yet kind, just as you wished. She is an especially suitable companion for me." A brief lull in the conversation seemed to have an awkward effect on her as she suddenly fixed her eyes upon her hands, nervously rubbing them together. Glancing down at them, she hesitantly inquired how the time had passed with Mr. Bingley at Netherfield.

"It went well." He paused, as if he was going to elaborate, but then did not.

Georgiana lifted her eyes up to her brother and appeared to wish to say something but she averted her eyes from him again. I wondered if there was something that was troubling her.

She hesitantly gave a sidelong glance at him and finally spoke, "Fitzwilliam, I am quite surprised you remained on at Netherfield as long as you did."

"Did you think me there too long?"

"Yes, I confess I did."

"I am sorry. I did write. Did you not receive my letters?"

"Yes, I had merely expected you to return much sooner."

I pondered her apparent struggle to look at her brother and found that she now had turned away to look down at me.

By the narrowing of my master's eyes, it was obvious that he could see that something was disturbing her, as well.

"Tell me, Georgie. What is it that has you troubled?"

As she continued to face in my direction, I could see the all too familiar pained expression take hold of her features. Her breathing became unusually laboured and her fists were clenched so tightly that her knuckles were turning white.

"I thought perhaps… perhaps…" She took a deep breath as she struggled to find the words. After a few moments, she continued, "Is there anything *you* wish to tell me, Brother?"

My master looked inquisitively at her. "Tell you?" He shook his head, trying to understand. "About what?"

"I… it is nothing. You enjoyed your visit with the Bingleys, then?"

"Yes. I am expecting them this afternoon."

"All of them?" Georgiana inquired.

My master seemed perplexed at her query and bringing up his hand to rub his chin, he answered, "Yes. Charles, Miss Bingley and the Hursts have all been invited." He reached out for her hand and cradled it in both of his. "Tell me, Georgiana. What is it?"

She pulled away and stood up, walking towards the window. Taking a deep breath and straightening her shoulders, she began, "Fitzwilliam, pray forgive me if this is none of my business."

Her eyes glistened and she pursed her lips together as she seemed to gather the courage to continue. Very slowly, she said, "I know these things happen and I have been anticipating it for several years now…" She confessed softly, "I suspect that you are now inclined to marry."

My master's eyes widened and he drew back. He paled and appeared unable to say anything.

She looked back up to him, and knowing her brother as well as I do, saw his reaction as a confirmation to her suspicions. She grasped her hands tightly together. "If you have indeed found a lady... found her to be *worthy* of your admiration, as I suspect you did whilst at Netherfield, I will embrace her with every fibre of my being. I will do everything in my power to welcome her into our family. It may be difficult, but I will promise to love her as if she were my very own sister."

My master, who quickly recovered from her words, asked, "Georgiana, pray tell me, of whom are you speaking?"

She looked down, nervously retrieving some letters from her reticule. "Miss Bingley, of course. You are settling on an offer to Miss Bingley this afternoon, are you not?"

He let out a gasping huff and exclaimed, "Miss Bingley? You believe me to have affection for Miss Bingley?"

Georgiana barely nodded. Seeing her brother's incredulity, she returned her focus to her hands on her lap, a stricken expression on her countenance.

"Why… yes. She was clearly quite constantly in your thoughts throughout your correspondence. In one letter, she was mentioned in practically every paragraph. 'Miss Bingley inquires after you… Miss Bingley longs to see you again… Miss Bingley is delighted to hear of your improvement on the harp.' I believed you chose to remain as long as you did at Netherfield and referred to her with such constancy as you did because you had formed a deep attachment to her."

My master walked up behind her and placed his hands on her shoulders. "My feelings for Miss Bingley are as they ever were, Georgiana. You need not fear that I have any plans to marry her."

I noticed the release of pent up anxiety as Georgiana's shoulders slumped and she seemed to let out a long breath that she had been holding whilst awaiting her brother's response.

"So, you did not form an attachment with Miss Bingley whilst you were at Netherfield?"

"No, I most certainly did not."

She turned and fell against her brother. "Pray, forgive me for any disrespect towards Miss Bingley, Fitzwilliam, but I am so *very* pleased to hear that. I believed with all your references to her, you were preparing me to accept her as my sister!"

He let out a bemused chuckle. "No, my dear, I would by no means ever do such a thing to you."

He pulled her closely and I could see the expressions on both of their faces. Georgiana's face was flooded with relief, whilst my master's countenance held no such respite, as he squeezed his eyes closed and tightened his jaw.

"Fitzwilliam?"

"Yes, Georgiana."

"I confess that with each passing year that you do not find a lady worthy of your regard, I fear that you will merely settle for someone suitable in status only and not as a woman suitable to you in essentials."

My master pulled away. "What do you mean, Georgiana?"

"I know your feelings about the ladies of the ton; that many look to a marriage of advantage rather than one based on love and respect. I know that who you marry is solely your decision, but I must be honest and tell you that it sometimes frightens me."

He pulled her chin up so that he could look into her eyes. "What exactly is it that frightens you, Georgiana?"

"Your wife shall be my sister and I would wish, with all my heart, to be able to love her as one."

"You would wish to love my wife as your sister?" He spoke it as if he had never considered this before. My master briefly looked away, and his eyes closed for the briefest moment before he finally turned back to her. "I am quite confident that you would love any woman I marry and that she would love you, in return." He glanced briefly at me and then out the window, as I recognized again that reflective countenance that suggested he was meditating upon Miss Elizabeth.

"But I would wish that you would truly love her as well, Fitzwilliam. Will you marry for love or will you merely marry for duty?"

I observed him as he looked down now, his brow furrowed and jaw clenched as he gazed wistfully at the floor. "I should hope that I will marry for love," he answered without looking up.

"And I am sure I would love anyone you loved, but I must confess…," and now Georgiana looked down. "I confess that it would be extremely difficult to feel a sisterly connection to someone like Miss Bingley."

A knowing smile touched each of their faces.

"Do not fear, Georgiana." Tilting his head and lifting her chin with his fingers, my master reassured her. "Miss Bingley may have designs on me, but she will never be Mrs. Fitzwilliam Darcy."

"Oh, Fitzwilliam, I am confident that there is a woman somewhere whose heart will be inexorably entwined with yours."

My master started at this, as I did, in hearing Georgiana use very much the same words as my master had in the carriage about Miss Elizabeth.

"Fitzwilliam, do you know that I imagine her to be just as I pictured our mother to be?"

My master looked at her oddly. "And exactly how have you pictured our mother?"

"As very handsome and intelligent; someone who made Father laugh and enjoy life. Even though I only knew Father as a man who preferred solitude, I imagined Mother as the one who gently encouraged him to put aside the hundreds of years of Darcy reserve and be the man he truly was deep inside. I saw it come through his quiet demeanour occasionally whilst I was growing up."

A smile lit up her face. "I enjoyed those few times when he allowed himself the liberty to laugh… really laugh and to enjoy life. I pictured our mother as one who touched his life in such a way that he felt truly alive when he was around her. She brought a liveliness to his life that he had never before experienced."

She pulled away from my master and looked at him askance with a shy smile. "Was she anything like that, Fitzwilliam, or is it just fanciful thinking?"

My master swallowed deeply, his eyes narrowing. "She was exactly as you described, Georgiana. Exactly as you described."

Georgiana smiled and my master pulled her close again. How I wished he had spoken to her about Miss Elizabeth or that Georgiana would have pursued her suspicion that he had fallen in love. She seemed content, however, to merely hear he had not formed an attachment with Miss Bingley.

My master and Georgiana had an enjoyable visit, albeit a short one. I was able to coax her to join me outside to make Sadie's acquaintance and I was quite proud that both seemed to enjoy one another's company.

Her visit ended far too quickly for my taste, and soon she was taking her leave to return to Mrs. Annesley. She and my master made arrangements to return to Pemberley for the holiday season. Before leaving, she gave me a fervent hug, which I hoped would linger with me. I anticipated a most unpleasant afternoon amidst company that was coming together for exceedingly distasteful purposes.

~~*

My master had been awaiting the Bingleys' and Hursts' arrival with no little anxiety after receiving a prompt reply accepting his invitation. Determination was clearly written across his face as he resolved to carry through with the formidable scheme he and Miss Bingley devised.

He issued orders to have fresh food and drink set up in the sitting room, but to my surprise, was adamant about not replacing the bowl of tainted fruit. It was apparent that he wished to maintain a rather relaxed atmosphere for his friend whilst being subjected to a verbal assault. However, I could not comprehend how the rotten fruit fit into his hospitality.

At the appointed time, Bingley arrived with his sisters and Mr. Hurst. As much as I objected to this scheme, curiosity prompted me to remain. I lay my head down upon my paws, feigning a posture of indifference whilst, in truth, I was very much attentive to their conversation.

Bingley walked in innocently and greeted his friend heartily and cheerfully. "Goodness, Darcy! Everyone following me into town has certainly taken me by surprise! But do not take me wrong, I am pleased to see you!"

He extended his hand and my master took it in a firm shake. "Thank you, Bingley. It was unfortunate you had already left when it was decided upon that we would all quit Netherfield."

Bingley's eyes were wide with bewilderment. "I truly cannot get over how sudden and unexpected it was. I had no notion you all were inclined to depart."

My master waved for everyone to enter and Miss Bingley swept into the room, taking command of the conversation. "We all began talking about how envious we were of you, Charles, in such superior society and…" she looked over to my master for confirmation, "…the next thing we knew, we were all quite in an uproar about joining you here. There was no other alternative."

Bingley gave his sister and friend a brief smile. "But Netherfield… I had hoped to return in a day or two."

"There is no need to rush back, Charles," his sister began. "We are all of the same mind and wish to enjoy the society here that was lacking in Hertfordshire. It has been far too long, would you not concur, Mr. Darcy?"

I eyed him carefully as he took a deep breath. "Entirely too long."

I apprehended it was now his turn to plant the seed of doubt.

"My cook has laid out refreshments. Shall we enjoy a light tea and some fruit?" He walked over to the bowl of fruit and picked up an apple. "Would you care for an apple, Bingley? They were just purchased this morning, fresh from the ship. They appear to be beautiful specimens, do they not?" He turned with a smile and Bingley nodded. To my astonishment, my master handed him one of the apples and then went to stand in front of him. I wondered why he would knowingly hand his friend the spoiled fruit.

"Bingley, Netherfield was a decent house in the country, but I fear it would not prove to be a wise purchase. I must agree with Miss Bingley that the neighbourhood lacked any sort of excellent society." I was not fooled by the affable tone of my master's voice. I could sense he was laying a foundation to betray Bingley.

"Just what are you saying, Darcy?" he impatiently inquired as he tossed the apple from one hand to the other whilst my master began pacing the floor in front of his friend.

"You say you found your neighbours to be a friendly lot, Bingley. Perhaps that is true, but unfortunately, I found them to be simple country folk. No one of any real great esteem lived in the vicinity. You must begin to think about those with whom you associate, mere amiability cannot be your only standard."

I watched as a flicker of concern crossed Bingley's face. "They were all good people," he protested.

Miss Bingley felt it was her turn to add some fuel to their argument. "They were, Charles. But therein lies the problem. They were merely *good*. They lacked the connections, the breeding, the status to which we are accustomed… to which we are *entitled*."

He turned back to my master. "Darcy, are you of the opinion, then, that I should *not* make an offer to purchase Netherfield?"

"I believe that would be wise."

Bingley suddenly stood up and shook his head violently, and waving his still uneaten apple through the air, cried out, "But what of Miss Bennet? I must go back so I can further our acquaintance!"

My master walked over to him, standing a few inches taller and commanding a presence that was unflinching.

"For what purpose, man?"

"What purpose? She is an angel! She is everything I have longed for! I intend to offer her…"

"Bingley," my master now subdued him by placing both hands firmly on his shoulders and looked at him squarely in the eye. "Certainly you viewed Miss Bennet as nothing more than a delightful distraction."

"Delightful distraction! Good Lord, Darcy! She was much more to me than that!"

"Was she?"

"Of course! Could you not see how taken I was by her?"

"But was she as taken with you?"

Bingley's eyes narrowed as he looked from his friend to his sister and then back to his friend. "Yes, I believe she was."

Miss Bingley stepped forward, and with a cunning, condescending smile said, "She is a very sweet, amiable girl, Charles; the most delightful person of whom I made acquaintance in all of Hertfordshire, but…" She looked beseechingly at my master for assistance.

"But what?"

My master, remaining characteristically restrained, spoke softly, but forcefully, to his friend. "Bingley, it pains me to say this, but she exhibited no outward regard for you. She received your attentions very politely."

"Politely?" Bingley interrupted, his countenance reddening and his whole demeanour shaken. "You are all quite mistaken!"

My master lifted his hand. "Bingley, consider this. You came to Hertfordshire and singled her out. Without taking into consideration her family connections, you deemed her worthy of your undivided esteem. Their home is entailed away with no immediate male heir to claim it. With the pressure from her mother to secure a husband of at least moderate fortune, she had no choice but to accept your attentions."

"No! It is much more than that!" He directed his attention to Louisa and her husband, who had been sitting quietly, observing the machinations of the twosome. "Certainly *you* beheld her admiration for me!"

Louisa raised her eyebrow and shook her head. "No, my dear brother. I honestly have to admit I did not."

In a fit of frustration, Bingley finally took a bite out of the apple as my master watched him closely.

He did not appear to perceive anything unusual and he continued, "You did not make her acquaintance as deeply as I, nor did you apprehend the admiration in her eyes as she spoke, the tenderness of her voice, or the warmth in her smile. She loves me! I am convinced of it! She loves me!"

"Bingley, I am willing to allow that she has a most serene nature, but there is more to consider than merely that and her *angelic* beauty." My master fortified himself with a deep breath and continued. "Her family connections are nothing, their behaviour time and again points toward their ill-breeding. She is continually pressured by her mother to marry a man of fortune, and she challenges every word you say!"

Every eye turned in astonishment to my master at his final point. I knew, of course, that though his words were directed against Bingley's beloved, his thoughts were on a very different Miss Bennet.

"Challenges my every word?" gasped Bingley. "How could you accuse her of such a thing?"

As my master made an attempt to recover, his friend took another bite out of the apple and as the others were looking between themselves at this last outburst, Bingley called out, "Heavens, Darcy! Where did you get this apple? It is completely spoilt on the inside!"

My master, no doubt grateful for the distraction, called for the servant who had been standing outside the door. "Hannington! Remove this bowl of fruit at once! All of it! This is inexcusable!"

Hannington looked penitently and most curiously as my master looked at Bingley, offering an apology. "Please accept my apologies, Bingley. I deeply regret that it occurred."

"Think nothing of it," he replied and sat down, completely spent. Shaking his head, he softly uttered, "You just do not know her. None of you know her as I do."

As Hannington carried out the bowl, my master reached over and plucked another one out. Holding it up to his friend, he asked, "Charles, does *this* apple look fit to be eaten?"

Everyone's attention was riveted to my master, who spoke calmly and deliberately, hoping, I was sure, to convince his friend of the seriousness of his words.

"Yes, of course it does," Bingley answered, somewhat reluctantly.

"On the surface, its edibility actually appears quite promising. The apple is firm and the skin is red and shiny." He leaned in to his friend and asked, "But can you truly evaluate it by merely holding it in your hand or looking it over?"

Bingley did not answer, but huffed and looked away.

He continued. "Miss Bennet may have *appeared* to be everything for which you have ever wished, you may have even considered making her an offer, but was she truly suitable?" Darcy deftly cut the fruit in half, revealing its sorry core. "Like this apple, my friend, it would be a grave error for you to realize your misapprehension after you have plucked her from the bowl. A wretched wife is not so easily disposed of as a piece of spoilt fruit."

"Exactly! A dreadful apple ruins everything," exclaimed Miss Bingley. "Like the apple in the Garden of Eden! Look what trouble was wrought when Adam and Eve bit into that!"

"Quite!" added Mrs. Hurst.

My master rolled his eyes at Miss Bingley's reference and I let out a grumble. I knew the story well as Georgiana's reading lessons were often from the Bible and even *I* knew it was not an apple, but some unspecified fruit that they had been admonished not to eat, but did so anyway. The fruit in Eden was not rotten either.

I felt that this picture my master chose to emphasize his point was greatly flawed in that, unlike the apple, Miss Bennet was *not* rotten on the inside. She was exceptionally superior -- as was her sister -- to most other ladies hoping to be *plucked from the bowl* by some man of great fortune; one lady in particular who was present in this very room!

Think upon that, Bingley! I wished to shout at him. *Do not let them sway you from what you know is right and good! There is nothing whatsoever wrong with the apple you want. It is actually the tree and the orchard from which the apple came that offends them most.*

I was much too distressed and in no humour to stand by and watch as moment by moment Bingley was persuaded to look upon his affection for Miss Bennet as errant and foolish. I recognized, from the change in Bingley's deportment, the instant he altered from challenging his sisters' and good friend's judgment to questioning his own. The stubborn fire in his eyes was displaced by pain and anguish. A look of defeat and resignation swept over his whole being.

Unwilling to be party to this unhappy scheme, I picked myself up and slowly made my way to the door, giving my master one last glaring look and an emphatic bark that appeared to startle everyone in the room. The last thing I heard was my master apologizing for my behaviour, saying something about my recent testiness and blaming it on my advanced years.

When Bingley quit the townhome with his party later that evening, I comprehended that we both felt the dejection to the same degree.

My master sequestered himself immediately thereafter in his library, tense and quite depleted from his foray into duplicity. When I walked in, after leaving him to himself for a good amount of time, he merely looked up at me and in his most convincing tone, uttered, "This was for Bingley's own good, Reggie. One day he will be able to look back and thank me for it."

And whilst he may have persuaded himself that everything he said had been truthful, I knew that deep down inside he felt a crushing sense of treason against his friend; being tantamount in his estimation to disguise, which he utterly and completely abhorred. He may have succeeded in convincing himself and his friend of both ladies' unsuitability and believed it was his duty to separate them, but I was quite convinced that he would eventually come to regret it.

Chapter 17

Before finally returning to Pemberley, my master accompanied Bingley to his club, the theatre, a concert, more than one ball, and other society events. Although this went against his deeply ingrained reserve, it had been agreed upon back at Netherfield as he and Miss Bingley sought how best to keep Bingley otherwise distracted as well as take every opportunity to reinforce their opinion of Miss Bennet upon him. In unguarded moments, I could see that the forced society was taking its toll on my master. The furrows on his brow took permanent residence and little joy could be found in his eyes.

That time in London took its toll on me physically and emotionally as well. Physically, the cold, damp air assaulted my every bone, rendering me stiff and hampering my activities. It was an increasing burden to move around and necessitated my remaining indoors for the majority of the time, much to my disappointment.

It was fortunate that the servants understood my infirm condition and were kind enough to give me reassurances regarding Sadie. She was perfectly content in her new environs and was well looked after. I found it distressing that it took great effort to venture out, as a short visit left me quite fatigued. I also felt as though it took more than the normal effort to merely breathe in the dirty, dank London air and found myself wheezing and occasionally gasping. The whole household expressed concern, but I knew all that was needed was the sweet, fresh country air of Derbyshire and I would be my old self again.

My emotions, however, were not so easily healed. Do not doubt that dogs have feelings. They most certainly do! I assure you I was quite despondent! I -- who have prided myself on my ability to be an excellent companion to my master, who took on the office of bringing liveliness to his burdened life -- felt all the guilt for my master's present unhappiness. And what was worse, I knew a particular person who could bring us both joy, and yet, I was powerless to persuade my master to follow his heart.

My master and I both indulged in a bit of self-pity. I missed the spirit of liveliness that had been a vital part of our lives and I expressed my displeasure with frequent disgruntled moans. My master exhibited his self-pity by throwing himself into various endeavours that normally would try his patience and test his self-control. Some of the activities in which he engaged were done with Bingley and for his friend's benefit, others he did out of obligation to his name and standing in society, and still others he was wont to do -- I suspect -- to convince himself that he was not affected by the loss of Miss Elizabeth's society. But by his very choice to exert himself in society and to the extent that he did, I knew he felt the loss acutely.

I was convinced that we both anticipated returning to Pemberley and the semblance of peace and contentment it promised.

When that happy day arrived when we once again entered the woods surrounding Pemberley, I felt an exuberant sense of vitality course through me. Not since arriving in London had I felt in such good form. The air, although brisk, was fresh and clean and I could breathe with little effort and constraint. Returning to Pemberley appeared to make a difference for my master, as well. An expression of serenity replaced the severe countenance that had been permanently etched across his features for the past month.

"We are home," he said softly.

When we exited the carriage, I immediately felt the energy that had evaded me in London. I eagerly glanced around, hoping to see what became of Sadie, who travelled two days earlier with the servants and some of my master's personal articles. I also hoped that Georgiana had already arrived along with Mrs. Annesley.

I lifted my nose to the air, grateful that I was finally able to breathe something other than the stale, putrid London air. I forthwith detected Sadie's scent, but not Georgiana's. Giving my master a glance and seeing that he was off for the house, I set off to find Sadie. I was exhilarated to have the strength and ability again to be able to wander about freely and hoped to find Sadie to acquaint her with my favourite place in all the world.

I discovered her by the stables, sitting obediently without a restraint and facing away from me, next to one of the stablehands. Upon my approach, I watched as she lifted her nose in the air, pricked up her ears, and then her tail began wagging excitedly as she turned to greet me. She promptly came to me, our noses meeting, and she gave a few exuberant prances to display her delight.

I was proud that she had obviously been behaving in such a mannerly way to be allowed unfenced and off leash. The young stablehand stood up and greeted me.

"Hello, Reggie. I have taken a liking to your new friend. She and I have become excellent companions since she arrived two days ago." He leaned down and patted her on the head as she fixed her admiration-filled eyes upon him. "I hope you don't mind."

On the contrary, I was pleased that she had someone seeing to her and trusting her with a trifle more freedom that she had ever had. She had come a long way since that first day we saw her at Netherfield. I doubted, however, that she would ever become the faithful confidante to my master that I had been over the years.

~~*

It was with great delight that we welcomed Georgiana the very next day. Our return to Pemberley and her arrival seemed to effect a kind of healing in my master. He seemed better reconciled to the lot that had been dealt him -- or that he had dealt himself.

Occasionally there would be that gentle reminder of Miss Elizabeth that would unexpectedly bear down upon us through some word spoken or simple action. It presented itself in many forms.

As Georgiana worked on her needlework, the manner in which my master attended to every meticulous stitch, gave rise to the belief that he was imagining Miss Elizabeth's same actions at Netherfield. Did he picture her joining our quiet family circle, with her ready smile and keen observations? When Georgiana played on the pianoforte, did my master recollect that evening Miss Elizabeth played for us at Netherfield? When we sat quietly in the evenings, did he think of Miss Elizabeth and her spirited conversations? I strongly believed that he not only thought of her, but believed she and Georgiana would have taken great pleasure in each other's society. I was also quite certain that he envisioned her as a most delightful Mistress of Pemberley.

While my master was obliged to take several short trips into London during the winter season, it was decided that I would remain at Pemberley. He deemed it wise for me to remain back, for which I was actually quite grateful. Throughout my life, my preference was to accompany my master wherever he went, but in my advancing years, I was now reasonably content to remain at Pemberley where I was not continually reminded about my age and condition.

There were several occasions when my master departed quite speedily and unexpectedly for London after receiving a letter bearing Miss Bingley's officiously floral scent. He would claim he was obliged to tend to some business there, but I suspected in truth that she had bid him come as a reinforcement to hamper any wavering her brother was inclined to make regarding Miss Bennet. I often wondered whether she was truly in need of my master's assistance or was using her brother as an excuse to throw herself in my master's path.

My master spoke little when he returned from those trips to London and almost appeared a bit more hardened in his demeanour. He was keeping his resolve and maintaining his regulation, and I believe it was taking its toll on him. For I, who knew him so well, could see the sense of loss pulsing under his forbidding countenance. Pemberley had always been his refuge, but now he walked through the halls as if he was searching for something, as if there was something missing, as if someone who belonged here was not. But to my disappointment, he refused to concede to himself that he had the means to attain that joy and fulfilment that was so lacking.

As the days and weeks passed, my master's eyes reflected a resignation more than the loss that I could so easily discern. He appeared to grow less and less affected by those things that unremittingly gave me remembrance of Miss

Elizabeth. Not for the first time, I found myself meditating on the mysteries of the human heart. Dogs possess no artifice, our devotion and loyalty steadfast to those who earn it. How is it, I wondered, that humans can so easily forsake those to whom they are endeared? Either he had put her out of his thoughts and heart, or he became very adept at hiding it from me. Either scenario left me bereft for my master's future happiness.

~~*

An unmerciful cold swept through Pemberley that winter. A thin layer of snow dusted the ground and mounded upon the branches of the trees, painting a pretty picture outside. But inside, although warmed by the fireplaces, another type of coldness had taken hold.

While outwardly my master was excessively attentive to Georgiana, he seemed to be lacking any trace of emotion from within. His smile did not reach the depths of his heart and he rarely gave way to laughter. Frequently I noticed Georgiana look at him inquisitively as if she perceived a change in him, but she never questioned him about it.

As Easter approached, I began hearing talk of Rosings Park. Georgiana, too frightened to contemplate being forced to endure the society of Lady Catherine, prepared to return to London in a week's time with Mrs. Annesley. However much I would miss Georgiana's gentle presence, it was with a great deal of anticipation that we awaited the arrival of my master's cousin, Richard. He was expected any day and while my master did not look too favourably upon their annual visit to their aunt's, he was anxious to see his cousin and spend some time with him.

With great fanfare, my master's cousin Richard arrived one afternoon. Loud and ebullient, he entered the house, passing off his hat and coat and demanding to know where his cousin was hiding.

My master and I were in his study and he lifted his eyes up to the door when he heard his cousin's voice. He looked back and me and announced, "It will only be a matter of seconds before that door will fly open and Fitzwilliam will enter unannounced and demand something to eat!"

My tail thumped enthusiastically as I heard his footsteps approach the door. And as always, the door opened wide and with a beaming smile, Richard asked, "When is dinner?"

My master and I both rose to our feet. The two cousins walked toward one another and extended a hand for an enthusiastic handshake whilst I nudged our guest's other hand, which was dangling down by my nose, to secure his attention. He favoured me with a vigorous tousle of my head.

After the two men's initial greeting and inquiry as to the other's well being, Fitzwilliam again asked about dinner.

"Do they not feed the officers sufficiently, Fitzwilliam?"

"Now you are beginning to sound like our aunt. It has merely been a long day of travel and I am famished! And you had better tell me that Georgiana is still here or I shall have your head!"

"She is, and your timing is impeccable, Richard. Dinner..." he glanced over at the clock perched prominently on the mantel over the hearth, "should be served shortly." He guided his cousin toward the door and told him, "I will wager Georgiana is in the music room. Shall we?" He gave a sweep of his hand to allow his cousin out the door.

The addition of Colonel Richard Fitzwilliam to our party added a certain spiritedness again that had long been dormant at Pemberley. I suspect he was the only person I knew who could tease my master most incessantly and get away with it. He knew precisely how to make Georgiana laugh (usually at her brother's expense) and he was a well-needed and appreciated guest.

Georgiana returned to London two days later with Mrs. Annesley and we prepared to depart for Rosings Park. As was the norm, we spent the night in London at the townhome, which afforded my master the opportunity to briefly tend to some business, and then the following day, made the remaining journey to Kent.

~~*

We spent a rather uneventful night in London and departed early the next morning for Rosings. Our journey thither took longer than anticipated and I found myself exceedingly restless. The muddy roads from the recent rains interminably slowed our progress and I was anxious to get to Rosings merely so I could get out and stretch my cramped legs. My master and his cousin were similarly affected, stretching their torsos one way and then another, rubbing their necks, and reaching out with their arms to loosen their muscles.

The two men passed the time alternately between reading and conversation with each other. Thankfully, we stopped for a brief respite where the men enjoyed a meal and I was allowed to scamper about a bit.

As they returned to the carriage, my master looked across the road and noticed some sort of establishment. He gave a slight chuckle as he announced its name, "The Good Apple."

"Why do you find that humorous, Cousin?" Fitzwilliam asked him.

"Oh," he waved his hand dismissively. "It just brought to mind some spoilt apples we had in town and how I made use of them to convince a friend of a very imprudent decision he was about to make."

"Is that so? This is intriguing, indeed. Pray, continue."

As they settled in the carriage, my master proceeded to tell his cousin about his friend (he politely refrained from mentioning that it was Bingley) who was quite apt to make hasty and unwise decisions. Just hearing him retell the story brought back a great pain that I had not felt in some time.

"So you used a rotten apple to convince him that this marriage into which he wished to enter would be most imprudent?"

My master proudly nodded his head. "A most objectionable match."

"And it worked?"

"Exactly as I hoped it would," he replied with more than a little self-satisfaction.

"You appear quite triumphant in your success, cousin."

"I must admit it was well thought out and carried off quite admirably."

I easily noticed the look of incredulity Fitzwilliam gave my master. I wondered whether he felt in awe of my master's ability at persuasion or perhaps he felt -- as I did -- that he had no right to be interfering with his friend's happiness.

I let out an irritated growl and closed my eyes, hoping to get some sleep.

"It appears, Cousin, that your faithful friend here does not look kindly on your interference," Fitzwilliam laughed. "I am not sure I would appreciate it either, if I were your good friend!"

When at length we entered the park at Rosings, the two men began collecting their belongings in anticipation of exiting the carriage as soon as it came to a halt. As we passed through the lane, however, I heard my master mutter something under his breath and the carriage came to a halt.

I looked up and beheld a tall, stout man bow slightly and then approach the window.

"Good day, Mr. Darcy, Sir." He bowed again. "I consider it an honour, as clergyman of Rosings, to welcome you."

He gave a deeper bow this time, clasping his hands together.

I saw my master and his cousin eye each other quizzically and when he arose, my master introduced his cousin to Mr. Collins.

Aha! I thought to myself. *So this is the man that was so often talked of and ridiculed by Miss Bingley and her sister.* I had never the occasion to make his acquaintance whilst at Netherfield, but had heard a great deal about him; in particular, that he was related to the Bennets, yet another mark held against the family if I believed Miss Bingley.

"It is my pleasure," Mr. Collins continued, "to extend an invitation for you to stop at the parsonage at your leisure. My wife and I and our guests would be most honoured to receive you."

"Thank you for the invitation, Mr. Collins," my master replied very politely. "We shall make every effort."

The man bowed again and as the carriage pulled away, my master uttered, "I had completely forgotten about Mr. Collins."

His cousin returned him a curious glance with a definitively raised eyebrow. "Who is this Mr. Collins and how is it that you are acquainted with him and I am not?"

"Consider yourself fortunate, Richard. He was in Hertfordshire while I was at Netherfield. He is… he is…"

My master stopped and his face paled.

"He is… what?" asked Fitzwilliam.

"He is a relative of a family that lived there. That is all."

While appearing to shrug off the effect this man's sudden and unexpected appearance had on him, my master could not veil from me the sudden harshness of his breathing or the nervous tapping of his fingers. If his thoughts had travelled the same direction as mine, he was now dwelling on Miss Elizabeth and the possibility that he might very likely hear something concerning her from his aunt's very own clergyman.

The carriage stopped and the door was finally opened, allowing me to jump out. Running over to the closest tree, I took care of a very pressing matter before returning to the men who were walking slowly toward the manor. As I was wont to do, I took in the scents around me, identifying those that were familiar to me and curious to find out about those that were not.

Just as I heard the sound of Lady Catherine's garish welcome, I detected the faintest hint of a familiar scent. With tail wagging and nose to the ground, I set off in search of a stronger source.

My master called me to come as they all walked toward the house, but I found it difficult to pry myself away from the aroma that was so compelling.

"Is there some explanation for Reggie's behaviour, Darcy?" his cousin inquired. "He acts as if he is on the trail of some great treasure."

My master may have made some excuse for my behaviour, as he had been prone to do of late, but as I was out of hearing distance, I could not tell you what he said. When I could find no stronger scent in close proximity, I resignedly ambled over to join the others.

I trailed everyone into the home and listened as Lady Cat inquired after the two men. Without waiting for their response, she began telling them news of the neighbourhood. Both men bore it civilly, as this was the norm. They knew that if they let her unburden all her cares and complaints upon them when they first arrived, the rest of their visit would be reasonably tolerable.

"You must know, my dear nephews, that I am prodigiously attentive to everyone's needs and just the other day, I had to insist that the Carltons, on the south side of the park, deal more firmly with their unruly children. It is not to be borne how some parents exert so little control over their own!"

She spoke of another family and their unfortunate predicament as we came into the sitting room. Anne was awaiting us there.

My master and his cousin both dutifully proceeded over to Anne and leant over, giving her a very familial kiss on the cheek, all the while her mother continued her recitation. My master, feigning interest in the prospect from the window, walked over to it and I eagerly rushed over to greet Anne. That scent from earlier, however, unexpectedly washed over me again in a much more pointed manner, completely halting me in my steps. It seemed to infuse one chair in particular, and I gave it a thorough sniffing. The sudden realization of it struck me with a thrilling jolt! Miss Elizabeth! Miss Elizabeth had been here!

And just as I looked over to my master, tail wagging with uncontrollable delight, Lady Cat made mention of the guests that were presently visiting her clergyman and his wife - Mrs. Collins' younger sister and her friend, Miss Elizabeth Bennet.

My master whirled about abruptly, paling at the mention of her name and I saw him reach for the edge of a nearby chair, as if to keep upright. The astonishment he obviously experienced went unnoticed by everyone but Anne and me, as we were the only two facing his direction. As I watched him struggle to gain back his composure, I thought it promising that the mere mention of her name would so easily disquiet him.

Lady Cat hastily went on to another pressing matter, but my master could no longer attend her words. His eyes turned again to the window that faced

Hunsford. Could he have been hoping to catch a glimpse of her? From the expression on his face, I knew he was calling to mind memories of several months past. He tightened one hand into a fist and with the other, straddled his mouth. He did not hear his aunt address him.

"Fitzwilliam! Did you not hear me? Are you quite well? Was the journey particularly difficult?"

"I beg your pardon, Aunt." He cleared his throat and brashly ran his hand through his hair. "I am well, perhaps a little tired, that is all."

"Well, that can be expected after travelling all day."

I watched as she threw her hands together in a most satisfied fashion. I knew this signified that she had concluded her account of the neighbourhood and was about to lavish her praise upon my master. He barely had time to recover from her announcement concerning Miss Elizabeth when she began, "I have so eagerly anticipated this visit, Nephew. I was most disappointed that both of you were forced to depart early last year. I insist that you extend your stay this year."

As my master seemed not inclined to speak, Fitzwilliam set the record straight. "I thank you, Aunt, but I shall only be able to remain for the expected three weeks." Looking intently at my silent master for further confirmation, he added "But I can only speak for myself."

My master's eyes widened. With only the slightest quaver, he stated, "I shall give it some deliberation."

My tail thumped to the ground in delight while Fitzwilliam eyed him with disbelief. My master was at least considering lengthening his stay! For my part, that was highly encouraging, for as decidedly as he had removed Miss Elizabeth from his thoughts these past few months, he could readily have decided to quit the place immediately, knowing she was in the vicinity.

"Now, I know this will prove tedious, but I must insist you both pay your respects at the parsonage. There is no need to stay on long, but you must do it for me." She turned to my master folding her arms firmly in front of her. "Their guests claim a prior acquaintance with you," she said in a most accusing manner.

"Yes, that is correct," he stated succinctly and offered no further information.

"Miss Bennet is certainly an impertinent girl if you ask me. Such decided opinions!" She dismissed her with a wave of her hand. "And Miss Lucas never utters a word! I find little to admire in their guests, but you must pay a visit. It can be deferred, however, until another day."

She turned to Mrs. Jenkinson. "Pray, return Anne to her chambers. This has all been too much exertion for her." Then she turned back to her nephews. "You may freshen up in your chambers now. Dinner is served at six o'clock."

Both men nodded in acquiescence and departed with little delay. I was torn between following Anne or my master. While I greatly wished to see how Anne was faring, I had an even greater wish to ascertain my master's deportment. There was really no other choice. I followed my master.

As we walked up the stairs to my master's chambers, his breathing deepened again and became quite irregular. The servants had brought up his trunk and were in the process of unpacking it when he said, "Pray, allow me some time to myself and you may return at a later time to unpack my things."

"As you wish, Sir."

As soon the servants departed, my master collapsed into a chair, his hands clutched together. "You knew she was here, did you not?"

It was more a statement than a question, but I wagged my tail decidedly and looked up at him with eyes that implored him to take every opportunity to put things right between him and Miss Elizabeth.

Shaking his head, he said, "I never once entertained the notion that she would be here!" He took in a few deep breaths to collect himself.

He looked down at me and turned his head askance. "How can it be that I have done everything these past few months to expel her from my head and heart and now, when I hear she is nearby, she has completely filled every thought in my head and invaded my heart as easily as if I invited her back in?"

I whined and offered him my paw, trying to constrain my excitement and anticipation that Miss Elizabeth's presence here might occasion a more pleasing turn of events.

He dropped his forehead into his hands and his fingers opened and closed repeatedly into a fist, grasping ringlets of hair with each clenching. "I can do this," he said softly. "I can do this."

Slowly he lifted his head. My tail wagged and I came and placed my head upon his knees. He took his hand and stroked the top of my head. "I know I cannot hide anything from you, Reggie." He lowered his head and let out a huff of air. "I can scarcely breathe for contemplating her presence across the lane. How shall I endure seeing her face, beholding her sparkling eyes, and listening to her sweet and bewitching voice?"

He stood up abruptly and walked to the window. "No, Reggie, I fear that I shall not be very attentive company this afternoon and tonight will be another matter all together. Every thought will be on that very first moment when I look upon her countenance again."

My master was absolutely correct. He was quiet in the company of the others. I do not believe that his reticence was noticed, as his cousin bore the responsibility of most of the conversation with his aunt. Whilst Lady Cat did make several attempts to engage my master, he answered her questions politely but did little to elaborate on any of his answers. Dissatisfied with his responses, Lady Cat turned her attention exclusively to Richard. It was only Anne sitting quietly in her frail but perceptive condition, who eyed my master with a knowing apprehension that something was pressing heavily upon him.

That night, as he lay in his bed, he tossed and turned, occasionally bringing himself out of his bed and pacing the floor, or gazing out the window. I wholeheartedly wished that he would get a good night's sleep so as to at least appear presentable on the morrow in the anticipation of a meeting with Miss Elizabeth. But it was not within my power to bring about and it was only in the early hours of the morning that sleep overtook him.

~~*

On the following morning, we were honoured with a visit by Mr. Collins, who came to pay his respects. I must admit he was an odd sort of character, ingratiating and obsequious to Lady Cat, which at times pleased her and at other times seemed rather to annoy her. Mr. Collins also appeared to take great pleasure in the fact that he and my master were previously acquainted; a fact in which Lady Cat for some reason derived no satisfaction.

Of all the parties at Rosings Park, I was most keenly attentive to my master. I wondered whether he would be eager to pay a call to Hunsford or steadfastly avoid it as long as possible. My ponderings were answered almost immediately.

When Collins began to take his leave and extended an offer for my master and his cousin to pay their respects to his wife and guests at Hunsford, my master quite unexpectedly suggested that they accompany him back.

"We shall walk back with you directly, Mr. Collins, if that would be acceptable to you."

Lady Cat's eyes narrowed at her nephew as she must have realized, as I did, that he answered far too swiftly -- at least for her satisfaction. I believed that she was somehow jealous of the fact that he seemed to have acquaintances beyond herself.

But I would not allow Lady Cat's odd behaviour to dispel my excitement. My master was off to see Miss Elizabeth on his own volition! Nothing could have made me happier.

To my great delight, he invited me to accompany them. He adamantly reminded me, however, that I must remain outdoors when they went indoors. As we spanned the distance from the park across the lane to the parsonage, Mr. Collins took short, quick steps, which put him quite a bit ahead of us. His separation from the gentlemen gave Fitzwilliam the opportunity to demand that my master shed some light on these guests we were about to visit.

"So tell me, good cousin. Do I dare hope that I will find these guests a preferable diversion from our aunt?"

Without looking at him, my master answered, "There is every possibility."

"But please reassure me that they will be more intelligent than this Mr. Collins is!"

"There is one in the party that I found... that is... if I recall correctly, she is quite charming and intelligent."

I watched as Fitzwilliam boasted an eager, confident grin and suddenly my master tensed, as if all his eagerness to expedite this first meeting with Miss Elizabeth was now leaving him fraught with anxiety. I began to sense that there was something else as well. He was feeling somewhat envious of his cousin! Could he believe that his cousin, who always exhibited a lively and self-assured demeanour, would prove to be more engaging to Miss Elizabeth than himself?

As we walked along, I looked up at the two men. My master's deportment was rigid whilst his cousin's was easy and relaxed. My master bore a severe expression whilst his cousin exuded ease and amiability. As the two men briskly took the steps up to the house, I sat forlornly at the base. My master turned back and glanced at me. Expecting a victorious smile, I sensed rather a look of apprehension.

I lay down on the gravelled path, feeling a rising sense of doom within me. I knew not whether to risk raising my hopes for a positive meeting between them.

~~*

   As I awaited their return, patiently hoping for an opportunity to see Miss Elizabeth again, I pondered the unexpected change in my master. Unquestionably, I hoped that he would choose not to abide by that vexing resolve he made months ago. But no, in truth I did not suspect that to be the case. I believe he merely wondered how Miss Bennet would receive him, especially after everyone's sudden departure from Netherfield and the fact that Bingley had never returned.

   After very anxiously awaiting their return, I heard the door open and voices coming from inside. I turned my head and there were my master and his cousin, followed by Mr. Collins, two young ladies, and finally, Miss Elizabeth!

   Mr. Collins walked out, vehemently and repeatedly thanking the men for paying their respects so promptly and he made it clear that they all were quite honoured at their particular condescension.

   I took notice of Miss Elizabeth's manner as she walked out with the others. Whilst she did not seem troubled by my master's presence, neither did she appear particularly pleased. I noticed no interaction between the two when they stepped out, however Fitzwilliam readily entered into conversation with her and his comments seemed to elicit from her a friendly smile.

   As I patiently watched them all slowly quit the parsonage, it was all I could do to refrain from rushing up and greeting Miss Elizabeth. Her eye had not yet turned to me, so I finally let out several hearty whines and she looked my way.

   When she saw me, her face lit up with great delight.

   "Reggie!" she exclaimed as she hurried down the steps and leant over to scratch the top of my head. She brought her hand down under my chin and lifted up my head to look up at her. "This is certainly an unexpected surprise!" she said as the others looked on.

   I greeted her with gentle grace and basked in the warmth of her merry eyes as Fitzwilliam came up behind her. "You are acquainted with Reggie?" he asked most curiously.

   "Indeed I am, Colonel Fitzwilliam. He and I are the best of friends."

   "I see," he said, as he looked over at my master, giving him a look that left little mystery as to his message, *It appears as though you knew Miss Bennet more than you let on!*

   Fitzwilliam's pointed glare at my master prompted him to turn away, allowing for neither a confirmation nor a denial of his cousin's silent supposition.

   It was with much regret that we finally took our leave. I lifted up a paw to Miss Elizabeth and she gently wrapped her fingers about it, exclaiming with a smile, "I do hope to see you again soon, Reggie."

   My master took his leave with a formal bow and few words whilst his cousin merrily thanked them for their generous welcome and a most delightful visit.

   As we crossed back over the lane to Rosings Park, Fitzwilliam could not stop speaking about Miss Elizabeth Bennet. "She will be a delightful diversion from our aunt, do you not agree?" He let out what sounded like a very contented chuckle and he continued, "She has certainly caught my fancy, Cousin. Why have I not heard about her before?"

My master did not answer, and as their aunt's great manor came into view, Fitzwilliam stopped and turned to gaze back at the parsonage. "I do believe I shall call on them again tomorrow!"

Chapter 18

The next day Fitzwilliam excused himself late in the afternoon to pay another call at Hunsford. I was greatly disappointed that my master did not choose to accompany him. He declined the invitation his cousin extended to him under the pretence that he had some business to which to attend. As he sequestered himself in his chambers and made every attempt to occupy himself, I indulged in some rather irritating moans to declare my discontent.

I quite frequently espied him merely sitting at his desk, quill in one hand, and chin cradled in the other, looking not at all as if he were attending his business. As his eyes were cast towards the window in the direction of Hunsford, I was most certain I knew where his thoughts lay. It appeared to me on several occasions that he was about to stand up, as he made the slightest movement, but alas, he did not arise.

When Fitzwilliam returned, we were regaled with tales from his visit. He happily professed how much he enjoyed the ladies' company and boasted immodestly how much they appeared to enjoy his. He was particularly delighted that Miss Elizabeth was such an agreeable addition to their party.

My master bore his cousin's enthusiasm with a most stern countenance. He moved not a muscle as his cousin poured forth his praise. But I sensed that underneath his staid exterior was an overwhelming surge of emotion that he could not dismiss.

So much pleasure did Fitzwilliam take in visiting the Parsonage, that he obliged himself with several more visits. Much to my disappointment, my master was still not inclined to accompany him. It was not until Sunday at church that an invitation was extended to the Hunsford party to come to Rosings that evening. I was ecstatic to be able to see Miss Elizabeth again!

Lady Cat's behaviour that evening struck me as quite odd and I thought that she had certainly earned her feline moniker. Incomprehensible as it was to me, she seemed almost annoyed that the guests would be coming; yet paradoxically, I believed it was she that had extended the invitation. When they arrived, she greeted them civilly, but like the inconstant creature of which she put me in mind, it was plain that she was not particularly delighted in their company. She directed most of her conversation to my master who bore it quietly and civilly. And the more she pressed him, the quieter he became.

It was disheartening to me as I studied what was transpiring in this room. Lady Cat was singling out my master while Fitzwilliam was singling out Miss Elizabeth. The Colonel seemed to relish the fact that he had no rival for her notice, taking advantage of his aunt's solicitation of his cousin. Although Lady Cat occasionally drew Fitzwilliam into her conversation, he would return his attentions to Miss Elizabeth as quickly as he could.

As I observed my master's pained expression under his aunt's tedious declarations, I also observed Fitzwilliam's and Miss Elizabeth's seemingly endless and diverting talk of books and music and who knows what else. There appeared to be a real ease and joy in their conversation and with one another that prompted me to drop my head down to my paws in an abnormal aversion to Fitzwilliam's amiability. I could sense my master's desire to engage Miss Elizabeth in conversation -- and I knew he could, as evidenced at Netherfield -- but he was unfortunately not being given the opportunity by his aunt.

At one point, their animated conversation even attracted Lady Cat's attention and she demanded to know of what they were speaking. While his aunt was distracted, my master regarded his cousin -- and his close proximity to Miss Elizabeth -- with displeasure. I could easily comprehend regret on my master's part, as he watched her bestow her sparkling smiles and wit freely toward his cousin and that he could not engage her as easily as he wished.

Miss Elizabeth must have promised to play for Fitzwilliam, for after dinner she obliged him with a song. She sat down at the pianoforte and I watched as Fitzwilliam drew up a chair near her when she began to play. *Now why can not my master be as attentive to her as his cousin? Why must he be so attentive to his aunt and allow his cousin to claim all of Miss Elizabeth's attention?*

I had barely finished pondering my master's peculiar traits -- and his aunt had certainly not ceased her claim on his attention -- when he resolutely stood up and placed himself at the other side of the instrument, facing Miss Elizabeth. I considered it a bold move for him, walking away from his aunt who most likely would take her umbrage loudly and long, and then purposely placing himself in front of Miss Elizabeth. He seemed determined to become a third party to the little tête-à-tête that up until now had remained elusive to him.

With an air of a challenge, Miss Elizabeth confronted my master. "You mean to frighten me, Mr. Darcy, by coming in all this state to hear me? But I will not be alarmed though your sister does play so well. There is a stubbornness about me that never can bear to be frightened at the will of others. My courage always rises with every attempt to intimidate me."

Ahhh! I thought to myself! *That is the Miss Elizabeth I remember!* I anxiously turned to him to hear his reply.

My master's demeanour softened as he spoke, "I shall not say that you are mistaken, because you could not really believe me to entertain any design of alarming you; and I have had the pleasure of your acquaintance long enough to know that you find great enjoyment in occasionally professing opinions which in fact are not your own."

Yes! He was making progress! *Tell her what your designs truly are! Tell her how much of a pleasure her acquaintance truly has given you!*

A light banter passed between them; I dare say it could have been considered flirtatious. She blithely exposed to his cousin his rude behaviour at the ball where they first met for his only dancing four dances when gentlemen were scarce. He struggled for the right words to answer her challenge as he told her of not being acquainted with the ladies in the room and his difficulty in conversing with strangers. He was exhibiting the same vulnerability as he had the evening at Netherfield. I hoped that she would appreciate just how much of a compliment he was paying her in being so forthright.

Allowing a smile to soften his features, he ended with, "We neither of us perform to strangers."

At that, after a long gaze between the two, Lady Cat interrupted, demanding to know of what they were so intently speaking. I looked back and forth between the two, my heart beating wildly as I recognized the effort my master was now making in paying particular regard towards her.

Later that evening, after the house was quiet, I sensed a new tenor in both my master's attitude and the direction upon which he was embarking. And I was quite pleased.

~~*

The next morning my master awoke and rose before the first rays of light formed to announce the dawning of the sun. He seemed to have no other agenda for the day but to pay a visit to Hunsford. And he was determined to do it without his cousin joining him.

It was later in that morning when we walked into the woods a bit -- perhaps to persuade any inhabitant of Rosings against our actual destination -- but then retraced our steps to walk across the lane to the Parsonage. As we approached, his gait became more hurried. At the base of the steps, he combed his fingers through his hair, straightened his coat, and inquired of me, "Am I presentable, Reggie?"

I barked affirmatively, believing that the alteration in his resolve was having a most striking effect on his person. Even to my canine perception, he was decidedly more handsome when he was listening to his heart.

He took the stairs up to the Parsonage in a light, confident manner as I remained below. It is my lot in life to comprehend that not everyone would receive the visit of a dog kindly, even one as well-mannered as myself. I had no fear of Miss Elizabeth, but I did have my doubts about her cousin, Reverend Collins. So I wagged my tail encouragingly as my master took the bell at the door, giving it a few sharp tugs and then turned to look back at me, a cautious smile dawning upon his countenance. The door was opened and he was let in. I stayed back, content to find diversion in observing Mrs. Collins' chickens, and hoped that his visit would be a favourable one.

That he did not return immediately I felt was encouraging. But an even better indication to me of his success with Miss Elizabeth was the surprising arrival of Mrs. Collins and her sister. I suddenly realized that he must have been visiting exclusively with Miss Elizabeth all this time. Oh! How I hoped that he made the most of this opportunity to secure her regard!

It was shortly after they walked in that my master returned. A rather amusingly triumphant grin told me everything, but I was eager to hear it from his own mouth. As we returned to Rosings, I continually nudged his swaying hand with my nose to garner his attention.

"Well, if you insist, Reggie, I will tell you. I was quite pleasantly surprised to discover Miss Bennet to be the only one at home." He took in a deep breath and let it out in a most satisfying sigh, staring out off into the distance with a faraway look in his eye. "While I recognize that it may not have been the most proper thing to do -- remaining with her as I did -- I do believe it will indicate to her my partiality and a purposeful singling her out on my part." He nodded his head. "Yes, Reggie, it went very well."

When we returned to Rosings, my master kept the particulars of his visit to himself -- unlike his cousin, who always insisted on enlightening us with every detail. In fact, my master spoke nothing of his visit, nor did he rise to the bait of his cousin's taunts. But for the following week, a day did not pass that one of the men, oftentimes both, did not visit the Parsonage.

And whilst I was grateful for my master's willingness to place himself in Miss Elizabeth's society, I began to doubt whether it was accomplishing what he -- what *I* -- wished. In the evenings, as we gathered at Rosings, Fitzwilliam's teasing led me to believe that all was not as rosy as my master characterized his time with Miss Elizabeth to be.

"I certainly find pleasure in their society," Fitzwilliam offered one evening before Lady Cat had come down for dinner. "Miss Elizabeth is intelligent and lively." He leaned over and whispered, with a knowing smile to his cousin so that Anne did not hear, "and most pleasing to the eyes, is she not?"

Fitzwilliam stood up and began to walk about the room. "Do you know, Anne," he said with a teasing glint in his eye. "I know not what to do with my cousin. He insists on sitting quietly throughout the visit, contributing very little." He looked upon my master with a friendly rivalry. "Unfortunately, he leaves it to me to exhibit evidence of my intelligence to the young ladies and he speaks only when he deems it prudent. So they are left with the impression that they are with a fool and a mute!" He let out a hearty laugh while Anne merely smiled and then looked down at her hands in her lap. Fitzwilliam pointed his finger at his cousin.

"And how often do I catch you sitting with such an absentminded gaze? I truly believe you to be quite bored in their company, though Lord knows, their addition has been most delightful to the society here. I wonder that you even choose to accompany me!"

My master bore his cousin's mocking words as he always did, silently and without retort. But I sensed he was feeling the effects of it more acutely. And while I did not believe Fitzwilliam suspected my master's true feelings for Miss Elizabeth, I watched as Anne gravely observed my master's demeanour and wondered if she noticed any difference in it.

~~*

Over the course of the next week, the Collins party was invited to Rosings several more times. It was after observing my master's conduct during these visits that I deemed it imperative for me to take things into my own paws, if you will. For my master seemed perfectly content, to -- as Fitzwilliam so aptly described it on one occasion -- 'sit as if he were merely a bump on a log.'

Perhaps, accustomed to the overt advances of Miss Bingley and the ladies of the ton, my master was of the opinion that his mere presence in Miss Elizabeth's society should be sufficient to indicate his singling her out. I knew, however, that Miss Elizabeth was not like those ladies who judged a man's worth by the size of his estate. Though I knew my master possessed the most admirable of qualities -- ones that Miss Elizabeth would certainly admire -- he did little to offer them for her approval. I knew -- as his most true and loyal companion -- that the office fell to me.

My master maintained a regular habit of rising early and walking about the grounds whenever he was in the country and the weather was obliging. I had occasionally picked up Miss Elizabeth's scent in certain areas of the park and knew she walked there as well, although the opportunity to meet her had never manifested itself. One morning, I caught a whiff of her scent as we were returning to Rosings and I was quite certain she had just set out.

I surmised that she rambled through the park a little later than my master each morning and pondered how I might delay my master on his walk so that the two might find themselves out in the park at the same time.

The next morning, he arose and we proceeded downstairs as usual, for his first cup of coffee. He normally did not take the time to sit, but walked about the room sipping from his cup. Inspiration came in the form of an idea that would probably put me in -- if you will pardon the expression -- *the doghouse*, but I knew not of any other way to postpone his walk the few minutes necessary.

As he walked past me, I suddenly jumped up, placing my front paws firmly upon him, causing him to spill his coffee on his waistcoat.

"Reggie!" he exclaimed. "What did you do that for? You know better!"

He quickly took a napkin and wiped off the excess of the spill, scrutinizing me with such an expression of disbelief that I think he knew not what to say.

Exasperated, he called for his man and the two returned to his chambers to change his clothes; my master muttering under his breath, suggesting that my advancing age may be altering my demeanour for the worse. It did not take much time to change his garment, but I hoped that it was long enough.

When he came down, he looked at me in a most disappointed manner. "I know not what got into you back then, Reggie, but that was the most reprehensible thing you have ever done! Had you done that in the presence of Aunt Catherine, she would banish you to the stables forthwith."

We walked outdoors and I lifted my nose into the air, hoping to catch that wafting scent that would prove to be a certain lady walking about the grounds. My master began to set off in one direction and just as he did, I caught her scent coming from the opposite direction.

Letting out an eager bark, I set off in that direction, not even turning to see if my master would follow. At length I heard his footsteps behind me and another irritated, "Reggie, if you continue to behave in this most disagreeable…"

He stopped abruptly. Suddenly he espied her, walking briskly just across a field from us. Without awaiting his command, and somehow knowing he would follow -- and forgive me -- I set off in her direction.

As I approached her, she seemed wholly enjoying herself. She paused to pick a newly blossoming flower and held it up to her nose to breathe in its scent. She ran her fingers along the branch of a tree, her fingers caressing its new leaves.

She turned away from us to proceed down a shelter of trees, so I let out a few barks to attract her notice. She halted her steps and turned toward us, a smile appearing upon seeing me, but quickly disappearing when she noticed my master not far behind.

"Good morning, Miss Bennet," my master greeted her.

"Good morning, Mr. Darcy." She leant over, placing her hands upon her knees. "And how are *you* this morning, Master Reggie?"

I barked in response and after an awkward pause, my master asked, "Would you be so kind as to join Reggie and me on our tour of the park?"

Miss Elizabeth did not appear to readily accept his invitation, however, with a little apparent discomfit, she politely agreed and the two continued their walk. I was exultant that they were in each other's company, but my high spirits were soon dampened as I realized that rather than engaging in lively conversation and spirited banter, they spent a good deal of their time in silence. Walking opposite my master, I nudged him a couple times with my nose, hoping to encourage conversation, but he appeared perfectly content to walk quietly. Repose and contentment exuded from his person; and from her I sensed an uneasiness and puzzlement that was no doubt due to his silence. My master seemed not inclined to engage her in any sort of dialogue. He continued to stroll with a satisfied expression on his countenance.

At length, Miss Elizabeth remarked that this part of the park was her favourite in which to walk; that she preferred it to anywhere else. I despondently interpreted her manner in informing my master of this as something other than an invitation to join her in the future. But regardless of her intent for divulging this information, my master appeared very pleased.

We turned back towards the Parsonage and it was soon within our sight. As the arrival there would bring an end to the walk, it appeared that my master was finally interested in conversing.

"Are you enjoying your stay with your cousin, Miss Bennet?"

She looked up at him oddly, answering a simple and direct, "Yes, Mr. Darcy, I am."

"Good. And you enjoy taking solitary walks about the park?"

She laughed and looked at him pointedly. "Yes, when I have the chance."

We arrived back at Hunsford and he released her at the gate to the Parsonage. "Good day, Miss Bennet. It has been a pleasure."

"Good day, Mr. Darcy. Good day, Reggie."

As we walked back, his gait was lively and confident. I was of two minds whether he was actually securing her regard. While I prided myself on my knowledge of my master and knew very well that this was his manner of exhibiting particular esteem, I also comprehended that Miss Elizabeth was completely oblivious to his true intent.

By design, we happened upon Miss Elizabeth the following two mornings. Her countenance reflected her increasing surprise that these 'chance' meetings occurred. She always greeted me in her warm, cheerful manner, but her greetings to my master could only be construed as awkward, as if she believed each time he had not anticipated encountering her.

He spoke rarely, asking but a few questions that seemed to puzzle her.

"Do you believe your cousin and Mrs. Collins to have found happiness in their marriage?"

"They have what I would consider an acceptable arrangement to the satisfaction of both."

"What think you of Rosings?"

"It is a grand estate. Your aunt has done much to make it suit her admirably, but I cannot answer for all of it as I am only familiar with a few rooms."

"But you will come to be familiar with all of Rosings when you return to Kent. It will take merely a few times dwelling there to come to know it well."

I suspected my master was hinting that she would return next year as his wife -- the boldest declaration he had made as yet, but as I gazed up, an appearance of complete bewilderment -- and no little distress -- swept across Miss Elizabeth's features. While I eagerly wagged my tail at his rather pointed statement, I sadly believed she did not understand his meaning.

We were too soon at the gates to the Parsonage and they bid each other farewell, each going their separate ways -- and each feeling very differently about the time the two had spent together.

When we returned to Rosings, we found Lady Cat to be highly distraught. Fitzwilliam cast a plea for help to my master by the look in his eyes. She was stalking back and forth across the room. It never failed that at least once during our yearly visits something would happen that would raise Lady Cat's hackles and thrust her into a tirade.

"Nephew, where have you been? This is most vexing, indeed!"

I must admit that I cowered a bit as her angry gaze was directed towards him.

"Out walking. What seems to be the problem?"

"This is not to be borne! Mr. Collins paid a call this morning... oh, I just cannot bear the thought of it! So imprudent!" She began pacing again and clasped one hand over her heart. In an angry tone, she hissed, "I shall not live to see this union realized. My heart shall fail me before it ever comes to pass."

My master paled, but Fitzwilliam appeared untouched by his aunt's demonstrative ranting, even casting a surreptitious smile in my master's direction.

"Exactly what has happened?" While my master appeared to remain calm, I knew he was apprehensive about what was to come.

"Mr. Collins... he came over right away! He brought intelligence of the most alarming nature!"

My master looked with apprehension at Fitzwilliam, who merely shook his head resignedly.

"What intelligence was that?" asked my master.

Why, Lord Lansing's son has made a most insupportable offer of marriage! He has asked for the hand of a commoner! He applied to Mr. Collins just this morning about performing the marriage ceremony!"

My master slowly expelled the breath he had been holding. "And exactly who is Lord Lansing?" he inquired, although I am quite sure he really did not care who he was.

"I know I have mentioned them before! They are a highly esteemed family whose estate is nearby. I am quite certain that young man must have lost the use of his reason! How can he even consider marrying her? Does he not know what he owes his family?"

"And who exactly is the young lady?"

"Anna Middleton. No connections, no family alliance, nothing substantial to recommend her. A nobody. I am quite certain she used her arts to draw him in." She strode to the door and announced that she would be in the library penning a missive to the family expressing her displeasure.

Fitzwilliam whispered to my master as their aunt quit the room. "Far be it for *us* to ever disappoint our aunt in our choice for wife. Can you imagine her wrath?" Then he gave my master a teasing look. "At least *you* do not have to fear her censure, as you are to marry Anne!"

My master shot him a glare that reminded me so much of when he was younger and his cousin would tease him. "You know I will not marry Anne!" he countered in a barely restrained whisper. He stole a glance at Anne, who sat motionless in the chair, a coverlet wrapped securely about her and her eyes closed. She appeared to be asleep, but I had my doubts.

His cousin smiled. "So you frequently remind me! But I see no evidence of any other prospective lady who has garnered your favour!"

My master turned away from his cousin, indignantly straightening his shoulders and expelling a frustrated huff.

Defensively, he replied, "I have much to consider."

"True," his cousin answered with a laugh. "To do justice to the title of Mistress of Pemberley, it would only do to marry a woman of considerable consequence."

My master turned slightly, peering at his cousin out of the corner of his narrowed eyes.

"Of course, it does not help that your standards are so exacting. I should wonder that you know any lady of whom you approve," he spoke teasingly, but unexpectedly, he became serious. "But then, you must also consider Georgiana."

My master turned abruptly. "What of Georgiana?"

"Your wife shall be her sister. I would only hope that you would take into consideration how the two would get on. Georgiana is still quite shy and impressionable." Fitzwilliam stood up and came around to face my master. "Considering the influence any potential Mrs. Darcy will have on your young sister, Darcy, I might prove to be an even greater opponent to your marriage than Lady Catherine if I deem the lady unbefitting. Your wife must love *your* sister as deeply as a sister herself!"

The conversation in which Georgiana had expressed the same hopes crossed my mind and I was quite certain my master was recollecting it as well. He looked down at me and I looked up at him. Such is the nature of our intimacy after all these years. It was apparent that we were both of like minds that Miss Elizabeth would love Georgiana as much as she loves her sister, Jane. Moreover, there was no doubt that Georgiana would love Miss Elizabeth as fiercely.

That evening the party from Hunsford was invited to dine once again at Rosings. Lady Cat had finally calmed down and no further mention was made of Lord Lansing. She apparently had every confidence her missive would be the final word in the matter. But her outburst and Fitzwilliam's strong counsel seemed to have an effect on my master that I could not properly ascertain. He seemed distracted; however it appeared that he continued to allow himself to surreptitiously enjoy Miss Elizabeth's company -- at least, to allow his gaze to rest upon her throughout the evening.

That night, as the Hunsford party was driven home by way of Lady Cat's carriage, I sought out Anne. She was of such a delicate condition during this visit that her frailty demanded that she be secluded in her room at rest for the greater portion of the day. Despite this, she had remained with the party the whole of the evening. I went and sat with her as the guests took their leave.

She gently patted my head and in a knowledgeable but soft voice said, "He is deeply in love with Miss Bennet, is he not, Reggie?" She let out a sigh. "I knew that someday this would happen, but I hoped it would be after…"

She paused, and I felt her hand tremble as it made its way down my back. "I fear for him that…" She was not able to finish as Mrs. Jenkinson returned to the room to take Anne to her chambers. A weak smile touched her lips and she bid me good night.

~~*

My master exhibited his restlessness the whole of the next day. The morning greeted us with a dreary mist and therefore prevented us from meeting Miss Elizabeth on our walk. Lady Cat demanded his diligence and for a good part of the day had occupied him reviewing estate papers with her steward. The late afternoon sunlight was streaming through the windows when Fitzwilliam peered into the study and announced that the weather had cleared sufficiently for him to take his yearly walk about the park.

Lady Cat shooed him off and my master resignedly shrugged his shoulders as he turned his attention back to his aunt and her steward. I was settled down in the corner; the only bright prospect of the day was that Miss Elizabeth would be joining us again later in the afternoon for tea.

At length, we gathered in the music room, anxiously awaiting our guests. Fitzwilliam had returned earlier from his walk with a report that he had encountered Miss Elizabeth and they had a most enjoyable visit. He spoke most animatedly about her and the more he made mention of her, the more on edge my master became.

When the bell rang, all eyes went to the door. The guests were brought in, but three pair of eyes looked beyond the party, as one appeared to be missing.

Fitzwilliam, my master, and I waited anxiously for Miss Elizabeth to appear, but she did not.

"And where is Miss Bennet tonight?" demanded Lady Cat, who at length also noticed her absence.

"I beg your pardon, Lady Catherine," Mr. Collins began as he nervously bowed. "But a headache prevents her from joining us this afternoon and enjoying your most generous hospitality..."

"She has a trifling headache and refuses to come?" Lady Cat inquired with irritation.

Mrs. Collins stepped forward. "She sends her regrets that she is not able to accept your gracious invitation to come tonight for tea. She is truly unwell."

"Well! If that is the case, let us move to the drawing room. There is no reason to remain here if Miss Bennet is not to play!"

We adjourned to the drawing room, which was definitely more comfortable and there was more sitting room. As Miss Elizabeth was absent, I remained alongside Anne, deciding to bestow my attention upon her.

We came upon the drawing room and everyone took a seat quietly, awaiting Lady Cat's introduction of a subject about which to converse. Fitzwilliam made no attempt to hide his disconsolation upon hearing Miss Elizabeth would not be present.

I turned to my master. At least, I *attempted* to turn to my master. I searched to the left and to the right and did not see him. I could not discern but the faintest trace of his scent. *Certainly, he followed us into the room, did he not?*

As I apprehended his disappearance, so did Lady Cat.

"Now where is my nephew? Did anyone see where my nephew has gone?"

Each person looked around and no one seemed to know what happened to him. Except Anne.

"He has gone to her," she said very softly to me. "And I fear the result will not be as he expects."

Chapter 19

At first I thought my ears had played tricks on me, so astounded was I by Anne's declaration. She believed my master to have gone to see Miss Elizabeth but the results would not be what he expected! What could Anne possibly have meant and how could she be so positively certain of the outcome? Quiet, frail Anne, who lived in the shadows of her overbearing mother, undoubtedly comprehended far more than one could imagine. How had she deduced my master's expectations, and more importantly, were they in line with mine?

Fitzwilliam was noticeably distracted and kept looking about for his cousin, expecting him to return at any moment. Lady Cat's displeasure that her favourite nephew had uncharacteristically and without explanation disappeared was expressed in no uncertain terms. The Collinses made every attempt to pacify Lady Cat while young Miss Lucas sat rigidly still, pale, and meek as if any movement might incur Lady Cat's wrath upon her.

Anne sat placidly with her hands resting in her lap as her mother continued her onslaught. At length, Lady Cat turned her attention to informing Mrs. Collins on the proper manner in which to manage her household, and I observed Anne's head tilt off to the side and her eyes closed. I knew now there would be little opportunity to ascertain her meaning as she would soon be taken up to her chambers. When Lady Cat perceived her daughter's sleeping form, she called for Mrs. Jenkinson. As her companion fussed to help her to her feet, Anne furtively opened one eye to catch my notice and whispered, "Come with me."

I obligingly followed them upstairs and Anne asked Mrs. Jenkinson to allow her some time to read, requesting that I would be allowed to remain. At Mrs. Jenkinson's worried look, she assured that she would ring for her when she was ready for bed.

When Mrs. Jenkinson departed the room, Anne looked down at me. She had not been fabricating her fatigue; I could see it and her weakness permanently etched in her features. But I also knew she wished to talk to me.

"I fear that more than one party will be distressed this evening. Did you not observe him tonight when we were informed of Miss Bennet's illness? There was great disappointment in his features, as if he was struggling deep from within." The toll of her efforts to relate this to me was great, for weariness clouded her pale eyes, yet she continued.

"Then I apprehended a sudden look of inspiration. He looked about quickly at everyone but me -- he rarely attends me, you know -- and as he thought everyone was distracted, he quietly removed himself." She looked toward the window and let out a pitiful sigh. "He has gone to make her an offer."

My tail thumped heartily against the floor upon hearing those words and I was sure my eyes showed my great pleasure.

She put a hand down as if to stop me. "No, Reggie. When he returns, he will be gravely distraught." She took in a deep breath, I suspect as much to give her strength as to give her a few moments' pause. Her eyes were like windows into the world, reflecting the tumult from without while sheltering what lay within. "She will not accept him. She is not even mindful of his regard. I have observed the looks she gives my cousin, and I do not believe she thinks well of him." She shook her head and sighed, closing her eyes briefly as I felt myself grow cold. "Miss Bennet is not one to marry solely for advantage; therefore she will not have him."

I did not want to believe her. If indeed he went to her to make her an offer, he must have at least truly believed she returned his esteem, would he not?

But in truth, I knew that Anne was correct, and I let out an agonizing howl. I recognized the only display of his particular regard had been when he sought Miss Bennet out on their walks; yet all the while, she likely believed the meetings had been purely accidental. She wrongly perceived the comfort he felt in walking silently by her side as a sure indication that he truly wished to be anywhere else. And the few disconnected questions he peppered in her direction left her more bewildered than flattered, whilst my master laboured under the misapprehension that they were a sure indication of his fervent interest. All those conversations where she challenged his every word left him with a sense of exhilaration whereas she believed there could not be two more dissimilar people in all the country.

Anne continued in a soft voice, "He always made certain that he never paid me any particular attention that might add encouragement to my mother's assertion that we would wed. When we were quite young, he would look at me and frown or stick out his tongue whenever the subject was broached, but soon thereafter, he learned that was not acceptable behaviour for a Darcy." She let out a weak laugh.

"It was always the most difficult just before he visited. Mother would remind me over and over that my future husband was about to arrive and that I was not to overexert myself. She would enumerate his good qualities and assure me how pleased she would be the day I became his wife." Anne sadly shook her head. "She never once considered that he might not hold as strongly to the promise that my mother and his mother made long ago."

She closed her eyes and I watched as she brought her small hand up to her heart. "Even though I knew there was very little chance of it, I held onto a very small hope that perhaps he would -- someday and somehow -- fall in love with me."

I let out a sympathetic moan. "If he did not," she continued, her voice growing increasingly soft, "I hoped that he would not enter into an engagement until after..." She paused as a single tear trailed down her cheek. "Until after I met someone who held *me* in deep regard." She looked down at me. "I knew it would be easier for me to see him with the lady he would wed if I knew someone else loved me, as well."

She was quiet now and closed her eyes. It had been a great effort, both physically and emotionally, for her to have spoken so deeply. And now we both awaited his return, wondering what his state would be.

~~*

My master returned a short time later, successfully escaping notice by entering through the servants' entrance and going directly to his chambers. Being upstairs, Anne and I heard his thunderous steps coming up the stairs and marching toward his chambers.

Anne looked at me and whispered, "You had best go to him."

I walked slowly down the hall and found the door to his chambers closed. I found it necessary to paw at the door several times before he opened it to me.

Keeping his eyes averted from me, he allowed me entrance, closing the door quietly behind me after I cautiously entered. He spoke not a word as he paced about the room, his hands interlaced together behind his back and his head down. As he walked by me, I could see the anger and anguish drawn upon his features and watched as his chest heaved as if it were a struggle to take each breath. Finally, stopping at a chair, he grasped the back of it and his eyes met mine. "She refused me!" he spat out and said no more, dropping his head down.

I knew not what to do to ease his pain. I felt a terrible weight lay upon me. All this had been *my* fault. *I* had been the one to encourage this match when my master had resolutely decided against it and Miss Bennet had never even considered it.

His head remained downcast and he brusquely ran his fingers through his hair, grasping a handful. My head fell in dejection and sympathy for my poor master, my chin all the way to the floor.

The only sound heard was the constant ticking of the clock on the mantel and an occasional heaving sigh. He finally allowed himself the luxury of collapsing in a chair, although his change in position did nothing to ease his pain or dispel his anger. He stared straight ahead, his eyes glazed over. An occasional pinching of his eyes indicated to me that he was recalling a most painful, unpleasant incident.

A sharp knock at the door startled both of us. My master closed his eyes and steeled himself to answer. He stood up and straightened his coat, taking a moment's pause before calling out, "Come."

In walked Fitzwilliam, who took one glance at my master and seemed taken aback by his cousin's comportment. "Pray, Darcy, what is it? You left without saying a word! You look quite dreadful! Are you unwell?"

At first my master shook his head, but then offered, "Yes, Fitzwilliam. Pray inform our aunt that I have taken ill and express my regret to the others that I was forced to quit the party without informing anyone."

"Shall I ring for the servant to fetch you something? Do you require anything?"

"No, no. I merely need some rest."

"Certainly, Darcy." I watched him scrutinize the slumped form before turning to step out the door. As he took the doorknob in hand, he gave his cousin a sly grin. "If you did not look so poorly, I would have sworn that you fabricated your ailment this evening. With Miss Bennet absent, the conversation tonight is dull, uninspiring, and wholly tedious! She always adds such a spark -- a liveliness to the conversation. I quite often find myself pleasantly surprised by some of the things she says!" With that, he departed the room and closed the door behind him.

"And I find myself surprisingly *distraught* by some of the things she says," he retorted quietly.

Once Fitzwilliam left, my master took to his feet again and paced the room. Despite what he had told his cousin, rest seemed to be the only thing he could not claim. For several hours that night, he tormented himself with the accusations I can only surmise Miss Elizabeth threw his way.

"*I have never desired your good opinion!* " His fist pounded the desk at which he was sitting, startling my senses. "You have no idea, Miss Elizabeth Bennet, how relentlessly that good opinion pursued me! Even when I made every attempt to disregard it!"

He stood up and savagely pulled off his cravat and flung it across the room. "*I had not known you a month before I felt that you were the last man in the world whom I could ever be prevailed on to marry!* " His fists tightened and his face reddened as he recollected her words. "There are many ladies out there, Elizabeth Bennet, who would be flattered by my attention and would readily accept any offer I would choose to make!"

"*Your character was unfolded in the recital from Mr. Wickham!*" He closed his eyes and shook his head painfully. "How has he deceived you, Elizabeth?"

He was silent for a few moments before softly uttering a final accusation.

"*Had you behaved in a more gentleman-like manner!*" He jerked his head to the side and appeared not to have a retort for a few moments. I know not how he behaved in making his offer, but as I had never witnessed anything but gentlemen-like behaviour from him in the past, I could not fathom this accusation was accurate.

His final words were uttered in a desperate whisper. "Why, Elizabeth? *Why*?" He closed his eyes and clasped his mouth with his hand. His body tensed and he extinguished the candle, darkness filling the room much like it had filled his soul.

It was disheartening for me to have seen the anguish and to feel that there was nothing I could do for him.

After long hours of chastising both himself and Miss Elizabeth in turn, he abruptly walked over to his desk, seemingly with purpose. He lit a candle, sat down, and drew out some paper and ink. He stared at it for some time before putting pen to paper. I suspected he was writing a letter to Miss Elizabeth, for there were parts that gave him great pain. He would stop, close his eyes, and shake with rage. He laboured greatly composing this letter and just as the sun was lighting the sky with a new day, he set his seal upon it.

At length, he picked up his letter and looked at me. Comprehending that he was going to seek out Miss Elizabeth, I scrambled to the door of the chambers, wagging my tail eagerly. My master shook his head sadly. "Reggie, you must remain here. This is not an occasion for you to accompany me. It will be difficult enough for me to face Miss Bennet, and she will most likely not be pleased with this encounter. But I must present her with this letter."

I lay my head down upon my paws and let out a moan. "I am sorry," he said. Abruptly he left and the door slammed behind him.

Chapter 20

Two months later

I was grateful our stay in London on our return to Pemberley lasted but a week. More than the dirty London air made our stay insufferable. My master was in such a state of disquiet that his cousin, Fitzwilliam was anxious to move on. After enquiring after my master's distress and receiving no satisfaction in reply, they bid each other a quick farewell.

My master tended to some business, but declined any and all invitations extended to him. He chose not to even notify the Bingleys that he was in town. I suspect that he was in no mood for any sort of social engagement and the only thing he desired was solitude.

It pained me to see my master suffer. Once we returned to Pemberley, he made every attempt to acquire a semblance of regulation again, but even there it seemed to elude him.

On one of our walks, he told me he sent for Georgiana, professing the hope that her presence would be a balm to his fractured soul. He did not think he could tell her what had happened, but at least she might bring some simple joy and pleasure back into his life.

Georgiana arrived shortly thereafter. Though my master greeted her warmly, I could see the flicker of concern behind her loving embrace.

It was clear she could see immediately that my master had undergone a dreadful ordeal. His features were gaunt and drawn and his eyes were dark and weary. Anyone could ascertain that he had suffered through too many ignored meals and sleepless nights. While he attempted to give her his undivided attention, his mind often drifted and it took a great deal of effort for him to respond with any sort of clarity.

I was visiting her in her chambers one morning after breakfast when she confessed to me how disconcerting it was to observe her brother behaving so unaccountably. That evening she played the pianoforte and she looked pointedly at me and then towards her brother across the room with great concern as he did not seem to be receiving any pleasure from her music. In the past, her playing had always been quite soothing to my master regardless of his state of mind, but tonight he remained restless and tense.

When he stood up and quickly quit the room, her stricken countenance made me realize that she felt she was somehow responsible for his troubled temperament.

"I am worried, Reggie. Fitzwilliam is so altered. Nothing pleases him. Could it be that he has not forgotten? It has been just a year since it occurred!" Her eyes glistened with the formation of tears. "Is he still tortured by my error in judgment?"

I walked over and extended my paw to her, wishing I could make her understand that something else prompted his behaviour.

But without the benefit of understanding canine communication, her suspicion persisted, until four days later, whereupon -- unable to bear it any longer -- Georgiana confronted my master.

We were in the music room again, and when my master neglected to compliment her on her playing when she had finished her piece, she stared at him most acutely. She slowly stood up from the instrument and walked over to her brother, placing herself directly in front of her. His eyes took a moment to register her presence.

"That was played very well, Georgiana."

"What did I play?"

"I beg your pardon. What do you mean 'what did I play'?"

"It appears you heard my question, but I cannot claim the same confidence that you heard my music."

He looked down and shook his head. "You are correct, Georgiana. My mind was engaged elsewhere. Pray, forgive me."

She moved to the empty space on the settee next to him and placed her hand upon his. "Tell me, Fitzwilliam, what has happened that has made you so despondent?"

He looked up and made an attempt to smile. "Nothing has happened."

Georgiana shook her head. "No, Fitzwilliam. That will not do." She looked down at her hands as her fingers nervously intertwined one another. "I cannot help but wonder if you still hold me responsible for those events at Ramsgate with Wick..."

My master quickly interrupted her. "Georgiana, no! It is not because of something you have done! Please, dearest, do not think it your fault."

"Then what is the cause of *it*?

Dropping his head back, he peered out of almost closed eyes at his sister. I believed him to be pondering whether he could tell her of Miss Elizabeth. I was of the opinion he should. It was crucial that he unburden himself to someone.

Finally, he whispered, "You were correct, Georgiana. Something indeed has occurred." He took in a deep breath. "When you suspected me of forming a deep attachment for a lady whilst at Netherfield, indeed I had."

Georgiana's mouth dropped open in astonishment. Very meekly, she asked, "Miss Bingley?"

He let out a small bitter laugh. "No, my dear. Someone else."

Georgiana's eyes lit up. "Who is she? Am I acquainted with her?"

He shook his head dolefully. "No. She is someone to whom I was introduced in Hertfordshire. Our acquaintance was furthered when I was last in Kent."

Suddenly making the connection between what he just told her and his despondency of late, a look of concern swept over her. "Oh, Brother, what happened?"

"She did not return my regard. I made her an offer, but she refused me."

My master stood up and walked to the other side of the room and then abruptly turned around. "I do believe you would have enjoyed her company, Georgiana." His measured tone could not hide the quaver in his voice.

The pain which held her brother in its grasp radiated from him, filling the room. She walked over to his side and slipped her hand in his arm. "I am so sorry, Fitzwilliam. What can be done?"

My master looked into the pleading eyes of his sister and I knew he wished to tell her about Miss Elizabeth. He sat quietly upon the settee relating to Georgiana all about Miss Elizabeth and why he found her to be so charming. He told of her deep love for her elder sister, so openly displayed as she cared for her while she was ill; that she was kind and good, with a disarming wit and vivacity that drew him in.

When he had finished, Georgiana wrapped her arms tightly about his arm and rested her head against his shoulder. "I do believe I would have enjoyed making her acquaintance. I am so sorry, Fitzwilliam, but do you not believe that in time she could come to love you?"

Although he had maintained his regulation when giving voice to all Miss Elizabeth's qualities, here my master looked down. "I will not be seeing her again." He buried his head into Georgiana's hair and I suspected that his eyes had grown moist. Without lifting his head, he confessed to her, "She believed me to be proud."

She pulled away sharply, looking at him with wonder. "Proud?" Georgiana vehemently shook her head. "Oh, no! Not you!"

"Oh, yes! She accused me of pride and arrogance." He leaned forward, clasping his hands and resting his elbows on his knees. "It is only now, after months of reflection, that I can reasonably look back at my time in Netherfield and understand her accusation."

"Why, you are the most admirable person of my acquaintance. Of what did she accuse you? Whatever could you have done?"

"It is what I did *not* do. I did not think it necessary for me to acquaint myself with the neighbourhood. I considered them beneath my notice. I even considered her own family beneath me."

"Truly?"

"Yes, and yet to my surprise, despite her connections, despite her familial lack of standing in society, I found myself with such a strength of attachment towards her that I found it impossible to conquer." Very softly, he added, "And I did not wish to conquer it."

Both my master and Georgiana dropped their heads in silence. She obviously did not know what to say to comfort her brother and he was visibly shaken. Suddenly, Georgiana's head lifted as she cried out, "Even with her lack of fortune and all of yours, she refused you?"

"Yes."

Georgiana lowered her head. "I am so sorry, Fitzwilliam."

My master clasped his hands together. "Come, Georgiana. Let us talk of other things. Shall we take some tea?"

"Yes! That sounds delightful!"

Georgiana took his arm tightly again, as if to bolster him up with all the strength she could bestow.

They took the flight of stairs arm in arm and when they reached the bottom, my master suddenly stopped.

"Georgiana, do *you* find me proud?"

Georgiana's eyes widened and she pondered a moment before returning with an answer. "I do not believe that you possess the type of pride that boasts about your fortune and standing in society and seeks to promote your good qualities in others' eyes. On the contrary, you prefer your wealth not be of general knowledge and you accept your standing in society but do not necessarily put it on display."

My master tilted his head. "But that is not the pride of which I was accused."

"No, I think not." Georgiana took a few steps away from my master and then turned back to him.

"Perhaps she mistook your reserve in new situations for an arrogant disdain towards them."

For some reason, my master started at these words. He abruptly walked away from her and stood in front of a window. Looking out, he answered, "I have done much deliberating about my character in these past months and I find myself wanting." He took in a deep breath and let it out all at once. Running his fingers through his hair, his voice grew soft and pensive. "I have realized that I do look down on those I perceive of inferior stations, not necessarily by acts of cruelty or displaying my superiority, but in neglect. I choose to avoid them -- have as little to do with them as *I* deem prudent. My associations with them… well, she was correct."

They exchanged little else on the subject, but I gathered that allowing himself to confide in Georgiana and receiving her words of comfort to him had put his thoughts in a different perspective and that lifted the heavy burden he bore.

~~*

Both my master and Georgiana determined they would return together to London. As his plan was to stay in town for a good length of time, he deemed it prudent that I remain at Pemberley. The stifling heat and choking air in town would not be healthy for me and I could not but agree. So, although regretful that I was eschewing my duties as companion, I stayed behind.

Once they departed, I spent the majority of my time with Sadie, and whilst I could not match her liveliness, I enjoyed her society immensely. She came of age early that summer and I surprised even myself to discover I could engage in rather pleasing duties as aptly as any dog half my age. The groundskeepers spoke among themselves that I gave them hope for their old age.

When I was lonely and missed my master and Georgiana, I would wander through the house, sleeping in my master's chambers, enjoying the scent of him, or I would place myself in front of his portrait in the portrait gallery. I was very fond of that picture, as I had been painted faithfully at his side and he had a smile upon his face. As I gazed upon it, I wondered how long it had been since I had seen that smile. It was a smile of contentment and peace. But it had been painted before Ramsgate. Before Bingley and Miss Bennet at Netherfield. And before Miss Elizabeth at Rosings. I also wondered how long it would be before I would see that smile again.

For the most part, I usually began each morning feeling in relative good spirits, but as the day wore on, sleep beckoned me more and more insistently and I would once again slumber. There was very little that could awaken me no matter where I lay or what time of day it was.

Several weeks into my solitary schedule, something quite astonishing caused me to awaken with a start!

The day had begun as usual. There was talk among the staff that my master would be returning the following day and preparations for his return had begun. I made every attempt to keep out of everyone's way as they scoured and scrubbed to make things spotless, while feeling a sense of anticipation of his return. Finally, I found myself a little corner of a room off the kitchen and settled down for my afternoon nap.

I remember barely apprehending the bell announcing visitors. In my younger years I would have made my way to the door if only to satisfy my curiosity and greet whoever had come. But this afternoon, I barely woke up at the sound.

Vague voices could be heard coming through the house. It was then that I began to stir, stretching out my legs and arching my back. Oh, how good it felt to stretch out those aching muscles!

But suddenly my nose was in the air. A scent permeated throughout the house that was very familiar! Still groggy, I turned my head around, sniffing deeply to ascertain its source. No, I knew it was not my master or Georgiana. It was not Fitzwilliam. But it was someone special… someone… At once, I knew! It was Miss Elizabeth!

I could not scramble to my feet fast enough! With my nose to the ground, I followed the scent trail before me. I scurried through the house, kicking up the carpets as I rounded corners and frightening a servant or two along the way at my sudden burst of energy.

As I came upon them in the gallery, I espied Miss Elizabeth standing in front of a portrait -- *our* portrait -- staring intently at it. Mrs. Reynolds was giving a description of some of the paintings to a couple who were evidently accompanying Miss Elizabeth. I quickly scurried past them and came right up to my friend from Hertfordshire.

Mrs. Reynolds let out a cry of surprise, no doubt at my uncharacteristic exuberance. However, hers was not the reaction that left me quite bewildered. Miss Elizabeth looked most apprehensive upon seeing me.

In a quivering voice she said, "Reggie, I did not expect to find you here." She nervously looked in one direction and then another.

"Oh, you know our Reggie, do you?" Mrs. Reynolds asked of her.

"Yes, I do. We became acquainted last year when Mr. Darcy was visiting Netherfield at Michelmas and then we were able to enjoy each other's society this past spring in Kent."

"As fine a dog as one will find. Just like his master; most polite and loyal." She looked down and smiled at the attention I was bestowing on Miss Elizabeth. "And I can see that he esteems you, as well. I have not seen him this lively outside of the company of his master."

"He… he is not with his master?" Miss Elizabeth asked.

"No, he does not fare well in town anymore. Our master could not say how long he might be in London on this trip, so Reggie remained back."

At Mrs. Reynolds' answer, a look of relief swept across Miss Elizabeth's face. She reached over and patted my head. "It is good to see you, Reggie. I regret I was unable to bid you farewell at Kent."

I watched her take another long look at the portrait of my master, with me sitting faithfully at his side. She looked down at me and smiled. "A very good likeness of you, Reggie." Very softly, she added, "And of Mr. Darcy."

The party continued to walk down the hall, but just before leaving it, I watched as Miss Elizabeth turned back. She went and stood once more in front of the picture and I saw a look in her eyes that was tinged with regret but also appeared to be seeing something for the first time.

I stayed with the party as they were shown a few more rooms. I could not ascertain the reason they were here, but I was quite certain they had not come anticipating my master's presence. I felt all the anxiety of knowing that they would leave this place and the likelihood that he would never know they -- that *she* -- had come.

I did not want to leave Miss Elizabeth's side, and Mrs. Reynolds commented several times on how I seemed to take a real liking to her. The faithful housekeeper escorted the party to the hall door, where the head gardener was waiting and suggested that if they wanted to see the grounds, he would be more than happy to give them a tour.

Unwilling to lose one moment in Miss Elizabeth's company, I cheerfully trotted ahead of the party, wagging my tail in invitation for her to join me. This turn of events clearly had Mrs. Reynolds surprised and she did not fail to let it pass unmentioned. "Miss, you *must* be a special friend, indeed, for Reggie to wish to join you outdoors. The heat does not suit him well."

I looked at Miss Elizabeth, who seemed a trifle embarrassed. But she did meet my glance and smiled wryly at me.

Once outside, Miss Elizabeth and the couple began to walk around. Not attending to the gardener's responses to the couple's queries, Miss Elizabeth walked off by herself across the lawn toward the stream. I enjoyed my amble across the grounds with her; it put me very much in mind of our walks in Hertfordshire and Kent. She seemed to have a great appreciation for the beauty before her and commented several times to me how perfectly situated was the house and how well groomed yet natural were the grounds.

I appreciated how perfectly suited Miss Elizabeth seemed to be here. A look of regret seemed to touch her features as she looked about her in admiration and I wondered if she felt as I did, that this was where she could have been mistress. But mixed with that regret, I also sensed a gentle sensation, and I truly believed her animosity toward my master had dissipated.

I followed her toward the path that would take us through the woods and to the rear of the house when suddenly the very familiar scent of my master began teasing my nose. Was it truly him? I turned my head in the direction of the house, knowing that if he had returned, he would come from behind the stables and head directly into the house from the courtyard, never coming this way at all.

I knew I had to do something!

With a few very excited barks, I set off in his direction, leaving Miss Elizabeth with quite an expression of bewilderment.

As I had discerned, my master had returned. *How fortunate!* When I found my master, he had just relinquished his horse to a stablehand and was walking toward the house. Miss Elizabeth and the rest of her party were already on the path down by the stream. From there, they would likely return to their carriage, which was on that side of the house as well. I needed to think quickly to get my master to follow me to Miss Elizabeth.

He turned at the sound of my bark, and when he saw me, crouched down and beckoned me to come to him. "Hello, Reggie. What are you doing out here?"

I barked several times and he laughed. "I am glad to see you, too! Come! I am tired, famished, and could definitely use a bath!"

As he proceeded towards the house, I took a few steps in the other direction and barked. He looked at me and waved me to follow him. I stood my ground and barked again.

"Go on, then, Reggie. I do not have time for your games. If you want to play, go seek Sadie, or someone else who is willing. It has been a long ride, I must see my steward, and I am in no mood for all these peculiar habits you have begun exhibiting in your old age!"

He set off walking towards the house again and I became fraught with apprehension that he would never see Miss Elizabeth. Without really thinking, I charged toward him, grabbing the fabric of his breeches with my teeth and tugging mercilessly.

He swooped down with his hand, slicing it right across my nose. I pulled away and let out a yip.

"Reggie! Where did you learn such manners?"

I determined it was most prudent to change my tactics and so I looked at him so pleadingly and whined so pathetically that I knew he would have to follow me. He planted his hands upon his hips and stared at me in clear exasperation.

I turned in the direction of Miss Elizabeth and then stopped and looked back, giving him an encouraging bark.

"So be it! I shall follow you, Reggie, but it had better be important!"

Chapter 21

As you might imagine, once I had secured my master's consent to follow me, I was eager to return to Miss Elizabeth. Though my master made a valiant attempt to match my pace, I found I had to force myself to stop and wait several times for him to draw nearer. As he lumbered down the lane breathing heavily, he occasionally paused and glared at me. I am quite certain he was either questioning my reasoning for leading him as I was or his good sense in following; but I barked emphatically, urging him on.

The most direct route to Miss Elizabeth took us to the road that came from the stables. From there, we approached the path upon which she had been walking, and when we came to a clearing, I stopped and looked at my master expectantly. There before us was Miss Elizabeth; her hands clasped in front of her as she looked down at the grounds about her.

Though my master at once saw her walking along the path, it was apparent he did not recognize her.

"Is this what I followed you all this way to see, Reggie? Visitors?" He let out a disgusted groan. "I am in no condition to receive anyone! I am covered in several layers of dirt, I am hungry, and I might add, not a little exhausted! You know I prefer to leave the showing of the house and grounds to..."

His voice trailed off as Miss Elizabeth looked up. "It cannot be!" He came to an abrupt halt and I noticed his face overtaken by a deep colouring.

Miss Elizabeth, upon glancing up at us, beheld my master, drew back, and instantly dropped her eyes back toward the ground. Her face paled and then blushed much like my master had and she abruptly turned away. Awkwardness exuded from both of them and for a moment I knew not whether I had done a prudent thing. *Would either acknowledge the other?*

My master recovered more quickly from his surprise and walked toward her, despite his discomposure. "Miss Bennet." He faltered somewhat as he bowed. "It... it is indeed a pleasure to see you again."

She stammered out a weak, "Thank you, Sir."

There followed a rather long pause and I looked from one to the other. Their discomfiture in each other's presence was so great that even I began to feel it myself. Sensing however, that Miss Elizabeth might now be more receptive to my master, I began to nudge him in the hopes that he might further the conversation.

My master finally seemed to recall how to display the basic civilities and asked, "May I.... may I inquire as to your health and the health of your family, Miss Bennet?" I detected the slightest quaver in his voice.

"They are all well, thank you." Miss Elizabeth looked everywhere but at him as she answered.

"Good. I am glad to hear it." He looked about him, as if beseeching the grounds for some sort of inspiration.

"How long has it been since you have been at Longbourn?" he finally asked.

"Several weeks, Sir."

I groaned in despair during another long pause, wondering why it was proving so difficult for an intelligent human to express the things of his heart! They had engaged in such lively discourse at Netherfield -- why could they not now?

"And you have been travelling about Derbyshire?"

"Yes, Sir." Her answers were uttered hastily and with marked distress.

"Where are you staying?"

"At the Inn at Lambton."

My master nodded his head and he shifted from one foot to another as I suspected he was struggling to find some other topic. Clearly his nervousness got the better of him as he inquired again, "Have you been long away from Longbourn?"

"Yes, several weeks." Only the faintest trace of a wry smile belied any amusement on Miss Elizabeth's countenance at the repeated question. His obvious uneasiness had the unfortunate effect of only increasing hers. Her eyes darted about as if to find some pathway to extricate herself. *Would they ever pass this point of awkwardness to find some sort of understanding?*

I looked from one to another, my tail wagging uncontrollably. Despite their uneasiness, I had high hopes that Miss Elizabeth's disdain for my master had diminished and that he might have the opportunity to win her esteem and approbation.

"And are you to remain long in Derbyshire?"

"I believe but a few more days."

This was disheartening to me, knowing she would not be here much longer. This meant my master must further the conversation to deeper and more meaningful subjects -- and very quickly! I was pondering this while my master lingered silently for a few more moments, seemingly at a loss for any further subject to introduce. He seemed to look down at himself and I noticed a brief look of concern darken his features. Then to my dismay, he abruptly excused himself with a quick bow and strode off towards the house at a brisk pace.

How could he leave her so suddenly with nothing spoken between them but a few niceties? How many times has he wished to walk the grounds of Pemberley with Miss Elizabeth on his arm? Here was his chance! Ought I not receive more reward for my efforts in bringing them together than this? I wondered whether I would every fully understand this man.

I was torn whether to follow him or remain with Miss Elizabeth. I looked from one to the other, fighting every impulse to run after my master and bring him down -- as a hound brings down a rabbit or fox -- so that he would have no choice but to remain with Miss Elizabeth little longer.

I made the decision to remain at Miss Elizabeth's side with the intent that I might forestall her departure if my master did not directly return. Every fibre in my being *hoped* he would return!

Once he was out of our sight, Miss Elizabeth stomped her foot against the ground. "Oh, Reggie! How could I have been so foolish as to come? Such impropriety at being found here!" She abruptly turned; arms folded tightly in front of her, and shook her head almost as if she were reprimanding herself.

"How could I have allowed my curiosity to rule over my good judgment? I should have known better! I had no business coming here! What must he think of me?"

As the rest of her party and the gardener slowly approached us, she looked down at me. "And to have placed him in such an awkward situation! How he must despise me for the words I spoke to him at Hunsford! How he must have wished to be out of my presence!"

No! I whined in disagreement and lifted up my paw to her. *Could you not sense his pleasure at seeing you?*

She turned and looked back in the direction where my master had walked. Very softly she said, "Yet there was something in his manners..."

My heart leapt! Perhaps my master's quick removal had not caused her to think poorly of him. She was interrupted from saying anything more by her friends joining her. The gardener expressed surprise at the unexpected arrival of my master and great pleasure in the fact that Miss Elizabeth was acquainted with him. In the ensuing conversation, Miss Elizabeth's companions expressed a most favourable opinion of him. Grateful for the reinforcements in my campaign to raise my master in Miss Elizabeth's esteem, I worked out quickly that she seemed incapable of forming any sort of reply.

Earlier, Miss Elizabeth had openly admired the house and grounds and now she seemed insensible of anything about her, remaining uncharacteristically silent. When answering an inquiry of either the gentleman or lady accompanying her, she spoke with little ease. She seemed anxious to depart whilst her friends seemed content to enjoy a leisurely walk and I comprehended with dismay that she wished to leave Pemberley directly. They continued on their walk through the grounds whilst I kept a concerned eye on Miss Elizabeth and an eager nose for my master's scent signalling his return.

Upon glancing up at her, a disheartening apprehension occurred to me at the stricken expression that took hold of her features. I fretted that perhaps her earlier appreciation of Pemberley had only been owing to my master's absence. How I wished her appreciation could include him!

As I pondered this most bewildering predicament, we entered the woods and

I knew it could be a rather lengthy walk to return to the carriage. To me, this was encouraging news, as it would allow my master sufficient time to return. If the man had any sense about him, I knew he must! I remained at Miss Elizabeth's side to assure of her my devotion, if not my master's.

We walked across a bridge that brought us to the far side of a small stream. I became a little concerned when it was determined that the party wished to take the shorter route back that cut through the woods. Knowing how long it usually took for my master to make himself presentable, a situation that lay squarely on the office of his valet, I doubted whether he would return in sufficient time. I cast about in my mind for a scheme that could delay the party's removal.

We walked alongside a small stream, where the gentleman commented on the likelihood of excellent fishing. I watched as Miss Elizabeth turned to glance down the many paths that led into the deeper woods. Though the distress she was feeling was readily discernible to anyone as attuned as myself, I could not decide if she either desired for an opportunity to explore each one more thoroughly or wished to disappear directly down one of them.

When the party stopped to peer into the crystal clear water of one of the streams and watch the trout swimming about, I caught my master's scent and looked up to see him returning. I emitted an excited bark, which caused Miss Elizabeth to look down at me and then abruptly toward my master.

I heard her take in several short, shaky breaths that betrayed her surprise at his returning. Watching my master approach, I noted that he had indeed made himself more presentable, if a bit hurriedly. He had changed out of his road dust-ridden clothing, putting on a clean shirt and waistcoat. His face was washed and his hair was somewhat damp, the curls playing unrestrained about his face. It was quite apparent to me that he deemed it more prudent to return to Miss Elizabeth than to take the time normally required to make himself impeccably groomed.

He was soon before us and Miss Elizabeth, with a little wavering in her voice and manner, began to express her admiration for the grounds.

"Mr. Darcy, the grounds of Pemberley are delightful and charming..." she looked down in the midst of the sentence and I could barely hear her utter 'delightful and charming' as her voice grew very soft. Again I noticed the colouring in her cheeks and another self reproaching shake of her head. Why she was overtaken by embarrassment by a simple declaration, I could not determine.

"Thank you," my master replied, sensing her uneasiness. "And pray, forgive me for my abrupt departure earlier. I had ridden all day from London and was not presentable to receive guests.

He turned his attention to Miss Elizabeth's friends, who were standing back, and solicited an introduction. An expression of satisfaction marked her features and she noticeably relaxed. The introductions were made and we learned that her friends were Mr. and Mrs. Gardiner, her aunt and uncle.

That they were her relations surprised my master as greatly as it did me. All I had heard from him were that her relations were inferior or very ill-mannered, excepting of course, Miss Elizabeth and her eldest sister. These people looked to me to be as well-mannered and as fashionable as any I had seen in town!

Miss Elizabeth watched incredulously, and I watched with great pride, as my master exhibited ease and affability in his conversation with her relatives, even extending an offer for Mr. Gardiner to come fish in his stream while they remained in the vicinity.

I knew that since his conversation with Georgiana about Miss Elizabeth, he had done some harsh evaluating of the charges that had been laid at his feet. His open manner and amiability proved to me that he had taken both Miss Elizabeth's and Georgiana's words to heart and was hoping that Miss Elizabeth could see he had attended to them.

How I wished for my master to have the opportunity to walk with Miss Elizabeth! They walked as a group for some distance, but as they came down to the river, Mrs. Gardiner took her husband's arm in support, presenting an opportunity for my master to walk alongside Miss Elizabeth. I could not have orchestrated this arrangement better if I had tried.

Through design or happenstance -- I know not which -- the Gardiners kept a slow pace and my master and Miss Elizabeth were obliged to walk just ahead of them. At length, I deemed it to their best advantage that they increase their pace to put a greater distance between them and Miss Elizabeth's relations, so I scampered up in front of them, inducing them to walk a little faster. My hope was that by creating an intimacy of sorts, away from the ears of others, that my master and Miss Elizabeth might have a chance to find a way to bridge the misunderstandings of the spring.

At first, neither spoke a word and I recollected their walks in Rosings Park where my master was perfectly content to walk with Miss Elizabeth in silence, yet she assumed his silence was indicative of his disapprobation. I knew they both needed something to dispel their uneasiness and to spark the conversation I could sense they were both eager to have, so I crossed abruptly in front of them, causing them both to hedge their steps to avoid me. They shared a nervous laugh.

"You must excuse Reggie, Miss Bennet, as he has taken to some odd behaviour in his old age." He looked down at me and smiled in mock consternation. "Particularly in this past year..."

"He is truly the most affable, well-mannered, and intelligent dog I have ever seen, Mr. Darcy. You have done an admirable job training him."

She kept her glance away and I suspected they both felt awkwardness at her compliment. I, however, felt quite elated! I always knew Miss Elizabeth's discernment to be of the highest calibre -- well, with dogs at least. And my canine sense was telling me that her discernment towards my master was definitely improving.

My master suddenly let out a small chuckle.

Elizabeth gave a cursory glance up to him. "What do you find humorous?"

"There have been times when Reggie has been anything but well-mannered. Not too very long ago he actually jumped up on me whilst I was drinking some coffee one morning at Rosings and..."

He abruptly stopped in mid-sentence and they both looked away from the other. I sensed a great deal of anxiety on their parts at simply the mention of Rosings. I feared they would lapse into silence again.

At length, Miss Elizabeth recovered from her discomfiture enough to venture a remark. "Please I beg you pardon our intrusion, Mr. Darcy. We had been given assurances that you were from home." She looked away with dismay. "For your housekeeper," she added, "informed us that you would certainly not be here till tomorrow. Indeed, we fully understood you were not immediately expected in the country."

"Please do not concern yourself, Miss Bennet. Business with my steward compelled me to return a day earlier." He stopped and looked into her pained face. "I would not wish for you to feel uneasy."

Wishing to change the subject, he told her of the Bingleys' arrival the following day. Again, in the silent pause that followed, I imagined both their minds were engaged in recalling what my master had done in separating Bingley from Miss Elizabeth's sister.

How I wished my master or Miss Elizabeth could venture forth with a subject that would not cause such discomfiture! Finally, my master did.

With a pointed declaration, my master informed her, "There is also one other person in the party who more particularly wishes to be known to you."

Miss Elizabeth turned to look at him; the first time she allowed her eyes to meet his.

He continued, "Will you allow me, or do I ask too much, to introduce my sister to your acquaintance during your stay at Lambton?"

I wagged my tail most gregariously now, being quite certain that if Miss Elizabeth agreed, it would ensure at least one more opportunity to see her and would also be a good indication of her favourable regard.

Miss Elizabeth's surprise at his application was very evident and she did not even attempt to hide it. Her eyes widened and her mouth dropped open for the slightest moment. Gathering her composure, she answered him very directly, "I should be more than happy to make her acquaintance."

My delight could not be contained. Even though I was quite fatigued by all that had occurred this day, I playfully danced about them. I was quite certain, by the light dawning in Miss Elizabeth's eyes, that she realized that my master must have spoken of her to his sister - and in a most agreeable light!

I detected a deep sense of gratitude sweep through Miss Elizabeth as she acceded to his request, although traces of nervousness still lingered. As they approached the house, they both turned back and saw that Mr. and Mrs. Gardiner were quite a ways still down the path. Together, my master and Miss Elizabeth stood on the lawn, looking at everything but one another, and struggled to make idle conversation until their friends joined them.

Their dialogue was stifled and tinged with nervousness and I wondered why it could not be as it was at Netherfield - a spirited confrontation would certainly ease their discomfiture! But I determined to be satisfied with the progress that had been made. After all, Miss Elizabeth did not appear inclined to treat my master with disdain and I knew he still had a place for her in his heart.

I watched my master intently, hoping to see the smile that Miss Elizabeth found so captivating in his portrait. I knew that his pleasure at seeing her at Pemberley would be sufficient to persuade that smile to appear, but I do not believe he trusted himself to bestow it quite yet. I suspect that he was just waiting for the slightest encouragement. And yet I had a strong sense that she would have gladly welcomed that smile! I wondered that he could not sense it as well.

When the Gardiners finally reached us, my master extended an invitation to come inside for refreshment, but they declined, informing him that they needed to return.

They all walked up to the carriage and my master politely handed them in. Mr. and Mrs. Gardiner appeared to be most pleased with his attention and made a point of thanking him for his gracious hospitality.

My master expressed the hope that they had enjoyed their tour of Pemberley and hoped to see them again. He looked pointedly at Miss Elizabeth. "It has been a pleasure seeing you again."

Miss Elizabeth smiled warmly at his words. It was the first time I had witnessed such a smile upon her face in my master's presence and directed toward his person.

I then looked toward my master and found that he was gazing upon her with the identical smile that he had gazed down upon her from the portrait! And I realized at that moment that this rare smile had been securely tucked away and reserved all this time for one young lady. It was a smile meant solely for her, and how grateful I was that it had finally wound its way from his heart to his countenance.

We watched the carriage drive away and then we slowly walked toward the house. I pranced with pleasure alongside my master, frequently glancing up at him. He looked down at me and caught me watching him. Reaching down, he tousled my head. "Forgive me for my anger and impatience earlier, Reggie, when you wished me to follow you. You did exceedingly well!"

As did you! I thought to myself! *As did you!*

Chapter 22

After an unusually exhausting -- but most *gratifying* -- day, I was more than ready to crawl up onto my master's bed and get a good night's sleep. But as had often been the case in the past, that was not to be, as my master was not inclined to sleep. This evening, however, it was not turmoil, anguish, confusion, nor broken resolve that kept him from slumber, but overwhelming anticipation of paying a visit to Miss Elizabeth with his sister at his side.

Throughout the evening he meditated upon Miss Elizabeth's estimation of him. "I truly believe her opinion of me has improved, Reggie." He paced the floor as he gave consideration to the events of the day. "Undeniably, she was quite alarmed when I came upon her as unexpectedly as I did, but I did not apprehend that she felt anger or resentment towards me."

I barked in agreement and he smiled.

His pacing gave way to a slight moment's pause as he stood at the window and gazed out. "How I wished to inquire what brought her to Pemberley, but I did not wish to cause her further discomfiture."

From the window he walked to a chair and sat down, however he did not remain there very long. With a gentle laugh he said, "I know not who was more stunned, Miss Bennet or myself!"

He walked over to the bed and lay down, folding his hands across his waist. "Her aunt and uncle are fine people, are they not, Reggie? I truly enjoyed their company and can now discern from where both of the elder Miss Bennets acquired their good sense and behaviour. Indeed, these are people with whom I would not mind furthering my acquaintance."

He abruptly sat up. "I believe I shall invite them to dinner once Georgiana and the Bingleys are here. What say you to that, Reggie?"

I let out a rather fatigued bark.

"Splendid!" He clapped his hands, startling me. "I shall discuss it with Georgiana as soon as she arrives. Perhaps I should arrange to take her to Lambton so that I may introduce her to Miss Bennet. Yes, yes... we will away to

Lambton as soon as she arrives! I would not waste a moment."

Continuing in that manner for the remainder of the night, my master spoke of all that he comprehended of Miss Elizabeth's gracious demeanour towards him and wondered aloud whether she had read his letter and taken his words about Wickham to heart. His person was as restless as his mind. He paced the room or stood at the window and peered out. Scarcely a moment later, he stretched himself out on the bed. Dashing my hope of rest, he then sat up and rubbed my belly vigorously. Even though I desperately required at least a little sleep, I would not have wished to pass the night any other way!

In the wee hours of the morning, he at long last climbed into bed, allowing his head to touch the pillow. His voice softened as he said, "I would have given up in despair as a mere lad, Reggie, if not for you." He turned and directed his attention at me. "When I brought you home that day, you added that spark into my life that I so desperately needed. With you, I could enjoy myself; I could put aside those demands placed upon me by my birth and the melancholy that overtook me at my mother's death."

Even in the dim moonlight, I could see my master's eyes shone warmly. "And it was the same with Miss Bennet. From very nearly the first moment I saw her, I noticed something about her that made me feel different; made me look forward to each day that I might see her; made my heart beat a little faster when I was in her presence; and made me feel that liveliness again that I find so elusive. I believe you knew that, Reggie. Do not think I am unaware that you have done everything in your power to bring us together. In many ways, I believe you have been wiser than myself."

After he had drifted off to sleep, it was I who lay awake for some time, feeling fully my devotion for this man and his words of gratitude to me.

~~*

The next morning, my master awoke and dressed fastidiously. He had much to say to his valet about what he wanted to wear; changing his mind several times before he was satisfied. His valet patiently accommodated him without uttering a word, even though I could see the surprise and questioning looks upon his face.

My master determined that when Georgiana and the Bingleys arrived, they would have a quick meal, and then whilst the Bingleys settled in, he and his sister would go directly to Lambton. As he pondered that idea, however, he realized there was one more in the party that he should invite as well. He owed it to him. He would invite Bingley to accompany them.

We awaited their arrival eagerly, and at the first sound of the carriages, we were both at the door. Georgiana expressed gratitude to be home as my master rushed to embrace her. Miss Bingley seemed pleased at his prompt welcome, perhaps wishing to be greeted as warmly as her travelling companion.

My master invited the party directly into the breakfast room. As I expected, Miss Bingley admired the elegance of the room and the care in which the meal was laid out. Whilst his sister was distracted by her effusions, my master quietly confided to Bingley that he and Georgiana would pay a call after the meal, informing him of his chance meeting with Miss Elizabeth just the day before. Bingley would not hear of remaining back, though he apologized that he was obliged to see his sisters settled and would follow shortly.

At my master's words, a sparkle immediately lit up Bingley's eyes. Although never without his amiability, one did not need the keen nose of a dog to sense these last months that Bingley had lost some of his ease of manner and replaced it with a sense of wistfulness. I knew for a certainty that his thoughts were with Miss Jane Bennet as he anticipated visiting her sister.

To my delight, I was fortunate to accompany them, as well. I believe my master felt himself forever indebted to me and therefore he allowed me to accompany them, but with the admonition that I was to remain in the curricle whist they were inside the inn. I was most displeased by this demotion in situation, until he promised me that he would invite Miss Elizabeth to step out and say hello to me at the conclusion of their visit.

On the way to Lambton, Georgiana listened with wide eyed astonishment as my master delighted her with details about his encounter with Miss Elizabeth. She laughed in unrestrained glee as he recollected to her their mutual astonishment and awkwardness. I suspect she was overjoyed to see such a heartening alteration in my master's demeanour from the last time they had spoken.

"Oh, Fitzwilliam! I am so pleased! I do so hope she will find me to her liking!"

My master smiled, which prompted Georgiana to smile pensively as well. He reached out and took her hand. "I am certain you will be delighted with her. And she with you."

Georgiana shook her head. "I truly hope so. I am simply glad for this diversion with you, Fitzwilliam. Upon arriving at Pemberley I felt quite wretched as Miss Bingley insisted on riding with me the entire way and I truly wondered whether she would ever cease talking! I really do not understand her, Brother. Does she truly believe that I am interested in where she dined, which balls she attended, and with whom she danced? How I began to wish that I had the courage to say something that might silence her!"

My master looked at her with understanding. "I do believe, Georgiana, I hope… that it will only be a matter of time before Miss Bingley's motive for seeking your undivided attention will no longer exist."

That unspoken hope… did I dare think upon that myself? I felt that if I had been wrong in my conviction that Miss Elizabeth was the woman my master needed more than anything… even more than me… I had failed in my sense of duty to him.

My master held tightly onto his sister's hand and his face grew sombre. "Georgiana, there is something I must discuss with you and I in no way wish you any pain by mentioning it."

Georgiana regarded her brother with curiosity. "What is it?"

He looked down at her hand as he spoke, "During my stay at Netherfield, there was a regiment of the militia quartered nearby at Meryton." He lifted his head and peered into Georgiana's questioning eyes. "George Wickham was in that particular regiment."

I saw her try to pull her hand away, but my master held it firmly. She looked down and her cheeks coloured.

"Georgiana, dear, I mention it only to help you understand that you are not the only young lady to be imposed upon by Wickham."

She glanced up cautiously. "There was someone else?"

"I fear that there has likely been far too many who have fallen for his deceptive charm." He took a deep breath. "Miss Bennet herself found him to be quite delightful."

"Oh!" was all Georgiana could say.

"His accounting of our relationship to Miss Elizabeth portrayed him as wronged by me with no provocation and I am sorry to say that my own refusal to answer caused her -- indeed, I suspect likely all of Hertfordshire -- to believe him."

"Did he... did he say anything about me?" she asked, worry taking hold of her features.

"No, no," My master patted her hand reassuringly. "I believe his only motive was to cast aspersions upon my character, lest I be tempted to make the truth known."

"Did you inform Miss Bennet of his true nature?"

"Not at first. You know how loath I am to make public something of such a delicate nature and potentially injurious to you, Georgiana. However, when Miss Elizabeth reproached me for my treatment of Wickham during her refusal, I felt I had no choice but to defend myself. I gave her the whole of my dealings with him in a letter. Fear not, I have every confidence of Miss Elizabeth's discretion." His comforting smile allayed some of the wide-eyed shock in Georgiana's eyes, before his countenance once again turned grim. "Unfortunately, I know not whether she read it or whether she believed me."

Georgiana tilted her head. "But the fact that she consented to being introduced to me... that is a good indication, is it not?"

"Yes, Georgiana. Her behaviour at Pemberley, discomfiture notwithstanding, leads me to hope that she no longer thinks ill of me."

Georgiana smiled weakly. "As do I, Fitzwilliam."

We pulled up in front of the inn and stopped. My master gave me a firm reminder to remain inside the curricle, however little I required it. I am well aware of the expectations of my behaviour when we travelled.

As Georgiana and my master remained within, I kept my eyes fixed on the door, awaiting their return. Each time the door opened, my tail wagged and I perked my head up, anticipating greeting Miss Elizabeth in my most amiable manner, but I was disappointed several times.

At length, Bingley arrived in his carriage. With long strides and a beaming smile, he entered the inn. Not for the first time, I railed against the inherent disparity of our stations. How fervently I wished to be allowed to join them! It was too cruel to leave me outside, simply for the fortune of being born a dog. Was I not a closer friend to my master and Miss Elizabeth than Bingley? Was I not as well mannered -- or even more so -- than some who are born with rank and privilege? I am not ashamed to say it was one of the longest waits I had ever experienced.

Finally, the door opened and I beheld my master holding it open as Georgiana and Miss Elizabeth stepped out together. It appeared that they were having a most amiable conversation and my master turned his eyes toward me in a most satisfied manner, giving me a triumphant nod of his head.

Immediately, I jumped down and Miss Elizabeth and I greeted each other enthusiastically. She came forward as the others remained back. I watched as my master engaged the Gardiners in conversation whilst keeping his eyes fixed on the lady who now had captured not only his heart and mine, but Georgiana's, as well. She stood quietly aside her brother, hands folded demurely in front of her, eyes upon her new acquaintance and bearing a most pleased countenance.

On our return to Pemberley, Georgiana expressed her delight in Miss Elizabeth.

"Oh, Fitzwilliam! Miss Bennet is more delightful than I ever could have imagined! I do so look forward to their joining us for dinner!"

I perceived the serene calm and sense of contentment that infused my master's posture at Georgiana's words. It was as though everything was suddenly as it should be.

"I am very pleased," was all he said.

A smile tugged at the corners of his mouth. He took in a deep breath and let it out with great satisfaction. And from the moment we departed Lambton and set off for Pemberley until we walked in the door, his smile did not depart.

When we returned, Miss Bingley rather presumptuously assumed that his smile was directed at her. How great was my satisfaction when my master informed her that he and Georgiana had extended invitations to Miss Bennet and her aunt and uncle to join them for dinner the day after tomorrow!

~~*

The following day, Mr. Gardiner joined the gentlemen at Pemberley for a day of fishing. My master took care to attend to him solicitously by pointing out the best places to fish, offering him his best bait and tackle, and giving him tips to ensure a successful day of sport. Hurst seemed intent on walking a ways down the stream to fish by himself, but both my master and Bingley chose to remain in close proximity to Miss Elizabeth's uncle. I was quite proud of the effort my master put forth to engage Mr. Gardiner in friendly conversation, as if to atone for his reticence at Netherfield. Although all manner of subjects were introduced as the morning flew, I noted with no little pleasure that Miss Bennet and Miss Elizabeth were mentioned with great frequency by my master, Bingley, or Mr. Gardiner himself.

I was sitting along the bank of the river, taking pleasure in the camaraderie that the men enjoyed when I detected Elizabeth's scent. I let out a few excited barks as I kept my eyes in the direction of the house. My master looked to me curiously and I knew the moment understanding came to him clearly. His eyes lit up in comprehension and he turned to Mr. Gardiner.

"It appears we have more visitors. Reggie has discerned a scent, and unless I am very much mistaken, it is someone he knows."

Mr. Gardiner, never taking his eyes off his fishing line, mentioned in an off-handed manner that his wife and Miss Elizabeth intended to pay a call to Georgiana that morning and perhaps it was they. He watched my master closely from the corner of his eye at this intelligence. A look of satisfaction crossed his features when my master looked several times back towards the house and eventually commented, "Perhaps I should see to Georgiana and how well she is receiving them. Georgiana is quite timid and shy and has had very limited experience at being hostess for even a small party. I fear this may be daunting to her. I think it would be best to see if she requires my assistance. Pray, excuse me, I shall return shortly."

Mr. Gardiner made no attempt to hide his amusement as my master turned to leave with long, hurried steps. I followed close behind, ecstatic that he finally recognized my bark alerting him to Miss Elizabeth's presence.

We came into the house and my master inquired after the ladies.

"They are in the salon, Mr. Darcy," Mrs. Reynolds replied.

"Thank you," he replied. He quickly turned toward the salon, but was halted from his progress when Mrs. Reynolds called out to him.

"Pardon me, Mr. Darcy, but might you not wish to first attend to your appearance before you greet the ladies?"

My master looked down at his clothes and chided himself for his impetuosity with a brisk shake of his head. "Yes, thank you, Mrs. Reynolds. I shall do that."

We hurried off in a different direction, but not before I noticed Mrs. Reynolds' bemused smile.

With the help of his man, my master quickly changed into more appropriate clothes and took a cloth to his face and hands to cleanse himself.

We finally made our way to the salon and my master paused in the doorway, perusing the room. The ladies were gathered around the table and at first he was not noticed. A plethora of meats, cheeses, and fruits had been set out for them.

Miss Elizabeth peered up from her plate with a start when she noticed my master at the door.

We walked over to the table and soon every eye was upon my master. Georgiana looked with grateful appreciation at him; Miss Bingley eyed him with a possessive stare and an unpleasant suspicion; Mrs. Hurst merely appeared curious; Mrs. Gardiner was markedly flattered; and Miss Elizabeth seemed to be subjected to both a little pleasure and pain at his arrival.

He greeted everyone and came over to Georgiana, putting his arm about her. He leaned down and whispered something in her ear. Though he was too quiet and discreet for the others to hear, with my superior canine hearing, I could discern quite easily, "Dearest, I am most anxious to hear if you have been able to further your acquaintance with Miss Bennet."

Very softly, she answered, "I have hardly had the opportunity, for there is another here who overshadows me much of the time."

They both turned to Miss Bingley, who made it her mission to pay admirable compliments to Georgiana -- in my master's presence -- of the young girl's performance as hostess.

"You have been an excellent hostess this morning, Miss Darcy. Your brother would be proud of the way you handled the unexpected arrival of two guests." She smiled thinly in the direction of Miss Elizabeth and her aunt and then turned to my master with a knowing nod. "I did give her some well-heeded advice in suggesting we adjourn here, where it would prove to be more comfortable and would provide more room to visit. Miss Darcy is a dear girl, but one should be able to rely on a lady with experience in keeping a house and entertaining, would you not agree, Mr. Darcy?"

Georgiana seemed dismayed by Miss Bingley's words, but my master merely proffered his subdued appreciation for her consideration.

He turned toward the table and I watched as Miss Elizabeth kept her eyes averted from my master and directed toward the cluster of grapes she held in her hand. With a concentration I was unused to seeing in the employment of eating, she brought each one up to her mouth, slipping it in with the very tip of her finger. I could only account that her diligence was to capture every morsel of juice that may have escaped from it.

I found my master's gaze fixed to the grapes as intently as Miss Elizabeth's were. He followed her hand with his eyes and each time she dipped a finger into her mouth, I considered it odd that my master, almost imperceptibly, licked his lips.

As a dog, observing behaviour like this among my peers would indicate some exceedingly tempting smell or prospect of a treat had presented itself. I had never seen humans, much less my master, display such a mannerism before and I knew not what to make of it. I confess I have never had much interest in grapes myself, but the intensity of his scrutiny -- and the desire suffused upon his countenance -- made me wonder if I should reconsider.

Miss Elizabeth looked up and her eyes met my master, who was still intently observing her. She smiled nervously before glancing at the others, noting that every eye turned to her most curiously. She blushed lightly before returning her gaze to the one looking admirably upon her.

Shaking his head slightly, my master seemed to realize that the conversation at the table had stopped. He introduced a subject that I suspected was intended to allow his sister the opportunity to converse with Miss Elizabeth. "Georgiana, Miss Bennet recently paid a visit to her friend, who is the wife of our aunt's clergyman, Mr. Collins. She was introduced to Lady Catherine and was invited to dine at Rosings Park several times."

In my consideration, given the events that transpired there between her and my master, Miss Elizabeth admirably retained her composure at the mention of Rosings. When Georgiana turned to apply to her in her halting, shy manner, she seemed to forget her own uneasiness and looked to soothe the young girl's. "Did you… did you enjoy your visit… with your friend, Miss Bennet?" Georgiana stammered, blushing.

"Oh, yes, thank you," Elizabeth smiled at the young girl, I believe in hopes of assuaging her shyness. "I had the pleasure of making the acquaintance not only your aunt, but your cousins, Miss de Bourgh and Colonel Fitzwilliam."

"I hope you enjoyed their company as well."

"Very much so, thank you, Miss Darcy."

Georgiana was about to speak again when Miss Bingley apparently reached her limit of not being included in the conversation. "Pray, Miss Eliza, are not the ---shire Militia removed from Meryton? They must be a great loss to your family," she declared.

I could not help but think that Wickham was the true reason Miss Bingley mentioned the militia. From the looks upon everyone else's face, the very mention brought him to mind elsewhere. Miss Bennet seemed at first disconcerted, but quickly composed herself.

"I thank you for your concern, Miss Bingley, but I believe it is of little importance to my family where they are stationed, as long as they are fulfilling their responsibilities."

A quick glance at my master and his sister revealed all the discomposure that the mere unspoken reference to Wickham produced in both. But my master quickly collected himself after hearing Miss Elizabeth's even reply. It appeared she had taken to heart my master's words about Wickham's true character. Poor Georgiana, however, was not so lucky in containing emotions as her face went pale and she was incapable of carrying on any further conversation for the remainder of the morning.

Gratefulness shone in my master's eyes as he turned back to Miss Elizabeth, nodding his head slightly in a gesture of appreciation. She reciprocated with a smile that lit up her eyes and for the very first time I felt assured that admiration for my master had begun to grow within her.

Miss Elizabeth and her aunt departed soon after. But the effect of their visit remained with all of us. My master and I escorted them to the carriage and when we returned, Miss Bingley seemed to have an endless supply of disparaging words against Miss Bennet. She spoke against her person, behaviour, and dress. As she enumerated her many faults, I could sense my master fighting for control of the anger elevating within him. I was confident her words held no power over either my master's or Georgiana's estimation of Miss Elizabeth, but how greatly I wished my master would come to her defence.

Georgiana excused herself, feeling no inclination for further conversation. When she had quit the room, Miss Bingley knew no bounds to her accusatory words.

"I remember when we first knew her in Hertfordshire, how amazed we all were to find that she was a reputed beauty; and I particularly recollect your saying one night, after they had been dining at Netherfield, 'She a beauty! I should as soon call her mother a wit.' But afterwards she seemed to improve on you, and I believe you thought her rather pretty at one time."

I watched as every muscle tensed, his face coloured, and he turned to Miss Bingley, his eyes boring into hers. "Yes," he replied. "But that was only when I first knew her; for it is many months since I have considered her as one of the handsomest women of my acquaintance."

I added a resounding bark in concurrence and gloated at my master's declaration and Miss Bingley's shrinking back at his words. When he excused himself, I followed my master as he sought out Georgiana.

We came to Georgiana's chambers and he paused and knocked at the door. "Yes?"

"Georgiana, may I speak with you?"

When she allowed us entry, it was not difficult to see that she was hurt and angered.

My master reached out for her, putting his hands upon her shoulders while I lay down at her feet.

"Am I correct in assuming," my master began, "that you have been upset by all of Miss Bingley's words against Miss Bennet?"

"She is so cruel! If she were not your good friend's sister, I would wonder that she even be invited here!"

I do not believe I had ever heard Georgiana speak so harshly. My master consoled her by putting his arm about her and she looked up at him with a mischievous glint in her eyes. "Fitzwilliam, I am quite of the mind that her dislike of Miss Bennet increases as your admiration for Miss Bennet grows."

"I believe you may be correct, Georgiana."

"Fitzwilliam, may I speak candidly?"

"Certainly."

"Miss Bennet and Mr. and Mrs. Gardiner have consented to join us for dinner tomorrow evening. I think perhaps it would be most fitting for you to pay a call on the morrow, first thing in the morning. And Fitzwilliam, you should attend to her without either Mr. Bingley or me, to assure her of your continued devotion."

"Truly? You are of the opinion that I ought to pay a visit alone?"

"Absolutely! I am convinced of it!" Georgiana grasped his hands and gave them an emphatic squeeze.

"Now, Georgiana, you seem somewhat undecided about whether or not I should."

A smile touched at my master's lips as Georgiana's eyes widened. "No, Fitzwilliam, I truly believe…" She paused and then a nervous laugh escaped. "You are teasing me, now."

"Yes, Georgiana, I am."

The shared a smile as they looked upon each other.

"It has been far too long since you have teased me, Fitzwilliam."

"I hope you do not mind."

"No, on the contrary. It is good to see that aspect of you once more. You have not been this light-hearted since…"

I knew Georgiana had Ramsgate in mind. Obviously, as did my master, for he pulled her towards him in an embrace. Georgiana's voice was thick with emotion.

"I believe that I have much for which to be grateful to Miss Bennet. I can only assume that her visit to Pemberley has improved your demeanour, which has been so despondent of late. Oh Fitzwilliam, God willing, you will ascertain that her opinion of you has improved tomorrow. I so want to see you happy."

A declaration with which I could not but wholeheartedly agree.

~~*

With eager expectation, my master arose the next morning. Again he dressed with the utmost care.

He looked down at me and asked, "How is this, Reggie? Too formal? Does it appear that I am emphasizing the differences in our station? Does the colour make me appear too severe?"

When he had finally decided upon the garment to wear, I barked in hearty approval. But it was not the garment of which I was approving -- it was his smile. As long as he allowed himself the liberty to smile, he appeared most handsome, indeed.

I was not to accompany him; he was determined to have nothing to distract his attending to her. Now, I admit that normally I would be unhappy to be deprived of the opportunity to see Miss Elizabeth, but this visit had taken such momentous portent that I thought it prudent to acquiesce to his preference.

He called for his horse and I walked out with him to await the groomsman. "Well, Reggie. I hope Georgiana is correct. I shall make a concerted effort to assure Miss Bennet of my continued regard."

~~*

I suppose I ought to have suspected that he would return from his visit with Miss Elizabeth in anything but an agreeable state. How many times had I allowed my hopes to be raised only to have them dashed? I cannot count.

But as he stormed into the house, barely acknowledging his guests, I knew that something terrible had happened. And I could not understand how my master, Georgiana, and I could have so misapprehended Miss Elizabeth's favour.

I followed him up to his chambers and was surprised when I heard him issue an order to have a bag packed for an indefinite stay in London. As I awaited an opportunity to be alone with him, I watched his eyes. They were not exhibiting despair and grief, but anger and even hatred. This could not be directed towards Miss Bennet; of this I was certain.

When the servant departed to carry out his orders, he collapsed into a chair and cradled his forehead in his palm. His whole body was seething with anger and he looked down at me. "It is Wickham again!"

I looked up at him, feeling a wave of distress course through me. How did this cursed man have the ability to defeat my master's happiness and well being again and again?

He sat silently for a moment; the only movement he made was the closing of his eyes. "He has deserted his regiment with Miss Elizabeth's youngest sister, a girl no more than fifteen years old!" Shaking his head, he continued, "Elizabeth had just received a letter from her eldest sister relaying this information when I arrived. Needless to say, she was quite distraught and it was all I could do to not give voice to this great sense of loathing and make her feel even worse."

He stood up abruptly and raked fingers from both hands through his hair. "It is entirely my fault," he said. "If I had not allowed my pride to prevent me from disclosing Wickham's true nature, the Bennet family would not be facing this unspeakable disgrace!" He shook his head silently for a few moments, as if reprimanding himself. "I would never do anything to intentionally hurt her, and yet look at all I *have* done!" He looked down at me with great anguish. "To see her in such distress… I wished for all the world to be able to reach out to her and comfort her, but I could do nothing but stand there and spew out trifling, placating words."

He began pacing the floor and then stopped. "I shall be leaving for London first thing tomorrow morning to find that reprobate! I must do everything in my power to right this wrong!"

His valet promptly returned and he said no more. He kept to himself for the majority of the day. He only owned to Georgiana and Bingley that an unforeseen emergency required his departure the following day and that Bingley and his family could remain at Pemberley as they had planned; with luck, he would return within the week.

It was with a great sense of anguish that my master firmly looked at me and informed me that due to my difficulty in town, I was not going to accompany him. I was most aggrieved!

Despite my age, my aching bones, and struggle with breathing in town, I was convinced that my canine sense of smell could prove to be very useful. This was a hunt, was it not? Had I ever failed my master in pursuit of his prey? I was determined to devise a plan to ensure that on the morrow I accompanied him to town!

Chapter 23

My master arose early in preparation for his departure for London, whilst darkness still hung like a heavy blanket over the day. I eagerly followed him about, hoping he would realize how great an asset I would be to him as he searched for Wickham.

At length, he regarded me sternly and admonished me. "Reggie! You are not to go! You must remember how taxing it is for you when you are in London and I will not have it!"

I growled my refusal at him and remained steadfastly by his side. I had resolved late last night that a fervent display of obstinacy was the only means to ensure I would have my own, superior way.

We stepped outside just as the sun spread out its glow across the horizon. The early morning warmth was a sure sign that the day would turn unbearably hot in the mid-day sun. But I was determined to go, and when the door to the carriage was opened, I jumped in ahead of my master. He stared at me and then forcefully pointed down to the ground in front of him to signal his desire for me to remove myself immediately from the carriage.

"Reggie, I said you were not to go!" The anger in his tone of voice sent a shiver down my spine.

I let out an equally emphatic bark, however, and settled down onto the floor of the carriage, keeping my eyes averted from him. It was not easy for me to disobey and I found it exceedingly difficult to meet his piercing gaze.

"Reggie, both you and I know what difficulties you have in town. You will regret this!"

I shifted my position, but remained steadfastly in place. With a huff, my master joined me in the carriage.

"So be it, Reggie, but mark my words, we will have been in town barely a day and you will find yourself wheezing and unable to catch your breath!" His voice was firm, but I also heard a slight tone of compassion escape in his words.

It was only after we had been on the road for a good part of the morning that I ventured my head off the floor to glance up at my master. His head was leaning against the window and his eyes were closed. It gave me satisfaction that he could rest easily knowing I was accompanying him.

Upon arriving at the townhouse after a full day's journey, my master quickly penned some letters and had them dispatched immediately. He received two replies before nightfall.

One letter was brought to him just before the evening meal and the second arrived later in the evening as we sat together in his study. He quickly read it and then perused the one that had arrived earlier. He glanced down at me and nodded his head. He leaned over, resting on his elbows and began informing me of his plans. It felt quite satisfying knowing that this time as he planned his strategy, we were not adversaries as we had been in regards to his actions toward Bingley, but we were now companionable allies.

"From this intelligence," he said as much to me as to himself, "I am confident that I should be able to discover Mrs. Younge's establishment with little trouble. It is unknown, however, whether or not Wickham and the youngest Miss Bennet are in residence there." He reached down and patted my head. "I do not expect Mrs. Younge to freely disclose Wickham's whereabouts, but if I am able to confidently persuade her that I know Wickham has recently been to see her, I may have more leverage. Reggie, I will need you to accompany me and reveal to me whether or not you pick up his scent."

I gave him a hearty bark to assure him that I would do all I could to assist him.

The next morning we set out in the carriage and my master instructed his driver to convey us to Edward Street.

For the duration of the ride, my master sat quietly and kept his eyes turned toward the window. He sat stiffly, moving nothing but his fingers as they tapped repeatedly against the sill. I knew that he was not looking forward with any pleasure to this meeting with Wickham and was steeling himself for the encounter.

When the carriage finally came to a halt, the door was opened and we slowly stepped out. My master pulled himself erect and he inhaled deeply. Holding one of the letters in front of him, he glanced down at it and then looked ahead at what appeared to be some small residences.

Before we walked on, he gazed down at me. "Reggie, Mrs. Younge's boarding house is likely just up ahead. I know not what she will do when she sees me, but when the door is opened, I want you to slip inside and see if you can discern whether Wickham has been there. Bark if you pick up any trace of his scent. All I need to know is whether or not he has been there recently."

My tail wagged in eager anticipation and I obediently followed my master down a narrow street. I could immediately determine, from the noxious smells of rotting food, refuse piled in the streets, and poorly tended houses and gardens, that the people who resided here cared little for the appearance of their neighbourhood. It was nothing like the area in which my master's town home was located. We came to a small brick house and my master glanced down at the letter again.

"This is it," he said as he narrowed his eyes, which darted about in disgust. With his jaw set sharply and his shoulders steeled, I realized that he was willing to confront his greatest enemy of all for the sake of Miss Elizabeth and her family!

We walked up to the door and my master gave a sharp tug on the bell. After a brief wait, the door was slowly opened and a pair of eyes peered out at us. Instant recognition and alarm flashed in her eyes and Mrs. Younge made a futile attempt to slam the door on us. My master stopped its closure with his foot.

"What do *you* want?" she spat out, pushing with all her effort to keep the door from opening any further.

"I want some information, Mrs. Younge."

"Well, I know nothing!" she cried out.

"How do you know you know nothing? You know not what information I seek!"

My master, with several easy shoves, was able to push the door wide enough for me to slip through.

"Get that dog out of here!" she screamed as I easily made my way into the dwelling, sidestepping her foot that swiftly tried to reach out and bar me from entering.

I walked in and began sniffing about, but I did not need to go very far. The scent of Wickham was very evident in several places about the room. I turned back to my master and barked several times.

"Get him out of here! I have a reputable establishment and do not allow dogs!" Her voice and hand shook wildly.

"Come here, Reggie," my master commanded coolly.

When I slipped back out, my master was able to step up inside the door to prevent its closure. "Now, Mrs. Younge, my dog is very much acquainted with Wickham and judging by his reaction, I can reliably say that Wickham has been here recently."

A look of dread swept her features, although she did not acknowledge the truth of my master's declaration.

"I have not seen Mr. Wickham in quite some time." The slight twitch of her mouth betrayed the firm stance she was taking.

"Is that so?" my master asked.

"Yes. Now if you will excuse me, I have patrons I must see to."

She tried to close the door again, but my master's presence prevented her from doing so. "I will not take up too much more of your time, Mrs. Younge, but I would strongly suggest you heed my words. I would advise you to give considerable thought to informing me of Wickham's and Miss Bennet's whereabouts. It would be highly in your favour to do so."

"All I know is that they are not here!"

"So she is still with him," my master said softly. "I will assume they have been here, Mrs. Younge, and as Wickham has a great number of debts and has taken a young girl only fifteen years of age without her parent's consent, you may find yourself having to answer a number of questions."

His eyes narrowed and seemed to bore into hers. "You say you have a respectable establishment, Mrs. Younge?"

"Of course!"

"Then if I were you, I would cooperate. If you truly do not know where they are, which I doubt, I would surmise that you can easily find out. I shall return in two days and expect an answer. If you find out anything sooner or if you suddenly realize how prudent it will be to inform me of his whereabouts, you can contact me here." Darcy handed her his card.

"I doubt that I will!" she insisted a bit too strongly for me to believe her, but took the card anyway.

"Oh," my master let out a mocking laugh, "for a plentiful compensation I am quite certain you will! Contact me at my townhouse. All the information is on the card, although I am quite certain you remember where it is."

He allowed her to close the door and his eyes met mine. "We shall see how long it takes her to realize that her devotion to Wickham is not quite as strong as her desire for money!"

I was grateful to return to the townhouse, although even there I was tormented with the stifling heat and the stale air that seemed to squeeze all energy from me. My master departed in the afternoon to tend to some business and apparently did some additional investigating, but when he returned, he informed me that he had not been able to discover anything more of Wickham's whereabouts. He would have to rely on Mrs. Younge turning over the information.

The following day, I felt an even greater sense of ill being and my master paid Mrs. Younge another visit alone. When he returned, he informed me that although she still was not inclined to talk, he had strongly hinted to her that he was close to finding Wickham. He hoped that she would begin to fear losing out on some sort of ample payment, prompting her to divulge what she knew.

His plan must have worked, for the very next day my master received a short, concise note from Mrs. Young informing him that it was possible she may know where Wickham had been staying, but she would not divulge it without first receiving payment for her hard work.

"Hard work, indeed! She has known all along where he was!" My master shook his head. "She may consider herself a loyal friend to Wickham, but those ties can be easily cut by the right price!"

My master smiled as he tapped his fingers against his desk. "Soon we shall know where he and Miss Lydia are located."

Apparently, the enticement of an ample sum was all that my master required to procure an address where, Mrs. Younge claimed, she only *heard* Wickham had possibly stayed, but she could not guarantee it.

My master settled down next to me and stroked my head in that particular spot behind my ears he knew I preferred. His tone was quiet and compassionate. "Reggie, I know with each day that passes, your health declines. But I have one more task for you. I promise you that after this, you do not have to accompany me on any further schemes. Moreover, I shall provide you the finest comforts my townhouse has to offer and the finest meals prepared until we return to Pemberley."

He was quite accurate in his estimation of my well being. I was feeling very poorly, even worse than the last time we were in town. I was more than willing, however, to do whatever it took to find Wickham and make things right for Miss Elizabeth and her family.

He expounded upon the details of his plan for the following day. He had an address that Mrs. Younge gave him. She told my master that Wickham may have let a room at this address, but if he did, she knew not which one in particular he was staying.

I came to understand, in overhearing my master's conversation with his driver, that this establishment was in an even more sordid neighbourhood than Mrs. Younge's.

"He likely has many acquaintances of questionable repute in that part of town who may not take a liking to my inquiring as to his whereabouts. They may assume I am attempting to collect my debts from him or worse. Once we are in the area, the prudent course is to not ask any questions."

He cradled my head within his hands. "It will be up to *you*, Reggie, to discern his whereabouts. There may be several rooms let out at this address. We must find the right one on the first attempt!" My master reached up with his hand and gave my forehead a good rubbing. I lifted my paw and placed it across his arm. I would do all I could to find him!

We set out early in the morning, quite convinced that Wickham would likely not be out of bed, let alone anyone else in that neighbourhood at that hour. The carriage stopped and we stepped out. Along this street, we had to step over several motionless forms that appeared to have lost all ability and intellect to find their way home during the night.

As we walked toward the row of buildings, the stench that emanated from them invaded our senses. My master let out a disgusted grumble.

But I diligently performed my duties in sniffing out the different scents. Amidst all the offensive and putrid ones, I very directly picked up Wickham's. Following the scent past several doors, I finally found the one to which it led.

"Good boy," my master said, patting me firmly on the head. "Now, be ready for anything!"

I stood back and watched him take the knocker and give it a couple sharp raps. From inside, I heard something tumble followed by a wave of cursing. At length, the sound of shuffling of feet could be heard coming toward the door.

The door swung open and Wickham stood before us, eyes glazed over, hair and clothes dishevelled, and he made a futile attempt to focus his eyes and determine exactly who we were.

I responded to this vile man with a vicious growl. He lowered his gaze at me and I noticed recognition flash across his countenance as he glared back at my master.

"What are *you* doing here?" His voice slurred and he seemed unable to maintain his balance.

"There is something of vital importance we must discuss!"

"Away with you!" Wickham ordered. Every one of my senses was heightened by the hatred and fear which emanated from him. He was unquestionably displeased to see us.

He attempted to slam the door, but my master thwarted him by propping his large frame inside the door so it could not be closed. Wickham pushed against my master, but he would not be moved. The inebriated state in which Wickham found himself made his efforts most ineffectual and he let out a stream of curses as my master remained coolly firm.

I bared my teeth and I was prepared to lunge at him if such measures were necessary.

"You have no right to be here!" Wickham snarled. "We have nothing to say to one another!" Wickham scowled at me. "You still have this worthless cur?" Wickham sneered and the fur down my neck and back rose. Letting loose with my most threatening growls, I stepped toward him.

I really did not see nor expect it, but suddenly his foot hit me right in my belly, sending me off balance and knocking me over.

The wind was knocked completely out of me as I struggled to take a breath and pick myself up. My master grabbed Wickham's shirt collar, bringing his face within inches of his own.

"I will not lower myself to respond in kind to you, however tempting it may be." My master hitched Wickham's collar a little tighter, the murderous rage in his eyes warred with the measured, calm tones of his voice. "But I warn you, Wickham, do not *ever* do that again!"

My master looked down at me to assure himself that I was not seriously wounded. I could see that his regulation was most seriously tested and that if he did not have the welfare of Miss Elizabeth first and foremost on his mind, he would have had no qualms in giving Wickham what he richly deserved. I struggled to my feet, pain searing through my belly. Although it was quite an effort, I was finally able to right myself.

"Is Miss Bennet here?" My master released Wickham, pushing him back into the house, allowing himself to fully cross the portal. Both hands were clenched in tight fists; clearly, he was anticipating having to use them.

"Who?"

"Miss Lydia Bennet."

"I know not who…"

At that moment, I dashed between their legs inside the room, my nose to the floor.

Wickham's lodgings were nothing more than a dirty, dank single room. In the dim light of a meagre candle, I could discern a battered table with plates of half-eaten food strewn about and a rather messy, small bed with tattered coverlets. I barked several times, confirming to my master that she had been -- and indeed, still was -- inside this room. I assumed, from the direction of her scent, that she was on the bed under the blankets, although I never saw her face.

"I know she is here, Wickham. But as I cannot vouch for the state in which I might find her, I will not step further into this residence. Accompany me outside, immediately!"

"And what makes you think I will do what you say?" Wickham demanded.

"Because with all the debts you have no doubt incurred, you are almost certainly down to your last shilling and I can have you hauled down to the debtor's prison… or worse! Now, Wickham!"

My master turned to go and Wickham slammed the door behind him. As I took a few more strides, the pain shot through me again. I did everything in my power to walk as if nothing ailed me.

We walked away from the residences and my master stopped and turned to face Wickham.

"So what is this about?" Wickham eyed me as if he was actually fearful I might suddenly retaliate and attack him. I cannot lie and must confess that thought passed through my mind as an attractive possibility if I had not been in such dire pain.

"I demand to know your intentions regarding Miss Lydia Bennet!"

Wickham laughed. "My intentions? She and I are merely having a little fun!"

My master's face burned with anger. "You have no intention of marrying her?"

"You want me to *marry* her?" He laughed in disdain.

My master's eyes bore piercingly into Wickham's. "No, I do not *want* you to marry her. I would never wish that for her or any other lady. But I *insist* that you allow me to speak with her to help her to see reason, and hopefully find another means to end this insupportable situation. And if that means marriage, you *will* marry her!"

In a harsh whisper, Wickham adamantly informed my master, "I have no wish to marry Lydia and there is nothing you can do to force me!"

"You are correct, Wickham. I cannot force you to marry her. However, I do not doubt that those to whom you owe debts will only be too happy to know of your location. Make no mistake; I hold no compunction that prevents me from making your life quite miserable if you do not do what is necessary to protect Miss Bennet from any further scandal. If you comply with my demands, I will provide you with what you cannot provide for yourself."

"Such as…?"

"Settling your debts and purchasing a commission in another regiment, to name a few."

Sneering, he shook his head. "I will never marry that girl! She has nothing to recommend her."

"You should have considered that before you impulsively removed her from the protection of her friends!"

By the expression on his countenance, I knew Wickham suddenly experienced clarity of mind as he looked intently at my master with a sly smile. "Why are you suddenly so concerned for the welfare of such a silly little nothing?"

"Why I choose to do this is of no concern to you!"

Opportunistic pleasure crossed Wickham's face as he considered acceptance of his adversary's help. "So you will purchase me a new commission and settle my debts?"

My master quietly nodded.

Wickham cocked his head to the side as he looked at my master with appraising eyes. "I do not believe that what you offered is sufficient for me to take on the responsibility of a wife. Perhaps, I might suggest some further negotiating to make it worth my while to marry *her!* I would need much more!"

"Do you think me a simpleton, Wickham? You have nowhere else to turn. Your creditors will find you as easily as I. Do not forget, even your *good* friend Mrs. Younge was only too willing to divulge your location to me for the right sum!"

Wickham turned away, grumbling and my master grabbed the collar of Wickham's shirt to command his attention once more. "I shall return on the morrow at nine sharp to discuss with Miss Bennet what is to be done. I trust I will find her in an acceptable state or you will answer for far more than you ever wish."

My master turned toward the carriage and then stopped and glanced back at Wickham. "And Wickham, I would advise you to not try to do anything so foolish as to run away. You know I have the resources to track you down… and I will!"

I was grateful when I heard Wickham's footsteps briskly walk away. I was anxious to get in and lay down, but was not expecting the shooting pain when I stood up. A yelp escaped me and my master leaned down.

"I am so sorry, Reggie." He reached down and took care to gently pick me up, his arms going carefully around me and supporting my feet with his large hands. "You most likely have a few bruised ribs. You'll be in pain for a few days… I hope it is nothing worse."

I could see the pain, anger, and concern intermingled in my master's features. The last thing I wished to do was interfere with what he had taken upon himself to do, so I tried not to let any whine or moan escape, despite the pain that flooded my whole body.

With little effort, he lay me down on the seat of the carriage.

His hand stroked my fur from my head all the way down my back and soothed me as he spoke, "You performed admirably back there, my good friend. You did not deserve what Wickham inflicted upon you. You have no idea how much I regret that he hurt you. Be still, boy, and we will be at the townhouse directly."

Weary and in pain, I found it increasingly difficult to focus. "Wickham does not deserve my assistance at all and if it were not for my error in judgment, the Bennets would not be facing this disgrace. If there was only some other way…"

As the carriage began moving, the jarring motion heightened my pain. I made a vain attempt to hold in a moan, but could not contain it any longer.

My eyes were now closed, but I felt my master's reassuring hand stroke my back. "Do not move, Reggie. Just try to rest. We shall be home shortly."

As the carriage made its way back to the townhouse, I closed my eyes tightly, hoping to lessen the pain. It was now an even greater struggle to take a breath. But my master was correct, because before I knew it, we had reached home.

Without really apprehending how or when it occurred, I realized we were now inside the townhouse. My master was leaning over me and calling my name repeatedly with great anguish!

Chapter 24

Vague impressions were all I could claim to possess for the next few days. I heard the murmur of reassuring voices and felt gentle hands probing my feet and ribs. At some point, a snug wrap was placed about my belly. Food was spooned into my mouth, the bed of rags upon which I slept was frequently changed, and with every attempt to arise, however futile, a firm reprimand to remain still sounded.

"You just lay there, Reggie," a woman instructed me. "No need to be getting up."

Another voice assured me, "You'll be healed in no time, Reggie, as long as you rest."

Then there was my master's voice, "I hope you are not in too much pain, my faithful friend. I deeply regret what Wickham's actions have cost you." His hand stroked lightly on the top of my head. "You did not deserve this."

My injuries made it very easy for me to sleep. There were only a few occasions when I awoke with an urgent sense that I needed to get up. At these times, I knew not whether it was day or night, let alone how many days had passed. I was aware that I was not in my master's quarters; from the sounds and smells, I determined that I was being kept in or close to the kitchen. It was a struggle for me to even open my eyes and when I did, I found that I could not focus on any particular object before me.

The few times I lay there and was able to form any coherent thought, I tried to recall what had happened. Whilst I could not recollect every detail, I knew that my master and I had found Wickham and that he had assaulted me with a sharp kick in my ribs.

I awoke one morning to the sound of voices and I finally was able to open my eyes. I looked about me and could actually see sunlight pouring in through an open window and a slight breeze played with the curtains. I lifted my head slowly and did not see anyone, but discerned the voices were coming from another room.

Although it caused a great deal of discomfort to move my legs and pull myself upright, I did that very thing and took a step forward, wincing at the pain that spread from my belly out. I dared not let out a whine. I did not want to alert anyone to the fact that I was up and making an attempt to walk!

I concentrated on putting one paw in front of the other and slowly made progress across the room. At the bottom of the stairs I looked up. It seemed a daunting task, but I was determined to make it up the stairs to my master's chambers. That was my place and where I wished to be.

I was able to lift a paw upon the first step, but I feared the rest of my paws would not be as proficient. The pain paralysed me. I closed my eyes and finally brought a second paw up. I was now straddling the stair, two paws on the first step and two paws on the ground.

This was an unexpected situation. I felt too weary to even return to my bed and so I simply lay down, not caring about the odd position in which I found myself.

Happily, it was not long before I heard footsteps from above and lifted my head to see my master descending the stairs at a brisk pace. When he noticed me, he stopped abruptly. "Now just where do you think you were going, Reggie?"

He came down and sat on the stair next to me. His voice shook as he spoke softly. "It is good to see you making an effort to get around, but you cannot expect to be ready to climb a flight of stairs."

He put his hand to my nose and his scent infused me with a desire to regain my strength. Although I knew he did not care for me to lick him, I could not stop myself from gently licking his hand as it lingered near.

His eyes misted as he told me, "I feared that you were not going to come through, boy. You suffered some internal injuries, possibly a broken or fractured rib."

He gently lifted me and carried me into his study, calling for a servant to bring in my bed. He had the servant place the bed next to his chair and after we were both settled in, he told me of his visits with Miss Lydia Bennet ("she is unfortunately younger than her fifteen years and far too naïve about Wickham") and the Gardiners ("they are exceedingly fine people"). He also told me of the upcoming wedding that would take place ("it will be a mockery to have it in the church!")

When he finished, he looked down at me and smiled. "I dare say the members of the ton would think I was behaving in a rather odd manner by telling you all this, Reggie, as if you understood. But I feel as though you deserve to know what has transpired after all you have been through."

I moaned and he let out a small laugh. "Besides, there are times when I am convinced you *do* understand all I say."

With the information my master gave me, I was able to rest soundly. It seemed he succeeded in what he set out to do. He was quite confident Wickham would marry Miss Lydia Bennet with the financial incentive my master promised. He informed me that we would return to Pemberley in a few days' time, although he would need to return to town to attend the wedding within the fortnight.

~~*

Each day thereafter, I felt a little less pain and a trifle more energy, but instinctively I knew not all was completely right with me. Not wanting to unduly burden my master with all that was already weighing upon his shoulders, I made a valiant effort, however, to assure him of my well being and we finally returned to Pemberley. Whilst I was eager to be home, the jarring from the carriage ride unsettled me and prevented me from getting the rest I so desired.

We were heartily welcomed by Georgiana; concern etched across her features as she rushed out to greet her brother and inquire after my health. Apparently he had written a letter informing her of my encounter with an errant kick. I was quite certain he did not tell her who was responsible for it.

Georgiana informed us that the Bingley party remained at Pemberley. She was too kind to say so overtly, but we soon discovered that Miss Bingley rarely gave the young girl time to herself, smothering her with her attentions. The sheer frustration of such relentless flattery was noticeably apparent in Georgiana's face.

We walked slowly toward the house, my master very considerate of my still pained ribs. Gratefully, I was able to slowly ascend the steps without assistance and we came indoors.

"Mr. Darcy!" Miss Bingley's animated welcome reverberated unpleasantly in my ears. "We were about to despair whether you would actually return before we took our leave!"

"Good day, Miss Bingley." He walked toward his friend. "Hello, Bingley. Please pardon my long absence. I encountered some difficulties in the matter that required my attention in town. It took longer than I had anticipated."

"Oh, Mr. Darcy!" Miss Bingley prevented her brother from even the most remote opportunity to greet his friend. "Your sister has been the most charming hostess! She was so gracious and helpful. Such a sweet girl!" Miss Bingley looked expectantly at her brother, then to Georgiana, and finally turned back to my master. "She shall make a certain gentleman a fine wife someday!"

Georgiana appeared quite dismayed by Miss Bingley's effusions and less-than-subtle intimations.

Bingley stepped forward; seemingly anxious to change the topic of conversation. "Darcy, I am afraid we can only remain on at Pemberley a few more days. Then we must be off to the north. Pray, will you be here in a month's time when I return, or should I expect to find you in town?"

My master eyed him thoughtfully. "Do you have any plans at that time, Bingley?"

"Besides returning to town to attend to some business, absolutely none! What do you have in mind?"

"Certainly, do stop at Pemberley upon your return and stay a few days." My master turned his eyes to Miss Bingley for but a brief moment and then looked directly at Bingley. "Then I would suggest you make plans to return to Netherfield."

"Netherfield?" both Bingley and his sister uttered at the same time.

"Yes. Your lease is almost up and I do believe you need to make some decisions regarding it. Perhaps revisiting it will help you make the proper decision."

"Netherfield?" Bingley asked again pensively.

Miss Bingley, however, had quite a stern and quizzical look on her face and directed explicitly toward my master. "Certainly, Mr. Darcy, you cannot believe that to be a wise decision!"

My master shook his head. "On the contrary, Miss Bingley, I believe a return to Netherfield is long overdue!"

Bingley looked at my master expectantly. "Will you accompany me, Darcy? Certainly, you ought!"

My master seemed oblivious to every eye that was upon him. His brow furrowed and he answered adamantly, "No, Bingley. I do not believe I will have that pleasure on this occasion."

Georgiana was as disappointed by his answer as Miss Bingley had been stunned from his mention of Netherfield.

For myself, upon hearing his answer, I felt a searing pain of disappointment, almost as real as the physical pain I had been experiencing. I watched as my master turned away and walked toward the table that had been set up with tea and coffee. He poured himself some of the hot liquid and stared into the cup. He had spoken little to me of Miss Elizabeth since informing me of her sister's situation. I wondered whether he had thrown out his violent feelings of love for Miss Elizabeth now that Wickham was to be a member of her family. Was he questioning the suitability of her familial relations again and to an even greater degree all because of Wickham?

~~*

Once Bingley and his party departed for the north, my master made plans to return to London. He informed Georgiana that once again business required his immediate attention, but assured her he would return within a few days.

The evening before he left, he enjoyed the company of his young sister. The stress and anxiety of having endured Miss Bingley's attentions, while being hostess to a party of four, was clearly seen in her features. Over the evening meal, they talked of everything save for that which was foremost on both -- nay, on *all* our minds -- Miss Elizabeth.

We adjourned to the music room where Georgiana eased her and my master's spirits with some pleasant pieces on the pianoforte. The first touch of her fingers had its desired effect and I noticed both master and sister relaxed considerably. I lay in the corner, enjoying the company of the two people for whom I cared most deeply. Georgiana's music proved to be the balm to soothe my lingering infirmities and broken heart, as well.

When she finished her first piece, she began playing another, less difficult piece. She cast a glance at her brother and then back down to her hands. Biting her lip, she turned to him again.

"Fitzwilliam?"

His eyes had been closed, and at her summons, he opened them slightly. "Yes, Georgiana?"

"I am so grateful for your return. I confess I found my duties to our guests to be very demanding. Please do not think me rude to say so, but I began to wonder if I would be able to endure Miss Bingley's presence very much longer."

"Did you find her presence here taxing?"

Georgiana played a few more notes before answering in a careful tone. "Yes, Brother. I found it exceedingly difficult to be the gracious hostess to her that I knew I ought."

My master laughed softly. "She can become quite exasperating."

"I know not where she learned her manners," Georgiana continued, "but she spent most of her idle hours either praising me, praising Pemberley, or abusing Miss Bennet!"

My master's eyes widened at this and he let out a deep breath. "I apologize, Georgiana."

She stopped playing and then turned to him. "What took you so abruptly to London?"

My master shook his head in surprise. Obviously, he was not expecting this line of questioning.

Georgiana continued, "And what is prompting your immediate return?" She turned her whole body on the piano bench so she faced my master. "I know it is none of my business, but you set off that morning to pay Miss Bennet a call in Lambton and then upon your return, you inform us that you are forthwith departing for London with scarcely a reason. I cannot help but think it had something to do with your visit. When you informed Mr. Bingley that you would not accompany him when he returns to Netherfield, I felt certain something dreadful occurred. Was Miss Elizabeth not pleased with your attentions? If she was not, I must shoulder the responsibility, as it was my suggestion for you to go to her."

Looking down, my master tightened his fists. When he lifted his eyes to his sister, they were filled with anguish. "No, Georgiana, my sweet. It was not my visit that has caused distress. Oh, that I could conceal the truth from you if only I knew you would never come to learn about it! But I know that cannot be."

"What is it?" Her eyes widened with alarm.

"When I arrived at the inn, Miss Bennet had just received a letter from her sister with some very distressing news about her family."

Georgiana waited for her brother to continue.

My master stood and walked over to his sister, sitting down beside her on the piano bench. He took her hand and squeezed it tightly. I stood up and walked slowly over as well, nuzzling up next to her.

"Apparently, Miss Bennet's youngest sister followed the militia to Brighton when they left Meryton. She had been invited by the colonel's wife."

When he did not continue, she leaned her head toward his. "Fitzwilliam?"

His hand went up to rub his furrowed brow and despite the pain, I lifted my paw up and placed it on Georgiana's lap. "The letter informed Miss Bennet that her sister had run off with Wickham."

Silence now overtook Georgiana as she paled and stared at her brother in disbelief.

"They have eloped?" she inquired meekly.

My master looked down at his hand that held and gently stroked Georgiana's. "In her letter, Miss Lydia indicated they were going to Gretna Greene to be married. I doubted whether Wickham had such plans and the letter informed Miss Bennet that upon Mr. Bennet's inquiries, there was no evidence they ever left London. I left immediately to see if I could find them and set right the situation."

"Did you find them?" a very soft voice asked.

"Yes. And just as I suspected, he had no intention of marrying her. I am sure he held out the hope of a more advantageous match. I remained in town to try to talk sense into one or both of them. When I was unable to persuade Miss Lydia to return to her family, I had to content myself with convincing them that they must marry. I return to London tomorrow for the wedding."

Georgiana looked down to her hands that were now both engulfed by my master's large hands. Shame and remorse seemed to overwhelm her, as she must have recollected her imprudent actions. Her eyes travelled down to where I sat at her feet and I noticed her wince. Keeping her eyes on me, she asked, "Was it… was *he* the one who inflicted the kick to Reggie?"

"Yes," my master answered softly.

Tears came to her eyes as she looked remorsefully down at me, "I am so sorry, Reggie!"

I lifted my paws toward her several times to assure her I did not place any blame on her.

A look of sudden realization prompted her to lift her head back toward my master and her eyes looked at him with deep concern. "He will now be…"

"Yes," my master nodded. "He will be Miss Bennet's brother."

"And that is your reason for not accompanying Mr. Bingley to Netherfield?"

Standing up, my master briskly rubbed his jaw. "I do not know. When at Rosings, she made her feelings quite adamantly known to me. She may have been civil to me while she was here, however I have no assurances that her feelings have changed. Now with Wickham…"

"But do you love her?" Georgiana asked abruptly.

My tail wagged in an affirmative response as my master sought how to answer. He walked towards the window and looked out. It was only a brief moment before he answered.

"Yes, Georgiana, I do. Very much. But to align myself with her family now that Wickham is a part of it…"

"Fitzwilliam, is your love for her stronger than your loathing for Mr. Wickham?"

"Of course, but Georgiana…"

"Please, Fitzwilliam, forgive me if I assume too much. I beg you not to think you must give up Miss Bennet for my sake. I know that you are trying to shelter me from any pain of seeing Mr. Wickham again. Whilst I still have regrets over my behaviour, I no longer harbour feelings for him."

Georgiana walked over to her brother and took his hands in hers. "You have been an excellent guardian to me for the past five years. You have loved me, protected me, and I am sure that Father and Mother would be pleased with the admirable example you have set. But allow me to exhibit that strength of character that I have so often seen in you. You will deeply regret it if you do not go to her and find out her true feelings. If she returns your regard, the two of you can then address the issue of Wickham. But please, do not keep yourself from her because of me!"

"Georgiana, are you certain that the slightest possibility of aligning our family with his would not cause you unease?"

"I am quite certain. He has caused you pain too often. Do not let him have this triumph over you!"

I was a little surprised that I had not comprehended this earlier. It was for Georgiana's protection that he had resolved not to accompany Bingley to Netherfield, knowing that an alliance with Miss Elizabeth would perchance throw Georgiana into Wickham's path. I chided myself for this lapse and wondered whether my quick mind was slowing down much like my body.

I watched as my master took in a deep breath and a smile came to his face. "You are too perceptive for such a young girl, Georgiana. I believe I *shall* heed your wisdom and join Bingley at Netherfield."

~~*

My master departed the next morning for London. Assuming that Wickham posed no obstacles, he planned to stay but three days. For a trip of such a short duration, it was agreed that I would remain at Pemberley. I was most grateful as I did not look forward with any eagerness to another jarring carriage ride. I spent the majority of the time resting, still not feeling completely healed. I enjoyed this special time with Georgiana. She allowed me into her chambers and often lay on the floor next to me, combing my fur with her hands as she read a book.

When my master returned, the only words he spoke on the matter of Wickham's marriage to Miss Lydia were, "It is done."

We tried to resume some semblance of our normal schedule. Our walks were necessarily short and oftentimes, I merely awaited his return as he went out on his own. Sadly, not only was I still experiencing too persistent pain, but my strength had waned far more than I would have expected from my injuries. I feared my convalescence would be a lengthy one.

As I watched him return from a solitary walk, I was filled with regret that for the first time in my life, I could no longer accompany him. I missed our camaraderie and hearing him verbalize his deepest thoughts to me. Though he would come back from these lone ventures refreshed as one would expect from exertions of this sort, it did not take the acuity of a dog's senses to perceive something was lacking. I knew he wished for someone to accompany him. He needed someone with whom he could share his joys and sorrows, hopes and fears; someone who would challenge him with lively conversation; someone who would be there for him once I was gone. I knew who it had to be.

The problem, as I saw it, was that there seemed to always be obstacles in bringing them together. He seemed satisfied that he had done what he could to salvage the Bennet family's reputation and Miss Lydia's honour. I do not know exactly the intricacies of currency, but I was quite certain he did so with a sizeable sum -- far greater than Wickham deserved! Even still, I knew that he would have paid ten times the sum to have the right to court Miss Elizabeth.

To his credit, my master became more content once he had determined he would see Miss Elizabeth again, but he confessed to me in his chambers one evening that he did not wish for her to know of his involvement and what it cost him to bribe Wickham to marry her sister.

"I only hope that it will be kept from her. I asked everyone to give me their assurances that they would inform no one I was in attendance at the wedding, let alone arranged all the details. I trust the Gardiners to keep silent; I can only hope the new Mr. and Mrs. Wickham do the same. I do not wish to go to Miss Elizabeth if all she feels is beholden to me."

We were in the study late one night and my master was expecting Bingley any day. He had been making a vain attempt at reading, but finally put the book down in exasperation. Obviously, his thoughts had been elsewhere.

"I cannot begin to know what Miss Elizabeth will do or say to me when Bingley and I return to the neighbourhood. She may still harbour resentment towards me, but whether or not she returns my regard, I intend to confess to Bingley my error of judgment regarding her sister. That is the least I can do!"

He leaned forward, clasping his hands together tightly. "I do not deserve her, Reggie, but I do hope to God that she would give me another chance."

It was but a few days later that Bingley returned to Pemberley and he was quite pleased to find that my master had changed his mind about accompanying him to Netherfield.

My master insisted upon me travelling, as well, for which I was grateful. Whilst I had improved slightly, I knew the long day's journey over muddy and rutted roads would only serve to aggravate my condition. For my master's sake, I would bear up under it, especially as the hopeful outcome would be seeing Miss Elizabeth and my master together.

He assured me that he would do everything in his power to provide for my comfort and provide an opportunity for me to see Miss Elizabeth again. Perhaps he hoped that I could have some influence to help him win her over. I overheard him speaking to his sister, however, and knew his decision to allow me to accompany was partly due to his concern with my well being. In hushed tones he told her that he would not rest easy if I were not with him, knowing how poorly I had been in recent days.

We extended our heartfelt farewell to Georgiana, who was to remain at Pemberley through Christmas. A short stop in London to set some affairs in order was all that Bingley and my master required before we all departed, in hopeful anticipation, for Netherfield.

~~*

My master invited Bingley to ride along in his carriage to give them ample opportunity to talk. I knew what was on my master's mind and once he had the opportunity to confess his errant interference to his friend, he would be somewhat more at peace with himself.

As we rode in the carriage, I easily sensed the comportment of the two gentlemen. Bingley had a heightened anticipation about him that prompted him to smile throughout practically our whole ride. My master kept his anticipation at bay. His expectations were more cautious.

At length, Bingley spoke. "I must admit, Darcy, I cannot help but hope to see Miss Bennet again. I do hope she will be happy to see me."

"Bingley, I..." my master spoke but was stopped as his friend put up his hand.

"Now, I know what you are going to say. I remember all too well what your opinion of her was." He looked toward the window. "That *blasted* apple!"

"Bingley, there is something..."

"No, Darcy. I must say this. Upon seeing Miss Elizabeth at Pemberley, I could not dismiss the feelings that I discovered I still had for Miss Bennet. I have every intention of calling on her!" He firmly folded his arms in front of him. "You cannot talk me out of it and I insist that you accompany me to Longbourn at the first opportunity!"

My master smiled. "Of course, Bingley. It would be a pleasure."

It was not difficult to miss the look of surprise that crossed Bingley's face upon hearing my master's words. Rather than question his friend, his thoughts returned to Miss Bennet.

"I only hope she does not think ill of me for quitting Netherfield so abruptly and not returning until now. I know Caroline wrote to her to explain our situation but I cannot help but consider that she might have wondered of my long absence."

I watched as my master looked down and nervously wrung his hands together. I knew he was contemplating an apology, but apparently it was not the time.

"I am quite certain a visit to Longbourn will answer any fears one might have, Bingley."

I closed my eyes now with every hope that once we arrived at Netherfield, all would go well for both men.

Chapter 25

With the days drawing to an earlier close each day, the sun was reaching toward the horizon when we finally entered the park at Netherfield. Our arrival was almost a year to the day since we first saw Netherfield last autumn. The concept of calendars is not something that comes easily to dogs, not even one as used to humans as I, so this information became known to me on the good authority of Bingley, who, I discovered, was very keen on remembering dates.

Whereas I formerly would bound enthusiastically out from the carriage with nary a concern and work off all my pent up energy from the full day's ride, it was all I could do to merely stand up and turn toward the open door once Bingley and my master had stepped out. The distance to the ground looked much greater than I ever remembered it. My body ached from the long, uncomfortable carriage ride and the very last thing I wished to do was jump out.

While pondering how I might best remove myself from the carriage with the least amount of discomfort, I felt large hands gently wrap themselves about me and I looked up to see my master, who placed me down on the ground.

"Here we go, good fellow," my master said with a reassuring, knowing smile.

It felt good to get out, but it was in a rather slow gait that I took to the nearest tree as Bingley and my master stretched their legs and looked about the park.

"The gardeners have done well in maintaining the grounds in your absence, Bingley."

"Yes, I am pleased. Shall we step inside and see how well it has been prepared for our return?"

I joined the gentlemen and we stepped inside. I cannot answer for them -- human noses being what they are -- but as I walked indoors, my nose drew in all the scents that evoked vivid memories of our previous stay here. The floral scents reminded me of the first time Miss Elizabeth came to Netherfield, when I found myself quite taken by this lively and amiable young lady. There was a pleasant aroma coming from the kitchen that brought back recollections of the meals we had as I sat at Miss Elizabeth's feet, bestowing upon her my singular attention whilst all others at the table, including my master, paid her little heed. The smoke from the fire wafting from the hearth turned my thoughts to the evenings we spent in the drawing room where Miss Elizabeth challenged my master's every thought and unknowingly tore his composure to bits.

I easily apprehended that the two gentlemen, as well, were directing their thoughts upon the former days when both Miss Bennets graced the halls of Netherfield. Bingley had a rather dreamy look affixed to his countenance as he glanced about him. My master's posture stiffened and he walked immediately over to a window and looked out. I was quite certain the window faced the direction of Longbourn.

Bingley's housekeeper, who had met us at the door and cheerfully welcomed us back, engaged Bingley in a discussion about the management of the estate. My master pulled himself away from the window and he called to me, announcing that he was anxious to freshen up from the long ride and wished to proceed up to his chambers. I eagerly followed as I greatly desired a nap.

My master must have realized this; for almost immediately upon crossing the threshold did he put my special blanket atop the bed and lift me upon it. I no longer had the agility to jump up on my own and depended upon him to assist me. I turned around several times, pawing at the blanket so that it would fluff up and afford me greater comfort. Once it was exactly as I wished, I lay down. My eyes closed and I welcomed the sleep that quickly came upon me.

~~*

Whereas I firmly believed a visit to Longbourn should be of the highest priority, neither of the men seemed inclined to pay a call. Over the course of the next few days, several neighbours called to welcome Bingley back and I fervently hoped that perhaps Mr. Bennet might call again, as he did when we first arrived. When he did not, I truly began to wonder whether a visit to the Bennets would transpire.

Oftentimes in the evening, as the men adjourned to the drawing room, I sat at my master's feet and looked up unremittingly at him. I wished to convey to him that I had not come all this way for him -- or me, for that matter -- to remain confined at Netherfield. But to my dismay, neither he nor Bingley seemed eager to broach the subject of a visit to Longbourn with the other.

I could only attribute their reticence to the possibility that Bingley feared my master's disapproval and my master feared the same from Miss Elizabeth, despite her show of civility toward him at Pemberley.

It was not until a full two days later that the decision was made at last and the long-awaited visit to Longbourn was planned for the afternoon. While seated in the breakfast room that morning, Bingley casually mentioned it.

"I was wondering, Darcy," he began.

My master looked up. "Yes?"

Bingley seemingly needed to gather up courage to continue. "Do you not think it would be neighbourly… to call on… to call on the Bennets at Longbourn?" Bingley kept his eyes directed at the plate of food in front of him and did not look once at my master. "Certainly we do not want to appear uncivil."

"I quite agree with you, Bingley."

"Perhaps we could…." Suddenly, apprehending my master's acquiescence, Bingley looked up. "You agree with me?"

My master brought his napkin up and dabbed his mouth. "Yes. In fact, Bingley, I think we ought to call on the Bennets this very afternoon."

It goes without saying that Bingley was both pleased and surprised at my master's willingness to call. Now that it appeared my master had agreed to see Miss Elizabeth again, I wondered when he would exhibit the same strength of spirit and admit to his friend that he had been wrong about Miss Bennet.

I enjoyed watching these two men as they each displayed completely different peculiarities that betrayed their nervous excitement in anticipation of seeing the woman each so deeply admired. Bingley's manner took the form of walking restlessly about the room, arms flailing as he spoke unceasingly about every topic imaginable. I wondered whether he even took the time to breathe, as his words poured out in a never-ending deluge.

It was quite fortunate, however, that he was so disposed to speak, as my master's inclination was quite the opposite. He stood and gazed out the window or planted his arm on the mantel of the fireplace and gazed at absolutely nothing outside or across the room. He nodded every once in a while to one of Bingley's effusions, but I truly believe he heard not a word.

My master remained perfectly still except for the nervous tapping of his fingers. On occasion I thought I heard his breath catch, letting it finally escape ever so slowly, as if a fleeting thought had caused him some uncertainty.

I must admit, much to my chagrin, that my master did not seem to exhibit what I would consider a confident deportment in this thing humans call love. In most every aspect of his life, I had known him to meet every challenge with assurance, but now I saw him questioning his own worth! I wished that he would receive some sort of encouragement on this visit that would allay any and all of his fears that persisted concerning whether Miss Elizabeth returned his favour or not.

Mindful that the rituals of human courtship were beyond my comprehension, I was quite of the opinion that if he only confessed his undying love to her, how could she not return it? Whilst he had done it once before, he had done it all wrong! I knew he had learned much about himself since those days at Hunsford and I hoped that Miss Elizabeth would take notice that he had tried to attend to her reproofs. I could only hope as well, that once my master saw her again, he would display a more outward show of regard towards her.

Unfortunately, I was unable to accompany them as Bingley wished to ride. I suspect it was so that he could pound the horse to Longbourn in rhythm to the pounding of his own heart.

~~*

I anxiously awaited the return of my master and Bingley from Longbourn. Despite the slight pain and overall weariness due to my infirm condition, I found it exceedingly difficult to rest and so I paced the floors of Netherfield. However, I knew not whether I anticipated or dreaded their return more. If they returned too soon, that would be an indication that they were not well received, and I did so want them to triumph.

When the men did finally return, I greeted them at the door. Bingley was more exuberant than I had ever seen him, which I perceived as a very heartening sign. However, my master's mien was as reserved as he was before they departed. I did not know what to make of it. Bingley talked of the joy of seeing the Bennet ladies again, how friendly and engaging they all were, and how angelic Miss Bennet in particular remained. But it soon became clear that my master's manner had not improved upon seeing Miss Elizabeth again. How could this be? Could Georgiana's words have had so little effect on him?

Bingley crossed his arms across his chest. "I only wish, Darcy, that you would make an attempt to be more forthcoming in conversation. If you would enter into some sort of dialogue, it would not appear so much that I dragged you along with me against your will!"

"Against my will?"

"Well, what are they to think? You hardly uttered a word there today. You stood there absolutely grave and silent!"

My master guiltily glanced down at me as I lowered my head onto my paws and let out a rather loud and long groan. I knew my master could be quite the conversationalist. He was knowledgeable of all manner of subjects and could discuss anything from literature to history to managing an estate. Indeed, I had been witness to many a lively debate between my master and his friends, sometimes going into the wee hours of the night. It seemed, however, that the basic civilities escaped him when was confronted with the presence of an engaging lady.

I would have been completely disheartened had not my master informed me that night in his chambers that they had received an invitation to return to dine at Longbourn in a few days. He also explained his behaviour to me.

"You cannot think ill of me, Reggie, for my behaviour today! I... I did not feel welcome at Longbourn, particularly by Mrs. Bennet. Her veiled incivility coupled with Miss Elizabeth's refusal to even look at me left me with lingering doubts. Nevertheless, I knew I was lost as ever in her mere presence and will do all I can to hold on to any hope of encouragement from Miss Elizabeth as to a change in her regard for me."

My master looked down at me solemnly. "I promise, Reggie, that I will attend to her at dinner in two days' time and attempt to determine whether now she might be receptive to my suit."

I reasoned that this would certainly give my master more of an opportunity to engage Miss Elizabeth in conversation; particularly during the meal. He would have ample time throughout this more prolonged visit to establish whether or not the elder Miss Bennets had genuine feelings for either gentleman.

Again, I waited expectantly for their return that night; hopeful that I would find that there had been abundant conversation and occasion to display singular attention. And apparently there was -- for Bingley!

When they returned that evening, Bingley entered the room as if he was the Prince Regent himself. His smile was permanently etched across his face and he could not praise Miss Bennet enough nor doubt her affections.

"Did you see her smile at me when I walked into the dining room? That was all the invitation I needed to sit beside her."

"Yes, Bingley, and I did not disregard your expression of alarm directed my way when you took that seat."

"I was quite afraid of you, Darcy. If you were not staring at Miss Elizabeth all evening, your stares were directed at Miss Bennet. How was I to know whether you would take me aside, declaring that Miss Bennet was unfit even to be my dining companion?"

"Surely, you do not believe I would do such a thing!"

"I would hope not, but I never before saw you so adamant about something, Darcy, than declaring Miss Bennet's unsuitability and her absence of feelings for me last year in London!"

The two men eyed each other and my master straightened and nervously pulled at his coat. With measured words he said, "I must beg your forgiveness, Bingley. It was very wrong of me to make such a declaration. I should never have interfered. It was absurd and impertinent."

A very surprised smile appeared and Bingley retorted, "I am quite astounded by your admission, Darcy, but quite pleased. I cannot help but wonder what has brought about this change of heart."

My master looked down. "On our recent calls at Longbourn, I easily perceived that my previous assessment of Miss Bennet's affections was quite misplaced. It is clear that she esteems you highly and I have no doubts of your happiness together."

"That is quite remarkable coming from you, Darce. In all our years of friendship, I cannot recall one time when you have been wrong!"

"You are mistaken, Bingley. I have made countless grave errors -- many of them quite recently."

A sly smile crept across Bingley's face. "I cannot help but wonder if there is something more."

A firm thumping of my tail acknowledged the truth of this, but my master did nothing to confirm his friend's suspicions.

"I… I only wish to set things right, Bingley. I have been confronted lately with the results of my interference. I can only tell you that I have been much distressed by my actions."

"Good! I am glad to hear it! It serves you right for causing *me* such unnecessary torment!"

"I am truly regretful, Bingley."

"I am pleased you no longer disapprove. So I have your blessing to ask for her hand?"

"Of course, good friend."

"Good!" He turned a stern gaze upon my master. "But I would have you know, I had every intention to make her an offer whether or not you gave your blessing!"

"I am most happy for you, Bingley." My master chuckled softly.

This confession to his friend had been difficult for my master but he bore it admirably. However, I knew he was not done with his apology. He grew even more grave as he took a deep breath and he shook his head slowly. "Bingley, there is one more bit of information I need to relate to you which does not reflect well upon me either."

"What is it?" Bingley asked nervously.

"I fear that although I abhor deception, I did *withhold* information from you in concert with your sisters."

"About what?"

After a rather long pause, my master finally answered. "When we were last in London, Miss Bennet was also there, staying with her aunt and uncle in Cheapside. She even paid a call to your sisters and we agreed… we agreed that information should be kept from you."

"What? Miss Bennet was in Town and you did not tell me? Lord, she must think me unfeeling! How could you?"

"For the reasons we had previously addressed. Although I thought myself to be acting in your best interests, the scheme was wrong in its entirety, Bingley, and I accept full responsibility for my part of it."

Bingley looked away. He seemed to know not what to say. I wondered whether he refrained from speaking so that he would not say something harsh to his friend. They both were silent for quite some time, both feeling all the awkwardness of the situation.

Finally my master spoke. "It is very apparent, Bingley, that Miss Bennet holds a spirit of such a generous nature that she will not hold this offence against you. You may tell her that in all truth you were completely unaware of her calling upon your sisters. I am quite certain she will forgive you. I can only hope you can find it in your heart to forgive me, as well."

Bingley breathed in deeply. "She is an angel, is she not?"

Bingley suddenly laughed and I was grateful that the tension bearing down upon my senses had broken and given way to levity.

"Although this incident is far more serious than the other, I cannot help but forgive you. I cannot tell you how much pleasure I have derived to have seen such an expression of distress upon your countenance twice in one day." Bingley's eyes danced merrily.

"Twice?" my master asked.

"Yes. Just now, of course, and earlier at dinner when you were seated next to Mrs. Bennet! I found it more and more difficult to stifle a laugh each time I looked over at you. You were either silently staring at your plate of food or if you *were* in conversation with her, you looked as though you were suffering from an excruciating toothache!"

The men continued their discourse; Bingley teasing and gloating at my master's expense, a situation I had never before had the occasion of experiencing. But I must say my master tolerated it reasonably well. Perhaps he viewed it as atonement for his interference.

"I fear, Darcy, that for some inexplicable reason, you are not in Mrs. Bennet's good graces. You might have made more of an effort today to change that."

"I do not… I find it exceedingly difficult to carry on a conversation with her." My master wiped his brow. "If I had been seated near you or Miss Bennet… or Miss Elizabeth, I would have proven to be more companionable."

"Well, my friend, I suggest you accustom yourself to it."

My master looked at the sly smile on his friend's face. "I beg your pardon?"

"She will be my mother-in-law, of course! I would expect we shall be invited to many such dinners! Besides, I would not wish for her to think too unkindly of my best friend."

"No, we would not want that."

The men discussed when they would next visit Longbourn and I became a trifle more fretful about my master's lack of progress where Miss Elizabeth was concerned. The housekeeper came in and presented a letter to my master. He opened it and frowned.

"What is it?" his friend asked. I was curious as well.

"My presence is required in London. I must make preparations to leave first thing in the morning."

"Will you be away long?"

"It is difficult to say. Hopefully no more than a week to ten days."

"Will you return to Netherfield once you have completed your business?"

I shared Bingley's hope that we would return to Netherfield.

"Yes. I shall return directly."

That night, after we retired for the evening, I learned that although my master only had a few moments with Miss Elizabeth, he had sensed that she would have gladly welcomed more.

"Indeed, Reggie, I did make several attempts to converse with Miss Elizabeth, but it seemed as though some young lady was conspiring against me. She refused to allow me within proximity of her! It only left me feeling an extraordinary sense of embarrassment."

My master closed his eyes. His hand stroked down my back as he said softly, "I felt so much but was able to say so little."

I listened to the sound of my master's deepening breathing as he fell into a sound sleep and thought of all he had told me. Whilst nothing happened that absolutely assured him of her regard, at least nothing happened that completely shattered his hope.

~~*

I accompanied my master to London so I would not be a burden to the staff at Netherfield, although truth be told, my upkeep was but a trifling thing. I slept a great deal, ate very little, and only required the necessity of being let outside a few times a day. Admittedly, it took me longer to move about. I could, at least, walk under my own power even though the pain from my encounter with Wickham lingered. But even with the anticipation of a most disagreeably jostling carriage ride, I welcomed the privilege of remaining at my master's side.

I found it exceedingly difficult, however, to bear up under this carriage ride. While my master had his man arrange for the thickest blankets and even an old pillow to be placed beneath me, I could not contain my moans. Though I heard my master more than once berate himself for placing me it such a situation, it was not so much the physical pain from which I suffered, but emotional. I wondered whether I could endure another disappointment.

I felt my years advancing resolutely. As a younger pup, I would have shaken off my injuries by that cad Wickham with scarcely a convalescence. The very fact that I found it so difficult to heal made me feel fully every one of my years. I knew I was growing weaker and did not believe I had all the time in the world. My greatest desire was to see my master situated blissfully with Miss Elizabeth, who I knew would make him truly happy. If he needed a little nudging, I would gladly do it, but sadly, I had not yet been given the opportunity to accompany him to Longbourn. There must some way to accomplish this!

~~*

When we arrived in London, my master met with his steward and set to work directly. He worked late into the night and then awoke the next morning with the hopes of making the necessary contacts required of him before afternoon. The staff was happy to see that I had tolerably recovered from my injury, but I heard them whispering to one another that I did not look well.

The days in town passed slowly. While my master was away on errands, I forced myself to walk as much as possible. Recently I had been experiencing more and more difficulty getting up after resting idly for any length of time. My legs felt stiff and painful. I had every hope that if I applied myself to exercise, my limbs would be less likely to ache and I would soon have the ability to walk as frequently and as long as I once did.

We were in his study on one of our final days in town. I was sleeping soundly at his feet after sharing a brief walk with my master when a knock interrupted our peace. At my master's bidding, a servant entered, presenting him with two letters.

As my master read the missives, there was silence save for an occasional chuckle. Thinking the letters were business related, I was quite surprised when he leaned down and spoke to me.

"Well, Reggie. We have some interesting news here. I have just received a letter from Bingley and another from Georgiana. I have determined from Bingley's much blotted and barely decipherable letter that he has made an offer to and has been accepted by Miss Bennet. He has requested that I stand up for him."

My tail wagged at this most pleasant news about his friend. At the least, this guaranteed more opportunities to throw my master in the path of Miss Elizabeth. Perhaps even as soon as our return to Netherfield!

He looked at the letter from his friend and then at me. "I wonder whether he is aware of my feelings for Miss Elizabeth. I was quite certain he suspected something, but I could not bring myself to tell him. I must be assured of her feelings before I tell him of mine."

He looked down at the other letter in his hand. "I believe you will find Georgiana's missive to be of particular interest, Reggie. She informs me that Sadie is about to have her first litter of puppies!" He looked down at me and smiled. "Could it be, old fellow, that you are the father as everyone suspects?"

My tail wagged even more intensely at this glorious news! I confess I was now torn whether I wished more to head back to Pemberley as soon as possible or remain hopeful and return to Netherfield. I determined that it was not my place to be selfish. I had to know that my master's life could be as full and rich as possible. It was a comfort then, to know at least I had something to look forward to once we made the journey home.

My master finally concluded his business and we both looked forward to our return to Netherfield. I was in one of my deep slumbers late in the afternoon and in a rather dreamy state. In my dream I was surrounded by an array of puppies, little balls of fur, nipping and yapping, pouncing on me and wearing me out. Sadie was watching with great delight as I attempted to get these little rascals under control. It was a futile attempt.

Suddenly I heard a shrill voice that caused all the puppies to quiver in fear and sent shivers up and down my spine.

That which I had been dreaming quickly became a nightmare! A large cat suddenly appeared, causing the puppies to run about frantically in fright.

I woke from the dream and lifted my head, trying to shake the grogginess that hung over me. My heart was pounding and I chided myself for allowing a mere nightmare to effect me so greatly. But I heard the shrill sound again and knew at once who it was.

Lady Catherine!

I heard my master murmur something harshly under his breath and I looked over to him. There was a soft knock at the door and as my master stood, it opened abruptly. Lady Catherine swept into the room with a determined step, leaving the housekeeper to whisper meekly, "Lady Catherine, Sir."

"Aunt Catherine, to what do I owe…"

"I must have a word with you this moment!" She turned to the housekeeper. "You may leave now!"

Her eyes were dark and narrow and I sensed such an anger that it caused me to tremble. I wondered what could possibly have put her in such a state. But being familiar with her temperament as I was, I knew it might be anything from a disrespectful servant to not receiving an invitation to a grand society event. Still, I could not imagine what circumstances would cause her to leave Rosings Park to demand an audience with my master.

I had little time to ponder this, for she soon spewed out such accusatory words against my master that he and I were exceedingly puzzled.

"I would never have believed this of you! Never! How could you? My own nephew! The son of my beloved sister and the one promised to my daughter! I insist you tell me that this is not true!"

My master shook his head slowly, "I fear that I do not have the pleasure of understanding you, Aunt."

She narrowed her eyes and shook her crooked, pointed finger at him. "You are just as evasive as she was! I can see that she has bewitched you!"

"Of whom do you speak?" My master spoke calmly, but I could detect the slight quiver in his voice as shock and bewilderment assailed him.

"That impertinent upstart Elizabeth Bennet!"

I watched as my master's mouth dropped and he paled. However, he seemed at a loss for words for only a moment. He regained his composure and used carefully measured tones.

"What is it that Miss Bennet has done to cause you such distress?"

"Do not be coy with me, Nephew! An engagement to her? It is not to be borne! I know of her family, the disgrace and shame of it all! I know of her inferior family relations!"

My master's eyes widened when she made this declaration. I could hardly credit what I was hearing and I suspect he was of a similar sensibility. How on earth did his partiality to Miss Elizabeth come to Lady Cat's attention?

"Where… where did you hear of an engagement between us?" he finally asked guardedly.

"That is of no import. I received no satisfaction from her and therefore, I must demand so from you. What have you to say of this most insupportable alliance?"

The colour of my master's face deepened and I sensed anger emanating from him. Very slowly, he asked, "You spoke with Miss Bennet?"

"I did, yesterday. I informed Miss Bennet that any such union is impossible." Lady Catherine suddenly took off her gloves and presumed to sit down in one of the chairs without invitation. My master stared hard at her, evidently unable to fathom her confronting Miss Elizabeth, though her countenance revealed little anxiety. However, it did not escape my notice that she readjusted her body several times, as if she could not find any comfort in it.

"Listen to me, Nephew. You are a man of reason, but you may have found yourself drawn in by her arts and allurements and forgotten what you owe your family. That is why I am here -- to help you see that."

She spoke very deliberately and I waited expectantly for my master to put her in her place. But I was rather disheartened that he did not.

My master turned away from his aunt and looked down at the ground. "What exactly did Miss Bennet say when you went to her?"

"Impertinent girl! She refused to directly answer my questions. After I had exhausted all attempts at reasoning with her, she finally claimed that you were not yet engaged." Lady Cat huffed. "I knew, however, by her one response, that she had every expectation of a proposal!"

My master bolted around to face his aunt. "What one response? What did she say?"

Lady Catherine answered in a most disgusted manner. "I asked her to promise me that she will never enter into such an engagement."

"And?" my master asked hesitantly.

"She stated that she would make no promise of the kind! Insolent girl! She had the audacity to claim that neither duty, nor honour, nor gratitude would have any possible claim on her and that no principle of either would be violated by her marriage to you! To think that she would be willing to enter into a marriage that would bring you ruin; that would dishonour your family; that would make you the contempt of the world! She refused to give me the assurance that I required; that would exhibit respect for your station!"

I suddenly saw my master relax and a small smile appeared on his face. I watched in utter disbelief as he walked around his desk and leaned over and placed a kiss on his aunt's cheek. She seemed as surprised as I was, and her features softened -- to an extent.

"Aunt, I greatly appreciate your coming by today. You have no idea how much your words have meant to me."

A relieved smile appeared on her face. "Then you have not forsaken your duty to your family. You know not how pleased I am. You will promise me, then, never to make her an offer!"

"I now know precisely how to act." I could not believe I was listening to my own master! Had he lost all reason? Was he agreeing with his aunt on the one thing that I believed would destroy every hope for happiness?

"Forgive me, Aunt Catherine," he took her arm and escorted her toward the door. "I have some urgent business that requires me to leave immediately. Are you staying at your town home?"

"Yes," she stammered."

"Good. You shall hear from me later."

My master walked her to the door and when he returned, I detected no sign of his former anger. On the contrary, he closed the door to the study and turned towards me, clasping his hands and smiling! "Did you hear what she said? Elizabeth stood up to my aunt and refused to promise her that she will not marry me! She will not refuse me! We must be away to Netherfield directly!"

I sat up, eagerly watching the transformation of my master's features. Gone was the dull ache from his mien that troubled me to no end. His eyes lit up and his smile simply beamed. "At long last I have hope that Elizabeth is no longer absolutely and irrevocably decided against me. There is every reason to hope her regard for me has improved. My aunt could not have brought me news that was any more encouraging if she tried!"

He reached over and patted my head. "Reggie, we must be away to Netherfield without delay!"

Chapter 26

We returned to Netherfield both harbouring high expectations. Never had I witnessed in my master such optimism that Miss Elizabeth might finally return his affection. He wore a genuinely pleased countenance unlike any I had ever seen grace his features. A broad smile remained affixed as he gazed out the window. He was clearly eager to arrive at Netherfield; as was I.

Buoyed by his hopeful expression, my spirits were in much better stead. Whilst the jostling of the carriage pummelled my body, it could not dampen my morale. There was something in my master's manner -- indeed, in even the air itself -- that instilled faith in me that we would not come away disappointed.

Again and again I pondered the conversation between my master and his aunt. I must admit I had been quite disheartened when at first I supposed my master would heed his aunt's words. I was grateful he was of a quick mind to grasp the import of the words she ascribed to Miss Elizabeth. I was rather surprised that *I* had not and came to the sad realization that I was perhaps not as perceptive as I once prided myself.

When at length we pulled into the park at Netherfield, my master looked down at me. "I promise you, Reggie. No more disappointments. I am determined to see Miss Elizabeth and let it be known to her that my feelings have not changed."

His hand gently stroked my back and his fingers kneaded that one place that elicited a pleasurable moan from me. "I think it safe to say *I* have changed, but my feelings have not."

The carriage drew to a halt and my master began gathering his belongings. We had finally arrived at Netherfield.

My master provided the assistance I required to get out of the carriage. I walked to the house slowly, and much to my dismay, with a slight limp. Having remained immobile for so long in the carriage, it was quite painful to move about. I had truly hoped that by now my body would have returned to normal, but it was not to be. I took consolation, however, in the fact that each step brought me closer to my master's and my deepest longing.

Once inside, Bingley bounded down the stairs to welcome us. "You have returned! Did you receive my letter?"

"Letter?" my master asked innocently.

"Yes, I dispatched a letter to you in Town!" He was beaming.

My master chuckled. "I do recall receiving something from you! I would hardly call it a letter, however. I think it would be more accurately characterized as an illegible note or perhaps a barely decipherable communication, but a letter? I think not!"

"Ha! I was far too excited to write as meticulously as you! Nevertheless," begged his friend seriously, "you did read it, did you not?"

"Certainly, I did, Bingley, and I offer you and Miss Bennet my warmest congratulations!"

Bingley seemed quite satisfied with his friend's approval and clapped his hands together. "Thank you! Now, good friend, I presume that you will wish to give the Bennets your glad tidings as well. Would you care to accompany me when I call tomorrow at Longbourn?"

My master smiled. "I would agree to a visit this very evening if it were not so late and if I were not so tired and strongly in need of a bath. Tomorrow suits me quite well!"

With that settled, I was able to rest easily. Bingley and my master spent the evening talking of the plans that had already been set for the wedding. I detected a bit of envy in my master's eyes as his friend talked of his upcoming marriage. I knew my master well enough to comprehend that although he was more secure in his belief that Miss Elizabeth held him in high regard, he wondered whether it was enough for her to consent to be his wife if he renewed his offer.

~~*

Over breakfast the next morning the subject of their visit to Longbourn was brought up once again. Bingley wished to ride, but my master requested that they take the carriage, hoping that his friend would not object if I accompanied them. Fortunately, Bingley did not object and they agreed to depart immediately after the noon meal.

During the course of the morning, Bingley asked my master for some advice on Netherfield and whether he ought to go ahead and place an offer of purchase. I did not understand all the details the men discussed, but in the end, my master advised Bingley to continue to let the place whilst he and Miss Bennet settled in once they married. Then he advised that they consider carefully where they might wish to establish themselves before seeking out a permanent more suitable estate.

As I watched my master give his friend counsel, I was prodigiously proud of him. I could see that Bingley appreciated his wealth of knowledge and to his credit, Bingley's open nature made it clear that he had not lost respect for him. He listened to my master, eager to avail himself of his wisdom and willingness to help.

I also detected in my master's comportment a peaceful serenity that I never before had occasion to note. He was a gentleman who had always kept himself under control and good regulation, but now I sensed he was far more relaxed and at peace with himself. It was quite a pleasure to watch.

In surprised delight, I listened as my master inquired of Bingley what it was that he himself wished to do and gave him the advice he needed, but assured his friend that the final decision was his to make. Not more than a year ago, my master would not have hesitated in telling Bingley the exact proper course, never accounting that his friend's point of view may not be what he wished. Before me now stood a man so softened by love that he encouraged his friend to make the consideration himself.

As the time neared for the two men to depart, they began discussing how they could best extricate themselves away from the rest of the Bennet family and enjoy the company of the two eldest sisters once they arrived at Longbourn.

My master eyed his friend curiously. "Do you always find yourself in the midst of the entire Bennet family?"

"Oh, yes! Especially now that there are wedding details to prepare. Mrs. Bennet wishes to discuss everything with me, whilst I would just as soon leave that to Jane. I would prefer that she spend her time planning when I am away so I can spend some time alone with her when I am there. To own the truth, I care very little about all the details. I care only that at the conclusion of the ceremony we are married!"

My master nodded and I could sense his discomfiture rising. It caused me similar uneasiness at just the thought of Mrs. Bennet being continually in our company.

"I think I may have devised a way for us to assure you of that opportunity."

"Yes? What do you have in mind?" asked Bingley.

"It is a rather fine day." My master nodded at the bright expanse of park just outside the window. "Perhaps you might suggest a walk as being most beneficial. I doubt that Mrs. Bennet would wish to accompany us. I trust that such a scheme would be most agreeable to Miss Elizabeth and I would like to ensure that it is she that shares the chaperoning duties with me!"

"Truly, Darcy. Miss Elizabeth?"

I watched as a look -- more of confusion than comprehension -- swept across Bingley's features but then just as quickly disappeared. "But how are we to do that?"

My master shook his head for a brief moment as if he was not quite sure how. I let out a frustrated bark and he looked down at me. "Reggie!"

"Reggie?"

"Yes, Miss Elizabeth was always fond of Reggie. I shall inform her that he is outside and invite her to step outside to see him!"

"Splendid idea."

With that decided, the two men went their separate ways to prepare for the visit.

As we entered his chambers, my master looked down at me. "I fully comprehend, Reggie, that you are still not well enough to accompany us on a walk, as much as you would wish to." Ruffling the fur on my forehead he added, "At least you shall have the pleasure of seeing Miss Elizabeth. I promise I will do everything in my power to bring her outside to you."

Although I was pleased he was going to bring her out to me, I was disappointed that I would not be accompanying them. Knowing his and Miss Elizabeth's proclivity for walking, I knew they could likely travel a good distance; far too great for me to endure in my present condition. How I wished I felt more improved than I did!

Saddened by the betrayal of my own infirm body prohibiting me from assisting my master as I should have liked, I clung to his pledge to bring Miss Elizabeth to me. We then set out for Longbourn; all three of us in eager expectation.

As the carriage slowed, I was anxious for my first glimpse. The door was opened and my master assisted as I eagerly stepped out.

"Remain here, Reggie. We shall hopefully return directly."

I could not sit down and rest. I discerned Miss Elizabeth's scent so very strongly and wished above anything to go to her. Why dogs are not allowed the same privileges that people are is a question beyond my comprehension. I pride myself on being remarkably well behaved and took umbrage at the fact that I was not allowed entrance into the home along with the gentlemen.

I knew not whether to sit idly and hope to diminish the pain through respite or to walk about, hoping to loosen my muscles and work out the pain. I chose the former, knowing that if I were given the opportunity to walk, I would wish to be as rested as possible. I was well aware, however, that even in taking but a few steps, I was still plagued by a noticeable and painful limp.

After waiting patiently for Miss Elizabeth, I heard the door open. Looking up, I forgot every aching rib and painful muscle as I watched Miss Bennet, one of the younger Misses Bennet, and finally, Miss Elizabeth step through the open entry. My tail wagged with increasing joy as I watched my master walk up beside her and wave his hand in the direction of the carriage by which I was dutifully waiting.

I saw her eyes light up and a delighted smile cross her face, taking that as a sign that I could walk toward her. With a determined effort, I slowly made my way toward her. I sat down when I came to her and lifted up my paw to her. Her bright eyes clouded with concern as she leaned down and gently grasped my paw in her hand.

"Reggie, it is good to see you!"

She tilted her head at me and ran her other hand back over the top of my head. She then looked up to my master with grave concern. I did not miss her questioning look. It was one I beheld often, as people noticed a difference in me since my injury. I had hoped that my display of enthusiasm would hide from her any sign of my weakened and wounded state, but apparently it did not.

She turned her attention back to me and caressed her hand over my head several times. "We are to walk, Reggie. Will you be joining us?"

My tail wagged in willing eagerness, but my master spoilt my hopes. "I fear not. He was injured recently and his recovery has been slow."

"I am so sorry to hear that. Your presence will be sorely missed, Reggie."

I gazed at my master in earnest and kept my tail moving, wishing to convince him otherwise, but from the looks upon both of their faces, I knew they would hold firm.

My master looked at me sternly, knowing my wishes. "Reggie, it is no good. You know that you are still not well enough for such exertion."

He looked over at his friend and Miss Bennet, who had already begun heading down the lanes towards the woods, and then to the younger sister who seemed to be waiting rather impatiently for my master and Miss Elizabeth.

"Shall we go, Miss Elizabeth?" He held out his hand and she turned to me and whispered, "Unfortunately, Reggie, I am needed by my sister, but I give you my word that I will spend some time with you upon our return."

She reached out and placed her small hand in my master's and he helped her up. I know it was with great reluctance that he released her hand. I was quite disappointed that he did for more than one reason, as he then picked me up and returned me to the confines of the carriage. "Wait in here, Reggie, where you will be more comfortable."

I sat upon the seat with my nose pressed firmly against the window watching them depart and let out a huff. I was even more dismayed as my breath obscured the glass and thus, my vision. I could not pull myself away, however, and remained fixed in that place until I could see them no longer.

As they disappeared around a bend, a sense of determination overtook me that I would prove my usefulness to them! I looked over at the door, which I had witnessed my master on occasion open himself and wondered whether I could do the same. It was merely a lever; certainly I could do it!

I walked over to it and scrutinized it. Pawing at it gently, it did not appear to be inclined to budge. I reached up underneath it with my nose and tried to give it a push, but it was just as immobile. Not wishing for them to put too great distance between us, I reviewed by options once more.

Pushing and pulling, nudging and poking, I tried everything. Occasionally, I jumped back upon the seat to look out, hoping to see them returning. With each failed attempt, the pain I felt increased greatly, but I became more resolute to open the door!

At length, after trying everything I could imagine several times, the door quite unexpectedly swung open. I know not what I had done differently, but apparently whatever it was worked. I stood there, disbelieving at first, and finally realized I had better set out. Looking down at the ground, I readied myself for the pain of the impact and leapt.

With a thud I landed and my legs practically collapsed underneath me. It was excruciating and I was momentarily rendered motionless. I truly had not realized how my master had taken such prodigious care of me by lifting and carrying me and ensuring that I did not do anything that would unduly aggravate my pain. Now I understood why and my gratitude was manifold.

It took a great amount of fortitude to take each step and I wondered how far I would be able to walk in this condition. I set myself in the direction I had last seen them, confident that my great sense of smell would alert me to any deviation to their path.

My progress was slow and I was forced to confront the fact that there was the strong likelihood that they would walk so briskly that I would not be able to reach them and my attempt would be futile. But I could not remain where I was, so I pressed on.

Each step became more gruelling and just when I thought I could barely proceed any further, I espied them up ahead. Though a heartening sight, all was not as encouraging as I would wish. They were walking, in my humble opinion, at a far too respectable distance from each other. They both had their arms regimentally held to their side and from the looks of the posture of each, I doubted that they had come to any understanding.

As I slowly approached, I watched as Miss Elizabeth's younger sister turned and set off down a side path. I did not see Bingley and Miss Bennet and wondered what had become of them. The answer soon came upon me as I found them standing off the path in intimate conversation as they gazed in each other's eyes, completely oblivious to my passing them by.

I slowly approached my master and Miss Elizabeth and heard them discussing Miss Lydia's wedding and my master's involvement in it. Miss Elizabeth seemed to be explaining to him how she had come to know of it. With my last final surge of strength, I overtook them, garnering their attention by letting out a whine. Elizabeth responded with a cry of surprise.

"Reggie! How did you manage to come all this way?"

I saw her look to my master with concern.

"You *are* a determined little fellow. You ought never to have come!" my master spoke sternly, however I could see his deep regard for me in his eyes.

"Yes. He is determined. I like that about him." Elizabeth looked back down at me. "And you know what you want. You came all this way, Reggie, despite your pain and discomfort."

She looked to my master with gratitude; her eyes sparkling as she tilted her head and softly spoke. "He is truly devoted to you, Mr. Darcy. He is an excellent dog and you are… you are an admirable master."

He looked down at me and met my gaze. If there was ever a time to proclaim his feelings it was now and I let out a soft bark to encourage him, but instead, Miss Elizabeth continued.

"Mr. Darcy, let me thank you again and again, in the name of all my family, for that generous compassion which induced you to take so much trouble, and bear so many mortifications, for the sake of discovering my sister and Mr. Wickham."

I know my master felt grieved that she had come to learn of his actions and I could only hope he would not allow that to prevent his declaration.

"If you *will* thank me," he replied, "let it be for yourself alone. That the wish of giving happiness to you, might add force to the other inducements which led me on, I shall not attempt to deny. But your *family* owe me nothing. Much as I respect them, I believe, I thought only of *you*.

We both anxiously looked to Miss Elizabeth. Her eyes were turned to the ground and I could sense she was deeply touched and somewhat embarrassed by my master's words.

I did not believe her to be feeling awkward because he was professing esteem unrequited. I nudged him with my nose to encourage him to continue.

After a brief pause, my master took in a deep breath, looked down at me, and then back to Miss Elizabeth.

"You are too generous to trifle with me. If your feelings are still what they were last April, tell me so at once. *My* affections and wishes are unchanged, but one word from you will silence me on this subject for ever."

I knew that my master's heart was pounding mercilessly. I could see from the sweat on his brow as he earnestly awaited her response, but the look of admiration and tender regard in his eyes was unmistakable and if I surmised correctly, quite persuasive.

It was silent for a moment as we awaited her words. Even the woods around us seemed to be holding its breath in anticipation of Miss Elizabeth's reply.

Though I noted she was unable to meet his gaze, Miss Elizabeth finally stumbled through her answer. "Mr. Darcy, I... my sentiments... I cannot... my sentiments *have* undergone quite a material change." As a most becoming blush coloured her cheeks, she added, "I own that I am very pleased to hear your present assurances."

A great sense of happiness radiated from my master. I had never quite before been witness to a more notable transformation of his features.

"Miss Elizabeth, believe me when I say that I am most delighted to hear those words."

My master reached for Miss Elizabeth's hand and held it in his as one would the most precious treasure. Turning it over, he clasped his other hand over it.

Miss Elizabeth was finally able to meet my master's gaze and I beheld the love and admiration in her eyes. All the trials of the past year were swept away as the liveliness and spark that I had witnessed at Netherfield between the two erased all the misunderstandings, replacing it with mutual love and respect. My master told her of his aunt's visit and how her words had given him much hope.

They playfully quarrelled over whose behaviour that day at Rosings was the most reprehensible. They talked of the letter that my master had written in the early hours of the morning and delivered to her. He inquired whether it had accomplished what he had hoped and helped her to see some things in the true light. Then my master confessed to the pride he had developed as a child growing up and gave credit to Miss Elizabeth for helping him see it.

"Such I was, from eight to eight and twenty; and such I might still have been but for you," he brought her hands to his lips, "dearest, loveliest Elizabeth!" He kissed her hand and then her fingers. "What do I not owe you? You taught me a lesson, hard indeed at first, but most advantageous."

I contentedly watched as he then took her hand and placed it against his heart. "By you, I was properly humbled. I came to you without a doubt of my reception. You showed me how insufficient were all my pretensions to please a woman worthy of being pleased."

The two then slowly turned and began walking as they continued to talk, insensible of their surroundings and caring little where they went.

I watched as my master placed Miss Elizabeth's hand atop his extended arm. Instead of leaving it resting there, she slid it around his arm, gently wrapping it with her slender fingers. My heart pounded as I saw the joy in both their faces.

They had each declared their feelings, there was no other care in the world except the two of them, and everything was as it should be.

Except for me. I could not take one more step. Unfortunately, my aching body decided to betray me and spoil the perfection of the moment. I could do nothing but lie down in the path. As they continued to walk, I dared not utter a sound and disturb their bliss.

Their ardent conversation came to an abrupt halt when Miss Elizabeth looked down and discovered I was not accompanying them. Turning her head and looking back at me, the joyful look in her eyes clouded over. She tugged at my master's arm, bringing him around.

"Reggie!" my master called out to me.

The last thing I wished to do was bring this perfectly grouped and very touching picture to a halt, but they both quickly returned to me.

My master reached down and picked me up. The pain shot through me and I whimpered.

Miss Elizabeth asked with concern reflecting in her eyes, "What is the matter?"

"He has unfortunately exerted himself far too much. He is likely in much pain. I fear I shall have to carry him."

I was quite dismayed that with my master carrying me, his arm was no longer available for Miss Bennet. But a few moments later, I felt her hand slip in around his arm, despite the fact that there was little room for it. She then brought her other hand over and stroked my head.

We walked a short distance and then my master inquired of Miss Elizabeth, "Is there some place nearby where we may go and sit? A bench? A rock?"

Miss Elizabeth nodded. "There is a fallen log just off the road up ahead. But I fear we will lose Jane and Mr. Bingley."

My master turned and not seeing them, he smiled and shook his head. "I fear that they have already lost us."

She looked back as well and returned his smile. "It appears they have."

We walked the short distance to where Miss Elizabeth indicated we needed to veer from the path. When we came upon the log, my master set me down on the ground and offered a seat to Miss Elizabeth. He then sat beside her, taking her hand in his.

"Elizabeth." He spoke her name softly, as if it were sacred. "I truly never believed I would have had another opportunity to…" He paused and I noticed him gently squeeze and stroke Miss Elizabeth's small hand. "Do I dare hope that your regard for me has improved enough that you will accept my offer of marriage? You can be assured of my love and your acceptance would truly make me the happiest of men."

I watched as tears filled Miss Elizabeth's eyes. "I would be honoured to, Fitzwilliam."

He smiled, I suspect as much from her acceptance as from her calling him by his Christian name.

He took her hand and brought it to his lips, letting it linger there. Speaking with her hand still pressed to his lips he said, "My love for you has continued to grow and deepen, Elizabeth." He stood up and brought her up so she was standing next to him. "Just as it is impossible to stop a tree or a plant from growing, my love for you has never... *will* never diminish, never falter." With the lightest touch, he kissed her forehead. When she lifted her face to his, glowing with love and admiration, he leaned down and kissed her lips.

It was a short kiss, but one that I deemed came forth from the deepest love. I confess that I have not had the opportunity to witness many kisses in my lifetime, but this one seemed to be the most heartfelt that I had ever beheld.

Being in such close proximity to the two, I determined that even a brief human kiss must inhibit breathing, as they were both quite out of breath when they pulled away. Indeed, they both exhibited qualities quite uncharacteristic for them: they were both quite flushed in the face and neither said anything right away. But when my master finally spoke, I was quite in awe that he spoke of me.

"Elizabeth, when I say that you have made me the happiest of men, I must also add that you have made Reggie quite happy."

They both looked down at me and I wagged my tail. That was the only thing I could move without any pain.

"He has, from the moment he first saw you, singled you out... for me. I sometimes wonder that he knew you even before you and your mother and sisters first visited Netherfield to call on Bingley's sisters, for he went immediately to you."

Elizabeth smiled. "I *had* seen Reggie before that day."

My master raised his eyebrows. "Truly? Where?"

"Over there." Nodding toward the road, she said, "Up that road, a little farther up the hill is where I saw Reggie for the first time."

"When was that?" My master sounded surprised.

"I believe it was when you and Mr. Bingley first came to Netherfield. I was on one of my walks and saw a carriage pass. I did not recognize the carriage and was unable to see the occupants, but I did notice Reggie with his head sticking out the window."

"You were skipping along the side of the road!" my master declared with sudden recollection.

Miss Elizabeth laughed. "Yes, I do believe I was."

Miss Elizabeth smiled and turned to me. She stooped down and stroked my fur from the top of my head and down along my back.

"I recognized him at once when we visited Netherfield. I marvelled that he seemed to know me, as well."

"Reggie has a very good memory." My master bent down and began to pet me as well. I enjoyed their ministrations so much that I did not mind that his hand and hers occasionally entwined.

Miss Elizabeth tilted her head, a laugh clearly playing on her lips as I let out a moan of contentment. "That day at Pemberley... did Reggie go to you and bring you back to me?"

My master chuckled. "A fortuitous scheme on his part. I was in no mood to follow him. I believed he only wished to play, but he was determined."

"I thought he had picked up your scent and merely left to greet you and then you just happened upon me. I had no idea Reggie was so instrumental in our encounter."

"Oh yes," my master declared. "All credit goes to Reggie. At Rosings, as well."

"Rosings?"

My master nodded. "He knew exactly where to find you in the park when you were out walking and led me to you."

Miss Elizabeth looked at me and placed her fingers under my chin. "Did you truly do such a thing, Reggie?" She looked at my master. "And I was of the firm belief that I was the last person you wished to encounter." She laughed and stood up, folding her arms in front of her. "Is there anything else you wish to confess on behalf of your altogether too smart dog?"

"Yes," my master looked down at me and ruffled my fur before standing up and facing Miss Elizabeth. "At Netherfield, when you were caring for your sister, he positively tormented me!"

Miss Elizabeth looked at him in surprise. "Pray, how did he torment you?"

My master reached over to Miss Elizabeth's face and gently reached for a lock of her hair that curled down the side of her cheek. "I was quite envious of Reggie as I watched you bestow attentions on him. You cannot imagine how I felt seeing you run your fingers through his fur!"

Miss Elizabeth let out lively laugh. "You were jealous of your own dog?"

"Absolutely. How was I to feel when I witnessed you dancing with Reggie when you had refused to dance with me twice before the ball?"

A very appealing blush spread across Miss Elizabeth's cheeks. "You saw me dancing with Reggie?"

"I most certainly did."

"I do not know what to think, Fitzwilliam."

"Think nothing save for the fact that Reggie has apprehended all along that you were the only one for me, and those times when I acted the fool, he was most displeased!"

Miss Elizabeth looked at my master with a mischievous smile and then cast a sly glance down at me as she winked. "Are you to tell me, Mr. Darcy, that your decision to ask for my hand was on the sole recommendation of your dog? You did think me only *tolerable* upon our first becoming acquainted, did you not?"

My master paled at her words. "I regret that you overheard me. I offer my deepest apology. It was very wrong of me."

"I am only teasing you, Fitzwilliam. You must learn some of my philosophy. Think only of the past as its remembrance gives you pleasure." A more reflective expression spread over her features. "I fear I have acted the fool, as well. I should have known from the beginning that such a fine, well mannered dog could only have the finest of masters."

"You are too kind, Elizabeth. But you must allow me to apologize for my aunt's unpardonable behaviour toward you. She had no right to come to you as she did and express her disapproval in such an unmerciful fashion."

Miss Elizabeth looked down and smiled. "As long as I have your approval… and that of Georgiana."

"You are aware of my sentiments, Elizabeth, and Georgiana is most delighted. She shall be most pleased that you have accepted my hand."

"Then there is only one other whose approval I seek."

"And who is that?" my master asked.

Elizabeth leaned over to me and kissed the top of my nose. "Reggie, of course!"

Chapter 27

It was a beautiful, clear winter's day. The air was crisp and the snow that had begun falling the previous evening merely left a slight, powdery dusting upon the ground. Fortuitously, the clouds that had so readily released the snow had opportunely moved on, allowing the sun to shine and bestow upon the landscape a glistening radiance. There could not be a more perfect day for a wedding.

The morning sun greeted a bustling of activity at Netherfield. I was stirred from my slumber by the sounds coming from below and when I lifted my head, I discerned that my master had already dressed and departed. I shook my head to rid it of its fogginess and pulled myself upright.

When I found my master, he and Bingley were making an attempt to eat before they prepared themselves for the wedding. Given their demeanours, I doubted very much that they had succeeded. Bingley was speaking in an endless chatter, betraying his nervous excitement. My master sat quietly, sipping his coffee, nodding his head every so often toward his friend, but I was quite certain he heard not a word Bingley was saying. My master was outwardly composed, but I could sense -- almost as strongly as if I could see -- the nervous, eager flutterings within him.

He glanced over at me as I entered the dining room and seemed almost grateful to be able to turn his attention to me. I do not believe he had ever felt such strong sensations of anticipation and he knew not how to regulate them. Bingley's nervous dialogue added nothing to his favour and as I walked to him, he turned down to me and eagerly gave me a going over with his hands.

"It is about time you awakened, Reggie. You were in such a sound sleep this morning, I was quite envious. You had no compassion on me last night for my inability to get the slightest bit of sleep, and this morning you slumber as though it is the most ordinary of days!"

Though his manner was teasing, it was this very thing that had me most disconcerted. How was it that I was able to sleep when my poor master had such acute feelings to which he could not properly attend without my help? I very much disliked this aging process that seemed to have taken me within its grip at a most inopportune time!

~~*

Later that morning, like a grand processional, family and guests that had descended upon Netherfield during the week set out for the old brick church in Meryton. Once inside, I was obliged to sit down at Georgiana's feet as we awaited the commencement of the ceremony. I would truly have better enjoyed the prospect from the front, alongside my master; indeed, I felt it my rightful place as the one instrumental in bringing my master to his beloved. But in the end, others who were perhaps not as mindful as to my connection decided that it would be preferable for me to be furtively seated, out of the view of the guests, at Georgiana's side. She cast a glance down at me and tousled the fur on the top of my head.

"It should not be much longer, Reggie," she assured me with a smile.

I found myself growing increasingly impatient, and consequently occupied myself with recollections of the past few weeks. I looked up at Georgiana, who sat demurely with her hands now folded together and resting in her lap. A shy smile tugged at her lips as she acknowledged others around her. I thought back to her first coming to Netherfield.

My master had been eager for her arrival; anxious to renew and deepen the acquaintance between his sister and his betrothed. She had arrived late in the afternoon with loving regard and warmest wishes of joy for her brother and tender expressions of care for me. She was almost beyond words with delight to see us!

"I was never more pleased, never more overjoyed, dear brother, to receive word of your engagement to Miss Bennet." Her cheerful exuberance took both my master and me by delighted surprise. "You could not have made me happier by your choice."

She grasped both of his hands and was rewarded with a beaming smile from my master.

"And I could not be happier by your approval of Elizabeth!" His countenance was all earnestness.

She then turned in my direction and proclaimed the most excellent intelligence for me. I was a father!

"Sadie has had her puppies, Reggie. Seven of them, at that! She and the pups are all doing exceedingly well," Georgiana assured me. "Sadie is an excellent mother and she takes prodigiously good care of her brood."

My tail wagged in animated contemplation of this marvellous report. I was most anxious to see my dearest Sadie and become acquainted with my very own offspring, my own flesh and blood, but I knew that would not transpire until after the wedding.

Immediately following our mutual greeting, expressing words of admiration, and being brought up to date on the latest accounts from Pemberley, my master informed Georgiana that arrangements had been made for them to pay a call on Elizabeth at Longbourn the following day. Georgiana looked forward with delight to their meeting once again.

When at last Georgiana and Miss Elizabeth came together, they greeted one another with embraces and smiles, tears and mutual admiration. It was quite clear that Georgiana could not have been happier with the sister she was about to gain, and despite the fact that Miss Elizabeth already had four of her own, she expressed her great pleasure in claiming the young girl as her sister as well.

Later that evening, I had a brief opportunity to be alone with Georgiana and she expressed to me the fears and concerns she had been harbouring about her brother.

"I confess, Reggie, that I began to doubt whether he truly would ever marry." Her gaze drifted over to the door through which my master had just departed. With a trace of melancholy, she continued, "Oftentimes I wondered whether his responsibility for me prevented him from doing so. When I met Miss Bennet at Pemberley, my hopes were raised that she would become his wife... my sister, as I so admired her. But my hopes were continually dashed." Her eyes suddenly brightened and she softly giggled. "To own the truth, I had to read his missive several times over when he informed me of his engagement. I could barely trust my own eyes that what I was reading was true!"

My recollections of Georgiana's arrival were halted as I happened to glance up and observed Miss Bingley as she took her seat in the pew. Her mouth was skewed in a forced sort of smile that betrayed her true feelings about this wedding. I imagine that she could not have been more displeased about either of the men's choices.

It put me very much in mind of the afternoon she arrived at Netherfield, several days after my master and Miss Elizabeth announced their engagement.

We had returned from a rather lengthy visit at Longbourn, as was the usual, and when we entered the house at Netherfield, we were informed that Miss Bingley and the Hursts had arrived. They were aware of Bingley's engagement, as he had written informing them of it. They were completely unaware, however, that my master was now also betrothed.

Miss Bingley realized immediately that she no longer had an ally in my master in her campaign to prevent an alliance between her brother and the Bennet family. When she dropped a few hints about the unsuitability of an engagement with Miss Bennet, she was met with firm assurances from both men that Miss Bennet was an exceptional choice. Without the support of my master, she seemed resigned to accept her brother's engagement.

If she had expressed surprise when my master gave wholehearted assurances of the suitability of Miss Bennet, the announcement of *his* engagement to Miss Elizabeth produced an even greater astonishment. Miss Bingley was quite unable to speak for what seemed an exceedingly substantial length of time. I had never before witnessed such a draining of colour from one's face, eyes growing abnormally large, and a look of complete astonishment as she vainly made every attempt to hide her discomfiture. I watched in amazement, however, as she inexplicably employed her strict self-command, which brought about a swift recovery to her loss of composure. In no time was she able to quite civilly offer wishes of joy.

As I now watched Miss Bingley wiggle and squirm in the pew in an attempt to hide her consternation and make an unsuccessful attempt to find a comfortable position, Georgiana turned to greet her Aunt and Uncle and Cousins Fitzwilliam. They sat down alongside of us and I received a most sceptical glance from the Earl. I suspect he was perhaps not too sympathetic of my presence in the church. But I was quickly forgotten as he turned his attention to Georgiana and those around him.

Fortunately, the Earl and his wife received the notice of my master's engagement with sufficient pleasure. A prompt reply had been received from them expressing their delight. I am quite confident it was the Colonel who gave Miss Elizabeth a glowing report and assured them of his approval. When they arrived at Netherfield, it was with much eagerness they looked forward to making her acquaintance.

The family members most conspicuously absent were Lady Cat and Anne. Yet it did not come as a surprise to my master and me, for we had previously received word from both of them after the engagement became known.

I recalled how my master made the missives known to Miss Elizabeth. We had a most pleasant custom of visiting her at Longbourn each day and I watched the love and admiration grow between her and my master. They each became more open and comfortable with one another and their outward expressions of affection and regard. My master seemed to breathe in the liveliness and expressions of love that Miss Elizabeth exhibited as if his life and his own happiness depended upon it.

My master was most gracious in allowing me to accompany him on his visits. He strictly forbade me, however, from accompanying them on their walks; mindful of keeping my exertions limited, fearful of another collapse on my part.

Nevertheless, they generously accommodated me by spending a good amount of time in the grounds about the house; in particular, in a little wilderness area surrounded by trees and large bushes. Concealed from any view from the house, it became a favourite place for my master and Miss Elizabeth to come and talk. It was here where Miss Elizabeth claimed Lady Cat had paid her a visit to dissuade her from any ambition of being the future Mrs. Fitzwilliam Darcy.

It was also here that my master produced the letters his aunt and cousin had written.

"I received these two letters yesterday afternoon," he informed Miss Elizabeth, as he pulled them out of his pocket.

Miss Elizabeth's fine brow raised in question at my master. I remained seated next to the bench that they occupied.

"Did you?" Miss Elizabeth asked. "Do they bear wishes of marital felicity for us?"

"Not quite. The first is from my aunt," he replied gravely. "Do you wish me to read it to you?"

I sensed Miss Elizabeth's entire body tense, but just as quickly she relaxed. "I endured her censure in this very place already; I can certainly do it again with you by my side."

He reached out and took her hand, while holding the letter in the other.

"She writes, *My Nephew, You know not how wronged I feel in your decision to go against the duties of your family and enter into this marriage. You have certainly disappointed me and I am sure, if your mother were alive, this would have grieved her intolerably. I cannot, in any fathomable way, give my blessing upon this marriage. As I so plainly explained to Miss Bennet, I am determined to carry my point in this matter. Let me make myself clear! This marriage cannot take place! You must also be made aware -- and it distresses me to inform you -- that news of this engagement, this travesty! -- has brought about a serious decline in Anne's frail health. Her spells have increased alarmingly and I must attribute them to an inconsolably broken heart! Unfeeling nephew! Do you truly realize what you have done? You shall hear from me again. Lady Catherine de Bourgh."*

Miss Elizabeth's face grew alarmed. "This is distressing indeed! Truly, I am sorry for your cousin for it appears she truly loved you. Her condition has worsened by the announcement of our engagement. And your aunt's threats! Do you expect her to attempt to disrupt our wedding?"

He looked down at her and cupped her cheek with the palm of his hand. "Fret not, Elizabeth. Let me read you the *other* letter now. It is from my cousin, Anne."

He read, *"My Dear Cousin Fitzwilliam, Please be advised that my mother and I will be unable to attend your wedding. Believe me when I say that I wish with all my heart that I could be there to witness this sacred and most joyous occasion, but my mother would only cause a scene, determined as she is to prevent this union. She has threatened to do as much, which leaves it to me to prevent us from being in attendance. I have been compelled to employ my spells quite frequently in recent days to keep her from any sort of travel and I will continue to do so as your wedding date grows nearer. These conveniently timed episodes ultimately force my mother to send for the doctor and remain by my side until I am fully recovered, as she is so faithful to do… and at my insistence. I am quite certain I will be in the grips of a most severe spell the day before your wedding and that I will not be fully recovered until well after the wedding breakfast; perhaps not even until the following day. Please accept my deepest congratulations and warmest regards. Miss Bennet is truly a lady worthy of your love and devotion. I am so pleased that, despite your long wait, dear Cousin, she has finally consented to be your wife. With love, Anne."*

Miss Elizabeth tilted her head and her eyes widened in surprise. "Anne is truly not as frail as she leads others to believe!"

My master kept his eyes down, looking at the letter. "I have always wondered if she were truly ill and frail as she sat quietly in our midst. I confess that I never really took the time to become better acquainted with her, for fear of encouraging this notion her mother had that we would marry."

Elizabeth laughed. "She always seemed to me to be weak in spirit as well as body, and yet it appears she makes use of it to have an advantage over her mother!"

"My aunt is formidable. This apparently has been Anne's way of having a measure of control over her mother."

"She mentions your long wait and that I finally consented to be your wife. Did you… did you inform Anne of your proposal when at Rosings?"

"No, I told no one."

"How did she come to learn of it, then?"

My master took Miss Elizabeth's hand and wrapped it within both of his. "I believe she knows more about the people that come in and out of Rosings than they know about themselves." He looked down at me and winked. "Unless Reggie informed her, I think she just knew that I was going to propose."

"And that I was going to refuse."

My master quietly nodded, a smile forming on his lips. And my tail thumped in hearty consensus of his estimation.

A rustle of fabric and a whispering hush brought my attention back to the wedding, and I watched as Mrs. Bennet and her two middle daughters took their seat in the front row of the church just opposite us. She looked about her and nodded at several of her acquaintances. To me it seemed not so much a nod of greeting and affection, but of pure smugness and self-satisfaction.

I was only in her company briefly on the occasion of finally being allowed inside the Bennets' home. Though I exhibited my excellent training and breeding, giving her no cause for alarm, Mrs. Bennet eyed me with a horror I would expect of a vicious cur. It was to my advantage, then, that she rarely stepped outside, and when she did, it was only to quickly bid farewell. This suited me fine, as I found her nervousness and excitability a little too excessive for my tender sensibilities.

My master bore up under her idiosyncrasies quite well, although more than once I witnessed his jaw and fingers clench at one of her effusive outbursts on the brilliance of the matches of her two eldest daughters or the fortuitousness of having three daughters married. She expressed great relief of her own situation in the event of Mr. Bennet's demise, which if I may be excused in saying so, she predicted with some glee. Do not think me unaware that the one who felt the impropriety most heavily was Miss Elizabeth, who made countless futile attempts to curb her behaviour, her cheeks prettily flushed in embarrassment. My master frequently suggested a walk outdoors, even when the weather was not inclined to offer any physical comforts. It was for his own personal relief, I believe, that he sought to extricate himself from his future mother-in-law's presence.

My attention was drawn back to the wedding as at length my master and Bingley stepped out and stood at the front of the church. My master stood with rigid comportment, though with unmistakeable eagerness, alongside his guileless friend, Bingley, who as was his wont, displayed his excitement and enthusiasm unashamedly.

I knew my master felt fully every eye upon him and heard the whispering and murmuring as he took his place. He knew he had been under much scrutiny in Hertfordshire and as his loyal companion, I must say much of it had resulted in faulty speculation and unkind words. If asked, I have no doubt he would have said he cared not a whit whether everyone's opinion of him had altered from what it was a year ago, but I could sense he truly felt ill at ease under everyone's scrutiny. I believe his only source of composure was in knowing this was all necessary to secure Miss Elizabeth as his wife.

He glanced over at me and I lifted up my paw to him to signify my support. I was pleased that he responded with a smile that demonstrated his great sense of happiness; one that I had beheld more and more frequently in recent days.

The evening that Miss Elizabeth welcomed his address, as my master and I retreated to his chambers, his demeanour spoke of his joy and of his satisfaction. His greatest desire had finally been achieved. I do not believe I had ever beheld such unrestrained delight on his part. And I knew Miss Elizabeth was the sole reason.

I looked up to him as he slowly lowered himself into a chair and sat idly for a few moments. "I am almost afraid to sleep tonight for fear that I will awaken and find that it was only a dream!" He looked up towards the heavens. "Oh, Reggie, there have been far too many dreams of Elizabeth over this past year. Either they have ended with Elizabeth turning away from me and my greatest wish was to awaken at once from it or I dreamt she returned my regard and accepted my hand in marriage and then, I wished never to awaken! If this is a dream, Reggie, understand me when I say I have no desire to awaken from this most pleasurable state."

He sat silently for a while longer, his eyes still shining in memory of her acceptance, and then finally summoned his man who helped ready him for bed. When we were left alone, he stood looking down at the bed with a rather contented look in his eyes. I raised my paw to him and he smiled, and then leaned down and lifted me up, placing me down upon my favourite spot next to him upon the bed.

"There you go, my faithful friend. Shall we both sleep soundly tonight do you think?" He extinguished the candles and I watched him through the reddish glow of the burning embers in the fireplace as he sat down next to me. He rested his elbows upon his knees and brought one hand up and cradled his jaw. He spoke in a soft voice, "Could I have done it without you, Reggie? How many times did you reprimand me in that way that only I recognize when you knew my actions to be faulty? How many times did you lead me to her only to have me cause you grave disappointment again and again by not openly declaring myself? And how many times were you the sole reason I was given one more opportunity to make things right with her?"

He leaned back on his elbow and lifted my jaw with his hand so that we looked at each other eye to eye. "Thank you, Reggie, for faithfully remaining by my side and helping me see what I needed to do to win her affections."

He said no more and when he crawled into bed, I saw him staring for quite a long time up at the ceiling. But I knew he was not being kept awake by unsettled feelings, but by a great sense of awe in what had transpired that day.

Whilst sitting obediently at Georgiana's side in the church, I kept my eyes on my master, awaiting the moment he beheld Miss Elizabeth coming toward him. I knew the moment he saw her.

For a few moments I could only enjoy the reaction of my master, for there were far too many people around me blocking my view of his bride. I noted that his breath halted briefly and he wobbled slightly, as if the sight of her had a dizzying effect upon him. His eyes shone with admiration and his smile reached to the depths of him, leaving no doubt that this was a marriage of true affection. I knew from the unguarded expression that everyone else in this church had disappeared from his view and he saw only her.

When at last she came into my sight, I could have sworn my own heart stopped. It quickly revived, however, and thundered within my chest. Miss Elizabeth was a vision of beauty with the ribbons and laces -- of which her mother had so often spoke -- elegantly woven through her hair and sewn on her gown. But beyond the fashion of her dress, Miss Elizabeth's charm lay in the perfect reflection of warmth and love of my master in her eyes. There was a tangible connection between the two that I am sure I was not the only one to perceive, given the approving looks of the wedding guests.

Miss Elizabeth and her sister, who looked equally lovely, walked slowly toward their two gentlemen at the front of the church, each on the arm of Mr. Bennet.

Oh, yes, Mr. Bennet.

My sole interaction with Mr. Bennet occurred one afternoon, soon after my master's engagement. I was sitting quietly alongside our carriage in front of Longbourn, waiting for my master and Miss Elizabeth to go on their morning stroll. To my surprise, when the door opened, it was not my master but Mr. Bennet who graced the threshold. He stepped outside and began walking briskly in my direction, although apparently not mindful of my presence.

His hands were folded behind him and his gaze was directed toward the ground. He came to an abrupt stop when he noticed me.

"Eh, Reggie, is it?" He looked at me and reached into his pocket, pulling a watch from it. He glanced down at it and said with a sly smile, "I should not remain out here longer than fifteen minutes, however tempting. That amount of time will be sufficient for me to gather my wits and good humour, yet not be so long as to appear impolite to my family and guests."

He let out a laugh and looked back toward the house. "You know not how lucky you have it, being allowed to enjoy freedom from the conversation that Mrs. Bennet so obligingly monopolises. Far too much talk of ribbons and lace, for my taste. Lace, ribbons, flowers…" He waved his hand wildly through the air.

His face suddenly grew serious and he turned his attention to me. "So tell me, Reggie, just what kind of man is Mr. Darcy, eh?"

I let out a hearty bark to assure him of my approbation.

"Ah, yes. Just as I would have expected. What a loyal companion you are!"

He took in a deep breath and I thought I saw his eyes grow moist.

"I have no doubt that society considers the match to her advantage; she will want for nothing materially. But is that enough? Is he *good* enough for my Lizzy?"

I know not whether he truly expected a response from me, but I could not let such doubts go unanswered. I stood up and wagged my tail. I offered up my paw to him, which I am happy to say he reached down and shook heartily.

"You see, Reggie," he whispered conspiratorially, "though it is not politic to say so, Lizzy is my favourite child, and I only want the very best for her. From what I have seen of your master, he is deeply principled, highly esteemed, very well educated, and… I must admit that being a man of generous wealth does not lessen him in my eyes."

He stood up and continued, "But will he love my Lizzy as deeply as I do? Will he treat her with the utmost admiration and respect that she deserves?"

I affirmed his hopes with an even more fervent wagging of my tail and he smiled, nodding his head. "I can see that you have been treated well by him; that he has not treated you harshly nor been negligent to you."

An enthusiastic bark assured him of my master's devotion.

"That is a good indication. I believe if a man mistreats his own dog, chances are he will mistreat his wife."

He did not speak again immediately, I suspect more from overwhelming emotion than uncertainty. Finally, righting himself again, he proclaimed, "Yes, Reggie, your loyalty comforts me. I do believe he *will* be good for her."

He slowly turned around and walked back to the house. Whether they continued to speak of lace, I know not, but I felt proud that I had once again played a small role in reassuring Mr. Bennet that my master would be an ideal husband for his favourite daughter.

The clergyman began speaking and my attention returned to the front of the church.

Miss Elizabeth's face glowed with love as she looked up at my master. Her face beautifully radiated back to my master all the admiration and regard that she now treasured within her heart for him.

I sat as an enthusiastic observer watching this ceremony. I understood nothing save for the fact that once they walked back down the aisle, they would be husband and wife. She would be Mistress of Pemberley, would always be by my master's side, would take walks with him, sleep alongside him, and have his children. That notion gave me nothing but the greatest joy!

The thought of little ones also caused an impromptu wagging of my tail as I thought of Sadie's and my little puppies. I was anxious to see them!

At last, the ceremony concluded with a joyful pronunciation of their being man and wife. They turned to face their guests and their faces beamed with joy. A grand sense of satisfaction filtered through me as I realized this moment, that I had so long awaited, had finally come to pass.

But just as quickly, and unexpectedly, I felt somewhat melancholy. I knew things would never be the same between my master and me. My whole life had been devoted to him and he had returned my devotion. I have protected him; comforted him; supported him in his good decisions and wrestled with him in his poor decisions; but most of all I have taken quite seriously my office as his companion.

Ever since that day we came to Netherfield, I became devoted to securing my master's happiness with Miss Elizabeth. Now that he was assured felicity with her, the place of honour by his side was hers, not mine. My one consolation is that she is not only his heart's delight, but mine. I no longer have to worry about leaving him without camaraderie and support once I pass from this life on to the next.

Following the ceremony, the guests travelled from the church to Longbourn, where an extravagant breakfast was served. I made every attempt to keep from getting underfoot as there were a great number of people there. As it turned out, it did not settle for me to sit beside my master and his bride -- I do not think they would have even noticed me anyway -- so I made my solitary way to the drawing room. Here, away from the hustle and bustle, well wishing and jubilation, I curled up in the corner and fell into a sound sleep. Although most of the day still remained, I was quite exhausted.

~~*

I know not how long I had been asleep, but I was awakened by someone's hand gently shaking me.

"Reggie, wake up!"

I lifted my head and gazed into the concerned face of my master and his new bride. I started to arise, but he kept his hand upon me preventing me from doing so.

"You lay there, Reggie. It has proven to be an exhausting day for you. We just wanted to come and wish you well. Elizabeth and I are about to depart."

Miss Elizabeth -- that is, Mrs. Darcy, my *mistress* -- smiled and her overt happiness warmed me through. "The next time we see you, Reggie, will be at Pemberley in a little over a week." Her words gave me great joy. "You must promise me to show me about the place again." She leaned in a little closer and in almost a whisper, said, "And I look forward with great delight in seeing your puppies as I am sure you do!"

They took a few moments to run their hands through my fur, their fingers intermingling as they did. I marvelled at the feelings of contentment and joy I sensed from my master. When they walked away, even though I knew it would be a while before I saw them again, it gave me great pleasure to know that it would be a short absence and that I would be returning to Pemberley on the morrow with Georgiana and finally become acquainted with Sadie's and my pups.

It was true that I was exhausted and knew it would not be long before I fell asleep again. With a great sense of satisfaction of all that had transpired this day and almost as much anticipation on what the next day would bring, I lay my head back down and closed my eyes. Morning would be here before I knew it and Georgiana and I would be returning to Pemberley!

Chapter 28

Georgiana and I departed Netherfield for Pemberley the very next day. Georgiana said her farewells and we eagerly climbed into the carriage. We were both anxious to return home. There was no reason for us to remain any longer, despite Miss Bingley's half-hearted solicitations for the young girl to remain. I could see the relief in Georgiana's eyes, more from pleasure than surprise, when Miss Bingley made little attempt to change her mind. It appeared to both of us that she no longer had a reason to dote on her.

Georgiana passed the time reading, doing stitchery, or gazing out the window, whilst I slept most of the way. I sensed her stirring at about the same time I began to smell the wonderfully familiar scents of home. I lifted my head and she looked down at me.

With a contented smile she told me, "We are home, Reggie. We are returned to Pemberley."

Once the carriage stopped, I stepped down carefully and lifted my nose, inhaling deeply. The fresh air invigorated me and for the slightest moment I forgot my infirm state as a trace of energy coursed through me. It washed over and comforted me as warmly as a soft blanket. But there was one scent I was most determined to seek out -- that of Sadie's!

I felt obliged to follow Georgiana, but paused and turned my head toward the stables where I knew she most likely would be found. Georgiana seemed most anxious to enter the great house as she took the steps quite briskly. I halted in my tracks at the bottom of the stairs and she happened to look down at me.

"Reggie, do you need some assistance getting up these steps?" She began to descend the steps, coming toward me, and I barked excitedly, turning completely around, facing the stables.

"Of course, Reggie," she smiled sympathetically. "You wish to see Sadie and your pups."

She shook her head. "How thoughtless of me! Can you ever forgive me?" Before I could bark my affirmation, she waved her hand and called to the carriage driver.

"Pershing, would you please take Reggie with you back to the stables so he may see Sadie?"

"Certainly, Miss Darcy."

"Off with you then, Reggie. Sadie is nestled in the back corner of the stables in an empty horse stall. You will easily find her. The puppies are most likely making a commotion if they are not sleeping."

As I turned and walked back toward the carriage, I heard Georgiana speak again. "Pershing, would you please accompany Reggie and return him to the house in a short while? I would not wish for him to walk all that way on his own."

He murmured his consent as he opened the door of the carriage. "In with you, Reggie."

Even though I was about to see my puppies for the first time, Georgiana's concern for me reminded me just how old and frail I truly was.

In no time, the carriage came to a halt and the driver opened the door for me. I jumped down and walked toward the stables. Finding the door open, I entered. Just as Georgiana had said, I could hear a commotion coming from the back corner stall. I slowly approached and came upon Sadie and the puppies. I regarded them curiously. Cute little furry black and white creatures were clambering all over her.

Sadie lay sprawled out, seemingly oblivious to the puppies' noisy and energetic activities -- and oblivious to me. But as I stepped in a little closer, her head slowly raised and she peered in my direction. Our eyes met and locked and in the briefest of moments, I believe, she assessed my intentions. She was quickly assured that I meant neither her nor the puppies any harm.

I could not go to her side as I was wont to do for the stall had been secured so the puppies could not escape. I searched for some access to no avail. Thwarted, my eyes were drawn back to the lively brood before me and my heart swelled with pride.

One little whelp suddenly noticed my presence and he climbed over the others toward me. I lowered my nose and he reached as high as he could with his. What struck me immediately were his very bright, fine eyes. Even without a proper introduction, I felt as though he knew I was someone special in his life.

I remained but a short while. Sadie was tired and I did not wish to unnecessarily disturb her. I cocked my head at her, saddened that I must take my leave of her and our pups and let out a whimper. She lifted her paw up ever so slightly off the ground and lay her head back down. Taking one last look at my puppies, Pershing and I returned to the house.

~~*

I visited the puppies at least once every day after that. As I observed them, I easily began to distinguish one from another and recognize certain traits. If a father may betray a favourite amongst his offspring, the puppy that had come to me the very first day seemed to be the brightest and most social. He and I grew very fond of one another.

A little female -- to own the truth, the runt of the litter -- had the sweetest demeanour. She was always willing to allow the other puppies the opportunity to nurse first, obliging her clamouring brothers and sisters. Like her mother, she seemed to enjoy licking the other puppies, bestowing her little gifts of affection with as open a nature as I have ever seen. Georgiana took a special liking to her and ensured that she got her due share of mother's milk and attention. She named her Molly and I was quite certain she had found a most loyal and affectionate companion. I was also quite proud to learn that the puppy to whom I had grown most attached had been named after me, Sir Reginald Ascott Hamilton Darcy II, Scotty, for short.

I must confess that just being back at Pemberley and seeing the puppies provided me with a great sense of fulfilment and contentment. As I watched them play, however, I longed for the days when I had an abundance of energy and could romp eagerly and endlessly across the grounds on long walks with my master.

I recollected those days when he let me off the leash and I would scramble ahead looking for anything to chase -- even a leaf blowing in the breeze. Now I was barely even able to walk on my own to and from the stables, much less keep up with my active pups.

One afternoon I had fallen asleep on a little patch of sunlight that came through the sitting room window. The rays of the sun blanketed me with warmth and soothed my weakening body. I felt as though I could sleep forever. I was awakened, however, by the sound of puppies yelping.

Startled, I looked up and saw Georgiana entering the sitting room with pleased countenance and holding Molly and Scotty in each arm. She closed the door to the room and set the puppies down. Scotty instantly came over to me and pounced on my belly, causing me to flinch. Rather than be annoyed at him, though, I could only watch in pride and admiration as he playfully tumbled about me. It was indeed a memorable moment that I knew I would carry in my heart always.

Molly stayed somewhat back, encircled in Georgiana's arms. Georgiana took a seat upon the floor next to me and we both watched these two puppies with great delight. I could only hope that my master and mistress would look as kindly upon these two as Georgiana and I did.

~~*

As eagerly as Georgiana and I awaited the return of my master and mistress, so did the staff. A heightened sense of energy and expectation pervaded as they prepared the house for their arrival. It was not unusual to observe the servants fervently whispering amongst one another, speculating what changes the new mistress would demand; what she would require of them; or how she would treat them.

The ones who remembered Miss Elizabeth (and no, I cannot keep from calling her by that name) from her short visit to Pemberley reassured the others that she seemed to be most amiable and pleasant and that they were quite sure their master would have married only the most excellent woman in every particular.

Whilst I joined in their anticipation of seeing my master and his wife again, I knew that all was not well with me. I was growing more and more feeble. It took an exceedingly great effort to arise in the mornings. My legs ached and they moved slowly. In addition, my hearing was not as acute as it once was and my sight was becoming more and more blurred.

The only thing that still remained as strong as ever was my sense of smell. That often alerted me to a meal being prepared -- with the tempting prospect of scraps given to me. I knew with absolute certainty when Georgiana approached, or a stranger came near, and at long last, when my master and Miss Elizabeth arrived at Pemberley.

I was seated at the feet of one of the kitchen help. She had offered me a rather delicious morsel of meat and upon finishing it, I sat obediently, hoping for another. The outer door was opened and another servant walked in carrying a load of wood for the fires. At that moment I detected a trace of both my master's and Miss Elizabeth's scent. They had just entered the park!

I know not who was more surprised, the servants or myself, but with a sudden burst of energy, my legs took me to the door and I slipped out just as it was being closed. With no thought of pain or age, I rounded the courtyard and came around to the front of the house. I was all excitement as the carriage slowly made its way toward me.

My actions must have alerted the household to their arrival, as servants began coming forth from the house with Mrs. Reynolds in the lead.

We watched in eager anticipation as the carriage finally stopped. The door was opened for my master and mistress and they stepped out. I waited back as they were greeted with a warm, "Welcome home!" from everyone.

In years past, my master would deal directly with his obligations as Master of Pemberley, heading straight to his study the moment he arrived. But I knew that marriage had changed him for the better when his steward approached with papers in hand, ready to give him a brief account of the past few weeks as he escorted his wife into her new home. But instead of glancing over them as he usually did, he waved his steward on. "Not now, Crawford. We shall meet about this later if you do not mind."

Mrs. Reynolds stepped forward and personally greeted them both, welcoming Miss Elizabeth... nay, *Mistress* Elizabeth, and they chatted briefly.

As they walked toward me, I noticed my master's demeanour. Usually when he returned from a lengthy trip he was tired and worn, travel-weary and sombre. But today he appeared quite rested and jovial. His colour was good, his eyes were bright, and a very contented smile readily emerged. This was a man exceedingly blessed!

Mistress Elizabeth -- yes, that is what she shall now be to me -- greeted the staff, occasionally requesting a name. I noted that she and my master glanced at each other frequently with warmth and good humour as they returned greetings and answered questions. I could almost feel the strength my master received from just Mistress Elizabeth's look and the reassurance she received from his.

Before they reached the stone steps, where I was patiently waiting, Georgiana rushed outside. With tears of joy, she welcomed them and was rewarded with an embrace from both.

"I am so delighted you are home! I missed you both so much!" she exclaimed gleefully. "I wish to hear all about your wedding journey!"

A sudden blush coloured her face and she looked down. "I mean to say… that is…"

Mistress Elizabeth drew the girl in her arms. "We missed you as well, Georgiana, and we have much to tell. We had a splendid time!"

My tail wagged with joyful expectation when they both looked over at me. My master gave his thigh a slap with his hand to signal for me to come. I most happily obliged. My master leaned down and cradled my head in his hands.

"I have missed you, good friend."

Mistress Elizabeth leaned over and patted the top of my head. "It is a delight to see you again, Reggie."

They were prevented from paying any further attention to me by their duties to the others, but I felt a great sense of peace surround me. They were now husband and wife and they were home.

It was not until later that evening that I received undivided attention from them. After dinner they sat together in the sitting room and I joined them. When I first came into the room, I had a dilemma. I did not know by whom to sit.

My master sat upon his favourite chair whilst Mistress Elizabeth was seated on the sofa at his side.

I decided to seat myself between them and quietly nuzzled Mistress Elizabeth. Without saying a word, her hand went to my head and began stroking the fur down to my neck. She twirled her fingers in my fur and I closed my eyes and let out a moan of great contentment.

"Try as you like, Reggie," my master said, a sly smile forming on his lips. "You will not find me jealous any longer of Elizabeth's attentions to you."

I felt his hand come down over hers and she stopped. In a moment, however, I felt his fingers between hers as they continued indulging me. But I had the odd suspicion that their attentions were not primarily directed towards me.

At length, I lay down and listened as they talked, laughed, and reminisced about the past year. Mind you, I found their recollections of the events were curiously absent of my role in bringing them together. If only I could have contributed to the conversation, I would have enlightened them both of a few situations in which I had some influence.

The conversation continued thus for quite some time. They did not seem in the least weary of the pleasure of each other's company; however, I fell asleep. In the late hours of the evening, a gentle prodding by my master alerted me to their departure for their bedchambers.

Sleepily, I made my way up the stairs behind my master and mistress. When we stopped at the door to Mistress Elizabeth's bedchambers, my master leaned over and kissed her. "I shall be waiting." A knowing smile passed between the couple before we proceeded to his chambers.

We entered and I watched as his man prepared him for bed. But on this occasion, my master dismissed him earlier than normal. I had the oddest notion that he had forgotten me. I was far too feeble to jump up on the bed on my own and waited patiently for him to pick me up and place me in my favourite spot.

But instead, his eyes were on the door that separated his chambers from Mistress Elizabeth's as he waited expectantly in a chair.

When a soft tap was heard at the door, he jumped from the chair and rushed to open the door. Mistress Elizabeth looked beautiful in a floor length white gown. It reminded me of the night we saw her in the library and I thought she looked like an angel.

My master drew her into his arms. "Are your chambers adequate, my love?" he asked as his fingers combed through her hair, which had been let down.

"They could not be finer, Fitzwilliam," she replied with a soft laugh, looking up at him with her very fine eyes.

"Good. I am glad to hear that."

An understanding seemed to be formed between them, for they talked very little and the next thing I knew, Mistress Elizabeth had joined him in his bed and he had extinguished the candles. I sat for a moment at the foot of the bed, perplexed that my master, normally so solicitous in attending me, could have overlooked my presence. Perhaps it was due to me being out of his presence since before the wedding.

I let out a small whine. I hoped that it was received as more of a gentle reminder rather than a complaint.

I heard my master let out a breathy chuckle.

"What is it?" Mistress Elizabeth asked.

"Something that had rather slipped my mind."

My tail began wagging as he slipped out of bed and came towards me. But instead of picking me up, he walked past me to a large chest of drawers and opened it, pulling out a coverlet.

"I fear, Reggie, that things will be different from now on. You will be sleeping in the corner."

I slowly turned and walked to the coverlet that he had put down for me, letting out a soft grumble.

"My dear, has Reggie been in the habit of sleeping upon your bed?" I heard Mistress Elizabeth ask.

"From the very first time he was allowed in the house, yes."

"I do believe, Fitzwilliam, that there is plenty of room on the bed for him."

"No, Elizabeth. I will not have it."

"Fitzwilliam?" Elizabeth said ever so softly and slowly.

My master breathed in deeply. "No, Elizabeth, and that is final!"

"Fitzwilliam?"

"Reggie will be just fine on the floor!"

"Fitzwilliam?"

"What?" He walked back around to his side of the bed and I sullenly climbed onto mine.

"I have never seen a bigger bed than this in my life, let alone sleep in one. I am quite certain there is plenty of room for Reggie at the foot of the bed if he sleeps off to the side."

"No, Elizabeth."

"That is unfortunate." In the darkness, I watched as she turned her head towards me and gave me an endearing smile.

"How so?"

"I am quite fearful of getting lost in this bed for its size. If Reggie slept on the other side of me, you would be assured of always having me close by your side."

There was silence for a moment, followed by another chuckle. My master climbed out of the bed, walked over and picked me up.

"There you go, Reggie. You have Elizabeth to thank for it!"

And that was how it was to be every night. True to her word, Mistress Elizabeth always ensured that I had plenty of room on the bed. I worried sometimes that she was perhaps being *too* considerate about giving me ample space, but I never heard a word of complaint from either on their close quarters.

~~*

The household changed quite a bit once Mistress Elizabeth came to Pemberley. Not that she demanded things to be run differently. No, the alteration was more subtle, and infinitely more satisfying, for there was a greater sense of liveliness. It pervaded my master's demeanour and overflowed to the servants and even into the very rooms themselves.

As the days turned into weeks and the weeks into months, the transformation in my master was most heartening. Mistress Elizabeth's encouragement and support strengthened him in his struggle to overcome his weaknesses. Whereas he had always felt very uncomfortable speaking to strangers, it came very easily to his wife and she made those situations much less arduous for him. When his implacable resentment refused to budge, she would exhibit grace, good humour, and mercy and her mere example helped him to find forgiveness.

It was very liberating for me to watch this lady grow in her position of mistress -- both of Pemberley and of the heart of my beloved master. I recognized theirs was a special love reserved only for each other. His love for me as his companion had been of a different nature and I sensed that in Mistress Elizabeth he had found what I have heard humans call "his other half."

Mistress Elizabeth grew equally in the deep, passionate love for my master and she very easily fell into the role of Mistress of Pemberley. She possessed an open and curious air and eagerly availed herself of the benefits of my master's wisdom and experience. They took advantage of each day that presented itself suitable for a walk about the grounds of Pemberley, always in spirited and warm conversation. In town, they walked the neighbourhood and parks.

With her on his arm, he attended balls and dinners without grumbling, eager to acquaint her with his friends and take her to places she had never been.

I am sad to say that as their attachment grew, I found my participation with my two favourite people diminishing. I was no longer able to accompany them on their journeys to Town as the foul air made breathing more difficult. Walking was an effort that took far too much concentration. I began eating less and less, having very little appetite anymore. Upon returning, however, they would share with me all that they thought would be of interest to me and I hungrily devoured every word.

Despite my condition, I was content and at peace that my master was happy.

~~*

It was in the heavy heat of summer that I found my strength and energy waning. I slept more often than not and frequently had to be reminded even to eat.

One hot afternoon, the scent of some delectably odorous food tickled my nose and I slowly opened my eyes to see my master crouched down beside me holding out a plate of tantalizing meat that I would have in earlier years inhaled in a moment's notice. I know not how long it had been since I had eaten and to own the truth, I had absolutely no desire to do so. It was strange that I felt no hunger pangs, no stomach growls, nothing that would indicate that I had not eaten in several days.

"Come on, Reggie. Eat this little bit. It is the very best portion of the goose. You used to love it."

I recognized the proffered treat as something I enjoyed in the past. But not only was I not hungry, I was tired. Too tired to even open my mouth and chew. I looked up mournfully at my master, hoping he would understand.

The effort to stay awake was more than I could bear. I fell asleep again and at some point awoke to whispering voices. I opened my eyes slowly to see Georgiana and Mrs. Reynolds hovering over me.

"Look!" Georgiana whispered. "His eyes are open!" She turned to Mrs. Reynolds and asked that she fetch Mr. and Mrs. Darcy.

She leaned down to me. "We are here, Reggie. We are here." Her hand felt warm against me as she stroked my head and back.

My vision being mostly obscured, I sensed rather than saw Georgiana's eyes glisten as they filled with tears. This was troubling to me and I tried to lift my paw to her to reassure her, but found I had not the strength. I was barely even able to move my head, and when I heard the sound of footsteps, it took a concerted effort for me to turn in that direction.

Mistress Elizabeth and my master entered the room and made their way directly to me.

"Reggie has finally opened his eyes. I had about given up hope as it has been two days." Georgiana's voice quivered as she spoke those words that took me by surprise. I had no idea I had been asleep that long.

I rested my head back down and closed my eyes. It felt so good to keep them closed, but an ominous feeling counselled me that I should make every attempt to keep them open and remain awake. But yet, I cannot deny at the same time, the thought of sleep beckoned me.

I heard Georgiana say in hushed tones, "His breathing is very slow and shallow. Fitzwilliam, is there anything we can do for him?"

Straining my eyes to see Georgiana, I could see that she was worried. I felt powerless to do anything to ease her distress.

"We have to let him know that he can let go." My master's voice reassured me.

Hearing a faint weeping, I turned to Mistress Elizabeth and saw that her head was buried against my master's shoulder and she was dabbing her eyes with a handkerchief.

I then glanced at my master and he looked down at me. He nodded his head, saying, "You have been a loyal and good friend, Reggie, and I shall forever be thankful for our time together. But, it is time, my friend, to let go."

His words gave me a sense of freedom and assurance that all things were as they should be. I looked one last time at each of my loved ones. Quite unexpectedly and suddenly, I was granted a burst of strength, clarity of mind, and clarity of sight to acknowledge my master, Georgiana, and Mistress Elizabeth. I breathed in deeply the scents of those I held most dear, looking at each in turn. I wanted their faces to be imprinted in my mind.

I then turned back to look at my master. The scared and unsure boy that brought me home so many years ago had grown to a man that any dog would be proud to call his master -- a man of honour, of principle, and of unyielding loyalty. I nuzzled the hand stroking my head gently and even dared to give him a little lick to display my steadfast affection. The last thing I remember was seeing a lone tear trickle down his cheek. Then I closed my eyes, embracing the seduction of the peaceful rest.

Epilogue

That heartrending day happened ten years ago.

While I do not remember the particulars of that day, I do recollect the gravity of his loss. It affected the Darcys, the whole staff, and my mother, as well.

My name is Sir Reginald Ascott Hamilton Darcy II. I am called Scotty by my master and mistress and the staff at Pemberley. I am named after my father and have heard many wonderful stories of his great wisdom and devotion. I am rather in awe of him as I hear of his excellent behaviour, remarkable intelligence and acuity, and his heroic actions.

I know I can never live up to his legacy. I have heard over and over about how he came to Pemberley and what a great support he was for my master when, as a lad, he was broken-hearted at the loss of his mother; how he stood by my master as a young man grieving the loss of his father; and how he knew Mistress Elizabeth was the perfect choice of wife for my master and did everything in his power to bring them together. The stories amaze me even still.

While I am fully over ten years old, I am constantly reprimanded for my unregulated playfulness and rambunctious bursts, much like I was as a puppy. But fortunately, I am kindly tolerated. I am most grateful that I am quickly forgiven when I do not behave as I should.

But there is a material difference between myself and my father. To this day, no matter how patiently my master or his groomsmen work with me, I still struggle to remember the difference between "sit" and "stay." I confess, usually it is a matter of me not wishing to stay when I am told to sit. Nevertheless, I hold out hope that I will be as highly revered as my father was.

Much has transpired in these ten years. The Master and Mistress of Pemberley have three children. They were blessed with two sons, Fitzwilliam and Edmund, and finally a daughter, Jane. I suspect the reason that I am indulged despite my lapses in discipline is due to my own excellent rapport with the Darcy children. Fitzwilliam and Edmund are rarely without my companionship. We enjoy excellent schemes and adventures throughout the woods of Pemberley and I have exercised my office on occasion to alert the boys to some unforeseen danger or to the presence of their little sister hoping to join us on our escapades.

Mistress Elizabeth's sister, Mrs. Bingley, and her husband have two girls and two boys. They moved within an easy distance from Pemberley that allows for the families to visit often and allow the cousins to be very close.

Georgiana took my sister, Molly, as her companion. Molly accompanied her everywhere and is now living with her and her husband, Lord Breighton, at their home at Leddenwood. Molly has had several litters of puppies. Unquestionably, she has been an excellent mother, but her most prized role is that of companion to Georgiana. She helps her a great deal entertaining her young son, Frederick. Sometimes I wonder whether Molly has more of my father's traits than I do.

My master's cousin, Miss Anne de Bourgh, was married soon after her mother -- a woman who reminded me the first time I saw her of the hens in the chicken coop, always clucking and fussing, the feathers of her hat shaking furiously -- died unexpectedly a few years back. Though I do not pretend to understand the restrictions that humans place on society, it was said that Miss de Bourgh married beneath her, a man of little fortune whom she had known for several years. From the discussions I have overheard between my master and his wife, apparently the devotion he showed her through years of disdain from Miss Anne's mother proved his worth. His love has daily given her back the strength and comfort, which had for so long been lacking.

Frequent guests at Pemberley include Mr. Bennet, though I rarely see him outside of the library; the Bingleys; Colonel Fitzwilliam, who has remained unmarried -- a fact about which my master appears to take great delight in teasing him; and the Gardiners, who are particular favourites of my master and mistress. Another sister of my mistress, Miss Kitty, is a welcomed guest and enjoyed the company of the Darcys and the Bingleys until she married and moved a considerable distance from Pemberley. Mrs. Bennet visits rarely -- it appears that travel does not sit well with her nerves. Neither does Mistress Elizabeth's sister, Mrs. Lydia Wickham, visit. When she does, she arrives alone, unannounced, and with the request of financial assistance.

Mistress Elizabeth's remaining sister, Mary, continues at Longbourn; her primary responsibility being to care for Mrs. Bennet and to moralize about every occurrence, whether good or bad, that she encounters in a day.

My life here is far different than my father's was. He was allowed greater liberties than I shall ever enjoy -- I have never been allowed upstairs, let alone sleep upon anyone's bed. There are times when I feel as though I suffer in comparison to my father and shall never meet their expectations.

But I remind myself that when my father came, things were very different. He had the full devotion of his master, who trained him well. I am exceedingly proud of him and have come to love to hear the stories about him. I only hope that one day, a fine offspring of mine might happen along when one of the Darcy children is old enough to choose him as his particular companion and he will be just as excellent as my good father was -- Sir Reginald Ascott Hamilton Darcy.

The End

Kara Louise lives in Kansas with her husband.
They share their 10 acres with
an ever changing menagerie of animals.
They have one married son who also likes to write.

Other published books by Kara Louise

"Pemberley's Promise"

"Drive and Determination"

"Assumed Engagement"

and

"Assumed Obligation"

Visit her website,
www.ahhhs.net
where you will find a variety of stories
written by her and Australian author, Sharni.

Made in the USA
Lexington, KY
08 April 2010